The Ralph Nader Congress
Project is the most ambitious
Nader undertaking to date, and the
most comprehensive survey of
the national legislature in our time.
Begun in 1972, it took shape from
interviews with the members of the
92nd and 93rd Congresses, with
hundreds of congressional
staff members, with lobbyists and
federal officials. The result is a
provocative and timely analysis of
congressional committees directly
and crucially involved in domestic
legislation. Earlier works of the
Congress Project include the set
of profiles of individual members
published in 1972 and updated
in 1974, which were called
"perceptive observations of the
inner workings of Congress" by *The
New York Times*, and the
best-selling paperback, *Who Runs
Congress?*, published in 1972
and updated in 1975.

THE COMMERCE
COMMITTEES

This book is printed on 100 percent recycled paper

A Study of the House and Senate Commerce Committees

David E. Price, DIRECTOR

The Ralph Nader Congress Project

Grossman Publishers

A DIVISION OF THE VIKING PRESS
NEW YORK   1975

THE
COMMERCE
COMMITTEES

Copyright © 1975 by Ralph Nader

All rights reserved

First published in 1975 by Grossman Publishers
625 Madison Avenue, New York, N.Y. 10022

Published simultaneously in Canada by
The Macmillan Company of Canada Limited

Printed in U.S.A.

Library of Congress Cataloging in Publication Data

Main entry under title: No - See Slip
The Commerce Committees.

     "The Ralph Nader Congress Project."
    Includes index.
       1.   United States. Congress. House. Committee on
Interstate and Foreign Commerce. 2. United States.
Congress. Senate. Committee on Commerce. I. Price,
David Eugene. II. Ralph Nader Congress Project.
JK1430.I532C65   328.73'07'65   75-4912
ISBN 0-670-23257-2

Contributors

David E. Price, Project Director
  B.A., University of North Carolina (1961); B.D., Yale University Divinity School (1964); Ph.D., Yale University (1969)
  Associate Professor of Political Science and Policy Sciences, Duke University

Deanna Nash, Editor

Steven Brown
  J.D., University of Wisconsin Law School (1973)
  Counsel, Trade Division, Wisconsin Department of Agriculture

Joan Claybrook
  B.A., Goucher College (1959); J.D., Georgetown University Law School (1973)
  Director, Public Citizens' Congress Watch

Robert C. Fellmeth
  Director and Co-author, *The Interstate Commerce Omission* (*1970*); Project Director, *Politics of Land* (1970)

Jonathan Low
  B.A., Dartmouth College (1973)

John Paris, S.J.
M.A., Harvard University; Ph.D., University of Southern California
Assistant Professor of Social Ethics, Holy Cross College, Worcester, Mass.

Bruce G. Rosenthal

Andrew Weiner
Harvard University Law School
Former Staff Member, New York City Planning Commission

Contents

ix

TABLES AND CHART

Introduction

Historically, the Senate and House Commerce Committees saw their primary purpose to be that of arbitrating differences between business groups over legislation drafted or backed by one or more of these groups. Other observers might have viewed their function as making sure that consumer interests were blocked or ignored. Indeed, opposition to hearings and legislation about the health, safety, and economic rights of consumers was the touchstone of the operations of these committees until the mid-sixties.

As Professor David Price and his associates show in this volume, the gradual and uneven movement toward consumer sensitivity by these committees (the Senate committee more than the House counterpart) came about as a converging result of staff changes, external consumer group advocacy, greater media disclosure of consumer abuses, and the efforts of a small number of legislators. In the past, membership on these committees was considered a "plum"; members spoke privately of the amount of campaign money from the various commercial and industrial lobbies that would accrue to these lawmakers. One representative, to his dismay, began receiving envelopes with cash at his office as soon as he became a member of the committee. Such envelopes were part of a Capitol Hill tradition which provided a very fungible mode of making campaign contributions to grateful legislators.

The "cash" approach to members of these committees by the very companies and industries that desire their favors may not be as strong today as in bygone years. Watergate and other exposures must have some chilling effect on the recipients if not the givers. But the campaign contributions still flow and the lobbyists still think up new ways of being friendly and influential. On the other hand, their reception is more skeptical and less fraternal. This is likely to be even more the case for the Ninety-fourth Congress, with its young, aggressive liberals and seniority shakeups in the House.

Although this report covers the committees through early 1975, the external environment in which the committees operate is not likely to change in the immediate future. The Ford Administration is proving to be as hostile to consumer interests and as indentured to special corporate interests as its predecessor. Only the absence of the Watergate ambience is different. A White House–big business combination is difficult for even a well-tuned and determined Congress to overcome. If the auto or detergent or textile or railroad industry knows that bills will be vetoed by the White House, its position can harden and its demands escalate in the wake of a required two-thirds override by both the House and Senate. On the other side, the consumer groups, while developing broader alliances and contacts throughout the country, face a similarly heavy burden. Assuredly, more progressive bills can be introduced, extensive hearings held, and legislation passed by Congress. But unless the White House needs to trade off the measures it wants with the committees, the likelihood of veto is omnipresent. Since the regulatory and subsidy structure favoring industry and commerce is already in place, the White House is not finding itself in a position to engage in such trade offs.

Within Congress, however, a base of strong interest in consumer matters and structural reform to avoid economic waste, economic concentration, and corruption is developing. The members of Congress are hearing more from their constituents on specific proposals and bills. The intensity of inflation and recession in recent months is making more people think about the economy, about their rights as consumers, about the need for new ideas and for old ideas like the extension of consumer cooperatives. Such interest undoubtedly helped elect candidates who took strong pro-consumer stands in the 1974 elections. Their impact has already been felt in the early days of the Ninety-fourth Congress. For example, Representative John Moss (D., Calif.), with the solid backing of most of the new members of the House Commerce Committee, led a successful coalition move to adopt new rules giving the committee majority members—not the chairman—the right to decide structural and procedural questions for the committee's operation, as the Democratic Caucus rules mandate. Moss also narrowly defeated Chairman Harley Staggers (D., W.Va.) in a contest over the leadership of the key Investigations Subcommittee. This move not only dealt the seniority principle a major setback but also reflected a substantive demand that the Investigations Subcommittee start investigating and stop doing so very little with its relatively large staff of ten professionals.

During the past several years the Senate Commerce Committee would obtain Senate approval of consumer bills only to see the House committee simply sit on comparable bills until the end of the session. A combination of hostility to these bills within the House committee and Chairman Staggers' lack of vigorous backing—some members called it lethargy—was instrumental. But perhaps just as important were the grievous understaffing of the subcommittees and the chairman's assignment of members to subcommittees in a way that assured deadlock or defeat. The House committee is undergoing greater change now than its Senate counterpart, and it is likely to be more productive of legislation—or else another upheaval of committee leaders will be in the offing in 1977, when the next Congress convenes.

Veteran Congresswatchers are not prone to jumping to conclusions about how much of an impact such internal changes will have on congressional output. Certainly the pace of consumer legislation and inquiries has picked up in the last decade. But the enforcement of these laws and the issuance of effective standards and procedures have not been impressive. Similarly unimpressive has been the stamina and power the committees have brought to bear on oversight. The Senate Commerce Committee has done a much better job of oversight than that feebly attempted by the House committee. But neither committee has shown interest in using its subpoena powers and calling top corporate executives to testify. In fact, once a new regulatory bill was enacted, such as the 1966 auto safety law, the primary witnesses called thereafter by the committees were from government departments. The reluctance to call top-level business executives is a measure of the flabbiness of the committees in using the very power they have decided to place under the rule of law. So too is the timidity with which the committees approach the need to require disclosure by companies of information that relates to serious health and safety considerations.

Given the recent changes in membership and rules during the Ninety-fourth Congress, the committees and their staffs would do well to shape a more comprehensive framework for their legislative missions. There is too much reactive and too little initiatory effort, whether in reviewing the agencies to see what remedies are required or in responding to deep-rooted abuses that merit more than regulatory Band-Aids or window dressing.

There are four categories of consumer legislation which the committees might well contemplate in going about their business. The first category is the one that receives the most committee emphasis—namely, the regulatory-standards law. The auto safety, pipeline safety, radiation control, and flammable fabrics and product safety acts fit that description. Some of these laws provided for experimental safety research and consumer disclosure programs, but these fell prey to White House or industry politics.

The second category is the development of countervailing advocacy functions within the executive branch and within individual agencies to offset the powerful pro-corporate leanings of these agencies and the costly barriers to participation by noncommercial interests. The Senate Commerce Committee has strongly espoused the creation of a consumer advocacy agency with authority to intervene before other federal agencies to represent consumer intercsts. (This bill was under the jurisdiction of the Government Operations Committee in the House.) A Senate filibuster blocked passage of the consumer advocacy bill in 1972 and 1974, notwithstanding overwhelming support by both houses. Other Commerce committee–sponsored laws have included provision for legal counsel hired by the agency (ICC) to represent citizens in rule-making proceedings (Regional Rail Reorganization Act of 1973), and funding for representation of views not otherwise able to be represented in agency (Federal Trade Commission) proceedings (FTC Improvement Act of 1974).

The third category consists of those proposals which place in the hands of aggrieved consumers the rights and remedies to defend their own interests and obtain justice. Improved small claims courts, class actions, ease of securing legal representation, and access with redress to the offending agencies and officials are in this category. The committees have been unsuccessful in securing passage of such legislation, although the Senate committee has some well-developed proposals in this area on its agenda for the Ninety-fourth Congress. In 1974 a Federal Trade Commission warranty reform bill was enacted which may facilitate the enforcement of consumer rights by consumers because it assists them in retaining counsel inexpensively.

The fourth category of consumer legislation relates to economic and membership institutions that focus consumer interests in both economic and political ways. This area is fundamental, and the Senate committee, as of early 1975, appears to be moving in that direction. Consumer cooperatives, long a small but heralded fixture in the history of American progressivism, exemplify the unifying of consumer purchasing power with consumer-controlled management at the local or neighborhood level. Given inflation and other economic instabilities, given enhanced consumer awareness of superior alternative products and services, and given the perceived need to find a unifying and need-related thread to preserve or rebuild urban neighborhoods, the consumer cooperative movement may come of age again. In 1975 Congress will probably be considering a proposal to establish a consumer cooperative bank to extend credit and technical assistance to consumer cooperatives much as the Banks for Cooperatives have done for farm cooperatives since the federal farm credit laws were passed in the 1930s.

The Commerce committees may give further attention to ways in which nonprofit mass membership organizations such as the American Automobile Association clubs can be more open and accountable to their own consumer members, and how professional membership organizations like the engineering societies, which set private safety standards that find their way into state or federal law, can be less industry-dominated.

Finally, the committees should try to find time for educational hearings to stimulate creative solutions by citizens or by state and local authorities. There are few enough forums of high visibility for airing the problems and remedies for abuses in business-consumer relationships; these committees should not forgo the opportunity to spotlight and inform. Where there are models of superior performance, the committees should describe their activities, to reach a wider audience who may never have heard of these examples and may thus be encouraged to emulate them.

For decades, fresh, significant thinking has been stalled in Congress by lip service to a competitive free enterprise that was not practiced. Instead, the myth served to hide the reality of monopolistic practices, government protection from competition, government subsidies to business—which grew inefficient and stagnant on such welfare—and an utter degradation of consumer rights and remedies. Now the corporate economy can no longer keep from the public the fact that it avariciously relies on the federal mantle and the federal dollar. Indeed, the competitive market is an unacceptable insecurity for the steel, oil, and banking industries—to name a few. More than ever, the Commerce committees should develop operating principles for a just economic system, if only to know better how to perform their designated missions and for whose benefit in society.

Ralph Nader

Members of the Commerce Committees

SENATE COMMITTEE ON COMMERCE, NINETY-SECOND AND NINETY-THIRD CONGRESSES

Majority:

Warren G. Magnuson, Chm. (Wash.)
John O. Pastore (R. I.)
Vance Hartke (Ind.)
Philip A. Hart (Mich.)
Howard W. Cannon (Nev.)
Russell B. Long (La.)
Frank E. Moss (Utah)
Ernest F. Hollings (S. C.)
Daniel K. Inouye (Hawaii)
William B. Spong, Jr. (Va.)*‡
John V. Tunney (Calif.)†
Adlai E. Stevenson III (Ill.)†

Minority:

Norris Cotton (N. H.)‡
James B. Pearson (Kans.)
Robert P. Griffin (Mich.)
Howard W. Baker, Jr. (Tenn.)‡
Marlow W. Cook (Ky.)‡
Ted Stevens (Alaska)
J. Glenn Beall, Jr. (Md.)
Lowell P. Weicker, Jr. (Conn.)*

* Not a member of committee in Ninety-third Congress.
† Indicates addition in Ninety-third Congress.
‡ Not a member of committee in Ninety-fourth Congress.

xvii

Subcommittee on Aviation

Majority:

Cannon, Chm.
Magnuson
Hart
Hartke
Hollings
Inouye
Moss
Spong*
Tunney†
Stevenson†

Minority:

Cotton
Pearson
Baker
Griffin
Cook
Stevens
Beall

* Not a member of subcommittee in Ninety-third Congress.
† Indicates addition in Ninety-third Congress.

Subcommittee on Communications

Majority:

Pastore, Chm.
Hartke
Hart
Long
Moss
Cannon
Hollings
Inouye†

Minority:

Baker
Griffin
Cook
Pearson
Stevens
Beall

† Indicates addition in Ninety-third Congress.

Subcommittee on Consumer Affairs

Majority:

Moss, Chm.
Hart, Vice Chm.
Pastore
Hartke
Inouye
Spong*
Cannon†
Tunney†
Stevenson†

Minority:

Cook
Pearson
Stevens
Beall
Weicker*

* Not a member of subcommittee in Ninety-third Congress.
† Indicates addition in Ninety-third Congress.

Subcommittee on the Environment

Majority:

Hart, Chm.
Moss, Vice Chm.
Pastore
Long
Spong*
Tunney†
Stevenson†

Minority:

Cook
Baker
Pearson
Weicker*

* Not a member of subcommittee in Ninety-third Congress.
† Indicates addition in Ninety-third Congress.

Subcommittee on Foreign Commerce and Tourism

Majority:	*Minority:*
Inouye, Chm.	Griffin
Hartke	Cook†
Cannon	Pearson†
Long	Baker
Moss	Stevens
Stevenson†	Beall

† Indicates addition in Ninety-third Congress.

Subcommittee on Merchant Marine

Majority:	*Minority:*
Long, Chm.	Griffin
Pastore	Stevens
Hollings	Beall
Inouye	Weicker*
Spong*	
Tunney†	

* Not a member of subcommittee in Ninety-third Congress.
† Indicates addition in Ninety-third Congress.

Subcommittee on Oceans and Atmosphere

Majority:	*Minority:*
Hollings, Chm.	Stevens
Pastore	Griffin
Hart	Cook
Long	Beall†
Inouye	Weicker*
Spong*	
Moss†	
Tunney†	

* Not a member of subcommittee in Ninety-third Congress.
† Indicates addition in Ninety-third Congress.

Subcommittee on Surface Transportation

Majority:	*Minority:*
Hartke, Chm.	Beall
Cannon	Pearson
Moss*	Baker
Hollings	Weicker*
Long	
Stevenson†	

* Not a member of subcommittee in Ninety-third Congress.
† Indicates addition in Ninety-third Congress.

Special Subcommittee on Science, Technology, and Commerce (Established March 27, 1973)

Majority:	*Minority:*
Tunney, Chm.	Pearson
Stevenson	

HOUSE COMMITTEE ON INTERSTATE AND FOREIGN COMMERCE, NINETY-SECOND CONGRESS

Majority:

Harley O. Staggers, Chm. (W. Va.)
Torbert H. Macdonald (Mass.)
John Jarman (Okla.)
John E. Moss (Calif.)
John D. Dingell (Mich.)
Paul G. Rogers (Fla.)
Lionel Van Deerlin (Calif.)
J. J. Pickle (Tex.)
Fred B. Rooney (Pa.)
John M. Murphy (N. Y.)
David E. Satterfield III (Va.)
Brock Adams (Wash.)
Ray Blanton (Tenn.)
W. S. (Bill) Stuckey, Jr. (Ga.)
Peter N. Kyros (Me.)
Bob Eckhardt (Tex.)
Robert O. Tiernan (R. I.)
Richardson Preyer (N. C.)
Bertram L. Podell (N. Y.)
Henry Helstoski (N. J.)
James W. Symington (Mo.)
Charles J. Carney (Ohio)
Ralph H. Metcalfe (Ill.)
Goodloe E. Byron (Md.)
William R. Roy (Kans.)

Minority:

William L. Springer (Ill.)
Samuel L. Devine (Ohio)
Ancher Nelsen (Minn.)
Hastings Keith (Mass.)
James T. Broyhill (N. C.)
James Harvey (Mich.)
Tim Lee Carter (Ky.)
Clarence J. Brown (Ohio)
Dan Kuykendall (Tenn.)
Joe Skubitz (Kans.)
Fletcher Thompson (Ga.)
James F. Hastings (N. Y.)
John G. Schmitz (Calif.)
James M. Collins (Tex.)
Louis Frey, Jr. (Fla.)
John Ware (Pa.)
John Y. McCollister (Neb.)
Richard G. Shoup (Mont.)

Subcommittee on Communications and Power

Majority:

Macdonald, Chm.
Van Deerlin
Rooney
Tiernan
Byron

Minority:

Keith
Brown
Collins
Frey

Subcommittee on Transportation and Aeronautics

Majority:

Jarman, Chm.
Dingell
Murphy
Adams
Podell
Helstoski
Metcalfe

Minority:

Devine
Harvey
Kuykendall
Skubitz
Thompson

Subcommittee on Public Health and Environment

Majority:

Rogers, Chm.
Satterfield
Kyros
Preyer
Symington
Roy

Minority:

Nelsen
Carter
Hastings
Schmitz

Subcommittee on Commerce and Finance

Majority:	Minority:
Moss, Chm.	Broyhill
Stuckey	Ware
Eckhardt	McCollister
Carney	

Special Subcommittee on Investigations

Majority:	Minority:
Staggers, Chm.	Springer
Pickle	Shoup
Blanton	

HOUSE COMMITTEE ON INTERSTATE AND FOREIGN COMMERCE, NINETY-THIRD CONGRESS

Majority:	Minority:
Harley O. Staggers, Chm. (W. Va.)	Samuel L. Devine (Ohio)
	Ancher Nelsen (Minn.)‡
Torbert H. Macdonald (Mass.)	James T. Broyhill (N. C.)
John Jarman (Okla.)‡	Tim Lee Carter (Ky.)
John E. Moss (Calif.)	Clarence J. Brown (Ohio)
John D. Dingell (Mich.)	Dan Kuykendall (Tenn.)‡
Paul G. Rogers (Fla.)	Joe Skubitz (Kans.)
Lionel Van Deerlin (Calif.)	James F. Hastings (N. Y.)
J. J. Pickle (Tex.)‡	James M. Collins (Tex.)
Fred B. Rooney (Pa.)	Louis Frey, Jr. (Fla.)
John M. Murphy (N. Y.)	John Ware (Pa.)‡
David E. Satterfield IIII (Va.)	John Y. McCollister (Neb.)
Brock Adams (Wash.)	Richard G. Shoup (Mont.)‡

W. S. (Bill) Stuckey, Jr. (Ga.)
Peter N. Kyros (Me.)‡
Bob Eckhardt (Tex.)
Richardson Preyer (N. C.)
Bertram L. Podell (N. Y.)‡
Henry Helstoski (N. J.)‡
James W. Symington (Mo.)
Charles J. Carney (Ohio)
Ralph H. Metcalfe (Ill.)
Goodloe E. Byron (Md.)
William R. Roy (Kans.)‡
John Breckinridge (Ky.)‡
Thomas A. Luken (Ohio)‡

Barry M. Goldwater, Jr.
 (Calif.)‡
Norman F. Lent (N. Y.)
H. John Heinz III (Pa.)
William H. Hudnut III
 (Ind.)‡
Samuel H. Young (Ill.)‡
Edward R. Madigan (Ill.)

‡ Not a member of committee in Ninety-fourth Congress.

Subcommittee on Communications and Power

Majority:	*Minority:*
Macdonald, Chm.	Brown
Van Deerlin	Collins
Rooney	Goldwater
Murphy	Madigan
Byron	

Subcommittee on Transportation and Aeronautics

Majority:	*Minority:*
Jarman, Chm.	Kuykendall
Dingell	Skubitz
Adams	Shoup
Podell	Frey
Helstoski	
Metcalfe	

Subcommittee on Commerce and Finance

Majority:

Moss, Chm.
Stuckey
Eckhardt
Breckrinridge
Luken

Minority:

Broyhill
Ware
McCollister
Young

Subcommittee on Public Health and Environment

Majority:

Rogers, Chm.
Satterfield
Kyros
Preyer
Symington
Roy

Minority:

Nelsen
Carter
Hastings
Heinz
Hudnut

Special Subcommittee on Investigations

Majority:

Staggers, Chm.
Pickle
Carney

Minority:

Devine
Lent

THE COMMERCE
COMMITTEES

The prosperity of commerce is now perceived and acknowledged by all enlightened statesmen to be the most useful as well as the most productive source of national wealth, and has accordingly become a primary object of their political cares.

—*Alexander Hamilton*, The Federalist, 1787

1

The Politics
of Commerce

Will the American consumer receive the protection of an independent agency enforcing meaningful product safety standards? Will
the stranglehold of commercial broadcasters on cable-television
development be broken? Will the nation's coastal zones be saved
from commercial overdevelopment and irreversible ecological
damage? Can the regulation of surface transportation in the
United States be directed toward bringing lower costs and more
reliable service to the consumer? The answers to such questions
lie, in large part, with the House and Senate Committees on Commerce.

Only a few congressional sessions had elapsed in the early
years of the Republic before both House and Senate moved from
the haphazard appointment of special committees to consider
single pieces of legislation to a system of standing committees. In
the House, where this process proceeded more rapidly, the third
committee created—on December 1, 1795—was Commerce and

NOTE: This section was written by David E. Price.

3

Manufactures. In the Senate, Commerce and Manufactures was one of eleven standing committees established in 1816. Early concerns included harbor improvements, canal construction, and the regulation of shipping and foreign trade. Commerce and Manufactures were made separate committees in the House in 1819 and in the Senate in 1825. The next major reorganizations came late in the nineteenth century, as problems of railroad regulation and interoceanic canal construction led to the formation of separate committees on Interstate Commerce (1885) and Interoceanic Canals (1899) in the Senate and to the addition of "Interstate and Foreign" to the name of the House Commerce Committee (1892), together with a gradual broadening of its functions.[1]

The Legislative Reorganization Act of 1946 consolidated these functions under single Commerce committees in both houses, the jurisdictions of which did not change until late 1974, when the House transferred much of the House committee's responsibility for aviation and surface transportation policy to a new Public Works and Transportation Committee. During the period covered by this study, both committees were responsible for civil aviation; interstate railroads, buses, trucks, and pipelines; radio, television, and other interstate communications; and large segments of the expanding fields of consumer and environmental protection. The committees oversee the Federal Communications, Power, and Trade Commissions; the Consumer Product Safety Commission; the Interstate Commerce Commission; the Civil Aeronautics Board; the National Railroad Passenger Corporation; the Corporation for Public Broadcasting; and most of the bureaus within the Departments of Transportation and Commerce. The House Interstate and Foreign Commerce Committee, in addition, exercises jurisdiction over public health and safety, railway labor, and securities and exchanges, and oversees the Food and Drug Administration, Public Health Service, and Securities and Exchange Commission. The Senate Commerce Committee's jurisdiction includes the merchant marine, fisheries and wildlife, oceanography, the Federal Maritime Commission, and the Coast Guard.

THE MEMBERS

Neither Commerce committee has any trouble attracting and keeping members. Since 1971 members on the House committee have numbered forty-three, and on the Senate committee, eighteen; only the highly sought-after Appropriations committees are larger in their respective houses. House Interstate and Foreign Commerce chairman Harley O. Staggers (D., W. Va.) views the recent expansion of his committee as a mixed blessing, but acknowledges, "Everybody wanted on it, so I guess they had to do something."*

If the number of members transferring *on* as compared to *off* a committee is taken as an index of "desirability," the Commerce committees rank sixth—just behind the top "prestige" committees in both houses.[2] In the period 1969–74, only two members chose to transfer off each Commerce committee,† and it was possible to accommodate only a small fraction of those junior members seeking seats. As the Ninety-second Congress began in 1971, the average House Commerce member had been on the committee 6.0 years,‡ while the average Senate Commerce member had put in 6.9 years of committee service.

* Quotations without citations are taken from interviews conducted in 1972–74 by the Congress Project team studying the Commerce committees. Eleven members of the Senate committee, twenty-six members of the House committee, thirty-nine present or former congressional staff members, seventeen lobbyists and group representatives, five journalists, and twenty-seven present or former executive-branch and commission personnel were interviewed. Member interviews were semistructured, focusing on the member's goals as a legislator and the perceived relationship of a range of committee characteristics and practices to the shaping and pursuit of those goals. Interviews with other respondents were more specific and less uniformly structured. Here the intention was ordinarily to get a picture, from the respondent's particular perspective, of the factors shaping policy outcomes in a given area or on a particular bill, with special attention to the congressional role.

A recording device was not used, and note-taking was restricted where it seemed to threaten rapport or hinder free exchange. A transcript, as nearly verbatim as possible, was prepared immediately after each interview; it is this from which the "quotations" in the text are taken.

† The House transfers were to Ways and Means and Appropriations, the Senate transfers to Appropriations and Foreign Relations.

‡ Discounting the four new seats just added.

Why do such large numbers of congressmen seek appointment to the Commerce committees? Most committee members cite the importance of Commerce's work to their state or district. A substantial minority mention the breadth of the committees' jurisdictions and welcome the opportunity to shape public policy in ways that go beyond constituency service—especially in health (for the House committee) and consumer affairs (more frequently mentioned on the Senate side). House committee members seem also to value their seats as a mark of prestige and power; there is a sense that their appointment is an important sign of preferment and advancement within the House. But the major reason members give for seeking membership is the committee's relevance to their district and the major, if not exclusive, goal they articulate is district service.*

TABLE 1.

Demographic Characteristics of Members of House and
Senate Commerce Committees, 1972

	Percentage of Members			
	Senate Commerce	Entire Senate	House Commerce	Entire House
Business or banking background	35	27	42	33
Represent state/district bordering on ocean or Great Lakes	72	64	49	42
Region represented:				
Northeast	22	24	28	28
South	22	24	30	25
Midwest	28	26	30	31
West	28	26	12	16

SOURCE: *Congressional Quarterly Weekly Report*, Jan. 15, 1971, pp. 126–133.

* The House committee thus fits imperfectly into Richard Fenno's categorization of House committees according to the goals motivating the bulk of their membership—prestige and power within the House for Ways and Means and Appropriations, constituent service for Interior and Post Office, and the shaping of public policy for Education and Labor and Foreign Affairs. See Richard Fenno, *Congressmen in Committees* (Boston: Little, Brown, 1973), Chapter 1.

Commerce committee members are disproportionately drawn from districts and professions to which the work of the committees is especially relevant, as Table 1 shows. A higher percentage of members of both the House and Senate committees come from coastal areas and from banking or business backgrounds than is true of their parent chambers, although the pattern does not compare with the predominance of westerners on the Interior committees or of coastal-state representatives on the House Merchant Marine and Fisheries Committee. Members from a wide variety of districts apparently find Commerce committee seats desirable. The relevance of merchant marine, fisheries, aviation, and surface transportation policy has traditionally made for an disproportionate number of western members on the Senate committee, and Alaska, Washington, Maryland, and South Carolina have long laid claim to "reserved" seats. House members often mention an understanding that tobacco districts have a claim to membership on the Interstate and Foreign Commerce Committee, and one analyst has concluded that some one-third of the seats on House Commerce are handed down on the basis of the "prescriptive claims" of state delegations.[3] But as Table 1 shows, the regional distributions of the committees' members do not differ markedly from those of the House and Senate as a whole.

A further indicator of the interests and priorities of members is the choice they make with respect to subcommittee membership. House Commerce members may belong to only one subcommittee and, as Table 2 shows, when the opportunity comes to make a choice, it is the Transportation and Aeronautics and Communications and Power subcommittees that are most successful in attracting and retaining members.* The subcommittee handling consumer affairs, Commerce and Finance, ranks lowest on both of our indices of "desirability." Transfer figures are less meaningful on the Senate committee, where multiple subcommittee member-

---

* It thus seems likely that the House's alteration of the committee's jurisdiction in 1974—removing most transportation matters (except railroads) and broadening the committee's responsibility for health policy—will have a major impact on Commerce's recruitment base and its members' priorities.

ships are permitted, but here too seniority figures suggest that transportation and communications are the areas of greatest interest, with consumer affairs weighing in more favorably than on the House panel.*

TABLE 2.

"Desirability" Rankings of House and Senate Commerce Subcommittees

A. Average Committee Seniority of Subcommittee Members, January 1971

Senate Commerce Subcommittee	*Mean (years)*
Aviation	6.7
Communications	6.2
Consumer	6.1
Surface Transportation	5.5
Environment	5.1
Foreign Commerce and Tourism	5.1
Merchant Marine	4.8
Oceans and Atmosphere	4.4

House Interstate and Foreign Commerce Subcommittee	*Mean (years)*
Transportation and Aeronautics	5.7
Communications and Power	5.4
Health and Environment	4.4
Commerce and Finance	3.9

B. Transfers of Membership among House Commerce Subcommittees, 1962–1974

Transfer to:	*Transfer from:*				
	T&A	*H&E*	*C&P*	*C&F*	*Net*
Transportation and Aeronautics	—	3	4	8	+9
Health and Environment	2	—	0	0	−1
Communications and Power	1	0	—	3	−2
Commerce and Finance	3	0	2	—	−6

* The average committee seniority of the members of a subcommittee gives some indication of how desirable a subcommittee it is, since requests for subcommittee assignment are normally honored in accordance with the member's length of committee service. Less senior members thus must often take less desirable assignments. Membership transfers are a meaningful index only in the House committee where, in contrast to Senate Commerce, members could (prior to 1975) sit on only one subcommittee and hence had to choose to remain or transfer (as seniority and the chairman's discretion allowed) at the beginning of each Congress.

There is little evidence that constituency-based or other groups play a decisive role in dictating who gets on the committees or in urging members to seek seats. In this respect Commerce differs from, for example, the House Education and Labor Committee, where the recruitment efforts of both labor and management are often quite conspicuous. But the difference is not absolute; the potency of interests such as tobacco in North Carolina and shipping in Washington are responsible for much of the fervor of state delegations in claiming their Commerce committee birthrights. Nor are interested groups necessarily averse to interjecting themselves into "internal" committee matters. For example, Senate Commerce chairman Warren G. Magnuson (D., Wash.) denied the Aviation Subcommittee chairmanship to Vance Hartke (D., Ind.) in 1968 largely on the strength of industry objections. In deference to labor, House chairman Harley Staggers has attempted to persuade Torbert H. Macdonald (D., Mass.) to take the chairmanship of the Transportation and Aeronautics Subcommittee in order to bump management-oriented John Jarman (D., Okla.) from the position, and Staggers, again at labor's urging, successfully "encouraged" J. J. Pickle (D., Tex.) to forgo his seat on Transportation and Aeronautics in favor of the Investigations Subcommittee in 1971.

Commerce committee members represent a "middling" group ideologically. As Table 3 indicates, Senate committee members are close to the Senate norm in their average "liberalism" score, and majority and minority members fall near the averages for their respective parties in the Senate. In both cases, however, the committee contingents are less widely *scattered* in their scores than are their fellow partisans as a whole. Commerce committee Democrats range in their 1971 Americans for Democratic Action (ADA) rating from Philip A. Hart's (Mich.) 96 to Russell B. Long's (La.) 19, but most fall within twenty points of Magnuson's score of 78. The Republicans range from Norris Cotton's (N.H.) zero to Ted Stevens' (Alaska) 48, but most are clustered around Marlow W. Cook's (Ky.) and Robert P. Griffin's (Mich.) modal score of 33. This ideological distribution makes for relatively easy compromise both among and between Senate committee Democrats and Republicans.

TABLE 3.

Mean ADA "Liberalism" Scores and Standard
Deviations from Means, 1971*

	Mean Score	Standard Deviation
Senate Commerce Committee	46.0	27.6
Democrats	62.1	24.1
Republicans	25.9	16.5
Entire Senate	45.9	33.7
Democrats	63.9	29.7
Republicans	23.9	24.1
House Commerce Committee	37.7	32.1
Democrats	56.7	29.6
Republicans	11.4	7.2
Entire House	39.3	32.2
Democrats	52.5	32.3
Republicans	20.1	20.2

* For the 1971 scores and an accounting of the votes on which they are based, see ADA World, January 1972. Mean scores have been computed for the chambers as they stood in 1971, but the committee rosters used for computation have been updated to 1972. Data processed by William Lunn.

Larger ideological divergences on the House committee cause greater difficulties in consensus-building in that group. House Commerce's liberalism score is close to the House average, though considerably below that of the Senate committee. Majority members are widely scattered between John Jarman's and David E. Satterfield's (Va.) scores of 8 and Bob Eckhardt's (Tex.) 94 and Henry Helstoski's (N.J.) 95, though their dispersal does not exceed that of House Democrats as a whole. House Commerce Republicans contrast with committee Democrats both in their low mean score and in the uniformity of their individual rankings; none fall above Hastings Keith's (Mass.) and James Harvey's (Mich.) 27, and half fall within the parameters of 8 and 11 set by Samuel L. Devine (Ohio), William L. Springer (Ill.), and Ancher Nelsen (Minn.), the committee's three senior Republicans.

A collective profile of the members of the two Commerce committees thus begins to emerge. They largely but not exclusively value their committee seats because of the special relevance of Commerce committee matters to their districts and to powerful economic interests; they are rather scattered in their regional and group ties; and they tend toward "moderate" voting. How does this influence the committees' policy roles? For one thing, it is important to note a syndrome that does *not* often appear on either committee: that of the large and/or urban-state liberal, cued to the media, often aiming at higher office, and attempting to project a national image of policy leadership. This type of legislator has become increasingly conspicuous in recent years, particularly in the Senate. But by and large such members have not gravitated to the Commerce committees (although John V. Tunney of California and Adlai E. Stevenson III of Illinois were added to the Senate committee in 1973), and the committees' agendas and levels of policy-making involvement have shown it.

It could be argued, of course, that in many areas of Commerce committee jurisdiction, ideological "flexibility" and strong constituency or group ties are just as likely, and perhaps more likely, to lead to extensive policy-making endeavors as are stronger sorts of liberal and programmatic commitments. The willingness of Howard W. Cannon (D., Nev.) to back major new aviation subsidies (see Chapter 4) and of Vance Hartke and Brock Adams (D., Wash.) to underwrite the railroads (see Chapter 3) are cases in point, as are the more independent entrepreneurial efforts of Senators Magnuson and Ernest F. Hollings (D., S.C.) on behalf of maritime affairs and oceanography (Chapter 7). But such ties and orientations more often lead to a *defense* of comfortable patterns of subsidy and anticompetitive "regulation." Committee membership is valued for the vote and the voice it gives one with regard to matters affecting his clients, but rarely as a platform from which one might search for policy gaps, advocate major new departures, or exercise vigorous oversight of the regulatory agencies.

On both committees the average member's level of policy-making involvement is rather low. Our interviews suggest, however, that for most members their level of performance is a fair measure of their aspirations. Commerce members are not, by and large, would-be activists frustrated because they cannot do more. Complaints of a lack of time and resources to "do this job right" are endemic, but few members can be credited with a full realization of the potential they *now* have for sustained lawmaking and oversight activity.

The rate of activism is somewhat higher on the Senate committee than on its House counterpart. A more active Senate staff bears considerable responsibility for this, but so do a number of members who are willing to make at least minimal efforts at policy instigation and oversight. Magnuson has assumed strong policy leadership in consumer and maritime affairs over the years; Frank E. Moss (D., Utah) and Ernest Hollings, as subcommittee chairmen, have become increasingly assertive in consumer affairs and oceanography, respectively; and Philip Hart, despite some retrenchment in recent years, is still actively identified with a range of legislative projects in consumer and environmental affairs. New members Tunney and Stevenson have already made their mark on committee output, mainly in the energy and consumer areas. Hartke must be credited with considerable energy and persistence, however open to doubt his effectiveness and the merits of some of his projects (see Chapter 3) may be. Chairmen Long and Cannon of the Merchant Marine and Aviation subcommittees have proved active and effective promoters of the industries under their care, although their efforts reveal little independence or creativity (see Chapters 4 and 7). Among the Republicans, James B. Pearson's (Kans.) active collaboration with Cannon on aviation promotion, Ted Stevens' occasional innovations on Alaska-related policy questions, and Lowell P. Weicker's (Conn.)* concern with Amtrak and other surface transportation matters are worthy of note.

---

* Weicker was bumped from the committee in 1973 because of a shift in party ratios. In 1975, however, he and James Buckley (N.Y.) filled the Republican slots vacated through Cotton's retirement and Howard Baker's (Tenn.) move to Foreign Relations.

Senate Commerce members are thus not paragons of legislative creativity or vigilant oversight, and many of those who are active take their cues from the dominant economic interests in their policy areas. But it is, as an activist staff member puts it, "a committee you can work with." A number of members are sufficiently alert and motivated to perceive the policy gaps and deficiencies in developing areas such as consumer and environmental affairs and to assume a modicum of responsibility and leadership.

Policy involvement is less intense and less widely distributed on the House committee. Table 4 reflects an estimate gleaned from

TABLE 4.
Estimated Levels of Legislative Activity
House Commerce Committee, 92nd Congress

Self-starters	Moss, Rogers, Adams, Roy, Eckhardt
Occasional activists	Staggers, Macdonald, Jarman, Dingell, Van Deerlin, Pickle, Tiernan, Springer, Nelsen, Broyhill, Carter
Largely inactive	Rooney, Murphy, Satterfield, Blanton, Stuckey, Kyros, Preyer, Podell, Helstoski, Symington, Carney, Metcalfe, Byron, Devine, Keith, Harvey, Brown, Kuykendall, Skubitz, Thompson, Hastings, Schmitz, Collins, Frey, Ware, McCollister, Shoup

interviews and from committee documents of the members' propensity to propose new departures or substantial refinements in policy in the areas under their care. As subsequent chapters will show, John E. Moss (D., Calif.), who was chairman of the Commerce and Finance Subcommittee until his election to the Investigations Subcommittee chairmanship in 1975, and Paul G. Rogers (D., Fla.), Health and Environment chairman since 1971, stand apart as the most productive legislators on the committee, although they differ markedly from each other in style and tactics. Full-committee chairman Staggers, Communications and Power chairman Torbert Macdonald, and Transportation and Aeronautics chairman John Jarman have periodically asserted themselves, but their efforts seem more a function of their formal responsibilities as chairmen and of the pressure placed upon them than of any independent, coherent, or sustained policy interests. The activism

of relatively junior members such as Brock Adams in transportation. William Roy in health, and Bob Eckhardt in consumer
affairs points up, by contrast, the inertness of the bulk of the
membership. It also suggests, however, that there is nothing im-
mutable about this situation: a more productive role is open to
those who will assert themselves.

The rarity of sustained legislative endeavors among House
Commerce Republicans reflects the fact that they are neither in
control of committee machinery nor held responsible for committee output. It also reflects the prevalence of conservative, *status
quo* orientations among them. Some minority members deserve
inclusion among the "occasional activists," however, by virtue of
their relatively creative and cooperative contributions to processes
of legislative refinement and compromise as proposals make their
way through the committee. It is no accident, of course, that it is
the ranking committee and subcommittee members who most
often assume such a role.

The paucity of individual *attempts* at policy-instigation, which
reflects nonactivist job orientations and underdeveloped policy
goals on the part of most members, constitutes a major explanation for committee nonfeasance. Conversely, the occasional instances of House Commerce leadership and the somewhat more
creditable performance of the Senate committee must be attributed in large part to the willingness of members to assume the
burden of legislative advocacy. This should be kept in mind as the
committees are examined in greater detail as work settings: a
focus on incentive-producing and -constraining conditions should
not obscure the basic fact that the kind of job a legislator wants to
do is largely up to him. One can say all he likes, for example,
about the particular advantages and resources that enabled freshman Congressman William Roy to have an impact on health policy (see Chapter 6), but the major explanation still lies in his
own purposefulness and persistence. That these qualities are in
such short supply on the Commerce committees goes a long way
toward explaining the policy-making and oversight disabilities of
both groups.

THE LEADERS

In a sense, both the House and Senate Commerce committees are weakly led. The consequences of this, however, are vastly different for the two groups. The difference stems not only from Staggers' and Magnuson's particular flaws and strengths, but also from the traditions and circumstances of the group each attempts to lead. Indeed, one could argue that Magnuson's laxity enhances the Senate committee's productivity, albeit under conditions that must be regarded as unstable and potentially dangerous. Staggers' weakness, on the other hand, contributes measurably to the House committee's high level of frustration and paralysis. Such judgments are relative; both chairmen want to run productive, responsive committees, and neither aspires to the kind of autocracy and obstructiveness for which past and present chairmen of the Agriculture and Armed Services committees have become notorious.

Staff members and other observers often speak of a dramatic transformation in Magnuson's role as committee chairman and legislative leader over the past decade.[4] In the wake of near-defeat in the 1962 election, Magnuson began to accept suggestions that he should take a more active role in promoting legislation with general public appeal. This led to important staff changes: Gerald Grinstein, a young, liberal, and aggressive aide was made chief counsel and was given considerable freedom to hire aides of his own choosing and to chart a more ambitious legislative course. Onto the old Magnuson, interested mainly in fishing, shipping, and Boeing aircraft, and running a rather sleepy committee, was grafted a new one: the champion of the consumer, the national legislative leader, and the patron of an energetic and innovative legislative staff.

At times it was uncertain whether the graft would "take." Magnuson's new role gave proposals like fair packaging, cigarette labeling and advertising regulation, and traffic safety a new lease on life. But the original advocates of these and other measures frequently expressed the fear that once Magnuson "gets hold of something . . . while he'll get it passed, he is likely to compromise it away in the process." Staff conflicts between old guard and new went on for years, feeding fears that Magnuson would revert to what one aide called "his natural tendency . . . to pull back, not to get any new fires started."* At present however, the situation has stabilized considerably. Michael Pertschuk, one of Grinstein's first staff recruits, is firmly entrenched as chief counsel; his own assertiveness, plus what one aide terms "a progressive lopping off from the payroll of the old cronies," has made for a new degree of staff consensus and unity around activist, reformist norms. And Magnuson himself is noticeably bolder, though still hardly a legislative zealot.

This is not to say that the "old" Magnuson is no more. In areas like transportation and communications he still sees himself as little more than a broker among dominant interests: "In some of these areas it's pretty difficult [to be a legislative leader]. All these interests pulling this way and that—you just have to work your way through as carefully as you can." Subsequent chapters will document how far the chairman was willing to go during the Ninety-second Congress in extravagantly underwriting the railroads, the airlines, and the merchant marine. The servicing of home-state interests is still a central concern, and it continues to pay off in votes and campaign support. It also apparently pays off for Washington: in 1971 the per capita expenditures of both the Commerce and Transportation departments in the state were three times the national average.[5]

---

* Quotes from David E. Price, *Who Makes the Laws? Creativity and Power in Senate Committees* (Cambridge: Schenkman, 1972), pp. 87, 78. The analytical underpinnings of the present study are to some extent spelled out in this earlier work, a comparative study of policy-making on the Senate Commerce, Finance, and Labor and Public Welfare committees. *Who Makes the Laws?* explores the conditions of legislative independence and creativity and thus, in its treatment of the Commerce committee, gives disproportionate emphasis to the emerging area of consumer affairs. The present study attempts to take a more comprehensive view of the committees' jurisdictional territory, examining not only major legislative endeavors but also policy areas where inaction or subordination to the dominant agencies and interests in the environment is the usual pattern of behavior.

Magnuson, however, can with justification claim a more creative leadership role in consumer affairs and oceanography. His capacity for toughness is borne out by his steadfastness on such matters as the enforcement and rule-making provisions of the Federal Trade Commission (FTC) Improvements Act and the provisions for citizen suits in the Consumer Product Safety Act (see Chapter 2). He was willing to fight two major industries in enacting, in 1970, a prohibition of the broadcast advertising of cigarettes, and to defy the scheduled airlines in 1974 by reporting a bill liberalizing the regulation of charter flights. Magnuson and his staff make prudential calculations in deciding which bills it is profitable to take up and when, but their notion of what is possible has expanded since the mid-sixties, and they are less likely to be intimidated by the prospects of industry opposition. Magnuson still dreads floor fights and seeks to avoid confrontations, but his persistence in pursuing no-fault insurance and other measures to which he has become committed has often been impressive.

While becoming bolder in his legislative stances, Magnuson has in recent years also become progressively disengaged from day-to-day Commerce committee affairs. His growing duties on Appropriations ("*That's* the kind of committee work Magnuson really likes," comments one associate. "All that horse-trading—he's really in his element"), his own and his wife's health problems, his noncomprehension of and impatience with close legislative work—all have in recent years increasingly left others at the Commerce committee helm.

The slack has to some extent been taken up by the subcommittee chairmen and other members. But the lackadaisical and over-extended commitments of many of those members, the chairman's continuing control of key committee functions and resources, and the staff's efforts to preserve Magnuson's prerogatives have inhibited decentralization in this direction. The main beneficiaries of the laxness of Magnuson's personal leadership have rather been those who speak in the chairman's name: Michael Pertschuk and the talented, aggressive staff he has assembled. The activist, reformist inclinations of these aides and their ties with consumer and environmental advocates make the committee output more prolific and "tougher" in terms of regulation than it might be if Magnuson or other members were more actively in charge. But subsequent chapters will point up several moments of truth during the Ninety-second Congress when organized interests found sympathetic allies among the committee leadership and the staff was reminded where the ultimate power lay. Activist aides, no matter how skilled they are or how much freedom they are given, are not an adequate substitute for active, informed, committed senators. The Senate Commerce Committee is strong in the former department, considerably weaker in the latter. As long as that is the case, doubts will persist as to the stability and steadfastness of its legislative role.

When one turns from "task" leadership to what sociologists call "social" leadership—the maintenance of an atmosphere of cooperation and harmony, the promotion of group solidarity—Magnuson's particular personal strengths become more apparent. When committee members are asked to comment on Magnuson's qualities as a leader, they almost always list traits that contribute to group cohesion. "Maggie is easy to work with," says Frank Moss. "He's tolerant and understanding. It's a good committee." "Maggie is an incredible man," chimes in Republican James Pearson. "I love the man. He's a great big bear. But he's not a buffoon, as some might assume. . . . Of course his strong point is his ability to bring people together." In some committees social and task leadership interfere with each other; committee harmony can be purchased by compromises that, while rendering legislation less controversial, also make it ineffectual. That, however, would not be a fair characterization of the way harmony and unity are achieved on the Commerce Committee. Bargains and compromise often do take place, but Commerce Committee bills are increasingly being reported with their teeth intact *and* with the support of a large and bipartisan majority of the membership. Most members believe that a large part of the explanation is to be found in Magnuson's low-key style, his fairness and tolerance, and in the homespun persuasiveness he possesses.

House Commerce members use many of the same adjectives to describe their chairman, Harley Staggers, as do their Senate counterparts in speaking of Magnuson: kind, warm, persuasive, decent. But the context in which such charitable characterizations are given is considerably different: they invariably insert a qualifying remark to explain how these admirable human traits do not result in effective group leadership.

Staggers' fifteen years of service on the committee resulted in his elevation to the chairmanship in 1966, when Oren Harris (D., Ark.) left Congress to become a federal judge. Harris was a conservative and controlling chairman whose legacy proved problematic for the rather indecisive and mild-mannered Staggers. Early in his term Staggers was confronted with the restiveness of members like John Moss and John D. Dingell (D., Mich.), who were anxious to increase the committee's output and their own contribution to it. Staggers' tendency was to be cautious and suspicious. As one member put it:

> Staggers doesn't like controversy. He's most comfortable when he's reporting out a bill that increases some railway labor welfare fund—or maybe a health bill reported out by Paul Rogers, who's a pretty conservative fellow. Some of these consumer bills that he doesn't know much about, but which look controversial to him—or maybe he's getting some objections from [ranking Republican] William Springer—then he'll hold back and it'll be hard to get a commitment out of him.

Such behavior cannot always be explained by the chairman's ideological and policy preferences. His cumulative ADA score is 77 and his AFL–CIO rating is a hefty 94. He is considerably to the left of Oren Harris. But Staggers has felt constrained to keep committee power centralized, and this has prevented him from delegating authority and dispersing resources gracefully. Staggers has tended on ideological and policy grounds frequently to identify with the aspirations of the liberal wing of the committee and the activist subcommittee chairmen, but he has become threatened and defensive as this group increasingly has questioned his own efficiency and effectiveness and has sought to share some of his powers. The result has been a series of struggles and uneasy truces between Staggers and his more active members, and the development of a legislative bottleneck at the top of the committee.

Subcommittee chairmen frequently complain of the difficulty of scheduling hearings and of securing full-committee action on subcommittee bills. These problems do not reflect any sustained and systematic effort to control or skew committee output, as was the case under Oren Harris; with Staggers, the holding back, the delays, the occasional outright obstruction are better understood in terms of the anxieties of the chairman, his fear of losing control of the committee, and his periodic impulse to demonstrate where the real power lies. Those who know Staggers best never characterize him as naturally power-hungry or aggressive. They do, however, acknowledge a tendency to become peevish and vindictive when pressed and to squelch those whom he suspects might be willing to take advantage of him. There is little doubt that his peculiar anxieties and sensitivities have had their inhibiting effect on the committee's work.

Staggers' leadership style affects the committee's external role and relationships as well as its internal operations. In 1972 he held up a repeal of the equal-time rule (which would have facilitated the televising of presidential campaign debates) as a way of "getting even" with the House leadership after they had rebuffed him in his attempt to serve a subpoena on CBS in connection with a Commerce Committee investigation (see Chapter 5). The House committee's frequent intransigence in Senate-House conference is also related to Staggers' style. As a Senate aide perceptively reports:

> Like a lot of weak people, Staggers will dig in on something and not give an inch. It's not a matter of "conservatism"—a

lot of these things he agrees with—but just this feeling that he's got to stand firm.

Staggers' background and legislative orientation do not give him any particular capacity or incentive for energetic and productive committee leadership. The electoral pressures that have goaded Magnuson are not present in West Virginia's safely Democratic, rural, and isolated second district. It is a district, however, to which Staggers is extraordinarily closely tied; he loves to talk of its history and landmarks, his early years as a coach and as sheriff of Mineral County, his weekly trips back to his home and around the district. He does not doubt that his committee position results in benefits for his district: he mentions the Department of Transportation's experimental "people-mover" in Morgantown, the Harpers Ferry National Monument, and a Bureau of Mines facility at Morgantown ("Scoop Jackson wanted that for Washington"). The commitments of the Commerce Department's Economic Development Administration in Staggers' district totaled $11.9 million through June 30, 1971—compared to a $2.0 million average for all districts represented by House Commerce members and a $1.9 million average for all House districts.* Department of Transportation outlays in the district in 1970 were almost twice the national average.[7] It was in deference to Staggers that Amtrak instituted a special turbotrain run from Washington, D.C., to Parkersburg, West Virginia. The train, known affectionately as "Harley's Bullet," was eventually canceled because of insufficient passenger use.

As a constituency-oriented representative, Staggers has good reason to value his Commerce seat, although he also perceives that most of his committee work counts for little among the constituents to whom he remains so finely attuned: "Sometimes you wonder if all the work is worth it. They don't know anything about all these things. What really matters are the local things, things close to the individual." Staggers speaks with genuine satisfaction of the way the committee has "helped people," particularly in the health field. But his references to legislative accom-

---

* The average for all House committee chairmen is $5.5 million.[6]

plishments and goals remain vague, and one suspects that his senses of efficacy and adequacy are rather fragile. Staggers is a man who probably would not have sought or gained leadership had it not been for the exigencies of the seniority system. He dutifully carries out his responsibilities as he sees them: "Being chairman of this committee takes half to three-quarters of my time. When people come in about one bill or another—maybe I shouldn't, but I agree to see every one of them." But he seems to derive as many burdens and anxieties as he does satisfactions from the job. Basically localistic in his orientation, with few well-developed legislative ideas and little innate taste or capacity for policy leadership, Staggers has not translated his good intentions into innovative or energetic or even expeditious legislative undertakings. The result is a committee where outright obstruction occurs less frequently than it did previously but where legislation nonetheless frequently gets bogged down. "It's not so much a matter of one guy or another setting out to kill a bill," said one Senate aide. "You just never see a lot of these things again."

Committee members are far from entirely negative in their assessment of Staggers' leadership. Most express some affection for the man, and some value the increased efficacy they have experienced because the committee is now "not as tight a ship." But members invariably comment on a weakness in the chairman which keeps him from effectively mobilizing the committee for action but at the same time leads him sporadically to attempt to assert his authority. The weakness might be acceptable if it led to an effective decentralization of the committee, a willingness to "let things happen." The self-assertiveness might be acceptable if it made for unified and sustained legislative endeavors. But Staggers' leadership qualities in their present incarnation contribute both to the committee's unpredictability and sluggishness and to the restiveness of its membership.

THE STAFFS

The differences between the House and Senate Commerce Committee staffs are just as striking as the contrasts between their chairmen—and perhaps even more determinative of the contrasting legislative roles played by the two committees. The Senate committee staff is larger and less thinly spread; as Tables 5 and 7 show, it has more than doubled in size since 1965. The more important difference, however, has to do with the *kind* of services the two staffs render, the way they view their jobs. In the Senate committee, the activist, "entrepreneurial" style fostered by men like Gerald Grinstein, William Foster, and Michael Pertschuk in the mid-sixties has become the established norm.[8] The House Commerce staff, in contrast, sees itself as a resource for the members' use more than as a source of ideas and initiatives. Neutrality and nonpartisanship are key norms.

The Senate staff is generally adequate to the committee's workload—although the committee by no means gets its money's worth from long-term patronage appointees like Frederick Lordan, Edward Stern, and Joseph Fogarty or from the numerous subcommittee aides used for personal staff work. The chairman himself is a major offender in this regard. *Washington Post* reporter Stephen Isaacs (February 20, 1975) found three aides on the committee payroll working in Magnuson's office, largely on matters unrelated to committee business. Another characteristic of the Senate staff is suggested by Table 7: there has been an easy movement between service on the committee and lucrative positions in industry or in law firms dealing with the government. Former staff members like Gerald Grinstein and William Foster have become highly skilled, highly paid lobbyists, often trading on their continuing access to the committee. To note such linkages is not necessarily to impugn them, but these career patterns do contribute to the accommodationist norms and practices that prevail in most areas of the committee's jurisdiction.*

The House Commerce staff includes seven full-committee professionals and ten assigned to the Investigations Subcommittee, all appointed by and responsible to the chairman (see Table 6).

---

* An interesting, if partial, exception is represented by Stanton Sender, who says his work as surface transportation counsel on the committee convinced him he wanted to work for a shipper rather than a carrier.

TABLE 5.
Professional Staff, Senate Commerce Committee, August 1, 1974

Name	Previous experience	Years on committee	Policy area	Responsible to:
Michael Pertschuk	Legislative assistant to Sen. Maureen Neuberger	10	Chief counsel; consumer	Magnuson
Lynn Sutcliffe	U. of Washington Law School	8	Surface transportation; transportation generally	Magnuson
Thomas Allison	U. of Washington Law School	2	Consumer, transportation	Magnuson
Leonard Bickwit	Lawyer (New York)	5	Environment	Magnuson, Hart
Michael Brownlee	Bureau of Sport Fisheries and Wildlife	3	Environment	Magnuson, Hart
John Butz		25	Case work (Magnuson's office)	Magnuson
Edward Cohen	Law student	4	Consumer	Magnuson
Paul Cunningham	U. of Washington Law School	2	Environment, transportation	Magnuson
Richard Daschbach	Legislative assistant to Sen. Long	5	Merchant marine	Long
Joseph Fogarty	Lawyer (R. I.)	10	General	Pastore
Robert Ginther	Press secretary to Sen. Magnuson	7	Aviation	Magnuson, Cannon
John Hardy	FCC	6	Communications	Magnuson, Pastore
John Hussey	Press secretary to Sen. Hollings	2½	Oceanography	Magnuson, Hollings
Barry Hyman	Professor, Geo. Washington U.	2	Staff engineer	Magnuson

Name	Background	Area	Years	Senator
John Jimison	Amer. Public Gas Assn. and Library of Congress	Energy	½	Magnuson
Robert Joost	Trial Lawyers Assn.; Judiciary Comm.	Legislative counsel	1	Magnuson
Frank Krebs	Staff of Sen. Cannon	Aviation	½	Cannon
Eric Lee	Legislative assistant to Sen Inouye	Foreign commerce; general	3½	Inouye Magnuson
Henry Lippek	U. of Washington Law School	Energy	3	Magnuson
Frederick Lordan	Administrative assistant to Sen. Magnuson	Staff director; tourism	7	Magnuson
Howard Marlowe	Law student	Surface transportation	1	Hartke
Linda McCorkle	Law School; HEW	Environment	1	Magnuson
Linda McKeough	Graduate school	Staff economist	1	Magnuson
Edward Merlis	Clearinghouse for Smoking and Health, Public Health Service	Consumer	3	Magnuson, Moss
W. F. Reid	State Legislature, Washington	HEW appropriations (Magnuson's office)	11	Magnuson
Loyal Snyder	U. of Washington Law School	General	4	Magnuson
Edward Stern	Northwest Airlines	General	19	Magnuson
James Walsh	U. of Washington Law School	Fisheries; oceanography	2	Magnuson
John Wedin	Edited Fisherman's News-paper, Washington	Fisheries	8	Magnuson
Nicholas Zapple	Counsel, CAB	Communications	25	Magnuson, Pastore
John Dale	IRS, Intelligence Division	Investigations	3½	Magnuson
William Gray	House Gov't. Operations Comm.	Investigations	4	Magnuson

TABLE 5. Professional Staff, Senate Commerce Committee, August 1, 1974 (Cont'd)

Name	Previous experience	Years on committee	Policy area	Responsible to:
James Kelly	House Commerce Investigations	3	Investigations	Magnuson
Arthur Pankopf	Minority counsel, House Merchant Marine and Fisheries Comm.	5	Chief minority counsel	Cotton
Tom Adams	Justice Department	2	Consumer	Cook
David Clanton	Legislative assistant to Sen. Griffin	3½	Merchant marine; foreign commerce	Griffin
John Kirtland	Staff, Sen. Pearson and Rep. Mize	3	Aviation	Cotton, Pearson
Malcolm Sterret	ICC	3½	Surface transportation	Pearson
Ward White	Legislative assistant to Sen. Dole	3	Communications	Baker

SOURCE: Committee records and interviews.

TABLE 6.
Professional Staff, House Commerce Committee, August 1, 1974

Name	Previous experience	Years on committee	Policy area	Responsible to:
William J. Dixon	CAB appellate division	10	Transportation and aeronautics	Staggers
Robert F. Guthrie	House legislative counsel	7	Communications; consumer	Staggers
Charles B. Curtis	SEC Counsel	3	Consumer; securities	Staggers
Lee Hyde	Public Health Service	2	Health	Staggers
John Gamble	Staff, Rep. Blanton	1½	Surface transportation	Staggers
Elizabeth Harrison	Electronics Industry Associates	1½	Consumer	Staggers
Jeffrey Schwartz	EPA counsel	1½	Energy; environment	Staggers
Dariel Manelli	Trial attorney, FTC; legal counsel, Dept. of Commerce	7	Chief counsel, investigations	Staggers
Michael F. Barrett, Jr.	Army JAG; trial attorney, FTC and SEC	4	Investigations	Staggers
Raymond Cole	Congressional investigations committees	2	Investigations	Staggers
James Connor	U.S. Army (ret.)	9	Investigations	Staggers
William Druhan	GAO	7	Investigations	Staggers
Lynne Finney	Law teaching and practice	1	Investigations	Staggers
Albert McGrath	FBI	3	Investigations	Staggers
Michael Parker	Private law practice	3½	Investigations	Staggers
Mark Raabe	FBI; FTC counsel	4½	Investigations	Staggers
Ben Smethurst	FBI	5½	Investigations	Staggers
Walter J. Graham, Jr.	Education and Labor Comm.	3½	Transportation and Aeronautics Subcomm.	Jarman

TABLE 6. Professional Staff, House Commerce Committee, August 1, 1974 (*Cont'd*)

Name	Previous experience	Years on committee	Policy areas	Responsible to:
Stephan Lawton	Staff, Rep. Jarman	3½	Public Health and Environment Subcomm.	Rogers
Michael Lemov	Product Safety Commission; Banking and Currency Committee	3	Commerce and Finance Subcomm.	Moss
Richard Krolik	Manager cable system, Columbia, Md.	2½	Communications and Power Subcomm.	MacDonald
Lewis E. Berry	Deputy Director, Office of Civil Defense	11	Chief minority counsel; transportation	Devine
Thomas Greene	U.S. Attorney General's staff; Riggs Bank trust officer	3½	Consumer; securities	Devine
Bertram Levine	Blue Cross; HEW; WH drug abuse office	1½	Health and environment	Devine
Thomas Sawyer	Teaching and administration, Ohio State U.	1½	Communications and power	Devine
Jan Vlcek	CAB counsel; EPA	1½	Transportation and aeronautics	Devine

SOURCE: Committee records and interviews.

TABLE 7.

Where Are They Now?

Professional Staff, 1965, Senate Commerce Committee

Name	Policy area	Subsequent employment
Gerald Grinstein	Chief counsel	Administrative assistant to Sen. Magnuson; now practicing law (Seattle)
William Beeks	Aviation	Air West (San Francisco)
Donald Brodie	Natural gas; power	Teaching, U. of Oregon Law School
John Burzio	Aviation	Post Office & Civil Service Comm. (under Monroney); now practicing law
Donald Cole	Consumer	Practicing law (Seattle)
Joseph Fogarty	General	Still with committee
William Foster	Merchant marine; fisheries	Ralston Purina (D.C. representative); now practicing law (D.C.)
Harry Huse	Fisheries	Retired (now deceased)
Daniel Markel	Press man; oceanography	Retired
Michael Pertschuk	Consumer	Still with committee (chief counsel)
Stanton Sender	Surface transportation	Sears, Roebuck (transportation counsel)
Edward Storn	General	Still with committee
Nicholas Zapple	Communications	Still with committee
Ralph Horton	General; chief minority clerk	Deceased
Walter Boehm	General	Staff, Sen. Scott; now retired
Raymond Hurley	General	Practicing law (D.C.)
Jeremiah Kenney	Chief minority counsel	Union Carbide (counsel)
Paul Molloy	Counsel	Practicing law (D.C.)

SOURCE: Committee records and interviews.

Recent staff additions include five minority professionals appointed pursuant to the Legislative Reorganization Act and four subcommittee aides appointed after a 1971 agreement with the subcommittee chairmen. The House committee staff is generally regarded as industrious and competent, but senior aides are widely perceived to be badly overextended—a situation that has not been helped by Jarman's and Macdonald's use of their subcommittee aides for service on their personal staffs.

A clue to the difference in orientation between the Senate and House Commerce staffs is to be found in their respective patterns of recruitment (see Tables 5 and 6). The House Commerce Committee has drawn its full-committee professionals mainly from the regulatory commissions and the executive bureaucracy. Robert Guthrie and long-time staff director James Menger (who retired in 1972) came to the committee from the House Legislative Counsel* staff; as one of them put it, "I guess I was pretty well sanitized [in terms of partisanship] over there." Senate Commerce aides, on the other hand, are recruited primarily from within Congress and often come to the committee with the partisan and policy commitments developed in a member's office intact. Younger aides are also drawn in large numbers from the University of Washington Law School; six current staff members were initially recruited through an internship program which Magnuson established with the school in 1964. The presence of these and other recent law school graduates is important in giving the staff a youthful, activist cast; it also builds an indebtedness and loyalty to Magnuson into staff operations and presents Pertschuk with a corps more amenable to his tutelage than a more experienced or politically heterogeneous group would be.

The basic premise of the entrepreneurial orientation on the Senate Commerce staff is that aides, far from being neutral or passive instruments, are expected actively to generate ideas and develop projects for the membership. Chief counsel Grinstein in 1966 defined the role he anticipated his staff recruits would play:

> We certainly don't think of our staff as you would some reference book, to be taken down off the shelf and used occasionally. We see it as part of our job to present alternatives to the senator, to lay out things before him that he might want to do.[9]

---

* A nonpartisan office where bills are drafted and information on points of law is given at members' requests.

The members' relation to these activities has more often been permissive than directive. The reflections of two staff members are especially revealing:

> With Magnuson's and Hart's blessing we sought out [William] Spong to take the lead on the toxic chemicals legislation . . . (We asked Hart if he would mind and he said, "Would I *mind?*"). That was a classic example of how the system is supposed to work. Now Hollings is a more complicated case—bright, aggressive—could be extremely valuable if properly channeled. . . .
>
> You know how things work around here: it's mainly a matter of developing ideas and then *finding* a senator who is interested in them. There's not much you're doing at the *direction* of a senator. . . . It's pretty well understood, and Pertschuk stresses this, that we want the kind of staff that moves out independently in these areas.

Magnuson and his committee members are not as unwitting as the staff sometimes supposes, but staff orientations and activities do have a major impact on the volume and the content of committee output. Their initiative is a matter both of floating new ideas and, once bills are in the works, of taking an extraordinarily free hand in "working out" difficulties and conflicts and in framing the way critical matters come to the committee for decision. As ranking Republican Norris Cotton rather wryly put it:

> We're inevitably dependent on staff to work out most of the language. They supposedly take our concerns into account. We sometimes go through five or six prints—we decided we should call them "staff prints," not "committee prints."

Staff roles vary considerably from area to area. It is in consumer and environmental affairs that the activist, reformist style set by chief counsel Pertschuk is most pervasive. Communications Subcommittee chairman John O. Pastore (D., R.I.) has been openly resentful of the majority staff, and communications counsel Nicholas Zapple is largely independent of Pertschuk's line of command (see Chapter 5). Zapple tends to define his role in terms of service and information functions; he also speaks of oversight, but by that he seems mainly to mean "keeping up" with the plans and needs of the Federal Communications Commission. Aides working on transportation matters reveal a wider range of goals and orientations. Surface transportation counsel and long-time Magnuson staffer Daniel O'Neal was understood, before his appointment to the Interstate Commerce Commission in 1973, to be *primus inter pares* among transportation aides. He exercised some coordination over the transportation "half" of the committee; Pertschuk's day-to-day involvement was not extensive. Aides in these areas tended to be less critical of established interests and less oriented toward legislative activism than those working in more visible, less stabilized areas like consumer affairs; this both reflected and reinforced the conservative, industry-oriented role of the committee in aviation, maritime, and surface transportation policy.

There are some scattered signs of change even in traditionally industry-oriented areas. The Surface Transportation Act found staff members stimulating counterpressures and actively developing major modifications of the legislation (see Chapter 3). An important precedent was set by William Foster in the merchant marine and fisheries area in the mid-sixties: the committee became no less inclined to "promote" the fishing and maritime industries, but it became considerably more creative and less tied to traditional approaches and specific interest-group proposals in doing so.[10] The present fisheries aide, John Wedin, has not approximated Foster's performance, but the development of Hollings' Subcommittee on Oceans and Atmosphere and the hiring of new aides John Hussey (1972) and James Walsh (1973) promises some new approaches in the fisheries area. Merchant marine counsel Emanuel Rouvelas (1969–1973) could claim some credit for the extent to which the committee's involvement in maritime affairs had come to include environmental protection and safety measures: "These promotional bills are not what I would choose to work on, but I'm willing to because the job also lets me do these other things." Perhaps the most significant single sign of change came in 1973 when O'Neal's transportation slot was filled by Lynn Sutcliffe, an aide who was closely tied to Pertschuk and whose experience and sympathies lay with the committee's consumer and environmental operations.

The staff's occasional misgivings about giveaway bills, impatience with traditional approaches, and concern for broader policy questions have had only limited impact on the bulk of the committee's work in the transportation areas. But an interesting process is going on, and it may have long-range policy implications: the orientation that set aides like Grinstein, Pertschuk, and Foster off from their more traditional, service-oriented colleagues a few years ago is gradually beginning to infuse the entire committee. One full-committee aide offers some tentative explanations:

> These are younger guys and they're not content just to service the industry like some of their predecessors. They're aware of some of the reform currents that are stirring. Also, they're ambitious; Manny [Rouvelas] has the idea, I know, that [developing innovative environmental and safety proposals in his area] is the way you get ahead around here

The ethos has not evolved by accident; Pertschuk's recruitment and promotion practices have been designed to foster it. The shift of Sutcliffe and of junior aides Tom Allison and Paul Cunningham into transportation areas has greatly strengthened Pertschuk's hand. He has also made a concerted effort to enlist the sympathy and aid of staff members appointed by and attached to senior committee members. These efforts have apparently met with some success in "bringing around" members on controversial or little-understood matters; in one instance an aide whose mentor was set to vote adversely managed to schedule another meeting so as to make the senator miss the Commerce Committee vote in question. Finally, during the Ninety-third Congress Pertschuk has increased his resources and his potential for influence and intervention across subcommittee lines by hiring an economist, an engineer, and a legislative counsel at the full-committee level for work in various policy areas, as needed. One explanation that is conspicuously missing from accounts of the spread of staff activism is any suggestion that the *members* have specifically prescribed it. This helps account for the fact that the new orientations have *not* penetrated many traditional patterns of service and accommodation, and suggests that emerging staff roles may be rather unstable, unpredictable phenomena. It is sometimes advantageous to Magnuson to portray himself as a prisoner of circumstances ("You've got to have an active staff to do what needs to be done in all these areas") and to allow others to blame the staff for the committee's alleged excesses. The fact is that Pertschuk could not do a fraction of what he does without the chairman's active or implied backing. As one lobbyist puts it:

> Mike isn't nearly as close to Magnuson as Jerry [Grinstein] was, but my impression is that it doesn't matter much. He's still pretty free to operate the way he wants to, and Magnuson gives him the kind of backing he's got to have. I've found that if Mike says that Magnuson won't oppose something on the floor, then it will turn out that Magnuson doesn't oppose it on the floor.

The fact remains, however, that the relation to staff operations of Magnuson, and of members like Hart and Moss as well, is permissive more than prescriptive. The committee as a whole is unlikely to realize its potential for creative lawmaking and sustained oversight until *staff* activism and reformism are more adequately undergirded with *member* involvement and initiative.

Staff activism on the Commerce Committee is channeled, and sometimes constrained, by the understanding that staff efforts are to enhance primarily the *chairman's* role and reputation. Subcommittee aides have occasionally learned that pushing another member's project at Magnuson's expense could imperil their job. One aide recounts the advice he was given on his first day of work:

> Mike [Pertschuk] told me I would have to be careful in balancing my responsibilities to Magnuson and [subcommit-

tee chairman]. Stan Barer [Magnuson's administrative assistant] was more blunt: "Remember," he said, "you were hired by *Magnuson*."

But here too some change is discernible. As a former staff man observes:

> My impression is that Magnuson is much less interested in keeping on top of what goes on in the committee than he was, less interested in getting the credit. A lot of that was more Jerry [Grinstein's] doing than Magnuson's anyway.

Many of the staff members frequently seem to be searching for a senator, any senator, to take up a pet idea; they are often willing and able to work with any member who shows an interest. The most viable and creative ideas, especially in areas such as consumer affairs, oceanography, energy, and the environment (the areas, generally speaking, where entrepreneurial staff orientations are most conspicuous), are still developed and publicized under Magnuson's name. This sometimes denies resources to potential activists and otherwise discourages them. But the fact that policy development and the promotion of Magnuson have been seen as interrelated objectives has undoubtedly both provided a focus and impetus for staff efforts and made the chairman bolder and more confident in countenancing them.

Senate Commerce's ranking minority member, Norris Cotton, is far from happy about majority staff operations: "We've got this aggressive, eager-beaver majority staff to contend with. They stir up so damn much it's all we can do to keep up with them." The minority staff furnishes a contrast to the majority. Although Jeremiah Kenney, chief minority counsel during the period when the committee's level of activity rose most markedly, set a pattern of moderation and cooperation that has continued to characterize Republican staff operations, minority staff members consciously differentiate their own role from that of the majority. Arthur Pankopf, chief minority counsel since 1970, elaborates:

> My own philosophy is not as "activist" as that of the majority. Maybe that stems from my experience on the House side.

There the members are much more involved, and the staff is more a *resource.*

Minority aides also distinguish their mode of operation from what they perceive on the House committee. As David Clanton puts it:

> My impression is that the House staff is more limited to *informing* the minority than we are. Our tendency is to work closely with one man in particular in helping him develop his own stuff and work through other matters.

Still, minority staff members almost never speak of developing a legislative idea and "finding" a member to sponsor it. They eschew any desire to "play senator" and likewise express disapproval of the majority staff's tendency to leak material to the press as a means of moving the committee or exposing recalcitrant members. "I still have the old-fashioned view," one minority staffer commented, "that senators ought to be able to work these things out without fear of its being all over the papers."

Minority aides stress the necessity of keeping "on top" of the flow of committee business and informing their mentors of the dispositions of the administration. Their legislative activity most often takes the form of working with the majority staff to get a member's interests taken into account as proposals are refined. This is a far more efficacious role than the isolation and opposition one often finds on committees with more severe partisan splits or more conversative minority members. But it does not approximate the kind of creative partisanship for which Jacob Javits, for example, has striven on the Labor and Public Welfare Committee. Commerce's minority aides have their impact on committee output, but it rarely takes the form of original or "alternative" proposals. More typical is an inconspicuous, cooperative attempt to modify legislation that is already in the works; they occasionally feed suggestions to their mentors or flag problematic situations, but often their proposals originate with an interest group or executive bureau seeking exemptions or qualifications to majority proposals.

The difficulties Senate Commerce Republicans have had with their staff—rapid turnover, inexperience, and individual deficiencies in ability and motivation—have been only partially alleviated by the stabilization of the minority staff contingent during the Ninety-third Congress. But as far as its orientation is concerned, the minority staff seems to behave much as the Republican members wish. Cotton and his colleagues do not expect a great deal of independence and initiative from their aides. Minority staff men thus generally mirror the aspirations and implement the stated objectives of their mentors.

The House Interstate and Foreign Commerce staff differs markedly from its Senate counterpart in orientation and role. It also displays fewer internal variations between subcommittees and between majority and minority. Veteran staff director James Menger freely expressed his distaste for Pertschuk types who pushed their "own ideas on the chairman." The House Commerce staff, he added, "does not think up ideas for the committee. It only responds to the felt needs of the members." A second long-time aide asserts, "I really can't afford to be identified with any proposals in my position." A third staff man is somewhat more reflective:

> To me, it's more important that the process work than that specific decisions be reached. It offends me when the staff use their positions to further their own points of view. I'm here to *implement*, to help the committee, not to set my own gun off.

House Commerce majority aides display a deep conviction, remarkably consistent from man to man, that personal and political preference should not intrude on their work. Some feel rather strongly that changes are needed on the committee, but all seem to feel that the agents of change must and should be the members themselves. Surely there is a grain of truth in their view: if the Senate committee shows the possibility of staff-induced change, it also displays its instabilities and limitations. But the orientation of House Commerce aides represents more than a factual assessment of their own limited leverage; it reflects a pervasive, internalized set of *norms* which set quiet restrictive constraints on behavior. The Interstate and Foreign Commerce aide, in short, conceives of himself as a "professional," not merely "competent," but "neutral" as well, performing "according to explicit, objective standards rather than . . . personal or party or other obligations and loyalties."[11]

The majority staff's aspirations toward "neutral competence" both reflect and facilitate chairman Staggers' quest for committee bipartisanship. The chairman, in fact, has shown some resistance to the minority decision to take advantage of the right to minority-staff appointments provided by the 1970 Legislative Reorganization Act. As Representative Eckhardt noted, "Staggers has opposed the idea of 'Republican' staff men. He says the whole staff is for the whole committee. And he once pointed out that over half the staff was Republican anyway. I guess he had a point." The minority appointments have been made, but the committee tradition has been maintained whereby the chairman and the ranking minority member must agree to every staff appointment. The Republican aides recruited under these conditions tend to share the majority's "professional" orientation; as one of them testifies:

> Here members look to the staff for advice, but they don't go to the staff for issues. . . . We don't work the way the Senate [Commerce] staff does. That type of behavior is bound to result in playing one member off against another. . . . A member will tell us what his view is, what type of amendments he wants, etc., and we prepare material that fits those specifications. . . . I don't show my political views. [Majority Counsel James] Menger doesn't either. You would never know his own views on any issue. . . . Staggers asked me if I was going to be kept on after [ranking Republican] Springer retired. . . . He told me that if I wasn't I could join the professional staff on the *majority* side. That gives a good indication of how this committee operates.

The new majority aides assigned to subcommittee chairmen in 1971 display somewhat different orientations than the full-committee veterans. The transportation and communications appointees have become little more than personal aides to Jarman and Macdonald. But Rogers' and Moss's appointees, Stephan Lawton and Michael Lemov, are gaining in expertise and developing policy ideas of their own. They do not expect to remain subservient to the full-committee aides responsible for their issue areas. Lemov explicitly differentiates his role from that of the senior aides:

> I'm not neutral: my job is to further Moss's legislative interests. On the other hand, I give members information and help them whether I agree with them or not. . . . I think it would be frustrating to work on the full committee staff, to work under the limitations they work under. It's not at all like the Senate [Commerce] staff. They're just supposed to process the bills and not show their own preferences.

At the same time, Lemov considers a Pertschuk-type role inappropriate to his own situation, probably for a number of reasons: his work load leaves him little freedom of movement; the composition and predispositions of the Commerce and Finance Subcommittee make it futile to aspire to more than getting a few Senate bills through each session; Moss's degree of involvement is such that he seems neither to want nor to need prodding; and, finally, Lemov is not immune to the pervasiveness of the "professional" norm and the related expectations of his mentors. In any event, Lemov does not often engage in independent efforts at policy instigation. In his partisanship and the strength of his political ties to Moss he represents a significant exception to the House Commerce pattern, but he still sees himself as primarily a "resource" and is largely content to process legislation coming from elsewhere.

Although staff orientations and roles in the Senate and House Commerce committees contrast considerably, the general level of competence on both staffs is high, the accessibility of aides to members relatively broad, and the incidence of pure patronage appointments relatively low. Both staffs spend a great amount of time simply processing committee business, member-generated and otherwise, and aides of various stripes generally recognize the need to hold their own preferences in abeyance in order to assist certain members. But within these limits there are significant differences in both style and purpose. The House Commerce staff sees the committee agenda as a "given" reality with which it must deal; the Senate Commerce staff, in undertaking a wider search for policy gaps and opportunities, seeks to shape and expand the agenda. The House staff aims at providing its members with the background necessary to make considered, informed decisions; the Senate staff takes more explicit account of the fact that the "options" are not self-evident—the *way* information is organized and presented and the *form* in which matters come to the committee for action may decisively affect the outcome. House Commerce aides see their job in terms of responding to the directives of their mentors, particularly those in positions of formal authority; Senate Commerce aides feel a particular responsibility to the chairman, but they are as concerned about feeding him ideas and encouraging initiatives as they are about following specific directives, and in areas where the chairman has no particular interest or concern they play a similar instigative role with respect to other members. On the House committee, personal and partisan preferences are seen as irrelevant to the staff's performance of its functions; on the Senate committee, where staff functions are seen in terms of creativity as well as of expert advice, partisan and personal loyalties often provide motivation and a focal point for effort. House Commerce aides portray themselves as wholly at the service of their mentors; Senate aides are more consciously seeking for the intersection between their mentors' actual and *potential* interests and their *own*.

To some extent the differences between the two staffs are related to more general differences between Senate and House: the "professional" staff orientation is better suited to the House with its less public and less dramatic legislative style, its relative conservatism, and the more specialized, closer legislative involvement of its members. Staff orientations on the two Commerce committees are reinforced, moreover, by the divergent patterns the two committees follow in recruiting their aides and by the desires and expectations their members convey. That the entrepreneurial orientation requires a supportive environment is borne out by its markedly limited successes in the more traditional areas of Senate Commerce jurisdiction. But if staff orientations "fit" with other aspects of committee life, they nonetheless acquire a life and impact of their own. Perhaps "entrepreneurs" could operate only in a restricted fashion in the Interstate and Foreign Commerce setting. But present staff roles, if they contribute to the House committee's capacity for painstaking and comprehensive legislative work, also do little to make it a creative or energetic source of legislation and oversight. On the Senate side, the staff impact is more independent and distinctive; the committee's output in consumer and environmental affairs during the past decade is scarcely conceivable without it.

THE SUBCOMMITTEES

The House Commerce Committee had four standing subcommittees from 1959 until 1975, when jurisdictional shifts and membership pressures forced the formation of an additional subcommittee and some alterations in subject-matter boundaries.* The number of subcommittees on the Senate Commerce Committee has multiplied from four to eight (adding Consumer, Environment, Foreign Commerce and Tourism, and Oceans and Atmosphere) since 1965. The responsibilities of these subcommittees, particularly for legislation in its formative stages, have steadily increased in recent years in both committees (see chart below). The process

* The new legislative subcommittees are Energy and Power (chaired by John Dingell), Communications (Torbert Macdonald), Health and the Environment (Paul Rogers), Consumer Protection and Finance (Lionel Van Deerlin), and Transportation and Commerce (Fred Rooney).

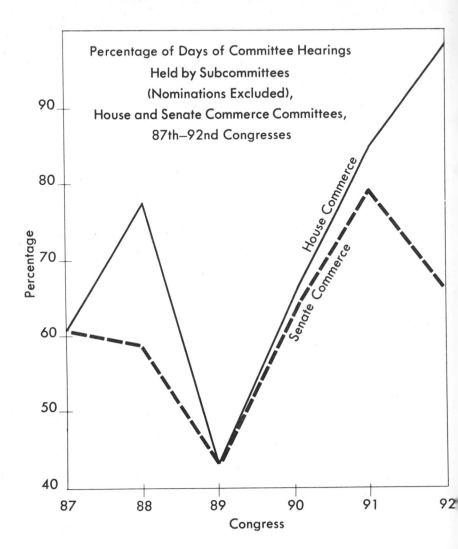

Percentage of Days of Committee Hearings
Held by Subcommittees
(Nominations Excluded),
House and Senate Commerce Committees,
87th–92nd Congresses

temporarily decelerated in the mid-sixties, partly because of an increasing flow of consumer and environment bills that did not neatly fit under existing subcommittee rubrics. In addition, both chairmen proved reluctant to delegate responsibility for the major new departures in policy proposed during the Eighty-ninth Congress (1965–1966) in particular.

The House pattern also reflects Staggers' attempt to assert control upon assuming the Interstate and Foreign Commerce chairmanship in 1966. During the Ninety-first Congress, Staggers reserved such matters as airport and airways development and cigarette labeling and advertising for full-committee consideration. A staff member remarked on the jurisdictional conflict between two Commerce subcommittees on the cigarette issue, "If you have these jurisdictional overlaps and in addition are edgy about the outcome, you might be inclined to keep it at the full committee level." But in the Ninety-second Congress Staggers held hearings at the full-committee level only on a few railway labor bills with which he did not trust Transportation Subcommittee Chairman Jarman; 99 percent of the committee's legislative hearings were in subcommittee. Members agree that the disuse of the full-committee technique, plus the resistance of the subcommittee chairmen, would make any large-scale reversal of this trend unlikely.

A similar trend is discernible in the Senate committee, but it seems to have leveled off. During the Ninety-second Congress two-thirds of the committee's hearings were held by subcommittees, but the chairman still reserved crucial matters like no-fault insurance, consumer product safety, and power plant siting for full-committee consideration. Nor has decentralization proceeded at the same pace in all policy areas. Magnuson and his aides were especially anxious during the sixties to keep the chairman identified with and in effective control of the committee's output in the consumer and merchant marine-fisheries-oceanography areas.[12] To some extent, the pattern still holds: Magnuson continues to maximize his control of various consumer measures by processing them in full committee, and subcommittee chairman

Hollings continues to tread deferentially in the oceanography and fishing areas. Magnuson is also reluctant to give Hart and his Environment Subcommittee free rein on matters such as power-plant siting and aircraft noise. Pastore, on the other hand, has for years enjoyed virtual autonomy in his communications fiefdom, as have Cannon and his predecessor, Mike Monroney (D., Okla.), in the aviation area.

Magnuson's willingness to delegate authority is only partially determined by calculations as to the policy areas in which it is important for him to retain a distinctive role. Also of considerable importance is the degree of compatibility he feels on personal and policy grounds with the subcommittee chairman in question. Thus has Magnuson been willing to give Cannon and Long relatively free rein in aviation and maritime areas where he retains a strong interest, while in surface transportation, where his interests are less strong, he has nonetheless been reluctant to spin off authority to Hartke or to his obstructive predecessor, Frank Lausche (D., Ohio).

The doubling of the number of standing subcommittees and their increased prominence in lawmaking are nonetheless indicative of a devolution of resources and responsibilities that has touched *all* policy areas to a significant degree. For this a number of interrelated factors are responsible: Magnuson's reestablished electoral security; Grinstein's departure and a certain toning down of the staff's zealotry in safeguarding Magnuson's prerogatives; and a desire for increased independence on the part of subcommittee chairmen, based in part on electoral considerations but also on decentralizing trends in the Senate as a whole. Magnuson's increased responsibilities on the Appropriations Committee have also encouraged him to delegate authority, as has Commerce's increased workload. The Commerce Committee's solidarity and homogeneity of outlook, moreover, make decentralization appear nonthreatening to the chairman and relatively inconsequential for the substance of policy outcomes. But crucial means of control, actual and potential, remain in the chairman's hands. All but a few staff members are hired by and responsible to Magnuson, and Pertschuk has carefully incorporated most of the others into his network. The committee budget is still centrally drawn up and administered, and Pertschuk and Sutcliffe perform clearance and coordination functions that are often, but not always, routine.

Queries as to what impact Magnuson's blend of permissiveness and control had on committee output often drew ambivalent responses from members and aides in the mid-sixties.[13] Most found the committee a relatively open and productive place to work, but some found in Magnuson's tendency to preempt or take over members' projects, particularly in the consumer and maritime areas, a significant disincentive to legislative involvement. By 1972, with the decentralization pattern farther advanced and relatively stabilized, such misgivings were much more rarely expressed. Committee aides were less preoccupied with balancing the interests and involvements of Magnuson and other members, and members and their staffs were less concerned about the perils of stepping on the toes of the chairman and his men. In fact, as Pertschuk notes, "the staff under Magnuson's directive" have in some instances "actively sought out the participation of junior members of the committee in taking leadership in important areas." Thus has committee decentralization given members, and subcommittee chairmen in particular, freedom, incentives, and resources to make a substantial policy input; this, in turn, has increased the *committee's* overall legislative and oversight capacities beyond what would be likely under more restrictive conditions. The actual and potential leverage of Moss, Hart, Hollings, Pastore, and Cannon in particular bear this out, though of course they utilize the organizational "slack" and resources at their disposal in quite different ways.

It is more difficult to pinpoint specific inhibiting effects. A member like Hollings must be taken at his word when he says, "There's been no conflict with Magnuson. . . . I had no trouble getting into the area [oceanography]." But certain leadership practices might have an impact on committee output that transcends the everyday awareness of individual members. Magnuson's practice of preempting certain members and giving his imprimatur to most committee proposals, it can be argued, improves the prospects of the measures that are thus "perfected" and made legitimate at the full-committee level. But the possibility that incentives for potentially active members are thereby reduced is still very real. The apathy down through the ranks of the Commerce Committee may be related to the degree of control exercised by the chairman and his staff. The Surface Transportation, Environment, and other subcommittees display low levels of member interest and can rarely even assemble a quorum. There are a variety of reasons for this, but it is worth asking if the situation might be marginally different if there were a stronger sense that the subcommittee's handiwork was "final"— that proposals developed there would sail through, with their original sponsor's name intact, at the full-committee level.

Many of the same questions apply to the House Interstate and Foreign Commerce Committee, though here the members' sense of the inhibiting effect of committee organization is much more vocal and acute. House members in general and Commerce members in particular are far more restricted in their committee and subcommittee memberships than are their Senate counterparts. Senators may hold seats on two "major" committees and one "minor," select, or joint committee, and members who held *more* seats prior to the enactment of these restrictions in 1970 have been allowed to retain them. Within Senate Commerce, subcommittee seats are roughly apportioned on the basis of committee seniority, but the size of the subgroups is flexible (only three members were *not* on the Aviation Subcommittee during the Ninety-second Congress) and overlapping memberships virtually unrestricted (most members are on five of the eight standing subcommittees). House Commerce members, by contrast, can hold seats on *no* other "major" House committee. Rules adopted by the Democratic Caucus in 1971, moreover, forbid any member to hold more than one subcommittee chairmanship. This rule forced John Moss to give up his chairmanship of the Government Operations Subcommittee on Foreign Operations and Government Information so that he could retain his Commerce and Finance Subcommittee post. On the other hand, John Dingell waived his Commerce prerogatives in order to retain the chairmanship of the Merchant Marine and Fisheries Subcommittee on Fisheries and Wildlife Conservation.* And House Commerce Committee rules have been even more restrictive. The long-standing prohibition of membership on more than one legislative subcommittee was extended in 1971 to the Investigations Subcommittee as well; rules changes promulgated in 1975 changed the limit on subcommittee memberships from one to two.

It is thus easy to understand why a representative such as J. J. Pickle would regard getting stuck on the Investigations Subcommittee as his effective "disenfranchisement" (see Chapter 8). For House members, subcommittee assignments are all-important determinants of legislative opportunities. There are few alternative outlets, much less the opportunities for independent action on the floor, of the sort that even the most junior senator often enjoys. One reason for the intense and persistent efforts of House Commerce subcommittee chairmen to wrest resources and authority from Staggers in recent years is surely the extent to which all their activities and ambitions as legislators are focused on this one position. Nor do they seem particularly anxious to share what they do obtain with those below them on the ladder. House Commerce subcommittee members are sometimes able to become active participants in team efforts to develop legislation, but there is hardly the same amount of power and initiative waiting to be independently picked up that one finds on several of the permeable and overlapping Senate Commerce subcommittees.

Structural factors, then, heighten the stakes that House mem-

---

* Moss and Dingell could retain their dual *seats* (as opposed to chairmanships) because neither Government Operations nor Merchant Marine and Fisheries is classed as a "major" committee. Those so designated are Interstate and Foreign Commerce, Agriculture, Armed Services, Banking and Currency, Education and Labor, Foreign Affairs, Judiciary, and Public Works. "Major" committee members, as opposed to those on the three "exclusive" committees (Appropriations, Ways and Means, Rules) may serve on one "nonmajor" committee as well.

bers have in committee and subcommittee operations. Trends toward decentralization abroad in Congress as a whole and the
political and policy-making ambitions of members like Moss,
Dingell, and Rogers have also contributed to the restlessness and
conflict on the House committee. And Staggers' sporadic, often
inept, efforts to assert control have exacerbated the situation. A
persistent sticking point has been the composition and functioning
of the Subcommittee on Investigations (see Chapter 8). Under
pressure from Moss, Dingell, and others, the subcommittee's
membership was increased to twelve in the Ninetieth Congress
and sixteen in the Ninety-first. But as Staggers continued effectively to stifle initiative within the subcommittee and many of the
activists obtained their own legislative subcommittees, the focus
of conflict shifted. Commerce members voiced few strenuous objections to Staggers' reduction of the Investigations Subcommittee
and the elimination of dual memberships as the Ninety-second
Congress began, though few supposed that these arrangements
would prove stable. But they did demand increased resources and
autonomy for the legislative subcommittees. Staggers agreed to
assign a $20,000-per-year staff assistant to each of the subcom-
mittee chairmen and continued to decentralize the hearing
process. But his controls over appointments, budgeting, staff hiring, and scheduling have remained. And the complaints have continued and intensified, not only regarding these mechanisms of
formal control but also with respect to the pace and efficiency of
committee operations—delays in scheduling hearings, postponed
and desultory markups, and so on.*
   It thus comes as no surprise that Interstate and Foreign Commerce members testify far more vocally than their Senate counterparts as to the constricting effect of organizational "tightness" on
committee productivity. The magnitude of that effect is difficult to
assess. There are, after all, important ways in which Staggers has

---

* Committee members have also attacked Staggers for his alleged violations
of House Democratic Caucus rules (see Chapter 2).

decentralized committee operations. As Transportation and Aeronautics chairman Jarman stated:

> [Oren] Harris made less use of the subcommittees. Chairman Staggers has wisely changed to almost full use of the subcommittees for hearings and preliminary consideration of bills. The result is a tremendous increase in legislative production. . . .

Bob Eckhardt points, in addition, to a growing presumption in favor of subcommittee-reported bills. Full-committee markup tends not to be protracted unless major problems and conflicts have been incompletely worked out in subcommittee or major pressures from outside the committee intervene. But Jarman, who was not one of the more aggressive subcommittee chairmen, nonetheless criticized Staggers' "one-man rule over the subcommittee agenda" and his attempts "to handle each bill on the House floor, even though he has not attended the hearings."*

The impact of Staggers' techniques is more evident in some areas than others. His pecuniousness with staff resources has visibly hindered Rogers and Moss, but neither Jarman nor Macdonald has made effective use of the subcommittee staff men they were given. Moss is the subcommittee chairman who seems most often to run afoul of the committee's "bottlenecks"; moreover, Staggers' prerogatives to name subcommittee members have been used in such a way as to make it difficult for Moss to report strong consumer bills to the full committee (see Chapter 2). But the situations of the Communications and Power and Transportation and Aeronautics subcommittees demonstrate that organizational variables do not offer a sufficient explanation of either the level or the direction of committee activism. For that one must examine the goals and ambitions of the members themselves, which organiza-

---

* Rules changes adopted at the beginning of the 94th Congress permitted subcommittee chairmen to schedule hearings without the full committee's approval, gave them the right to manage their subcommittees' legislation on the House floor, and increased their control over subcommittee budgets.

tional conditions may facilitate or frustrate but do not conclusively determine.

THE MINORITY

The House and Senate Commerce Committees both display relatively harmonious majority-minority relationships, although recent years have seen some trends in the opposite direction: the accession of the Republicans to power in the executive branch and their need to maintain distinctive positions and to build an identifiable legislative record have created certain pressures on committee Republicans and have somewhat altered past patterns of mutual accommodation. The slight movement of Interstate and Foreign Commerce leftward from the comfortable (for Republican members) conservatism of Oren Harris has created some difficulties for the minority, while Magnuson's growing legislative boldness and the increase in the number and comprehensiveness of consumer and environment bills on the agenda have had a similar effect in the Senate committee. But neither committee is highly partisan. Republican and Democratic members of both committees are drawn from the relatively "moderate" wings of their parties (see Table 3). Moreover, the leadership style of the chairmen and ranking minority members of both committees generally fosters partisan cooperation. Staggers points with considerable pride to his and Springer's working relationship and expresses a desire for a similar relationship with Springer's successor as ranking Republican, Samuel Devine: "[Devine] is more conservative but we'll do our best to be accommodating. I think it'll work out." As Norris Cotton, the Senate committee's ranking Republican from 1963 until his retirement in 1974, put it:

> Now Magnuson and I serve as chairman and ranking minority member on Commerce and also on the Labor–HEW Appropriations Subcommittee. I've often said, there are two people I *have* to get along with in this world, my wife and

Magnuson. And I do get along. We manage to work together well.

Similar patterns are generally replicated at the subcommittee level; subsequent chapters will point up the cooperative working relationships that exist between Chairman Moss and ranking Republican James T. Broyhill (N.C.) (House Commerce and Finance Subcommittee), Rogers and Nelsen (House Health and Environment), Cannon and Pearson (Senate Aviation), and Hollings and Stevens (Senate Oceanography).

But expressions of amity and appearances of harmony can be deceptive. Conflicts of value and interest do exist, and obstruction and opposition can take on a quite gentlemanly guise. "The record will show," Cotton noted, "that it's not been quite as cooperative as you suggest." Indeed, a survey of the consumer measures reported by the Senate Commerce Committee in recent years—from the fair-packaging and cigarette-labeling bills in the Eighty-ninth Congress to the consumer safety agency, no-fault insurance, and fish-inspection bills in the Ninety-second—finds Cotton more often than not filing minority views and offering weakening amendments in committee and on the floor.* This opposition in recent years has been rooted partially in the obligation the senator feels to speak for the Republican administration and partially in his own personal reservations:

> My own feeling is that the basic stake we have in these consumer bills is in assuring *safety* and preventing *fraud*. When you get beyond that, you're approaching the point at which the costs are going to outweigh the benefits.

Two factors have greatly mitigated the effect of Cotton's dissent on committee output. In the first place, he has generally been willing to have his say, take a vote, and let the majority work its will.

* The Consumer Federation of America found him "wrong" on all five key votes in 1971. See the discussion in "Norris Cotton," *Citizens Look at Congress*, Ralph Nader Congress Project (Washington: Grossman Publishers, 1972), pp. 16–17.

Chief Counsel Pertschuk leaves no doubt as to the importance to the committee of Cotton's preferred mode of operation: "We couldn't do one-tenth of what we do if he chose to obstruct." Second, Cotton has almost never attempted to galvanize the minority into a cohesive opposition bloc. For example, administration-backed amendments on product safety and no-fault insurance were supported in committee by only four and three Republicans, respectively, in 1972, and in both cases Cotton and a scattering of other Republicans submitted their "minority views" individually. Cotton showed little interest in developing a Republican "line" on committee bills or formalizing minority alternatives. "I've never had all eight [Republican members] together in the same room," he says. And he is keenly aware of the obstacles that would hinder such an effort:

> Five of our members are up for reelection this year, and it really would look bad for them to be opposing [the independent Consumer Product Safety Agency]. . . . I know what the realities are in a situation like this, and I didn't try to push anybody.

For Magnuson and his majority colleagues this cooperative, bipartisan style is obviously a resource to be cultivated. Although they sometimes incur costs in the form of painful compromises or a restricted agenda, the bargaining strength that a cohesive majority gives Magnuson and the disinclination of many of the Republicans to seek or push hard bargains in the first place usually limit such costs. What costs and benefits accrue to the Republicans is a more complicated question. Some bills are reported more quickly or in a stronger form than some of the Republicans would like; this might occur less frequently on a more partisan committee. Moreover, the Republicans often leave a less distinct imprint on legislation and receive less credit for it than they might if they articulated their dissent and formulated their alternatives more explicitly. But Commerce Republicans believe that their gains in efficacy more than offset such liabilities. Cotton commented:

If we have a bill we know that the way to get it through is to get a majority member interested in it and then to offer it jointly: the Magnuson-Cotton bill. That means you don't get exclusive credit, but it means the thing has a much better chance of passing.

Committee bipartisanship makes such ventures more viable. It also enables the Republicans to influence more and earlier *stages* of policy-making. Cotton and his colleagues are capable of non-cooperative, partisan strategies, and sometimes—for example, striking a cargo-preference provision from the 1972 maritime authorization on the floor (see Chapter 7)—they succeed. But it is obviously more efficacious to participate in the formulation and modification of bills within the committee, and this the Republicans generally manage to do. As chief minority counsel Arthur Pankopf testifies, "We usually don't get in on things at the drafting stage, but we do soon thereafter. Unless our member is clearly opposed, we work along on it."

Cotton's style has also made for a wide dispersal of policy-making endeavors *within* the minority. Cotton has run his side of the committee with a looser hand than Magnuson has run his. Cotton's sensitivity to his colleagues' electoral situations underlies his reluctance to try to develop minority discipline (as on consumer safety) and sometimes leads him to abandon his own prerogatives (as when he temporarily left the ranking minority member's seat on Aviation to James Pearson, who was up for reelection and whose state has a vital stake in small-aircraft production, in 1971). Commerce Republicans are a relatively diverse and active lot, and Cotton's inclination is to give the ranking subcommittee members considerable autonomy and to dispense the resources at his disposal rather generously. This is particularly evident in staff hiring: Griffin (Merchant Marine), Pearson (Aviation), Baker (Communications), and Cook (Consumer) each had one appointee among the six minority professionals in 1972:

I've changed staff hiring considerably over the years. I still appoint the top two minority staff, to keep some sort of control, but the others I've passed on to those down the line according to seniority. I said to myself, "Now look, Cotton, you're 72; you've got to bring these other fellows forward a little." . . . It's generally worked quite well, though in a couple of instances we've had the senators taking the staff members off for work on their personal staffs. I've insisted that they've got to be up there in the committee office, doing committee work.

Cotton's low-key and cooperative style is thus often cited by committee Republicans as crucial to their accomplishments.

The working relationship between the majority and minority on the House Commerce Committee is not as smooth or as productive as it is on the Senate committee, for a number of reasons: the House Commerce minority is considerably more conservative and less diverse than Senate Commerce Republicans; the majority is less liberal and less unified; and the chairman is less firm in his own legislative commitments and less able to prevent defections and attempts at sabotage on his committee. Staggers' efforts to be conciliatory and avoid conflict take on a considerably different coloration from Magnuson's and have a much more dubious impact on committee productivity. Republican opposition is more frequent and more monolithic on the House committee, and Staggers' reluctance to provoke or offend has a constricting effect on the committee agenda. The slow rate of flow of consumer bills can be partially understood in these terms.

The role of William Springer, ranking Republican in the House committee from 1964 to 1972, often contrasted with Cotton's in the Senate. As one member put it, "Springer can really obstruct if he wants to." His tactics ranged from the protracted questioning of witnesses to the forcing of vote after vote on amendments in subcommittee, and then full-committee, markups. And the Republicans often united behind such efforts. "When it's partisan, it's clearly so," testifies one member. "The Republicans stick pretty closely with Springer." Another member commented on the Republicans' successful attempts in 1972 to add the "manu-facturers' amendments, *verbatim*" to the "already damaged" Motor Vehicle Information and Cost Saving Act in full commit-tee: "The *coup de grâce* was Springer's move to recommit [to subcommittee]. When he speaks, you know, all those Republi-cans 'spring' into action." Such solidarity seems to have been as much the result of a natural homogeneity of outlook as of explicit attempts at organization or discipline on Springer's part. In fact, Springer, like Cotton, left the Republican subcommittee blocs a good deal of autonomy, although, like Staggers, he was capable of exercising his *ex-officio* voting rights on subcommittees in tight situations.

The cautious and accommodating style of the Interstate and Foreign Commerce leadership makes for an increased Republican policy-making role. This participation sometimes spells trouble for projects of the activists. But the contrast with Senate Com-merce should not be drawn more starkly than the facts warrant, for House Commerce Republicans likewise have "constructive" contributions to make and have at times facilitated legislative production. The later history of the automobile Cost Saving Act is instructive: James Broyhill, ranking Republican on the subcom-mittee to which it was recommitted, agreed to send a compromise bill back to the full committee. Ancher Nelsen's and John Y. McCollister's (R., Neb.) mediating efforts were crucial to the emergence of cancer research and product safety agency bills dur-ing the Ninety-second Congress (see Chapters 2 and 6). It is certainly plausible to argue that Staggers, Rogers, and Jarman defer inordinately to the Republicans and other conservative de-tractors on the committee; more "toughness" would make for better legislation and sometimes for a more credible political posi-tion as well. On the other hand, given the composition and slug-gishness of the committee and the norms and disposition of the House, the relatively open channels of Republican participation and the bipartisan working relationships must be deemed, on balance, a positive factor. Without them, the House committee would probably be even less productive.

THE POLICY-MAKING ENVIRONMENT

The House and Senate Commerce committees must deal with an array of groups, agencies, and publics, some of them offering competition, most of them making demands. What the committees do or fail to do often depends on the incentives and constraints these "outside" agents offer. The committees do not operate in a vacuum; the character of their "environment" often influences their behavior just as decisively as the patterns of recruitment, leadership, staffing, and organization that we have just examined.

The Commerce committees' environment is not populated by large groups or classes seeking "redistributive" ends. The distributive* and regulatory policies with which the committees characteristically deal usually involve organized labor only peripherally and seldom raise the specter of a massive reallocation of national resources. Business interests generally seek industry-specific benefits or exemptions, although this pattern is changing somewhat as consumer and environmental initiatives become more ambitious and more general in effect. The result is an environment where group conflict is, relatively speaking, muted and limited in scope; one need only look at the setting of the Education and Labor or Finance committees to appreciate the difference.

A second general characteristic of the Commerce environment is that the policy-making efforts of the executive branch in the areas of committee jurisdiction generally lack coherence and intensity. The initiatives of the Commerce committees in consumer affairs, oceanography, environmental matters, health, merchant marine, and aviation often represent an attempt to counter de-

---

* The terminology is taken from Theodore Lowi: a "distributive" interest is one whose policy preferences can be implemented "more or less in isolation from other [interests] and from any general rule." "American Business, Public Policy, Case Studies and Political Theory," *World Politics*, XVI (July 1964), p. 690. See also the discussion of maritime policy in Chapter 7.

clared administration policies and priorities, but they just as often —and this applies to the Johnson as well as the Nixon years— take place under conditions of administration indecisiveness and neglect. Why this should be so in parochial areas such as fisheries aid is evident, but in a burgeoning field like consumer affairs one suspects that the executive, by giving in to bureaucratic misgivings and opposition pressures, has forgone substantial opportunities for political leadership and profit.

The Commerce committees, then, are *not* generally faced with large-scale or sustained group conflict, with redistributive demands, or with a comprehensive and strongly advocated party or administration program. Many of the issues that come to the committee have a broad, nonpartisan, middle-class appeal: a touch of regulation here and there promises to benefit almost everybody. Alternatively, there is the distributive formula: groups and regions with special needs can be benefited with negligible apparent cost to the whole. And both regulatory and distributive measures generally seem within the grasp of the average legislator. They are often readily understandable; dealing with them does not generally require massive bureaucratic and informational resources; and many of them can be effectively "sold" to a local constituency or publicized among a wider audience.

Legislative efforts and successes in the consumer, environment, and health areas can be understood against this backdrop, as can the patterns of bipartisanship and cooperation that distinguish both Commerce committees. It is striking, however, that relatively few members of either committee seem fully to exploit the opportunities their situation offers. This is in part attributable to the foreshortened goals and perspectives of the members themselves; how the committees are run and their resources deployed also plays a critical role. But the particulars of the committee environment are also important, for the configurations of incentives and constraints vary considerably from area to area and in some cases seriously qualify generally "favorable" circumstances.

There is nothing absolutely fixed and predetermined, for example, about the Senate's lethargy and the House's ineffectuality in the communications area (see Chapter 5); one senior Senate Commerce aide in fact asserts, "If I were coming to the committee now, that's what I would want to work in. With some live-wire senators there's no limit to the things you could do there." The resources and the leverage are available for an altered and expanded Senate role, if the principals would take advantage of them. It is important to realize, however, that the actions and inactions of the Pastore and Macdonald subcommittees (see Chapter 5) do not take place in a vacuum; a look at the agency and group context sheds considerable light on the shape their behavior assumes.

Two characteristics of the environment are especially pertinent to the Communications subcommittees: the preeminence of commercial broadcasters among the "groups" in the field, a well-organized industry with ample means of rewarding its friends and with a strong interest in preventing major new policy departures; and the dominant, if hardly bold or innovative, policy-making role of the Federal Communications Commission (FCC) and the White House Office of Telecommunications Policy (OTP). There have been occasions when FCC, OTP, and broadcasting industry perspectives have diverged, but the industry generally finds the agencies cordial to its interests and has no desire to stimulate large-scale congressional interference. Legislators thus find themselves frequently preempted and perceive new policy departures and critical oversight as distinctly unwelcome. Nor are there sufficient positive incentives to override these constraints: no public-broadcasting or other groups can match the resources of the commercial broadcasters, and many broadcasting issues are arcane and dimly perceived by the public. This is not to say that issues could not be dramatized and public interest heightened in areas such as cable television or public broadcasting, but the House and Senate members responsible for communications policy have generally not shown the will or the capacity to exploit these opportunities. Instead, they have allowed themselves and their policy area to become dominated by the strongest forces in the environment. Commerce committee handling of communications thus remains a prime example of both policy *stasis* and congressional abdication.

Comparable results are produced by slightly different configurations of environmental forces in the aviation and surface transportation areas. Here there is a more obvious pluralism of interests than in the communications area; congressional abdication is prompted by conflicts among contending interests—rail and motor carriers, regulated and unregulated carriers, supplemental and scheduled airlines, general and commercial aviation—as much as it is by the influence of any one dominant interest. Members are sometimes deterred from entering the fray; at other times they enter on behalf of particular interests only to cancel out one another's efforts. But what is at stake in transportation and aviation are not merely questions of regulation but also massive governmental subsidies and support. And as a Senate transportation counsel puts it, while there may be disagreement on the "brand," the contending interests "all want champagne." Thus when these interests can get themselves together, as Chapters 3 and 4 show, many of the political perils that otherwise would attend legislative involvement can be avoided. In fact, there may be substantial political and financial incentives to champion such packages. Here too the level of public knowledge and interest are not generally high. If this reduces the incentives to broader sorts of policy innovation and oversight—except on such widely perceived "crisis" matters as hijacking and air safety—it also means that legislators can usually champion industry requests without any great fear of public outcry.

In transportation and aviation, as in communications, the operations of the regulatory agencies, if they do not make for bold new departures in policy, still tend to preempt congressional involvement and concern. This is all the more true by virtue of the industry ties and orientations to be found on the Interstate Commerce Commission, Civil Aeronautics Board, and Federal Aviation Administration (see Chapters 3-4). Legislators are seldom urged to interfere and are often urged not to rock the boat. In the Department of Transportation Congress confronts anything but a monolith, and this fragmentation has proved more debilitating than a unified executive with a coordinated transportation program would be. The fact that they have jurisdiction over neither highways nor urban mass transit naturally inhibits the Commerce committees from assuming any kind of coordinating policy role. Magnuson did attempt in 1967 to combine Surface Transportation, Aviation, and Merchant Marine into a single transportation subcommittee; he attributes his failure not only to the objections of the dispossessed chairmen but also to the continuing fragmentation of the executive establishment:

> That [kind of reorganization] won't work until we have a Department of Transportation. I mean a *real* DOT and not just this collection of agencies with each one going off on its own. My idea [in pushing the 1966 legislation creating the DOT] was to force Johnson to do that; then *our* reorganization would follow. Of course now it would be much more difficult, with all these subcommittees and each fellow so worried about getting cut out of something.

In any case, given the fragmentation of committee jurisdictions and the fixation of many legislators on a single mode of transportation, it seems clear that executive fragmentation, far from being perceived and utilized as an opportunity for congressional leadership, instead discourages any kind of broad overview and tends to channel legislative activity into the promotion of one mode or another.

Congressional policy leadership has been more evident in merchant marine than in other transportation areas, though it still has aimed mainly at subsidy and promotion. Certain environmental factors help explain the pattern. More than surface transportation or aviation policy, merchant marine policy is "distributive" with respect to specific states and congressional districts. This helps explain both the low priority maritime matters often receive in the executive scheme of things and the intensity of the merchant marine's congressional champions. Maritime interests—

shipbuilders and operators, management and labor, carriers affected differently by the regulatory and subsidy programs—have numerous conflicts among themselves, but they generally are unified in their promotional concerns. They are, moreover, seasoned and skilled, if sometimes inflexible and unimaginative, at the lobbying game. Agency jurisdiction has been divided since 1961 between the independent Federal Maritime Commission, responsible for the enforcement of the Shipping and Merchant Marine Acts, and the Commerce Department's Maritime Administration, responsible for the administration of construction and operating-differential subsidies. Under Administrator Nicholas Johnson (who went on to raise hell on the Federal Communications Commission) early in the Lyndon Johnson administration, the Maritime Administration was seen by the industry as a skeptical, even hostile, patron. Circumstances have since changed, and the Commerce Department in fact took the lead in developing a "new" maritime program in 1970 (see Chapter 7). But the Maritime Administration still has a reputation as something of a bureaucratically hidebound outfit; this, plus the relatively low ranking the executive gives to maritime affairs in its overall priorities, still often turns those interested in new policy departures to Congress. There, of course, legislators from maritime districts prove quite receptive. For if the servicing of the merchant marine promises little in the way of broad-scale publicity, it is often uniquely profitable in terms of campaign contributions and the support of powerful local interests. Needless to say, the environmental conditions that made for a certain congressional preeminence in the field do little to prompt a critical concern for regulation or oversight.

Oceanography touches many of the same regions and groups as merchant marine and fisheries policy, but the fact that policy options and expectations are much less firmly set gives potential policy entrepreneurs a greater degree of flexibility. Senate champions of oceanographic exploration and research, antipollution measures, and coastal zone preservation and development have seldom been under heavy group or constituency pressures. While the merchant marine environment evokes faithful responses to rather predictable and often inflexible industry demands, the oceanography situation places a greater premium on *stimulating* relevant interests and publics. That this is perceived as a rewarding enterprise is suggested by the initiatives undertaken by coastal senators such as Magnuson, Bartlett, Hollings, and Stevens during the past decade (see Chapter 7). Nor have they been particularly "crowded" by the executive branch. The establishment of the National Oceangraphic and Atmospheric Administration (NOAA) in the Commerce Department in 1970 gave oceanographic programs a new measure of visibility and administrative coordination, but the reorganization reflected less the administration's priorities than an anticipation of those of the Congress. NOAA officials admit that they have little clout within the administration and are highly dependent on their congressional supporters:

> This administration is just not marine-oriented, just like the last one wasn't. The pressure comes from Congress on this. . . . We might do better if we could get some understanding of our problems down at OMB. . . . One problem is that we don't really have any constituency. . . . Bob [NOAA Administrator Robert M. White] and I sometimes say that we aren't really very good bureaucrats.

Oceanography champions in Congress, for their part, find in NOAA and its constituent bureaus (including the old Bureau of Commercial Fisheries, with which Senate Commerce has long had a cooperative and mutually beneficial relationship) a crucial source of information and political support. But the configuration of environmental forces in the oceanography area is such as to give Congress a preeminent role.

Consumer, environmental, and health affairs are the policy areas where Commerce committee members have found their greatest opportunities to stimulate public support and where other environmental conditions have likewise proved relatively congenial to congressional leadership. The health area, within the jurisdiction of House but not of Senate Commerce, differs from the others in the extent of both executive and group involvement. Both the Johnson and Nixon administrations have put forward programs designed to exploit health's broad political appeal, though overall budget considerations have imposed certain constraints. The National Institutes of Health (NIH) have lost some of their fabled independence and political invulnerability in recent years, but the 1971 cancer bill (see Chapter 6) and most appropriations for health research demonstrate their continuing capacity to make end runs around their executive superiors and to secure mutually profitable ties with well-placed legislators. This situation provides Paul Rogers and his Health and Environment Subcommittee with obvious opportunities, although in 1971 Rogers paid for his support of NIH by alienating Mary Lasker, the American Cancer Society, and others supporting the concept of a new cancer agency independent of the NIH line of command.

The 1971 episode is not indicative of any general inclination on Rogers' part to take on the organized groups in the health field. On the contrary, he takes strong cues from the American Hospital Association, American Medical Association, American Association of Medical Colleges, and other medical groups, if this has moved him to defend established programs against the Nixon administration, it has notably inhibited his support of health maintenance organizations (HMOs), national health insurance, and other health-care delivery measures.* The tremendous public appeal of health policy remains an overriding environmental consideration. The incentive for legislators to boost administration requests and to strive for recognized leadership in the field is thus quite powerful. But in the House Commerce Committee, unlike Senate Labor and Public Welfare (which has jurisdiction over health issues in the Senate), the members have yet to "go public"

---

* On HMOs, see Chapter 6. On Rogers' reluctance in 1974 to oppose the AAMC on the question of grants to medical schools for student support, see *National Journal*, June 8, 1974, pp. 842–843. Health Subcommittee member William Roy, in contrast, was willing to see aid provided directly to students and used as an inducement for them to practice in medically underserviced areas.

in their strategies, especially when they move from research and reorganization into the more controversial questions of health-care delivery.

The administration gained a measure of coordination and initiative in the environmental field by the organization in 1970 of the Environmental Protection Agency and by Administrator William D. Ruckelshaus' (1970–1973) political adroitness. Less executive leadership has been evident in the consumer area, although President Nixon established a White House Office of Consumer Affairs in 1971 to succeed President Johnson's Special Assistant for Consumer Affairs and her staff. In both areas, however, the executive has often failed to speak with a single or decisive voice, and congressional Democrats, including several from the Commerce committees, have periodically moved to fill the vacuum. The incentives for such action are rarely furnished by organized group or constituency pressures; the main effect of organized interests, on the contrary, has been to restrain support and encourage compromises. Countervailing consumer and environmental lobbies have in recent years reached new levels of constituency support and political astuteness, and in a few instances have displayed an impressive ability to affect electoral outcomes through targeted fund-raising and publicity. But the most striking feature of the policy-making environment in consumer and environmental affairs is the opportunity these issues offer the legislator to appeal over the heads of the dominant industry groups to a largely unorganized, quite diffuse, but still politically potent public sentiment.

This is not to say, of course, that legislators are generally inclined to make such a public appeal. Entrepreneurial approaches to public policy are still rare; the easier and "safer" course is often to hold back in deference to the most visible and best organized "affected" groups. That is why the efforts in the Ninety-second and Ninety-third Congresses to shift the balance of forces impinging on policy-makers in the consumer area (see Chapter 2) were and continue to be so important. But the group and agency environment in which consumer and environmental policy is made is relatively pluralistic and in flux. Congressional policy leadership entails some perils, but the opportunities for successful and profitable entrepreneurship are there.

INTERCOMMITTEE RELATIONSHIPS

The Commerce committees must contend not only with agencies and groups, but also with other congressional committees. Overlapping and competing jurisdictions, for example, create severe problems for Commerce committee members interested in transportation, health, and environmental policy, and often bring them into conflict with the Public Works, Interior, and Ways and Means committees. Quite another sort of intercommittee relationship is pointed up by the high degree of overlap in membership (permissible only in the Senate) between the Commerce Committee and the Appropriations Committee. Six Senate Commerce members were also on Appropriations in 1974. Pastore headed, and Hollings, Magnuson, and Cotton served on, the Appropriations subcommittee voting funds for the Department of Commerce, while Magnuson, Pastore, Cotton, and Stevens occupied slots on the subcommittee handling Department of Transportation appropriations. Such combinations of authorization and appropriation authority naturally increase the ability of members to shape the programs and policies under their care. The overlap in membership also increases Senate Commerce's bargaining power *vis-à-vis* other members and committees; Magnuson and Cotton, for example, were chairman and ranking minority member, respectively, of the Labor–HEW Appropriations Subcommittee, while Hollings headed the subcommittee handling appropriations for the legislative branch. Such patterns contribute to the deference Magnuson and his committee enjoy and the support they can muster in the Senate.

The most important intercommittee relationships affecting the Commerce committees, however, are those they have with each other. They share jurisdiction on most bills that each processes. The Senate committee shares jurisdiction on maritime, oceanography, and conservation matters with the House Merchant Marine and Fisheries Committee, while House Commerce shares jurisdiction on health and railway-labor matters with Senate Labor and Public Welfare. Table 8 gives some indication of the interhouse patterns of initiative and response in the major policy areas for which one or both Commerce committees are responsible.

The figures on House Commerce–Senate Labor and Public Welfare interaction point up a solicitude by Staggers for railway labor and Rogers' desire to assert leadership in the health field. During the Ninety-first Congress, when Jarman headed the Public Health Subcommittee, 38 percent of the public laws enacted in the health area were first passed in the House. Under Rogers' chairmanship during the Ninety-second Congress, this figure rose to 65 percent. At the same time, however, Edward M. Kennedy (D., Mass.) succeeded Ralph W. Yarborough (D., Tex.) as chairman of the Senate Health Subcommittee, and the number of Senate-passed health bills that died in the House Commerce Committee rose from zero to seven. Kennedy thus stepped up Labor and Public Welfare's productivity, and Interstate and Foreign Commerce, for all of its increased prominence in health affairs, held up more of the Senate's bills than it reported. Such was the fate of a proposal underwriting health maintenance organizations, and also of bills establishing dental health projects for children, expanded public health and community mental health assistance, and health services for migrant workers.

The HMO episode (Chapter 6) reveals how Rogers' and Staggers' quest for consensus and their deference to established health interests inhibit the House committee's legislative role; comparative ADA scores provide an added dimension. The average 1971 liberalism score of Labor and Public Welfare members is 70.2; Kennedy is greatly strengthened by the presence of an extraordinarily liberal and cohesive Democratic bloc with a mean score of 91.9 and standard deviation of only 9.9. On comparable but not identical votes, Staggers and Rogers themselves score only 32 and

TABLE 8.

Patterns of Committee Initiative and Interaction
House and Senate Commerce Committees,
91st and 92nd Congresses

Committees handling bills	Subject matter	Public Laws		Bills passed by:	
		House passed first	Senate passed first	House only	Senate only
House Commerce– Senate Commerce	Aviation	3	6*†	0	1
	Surface transportation	5	5†	0	5
	Railway labor	2	1	0	0
	Communications	2*	7*	0	2
	Power	1	0	0	0
	Consumer	4	7	0	6
	Environment	1	2†	0	3
	Foreign commerce and tourism	1	1	0	2
	Other	2	4	1	3
	Subtotal	(21)	(33)	(1)	(22)
House Commerce– Senate Labor	Health	19*†	16*	3	7
	Railway labor	6	0	0	1
House Merchant Marine– Senate Commerce	Coast Guard	9	0	0	0
	Merchant marine	21	2	6	0
	Commercial fisheries	8	4	0	2
	Fish and wildlife conservation	14	0	3	1
	Oceanography	5	2	2	0

* Includes one vetoed bill.
† Includes one bill passed by both houses but not agreed upon in conference.
SOURCE: Legislative Calendars of the four committees, 91st–92nd Congresses. Computations by William Lunn.

19, respectively. The full House Commerce Committee averages 37.7 and majority members, 56.7 (see Table 3). So Labor and Public Welfare must increasingly think of the House committee as a competitor for headlines and initiative on certain kinds of health measures—research, reorganization, and student aid in particular. But on health care delivery and other proposals that require sizable authorizations or excite the opposition of organized medicine, the House committee seems inclined toward a decidedly more cautious, even obstructive role.

The House and Senate Commerce committees diverge only moderately in their mean liberalism scores (37.7 and 47.0 respectively), but Table 8 reinforces our observation of wider divergences in legislative productivity and style. Most consumer bills of recent years have had their start in the Senate, and several major ones—warranty standards in 1970 and 1972, fish and other food processing inspection in 1972 and 1974, no-fault insurance in 1974—have gotten no farther. The Senate committee likewise appears to take the lead in aviation, surface transportation, and communications matters, though the presence of a large number of minor bills distorts the picture somewhat and conveys an impression of activism that is not really warranted. The House and Senate Commerce committees have in recent years shared rather evenly such responsibility as they have chosen to assume for public television, but on COMSAT and political broadcasting matters the Senate committee has generally taken the lead. Table 8 also reflects the promotional orientation of Cannon, Magnuson, and Pearson toward the aviation industry. One Senate aviation aide goes so far as to claim that he "can't think of an instance where the House committee initiated a single original piece of [aviation] legislation." Nor is Interstate and Foreign Commerce always willing to ratify Senate moves; the House committee during the Ninety-second Congress rebuffed Senate initiatives on antihijacking and sonic-boom regulation measures.*

---

* The Senate passed the antihijacking bill again in 1973; for Cannon's account of the conferees' failure to reach agreement in 1972, see *Congressional Record* (daily ed.), February 21, 1973, p. S. 3089. During this effort

Patterns of initiative in surface transportation are less striking, though here too the House committee has rebuffed several Senate initiatives (dealing with such matters as freight-car shortages, rail-passenger service, and transporting of dangerous materials). Other policy areas—power, foreign commerce, and the environment—are conspicuous mainly for the low levels of legislative productivity on *both* committees, although the Senate committee's emerging activism in the environment area was discernible during the Ninety-second Congress in a bill regulating toxic substances (on which the House acted too late for a conference to be convened), a pure-drinking-water proposal (passed by the Senate and promoted but not reported by House subcommittee chairman Rogers), and bills on sonic boom, pesticides, and ocean dumping. In any case, the overall House-Senate Commerce pattern seems relatively clear. The Senate initiates action on most of the bills that the Commerce committees jointly process, and the House committee refuses to act on almost as many Senate-passed bills as it chooses to report.

In the areas that Senate Commerce shares with House Merchant Marine and Fisheries, however, the Senate committee often waits for the House to act. Table 8 points up the extraordinary productivity of John Dingell's Subcommittee on Fisheries and Wildlife Conservation and the willingness of Commerce to let House Merchant Marine and Fisheries take the lead on conservation and Coast Guard matters. "We get so much stuff from that Dingell subcommittee," reports one Senate aide, "and these bills aren't the kind [of environment proposals] that we're most interested in. So we often wait for the House, to make sure what they're serious about." The Senate acted first on the 1972 bill protecting coastal zones (see Chapter 7) and on several bills aimed at the development of the commercial fisheries. But former

---

and a comparable attempt to liberalize the terms of the 1970 airport and airways development program, Senate aviation champions portrayed the House's 1972 legislation as weak and negotiations with Interstate and Foreign Commerce as "very difficult"; see *Congressional Record*, February 5, 1973, p. S. 2088.

Senate maritime aide Emmanuel Rouvelas acknowledges that Magnuson and the Senate committee seem somewhat less concerned than they did in the sixties to get the jump on their Merchant Marine and Fisheries counterparts in maritime affairs:

> There's been some change in priorities on the part of the Senate Committee. Also, we've now got the basic law on the books [the Merchant Marine Act of 1970, on which, in fact, the House acted first], so there's less pressure to be in there pushing new promotional bills all the time.

By a "change in priorities" Rouvelas refers to the Senate committee's new concern for consumer and environmental affairs. By way of verification he can point to the Senate committee's strengthening of a House-passed bill establishing construction standards and safety programs for recreational boats, and its development of provisions requiring DOT to establish construction standards for vessels carrying oil or other hazardous bulk cargoes. Still, Magnuson's fortunes and those of the maritime and fishing industries remain intertwined. His increasing deference to the House Merchant Marine Committee on promotional matters thus does not stem from indifference as much as from his confidence that the proclivities of the House committee closely resemble his own.

The most direct encounter between the members of the two Commerce committees comes in conference.* Table 9 suggests that the House committee prevails in some two-thirds of those conferences with Senate Commerce in which a winner can clearly be discerned.† Senate Commerce fares somewhat better, with an

* Conferees appointed to resolve the differences between House and Senate-passed bills are almost always drawn from the ranks of the committees handling the legislation.

† David Vogler's examination of 14 conferences between 1945 and 1966 produced similar results. His cases included those reported by *Congressional Quarterly* at the time *and* described in terms of a clear House or Senate victory. He found Senate Commerce prevailing in 35 percent of its conferences and House Commerce winning 71 percent of its conferences; most but not all of the bills on which these tabulations were based were shared between the two committees. David J. Vogler, *The Third House: Con-*

TABLE 9.

Conference Outcomes on Bills Shared Among House and
Senate Commerce, House Merchant Marine and Fisheries, and
Senate Labor and Public Welfare Committees, 91st-92nd Congresses

Committees handling bills	Number of conferences		
	Senate wins*	House wins*	Draw
House Commerce–			
Senate Commerce	5	10	5
House Commerce–			
Senate Labor	1	12	10
House Merchant Marine–			
Senate Commerce	6	1	2

* For purposes of this tabulation, the house "winning" is the one whose bill the conference report most closely resembles. Determinations of conference "victories" are based on case material and on the accounts in *Congressional Quarterly Weekly Report*; we have not merely tabulated a balance sheet of provisions gained and lost but have concentrated on *major* provisions and those of particular salience to the participants.

86 percent "win" record, in its encounters with House Merchant Marine. The House Interstate and Foreign Commerce Committee matches its 67 percent record against Commerce with 92 percent against Labor and Public Welfare.

A closer look at these outcomes reveals certain recurring patterns. All but one of the Commerce–Merchant Marine bills that went to conference passed the House first, and on several of these the Senate was able to add "strengthening" amendments (mainly relating to the environment) and to make them stick in conference. The House Commerce Committee, on the other hand, is inclined to pass "weaker" and/or less expensive bills than either Senate Commerce or Labor and Public Welfare, and it is quite common for conferences in which its members are involved to settle on something close to the House version as a least common denominator. This took place during the Ninety-second Congress both on bills the Senate had initiated and on House bills that Commerce or Labor had attempted to strengthen. Senate Commerce is sometimes able to make its strengthening amendments

ference Committees in the United States Congress (Evanston: Northwestern University Press, 1971), pp. 64–74.

stick, but less often in its interactions with House Commerce than with Merchant Marine.

Conference outcomes sometimes reveal important committee strengths and weaknesses; Paul Rogers' expertise and persistence, for example, are widely perceived as giving him marked advantages over his Labor counterparts in conference. But Table 10 suggests that there may be a *negative* relationship between *initiating* a bill and "winning" in conference. The committee that has given a proposal its broad outlines often finds it possible and prudent to acquiesce in most of the (usually marginal) adjustments made in the bill by the other house; the conference outcome may be more indicative of that strategic situation than of persistent patterns of intercommittee domination.* Moreover, the House Commerce results suggest that substantial advantages may accrue to the chamber whose bills, because they are more modest, provide a natural fall-back position for compromise. This is not always the case, as Senate Commerce's success in strengthening Merchant Marine bills attests. But it is important to note that a favorable balance of conference outcomes may derive not so much from a committee's legislative boldness as from quite contrary traits. Such is certainly the case with Senate and House Commerce; the Senate's weak conference record detracts from its

TABLE 10.

Relationship Between Initiation and Conference Outcome
on Bills Shared Among House and Senate Commerce,
House Merchant Marine and Fisheries, and Senate Labor and
Public Welfare Committees, 91st-92nd Congresses

Number of bills	Conference won by:	
	House	Senate
Initiated by: House	7	10
Senate	16	2

* This makes more understandable the pattern of Senate victories several analysts have discovered in conferences involving the appropriations and revenue committees; on most of these matters, of course, bills are constitutionally required to originate in the House. See Price, *Who Makes the Laws?* p. 358, n. 16.

leadership role, but far from *contradicting* that role, it in part *stems from* it. The Senate committee could no doubt improve its batting average in conference by cutting back on its initiatives and commitments, but the result would hardly be an overall heightening of committee impact or influence.

These patterns of intercommittee action and reaction are mirrored in the images and perceptions of the participants. Senate Commerce Committee members frequently perceive House Commerce as sluggish, stubborn, and conservative. Magnuson's comment is typical:

> Well, Staggers, I don't know. It's not that he's so bad, but he does sit on things. *The delay!* They can't seem to get hearings scheduled. . . . The conferees over there meet ahead of time—we never do that—and then it's hard to budge them. And they're a damn sight more conservative than we are.

House Commerce members, on the other hand, tend to see their own operations as a "responsible" and deliberate filtering of the extravagant, unworkable, and carelessly drawn measures Senate Labor and Commerce send over. Staggers' comments are frequently echoed:

> I think we do a lot better than the Senate. We hold longer hearings and work the bills through much more carefully. . . . Often we'll win in conference because they just have to admit we have the better bill.

These perceptions often override whatever differences the conferees from one chamber or the other have among themselves; subsequent chapters will point up instances where ranking Republican subcommittee members Nelsen (House Health and Environment), Stevens (Senate Oceanography), and Pearson (Senate Aviation) stuck with their Democratic fellow conferees even when it meant opposing a Republican administration.

James Madison's defense of bicameralism in the *Federalist Papers* anticipated that it would be a prime function of the Senate to *check* the House, subject as that chamber was to "the propensity of all single and numerous assemblies to yield to the impulse of sudden and violent passions, and to be seduced by factious leaders into intemperate and pernicious resolutions."[14] Today's House Commerce member would be prone to claim that the roles of the two chambers have been reversed, but the explanation he might invoke would not differ greatly from Madison's. The *Federalist's* apprehension that short terms and democratic pressure might lead to irresponsible behavior in the "popular" chamber is now matched by a view, widespread among House members, that presidential ambitions and the lure of the media make for extravagant and misconceived legislative ventures in the Senate. This disapproval is not unmixed with envy, of course, but even activists such as John Moss and William Roy portray the House as doing "closer" and more "responsible" work.

The House Interstate and Foreign Commerce picture of the Senate contains a grain of truth, as do most stereotypes. Senate Commerce and Labor members are more thinly spread and less intimately involved with specific measures than their House counterparts, and both they and their staff members often leave something to be desired in terms of legislative craftsmanship. But to portray Senate Commerce and Labor as radical committees producing extravagant measures is to betray an insensitivity to the enormity of the policy problems they face and the demands of effective congressional leadership. In House Commerce, pride of workmanship and a concern for due deliberation are too often used to obscure or rationalize harmful compromises and the squelching of promising legislative initiatives.

The "other body," then, is an important feature of the policy-making environment for House and Senate Commerce members. Patterns of initiative and response, filtered through intercommittee perceptions and stereotypes, greatly affect committee behavior —influencing the priorities set by the Senate committee among various bills; justifying a solicitude for one interest group or another which the other chamber supposedly ignores (such as House Commerce and the AMA); and reinforcing House Commerce's self-righteousness and intransigence in conference. Relationships between committees may be cooperative and mutually beneficial as well as conflictful and competitive. Certainly House Commerce is less obstructive now than in the days of Oren Harris, even though Senate Commerce has at the same time grown bolder and more assertive. But there is a kind of built-in tension in the bicameral system, so that a committee's policy moves are in large part determined by its view of its own particular role in the constellation of policy-making forces. Senate Commerce sees itself as the creative, energetic force in the inter-committee system, while House Commerce sees itself as the "responsible," frugal force. These perceptions not only (however imperfectly) mirror "reality"; they also have a great deal to do with the kinds of enterprises each committee undertakes.

2

Consumer
Protection

In October 1972, a Senate-House conference agreed on a compromise Consumer Product Safety Act, one of the most important pieces of consumer legislation in a decade. This final stage
mirrored many of the legislative maneuverings that finally produced this controversial bill.

> There was fierce opposition within industry to this landmark
> [1972 product safety legislation]. And industry found its
> advocates among the House conferees.
> Those who were privy to the conference described it with
> some awe:
> When Maggie lumbered into the conference it was as if
> the wise and seasoned kindergarten teacher had suddenly
> come into the room where a group of unruly . . . children . . .
> had been squabbling and a mini-filibuster was in progress,
> the conferees suddenly became quiet and respectful.

NOTE: This chapter was written by Joan Claybrook. Steven Brown did significant research for the chapter.

With a mixture of good-natured camaraderie and a deceptive shrewdness, Senator Magnuson announced that as a gesture of good faith he was going to move that the Senate conferees adopt the "Springer Amendment," giving citizens the right to sue.

Now the "Springer" whose name he gave to this amendment was none other than the ranking Republican member of the House Conference Committee, no great hero to the Consumer Federation of America. In fact Congressman Springer was one of the most quarrelsome of the House conferees. But, in an off-guarded moment he had suggested that the staff try to revise the Magnuson citizen suit amendment and Magnuson knew that the staff had come up with a solution that was just as good as the original. When Senator Magnuson generously offered to accept the "Springer Amendment," he threw the negative-minded Congressman so off balance that he never did recover. So the "Springer Amendment," a milestone in consumer protection, is now enshrined in law. And it was done with a smile and a handshake.[1]

If the American consumer surveyed the senior members of the United States Congress, few could be found who have taken stronger public positions on consumer legislation than Senator Warren Magnuson. And if they could punch the voting lever to select the leaders of the key consumer subcommittees in Congress they could choose few individuals more dedicated to their cause than Senator Frank E. Moss of Utah and Representative John E. Moss of California. And if consumers could choose the staffs for the consumer subcommittees, they would have a hard time finding more concerned, hard-working, bright individuals than Lynn Sutcliffe, Edward Merlis, and Edward Cohen in the Senate (under the shrewd direction of Commerce Committee chief counsel Michael Pertschuk) or Michael Lemov in the House.

In the loosely structured world of Capitol Hill, where the force of personality often spells the difference between achievement and ineffectiveness, such a combination of advocates should be overwhelming. But while there is a clear list of past achievements, the early seventies have been lean years for consumer-protection programs. Only product-safety and auto-bumper legislation passed through to enactment in the Ninety-second Congress (1971–1972), and key sections of both these bills were mangled by opponents. Few of the existing programs have been scrutinized in oversight hearings, and the appropriations for many of these programs were downgraded in the Nixon budget and not restored by the Congress.

Consumer issues are within the purview of a number of subcommittees in each Commerce committee, but the majority of consumer legislation originates in the Senate Commerce Committee's Consumer Subcommittee and the House Commerce Committee's Subcommittee on Commerce and Finance. Among the topics in these subcommittees' jurisdiction are auto safety, gas pipeline safety, truth-in-advertising, warranties, toxic substances, cigarette labeling and advertising, toy safety, Federal Trade Commission (FTC) regulatory powers, fair packaging and labeling, flammable fabrics, no-fault insurance, and class-action lawsuits.* During the last half decade, the expertise, talent, and capabilities of the consumer subcommittees' staffs have vastly increased, particularly in the Senate. But these same years have seen a shift from a White House sympathetic to consumer interests to one dedicated to trading governmental favors for corporate campaign funds. The Nixon appointees, with a few exceptions such as Miles W. Kirkpatrick and Lewis Engman at the Federal Trade Commission, have been disposed to cooperate meekly with industry requests for lenient safety regulations and have refused to use their offices to inform consumers about unsafe or adulterated products. The shifting focus of White House concern has counteracted the increased energies of congressional consumer advocates and has

---

* Other subcommittees of the House and Senate Commerce Committees are responsible for air and surface transportation rates and safety, utility regulation, energy and communications, drinking water, noise pollution, and, in the House committee, for air pollution and drug efficacy and safety. Consumer areas not under the jurisdiction of the Commerce committees are occupational health and safety, food wholesomeness and prices, highways, housing, credit, antitrust, and water pollution.

left consumers with a net loss in representation at the highest levels of government.

Only since the scope of the Watergate scandal began to be revealed in the spring of 1973, severely weakening White House credibility, have many consumer-oriented members of Congress been willing to openly and directly criticize the Nixon White House for its emasculation of consumer programs. But this break with traditional congressional courtesies has not yet been reinforced by significant use of available congressional resources to really challenge the administration's anticonsumer policies.

The first contest occurred in June 1973. After consenting to a plethora of corporate-schooled nominees of little distinction for regulatory-agency posts, Senate Commerce Committee chairman Magnuson finally took a firm stand on Federal Power Commission (FPC) nominee Robert Morris. Morris was an attorney associated for fifteen years with the San Francisco law firm of Pillsbury, Madison and Sutro, whose principal client was Standard Oil of California, a company subject to regulation by the FPC. Magnuson explained his position on the floor of the Senate:

> If public confidence is to be restored in the fair dealing and integrity of government during these troubled times, there would seem to be no better way to begin than with conflict-of-interest-free appointments to Federal offices.
>
> The Senate should serve notice on the President that it expects revision of his criteria for the selection of nominees to all regulatory agencies. Now, more than ever, the Senate should not be asked to confirm appointments to regulatory agencies which appear to have been designed as rewards for politically supportive industries or other special interest groups. . . . Instead, the Senate should be asked to confirm nominees who have demonstrated competence and commitment to the public interest.[2]

The Morris nomination was defeated by a vote of forty-nine to forty-five, the majority having been aided by the votes of five staunch Nixon supporters who disagreed with Morris' opposition to deregulation of natural gas.[3]

It was the first time since 1927 that a presidential nominee to a regulatory agency had been rejected by the Senate. For years the distinction between regulatory agency appointees with a set term of office and executive agency appointees serving at the pleasure of the president had been ignored. But because Magnuson had not asserted himself earlier and exercised his considerable powers, he in effect acquiesced in dozens of second-rate appointments over the first four years of the Nixon presidency on the basis that a nominee should routinely be approved unless he evidenced gross disqualifications or notoriously aberrant behavior.

In a speech on May 7, 1973, to the Consumer Federation of America, Senator Magnuson described the traditional deference given by the Congress to White House nominees:

> We have always given the President—without regard to party—the benefit of the doubt on these appointments. We have always believed that the President, elected by mandate of the people, is entitled to have serve him the men and women he chooses—unless they are clearly disqualified. But I must tell you that we have swallowed nominees by this Administration who have left a bitter aftertaste and our tolerance for mediocrity and lack of independence from economic interests is rapidly coming to an end.

Several months later, in an August 1973 speech to the conference of State Attorneys General Magnuson expressed irritation with the quality of regulatory-agency performance under the Nixon administration:

> But the American public is now confronted with one more bitter lesson. Laws, even the best of laws, are meaningless where government lacks the resources, the commitment and—yes, the *integrity* to enforce them vigorously and even-handedly.
>
> For what we have come to see in these past weeks and months has been that same failure in the integrity of our institutions of government as we had earlier come to see in many of our business institutions.
>
> Government must not only bear the responsibility for en-

forcing the laws, but it must create a climate of integrity in which the highest standards of ethical behavior are set and demanded. This is where government has failed. . . .

We have seen unraveled, thanks to a healthy and persistent press, an ugly tapestry of *favoritism* to special interests, of laws enforced punitively against "enemies," while friends —especially those who are the source of huge campaign contributions—are never brought to trial.

I have come here today to tell you this—the American people have had enough!

The President got the message. White House operative David Wimer contacted Senator Magnuson to discuss future presidential nominations, including pending openings on the Federal Trade Commission and a final opening in the newly created Product Safety Commission. To avoid embarrassing rejections in the future, the White House decided to get informal clearance from Magnuson's staff on positions of interest to consumers prior to publicly announcing the nomination. This policy in effect gave Magnuson a veto power—or appointment power—over potential nominees.[4]

Magnuson and his staff have taken advantage of this new cooperation by the White House. Magnuson publicly insisted that the nominee to replace Mary Gardiner Jones at the Federal Trade Commission be a consumer advocate.[5] (Elizabeth Hanford, Virginia H. Knauer's deputy in the White House Office of Consumer Affairs, was cautiously accepted.) Magnuson also recommended the nominee for the Product Safety Commission, Dr. R. David Pittle, an assistant professor of electrical engineering and public affairs at Carnegie-Mellon University in Pittsburgh and president of the Alliance for Consumer Protection, a large Pittsburgh consumer group. The new nominee for the FPC post lost by Morris was Donald Smith, a Democratic member of the Arkansas Public Utilities Commission who garnered the backing of all the leading consumer organizations in Arkansas to assure his acceptability to the Commerce Committee.

These were important gains for consumer representation in

government decision-making. But their impact must be seen in the perspective of intense, continuing, and often successful industry pressures against proconsumer action by government and a much weaker, although growing, pressure by consumer interests.

THE LOBBIES

The regulated industries are sophisticated, coordinated, and experienced players in the political game; they locate their House and Senate friends, establish networks for nationwide dealer or local association (local Chambers of Commerce, for example) lobbying, and hire a capability for public relations responses to legislative initiatives they don't like. The private corporate lobbies in Washington can fly experts in to testify at hearings, hire $100-an-hour-plus Washington lawyers for their influence, and produce campaign contributions and honoraria in the thousands to reinforce their requests for consideration.

Armed with White House support under Nixon, the industry lobbies have been tough to beat, especially since their adversaries —the consumer lobby groups—are few, small and without access to the type of money corporate lobbyists can call on from their corporate profits.*

Commerce Committee counsel Michael Pertschuk, who has dealt with both corporate and public-interest lobbyists for the last ten years, described the operation of the lawyer-lobbyists—the corporate specialists:

> The relevant events take place in a quaint shifting forum. To be sure there are several minor scenes played out in the traditional court-like setting of a Congressional hearing room. . . .
> But the scene—and the forum—shifts abruptly—like a floating crap game!
> —now to the cramped enclave of a beleaguered junior staff counsel;

---

* Business corporations can deduct lobbying costs on income-tax returns as business expenses.

—next to the sixth hole at Burning Tree Country Club;
—back to a spare, obscure Committee room, packed with a curious amalgam of Administration bureaucrats and corporate lawyers and sprinkled with select, sympathetic Congressional staff;
—next a circuit of quiet, *ex parte* sessions in Senatorial offices;
—on to Redskin stadium;
—and final argument over the diet special at the Federal City Club. . . .

As for the distribution of legal talent, it's like the New York Yankees taking on the Bushwick Little League irregulars. On the bench for the corporate interests sit a rich assortment of power hitters: an assortment of specialists—administrative law specialists, litigation specialists, FDA specialists, FTC specialists, home state local "counsels" steeped in the warmth of key Congressional friendships—a half dozen house counsels steeped in industrial know-how, a sprinkling of legal academicians with impressive credentials, and a handful of eager gleaming rookies from the editorial boards of Harvard, Yale and Columbia law journals.

Representing the opposing parties is, quite often, no one. Occasionally, the corporate interests are challenged by a government lawyer whose agency's powerlust pits him temporarily in opposition to an industry which later he may either accommodate or join. There may also rise up to advocate the public interest, from time to time, a handful of in-house, Congressional public interest advocates, committed, but suffering from sharply circumscribed time and resources and dissipated energy.[6]

The *pièce-de-résistance* on top of this stacked deck, as Pertschuk describes it, is the prominent attorney specializing in the art of gentle, sure-fire persuasion. One example is "a former cabinet officer and confidential advisor to half a dozen presidents, not the least of which is the present incumbent. He calls the ranking committee member of his own party and he says: 'George, *we* don't like this one.' He leaves to his colleague the task of fleshing out the content of the collective pronoun."

Attempting to counteract this kind of influence are a number of small consumer and environmental groups, assisted from time to time by individual public-interest attorneys.

One of the few consumer lobby organizations, the Consumer Federation of America, is a loosely associated group of local consumer organizations and labor unions representing some 30 million consumers through its member organizations. In 1972 it had an annual budget of only $90,000 and three full-time Washington, D.C., staff members, a paltry amount for any lobbying group. Common Cause, financed by small contributions and headed by former Health, Education, and Welfare Secretary John Gardner, has five full-time lobbyists who concentrate on such important issues as congressional reform, campaign finance, and the Indochina war, but infrequently on consumer issues. The labor unions have significant lobbying expertise and persuasive powers because of their capacity to raise large amounts for campaign contributions, but seldom employ their energies for major battles on consumer issues (although they tacitly support most consumer legislation). Recognizing the void, Ralph Nader in mid-1973 established a new group of six full-time professionals (Congress Watch) to concentrate on consumer legislation.*

On environmental issues a number of small, often one-issue groups occasionally emerge (as on the supersonic transport, mass transit funds from the Highway Trust Fund, and the Alaska pipeline) to supplement the Sierra Club, Environmental Action, and the League of Conservation Voters.

Consumer lobbyists have the burden, in addition to their formidable competition, of attempting to change the *status quo* on issues that are complex, where up-to-date information is uniquely in the hands of industry (consumer advocates are often not experts in a given field), and where the consuming public is tough to mobilize. Although the various public-interest groups occasionally form coalitions on a given bill to increase their strength, their

---

* Nader himself has had input on such consumer legislation as auto safety (1966), clean meat (1967), radiation safety (1968), pipeline safety (1968), occupational health and safety (1970), and others.

independent-minded members often get weighted down in substantive or strategy disagreements. The consumer lobby depends on the support of citizen groups around the country to contact members from their home districts, on the interest of the press in their battles, on personal drive and energy, and on an ability to become extraordinarily well-informed about an issue, preparing or supporting legislation *they* consider desirable and fighting for it. The success of these lobbyists depends on their personal skills, articulateness, timing, and ability to anticipate the direction in which the legislation can be moved.

These are the meager resources available to push consumer issues in the House and the Senate. Although consumer lobbyists are quite successful when they concentrate on a particular bill, the consumer lobby on Capitol Hill is meager, and it suffers from lack of resources and turnover of personnel. Through a gradual, almost invisible process, in part because of seniority and resources, but mostly inclination and talent, Senate Commerce Committee counsel Michael Pertschuk has become one of the consumer power brokers in Washington. His shrewd tactical analysis and sensitive, initiatory approach to problems have led many consumer activists to depend on him for advice.

CONSUMER AFFAIRS IN THE SENATE

The Senate Commerce Committee Consumer Subcommittee is chaired by quiet-mannered Senator Frank Moss, but it retains the stamp of Magnuson and Pertschuk. The subcommittee was formed in 1966, when Magnuson, who foresaw difficulties in getting reelected in 1968, was seeking a new image as an activist legislator concerned about the plight of the consumer and other national issues. On the landmark bills of the Eighty-ninth Congress—fair packaging, cigarette labeling, auto safety—a pattern developed whereby Magnuson "took over" issues publicized and proposals generated by other members, sometimes tempering them in the process but increasing their political viability. Magnuson stressed consumer issues in his 1968 campaign, whose theme was "Keep the Big Boys Honest," and the favorable result was interpreted by the chairman and those around him as proof of the political payoffs in identification as an activist in this emerging policy area.

Newly secure after his reelection, Magnuson and his staff became more willing to delegate responsibility and to relax their hold on committee resources. Magnuson turned the Consumer Subcommittee over to Moss in 1969, though he continued to reserve some key consumer measures (for example, no-fault insurance) for full-committee consideration and to sponsor most of the subcommittee's initiatives (Magnuson's name was on every significant consumer bill in the Senate in the Ninety-second Congress). The chairman and the activist staff that Pertschuk assembled increasingly attempted to encourage members down through the ranks to choose a topic of interest, introduce legislation, and chair hearings, thereby becoming knowledgeable about an issue and publicly identified as the advocate of that issue. The result was often to interest senators in following proposals through the long and sometimes tedious legislative process—and greatly to increase committee productivity.

Moss, uncertain of the possibilities of "breaking into" an area so effectively dominated by the chairman, had at first been reluctant to chair the subcommittee. But as a Democrat from predominantly Republican Utah, Moss found that identification with consumer issues helped him win reelection against a tough opponent in 1970. Especially recognized in the Mormon stronghold of Utah was Moss's driving force behind the bill to ban cigarette advertising on television and to require the labeling of cigarette packages with a warning of health hazards. In the Consumer Subcommittee Moss has concentrated particularly on advertising and the Federal Trade Commission, while other senators on the committee have been the primary sponsors of other key consumer bills: Hart of no-fault automobile insurance, auto cost savings, and bumper standards; Magnuson of the consumer product safety agency; and Hartke of auto safety legislation.

During the Ninety-second Congress the Consumer Subcommittee considered some twenty-four pieces of legislation, but held hearings on very few of them. The Consumer Product Warranty and FTC Improvements Act (four days of hearings) and the cigarette tar and nicotine content bill (two days) were the only hearings of any importance. Rather, the key consumer bills during the Ninety-second Congress were kept at the full committee level (for example, no-fault automobile insurance; consumer product safety agency, a bill to establish the National Institute of Advertising, Marketing and Safety within the FTC; hearings on Corvair heater defects; and a bill to encourage competition among auto manufacturers in the design and production of safer motor vehicles for a greater resistance to damage.) Only the product safety agency bill and a bill advocating safer automobile bumpers were enacted into law in the Ninety-second Congress.

Since consumer legislation often impinges on the jurisdictions of other subcommittees, and since Magnuson likes to have the "last say," most bills are marked up* in the full committee. Moss does not appear to be bothered by Magnuson's continued involvement:

> Well, as you know, Chairman Magnuson and I share ideological positions. We're very, very close on the issues, and Maggie is easy to work with—he's tolerant and understanding. . . . It's a good committee.

Most consumer legislation originating in subcommittee has Magnuson's blessing and sponsorship and is thus usually quickly approved by the full committee, although there is sometimes Republican opposition. One frequent critic of the committee's consumer legislation is ranking Republican Norris Cotton, who stated:

> My own feeling is that the basic stake we have in these consumer bills is in assuring safety and preventing fraud. When you get beyond that, you're approaching the point at which the costs are going to outweigh the benefits. . . . I cosponsored some of those early bills, like flammable fabrics —but I do think we've gone somewhat overboard lately.

* Reviewed and changed by members before being sent to the Senate floor.

But Cotton, as already noted (see Chapter 1), has a good working relationship with Magnuson; he cooperates with the chairman
to attain consensus on the committee rather than rallying the
Republican minority against Magnuson. Of the eighteen senators
on the committee in the Ninety-second Congress, only Senator
Cotton voted against final passage of the consumer safety agency
bill[7] (even its most controversial provision, criminal penalties,
was opposed on the floor by only three committee Republicans
and one committee Democrat).[8] Cotton does occasionally propose limiting amendments to consumer bills, which Magnuson
generally accepts for the sake of committee harmony.

One Republican subcommittee member, Marlow Cook of Kentucky,* has complained loudly about some of the committee's activist positions and has heaped blame for them on the committee
staff. He is even rumored to have joined the Rules Committee because it has jurisdiction over allocation of funds for committee
staffs.

One Cook outburst occurred following a May 30, 1971, article
by Washington correspondent Ward Sinclair in the *Louisville
Courier-Journal* entitled "Marlow Cook Draws the Fire of Consumer Groups." It charged that Cook had obstructed consideration of the Consumer Product Warranty and Federal Trade
Commission Improvements Act of 1971 in secret committee executive sessions where the public could not see what he was doing.
The bill would have given the FTC new injunctive powers and the
authority to set industry-wide standards governing fair competition and consumer protection. Cook claimed that the Sinclair story
had been planted by the Commerce Committee majority staff to
bully him out of fighting for his own proposal in Title III of the
bill—an Institute for Consumer Justice, a nonprofit corporation
to provide remedies for individual consumers through a nationwide system of small-claims courts.

Cook's proposal was actually a delaying tactic; its net effect
would have been to postpone for at least eighteen months *any*

---

* Cook was defeated in his 1974 reelection attempt. His opponent, Wendell
Ford, was subsequently appointed to the Commerce Committee.

federal action on behalf of consumers under the provisions of the bill. Cook was also against the rule-making provisions in the bill, and his opposition warranted a note in *Advertising Age* that "some business groups . . . expect Marlow Cook to do battle in their behalf." Sinclair had cited the *Advertising Age* article as well as alleged absence from the committee hearings as proof that Cook has been a probusiness staller on consumer affairs.

The Sinclair story enraged the hot-tempered senator. A subsequent story on June 17, 1971, by Sinclair reported that Cook had questioned every member at the June 2 executive session of the committee demanding to know Sinclair's source and promising to "burn" any staffer who had leaked the story.* Cook also inserted a complimentary letter from ten of the twelve members of the Consumer Subcommittee in the June 14, 1971, *Congressional Record.* Concluding his defense, Cook told the Senate that "in spite of such ill-founded attacks, such as appeared in [the Sinclair] article, I pledge to continue my efforts to enact truly effective consumer legislation."

Oversight

While the committee has generally been responsive and innovative on new legislative proposals, a major omission is oversight of agencies already set up by legislation that originated in the committee, such as the Federal Trade Commission, the Food and Drug Administration, and the Consumer Product Safety Commission. For example, although for years the FTC assigned its hundreds of lawyers to minutiae such as the monopoly in bull semen, gift shops in the Virgin Islands, and textile labeling, reform was initiated not by the Commerce Committee, but by a group of law

---

* The secrecy afforded members of Congress by executive sessions is coming to an end. In 1973 the House adopted rules which require such sessions to be open unless the committee votes specifically at each session to be closed. House Consumer Subcommittee chairman John Moss has opened every executive session since then. The Senate adopted rules merely *permitting* the committee to vote to open the executive session to the public. The Senate Commerce Committee held no open executive sessions in the first session of the 93rd Congress.

students under Ralph Nader's auspices who studied the commission's idiotic priorities and slothful habits.* President Nixon responded by asking the American Bar Association to study ways the structure and activities of the commission could be improved. The ABA agreed with the Nader study group recommendations, and in August, 1970, Nixon appointed as FTC chairman Miles W. Kirkpatrick, who headed the Bar study. A considerable staff turnover took place under Kirkpatrick and the FTC's enforcement procedures were toughened and invoked against major corporate violators. The FTC became so activist, though, that Kirkpatrick submitted to White House pressure and resigned in January, 1973. He was replaced as chairman by Lewis A. Engman, a former White House aide.

Since 1969 the agency responsible for auto safety, the National Highway Traffic Safety Administration (NHTSA), has been trying to get the auto companies to install passive restraints in all new cars, a concept in auto safety that could save thousands of lives each year. The automobile industry employed all the typical delaying devices: petitions for extension of time, adverse comment on rule-making proposals, petitions for reconsideration of the rule as issued, lawsuits and threats of lawsuits, refusal to initiate field testing, intimidation of suppliers who might otherwise publicize the advantages of passive restraints, misleading advertisements proclaiming fictional dangers, and political interference by White House operative Peter Flanigan.

During all this time, while witnessing one delay after another, the Commerce Committee did not hold a single day of hearings to assess the arguments by each side or to determine whether the NHTSA was properly fulfilling its responsibilities to the public. Finally, on August 1, 1973, the committee invited the auto companies, Allstate Insurance Company, crash victims whose lives had been saved by the passive-restraint air bags in test cars, and the NHTSA to discuss why the goal of passive restraints in the front-seat positions of all new 1976 model cars might not be met.

* *The Nader Report on the Federal Trade Commission* (New York: Grove Press, 1969).

Ford and Chrysler, which had been considering a lawsuit against the agency on the test-dummy specifications, assured the committee in public testimony that they did not in fact intend to file such a suit. General Motors guaranteed that cars equipped with air bags could be purchased by January 1, 1974, from among the approximately 100,000 test cars it would produce. While perhaps a minor item in the complex history of passive restraints, these were important promises which might otherwise never have been made, but which committee oversight could frequently achieve if only used.

Since 1969 the committee has been considering hearings on small cars, especially imported vehicles, and their relation to the experimental safety vehicle (ESV) mandated by the auto-safety law and on which the NHTSA has spent about ten million dollars with little result. That hearing had not been held by the close of 1973. Although the schedule for 1974 listed oversight of the ESV program, such a hearing was never held.

In 1968 Congress passed a gas-pipeline-safety law after it was reported out of the Commerce Committee. It set up a new agency, the Office of Pipeline Safety (OPS), in the Department of Transportation to issue standards for and inspect the nation's one million miles of natural-gas pipelines, and, in cooperation with the states, to reduce the number of pipeline explosions which damage millions of dollars of property each year, kill some twenty to fifty people, and injure three to five hundred.

The Natural Gas Pipeline Safety Act clearly mandates the federal government to set safety standards for all gas-pipeline facilities (other than gathering lines in rural areas) but does permit a state agency that adopts a safety standard that is as high as the federal standard to assume responsibility for intrastate gas pipelines. If the state refuses to assume such responsibility, as have Louisiana and New Jersey (with many miles of pipelines), the federal agency automatically retains it. The Office of Pipeline Safety has recklessly adopted existing industry guidelines as federal standards, forcing some states, for example New York, to be content with interstate pipelines (under the jurisdiction of the

OPS) running through its state which do not meet the high standards applicable to New York intrastate pipelines.

OPS has rejected the responsibility conferred upon it by Congress in the 1968 act. The agency, when it was five years old, had a staff of only seventeen professionals, and although he has not tried to increase the agency's budget, OPS director and former petroleum engineer Joseph C. Caldwell admitted, "Obviously, with the limited staff that we have, a very little monitoring goes on." Caldwell boasts about the "operational responsibility" of the Office of Pipeline Safety and rejects the charge that his office is understaffed or underbudgeted. He said:

> I don't think the federal government should be in the position of running a complete regulatory program. We have the authority to see that a safety program is laid out at the lowest local level. If a state doesn't do it, we have to do it at the federal level.

His views are apparently colored by his philosophy of federal regulatory authority. He is quoted in the August 4, 1973, *Business Week*: "Regulation is a last resort. . . . When you're in business every regulation costs money." And he told us that "The act was designed for regulatory authority in decentralization."

In 1973, five years after the pipeline-safety law was enacted, the number of pipeline disasters, the number of deaths and injuries, and the amount of property damage from pipeline explosions was on the increase. Its director disapproves of the federal statute he is charged with executing and has failed to request either funds or staff sufficient to do his job. Yet the Senate Commerce Committee subcommittee has held only one oversight hearing on the program. With the recent assignment of a committee staff member to cover pipeline safety, it is anticipated that there may be more activity in this neglected area.

Senator Moss acknowledged, when asked about the low priority given to oversight, "There are some problems here. It's important to work on those problems so they don't slide." He also expressed frustration with the imbalance between the executive and legislative branches:

Congress relies too much on the executive department for information and data. We don't have the resources or personnel to do it. I don't want to see Congress grow any more, but I'd like to see independent staff, expertise and other outside resources available without going to the executive department.

During the lean Nixon years 1969 through 1973, the committee held only fourteen oversight hearings on consumer programs, including natural-gas-pipeline safety, or an average of three oversight hearings per year—a paltry showing indeed (see Table 11). Although much oversight can be accomplished by committee counsel through personal exhortations via telephone and visits, few agencies will effect any significant turn-around in their activities without public prodding. In comparison to other committees, the Commerce Committee conducts oversight well. But few committees devote any resources to overseeing the multitude of programs they have created.

TABLE 11.

Senate Commerce Committee Oversight Hearings on Natural Gas and Consumer Issues, 1969–1973

Date	Topic
July 9, 1969*	Gas-pipeline-safety oversight
July 25, 1969, Jan. 16, and Feb. 23, 1970*	Fair Packaging and Labeling Act oversight
June 2, 1970*	Flammable Fabrics Act oversight
Feb. 24, 1971	Corvair heater safety
Oct. 8, 1971*	Mercury and halibut situation
Feb. 16, 1972	Corvair heater safety
Mar. 2, 1972*	Nutritional content and advertising/dry cereals
July 19 & 25, 1972	Auto safety oversight
Mar. 8, 9, & 12, 1973	Radiation
Mar. 17, 1973*	Consumer impact of gasoline marketing
Aug. 1, 1973	Auto airbags status
Aug. 16, 17, 20, and 21, 1973*	Consumer redress
Aug. 31 and Sept. 4, 1973*	Federal Incentives for Innovation

* Subcommittee hearings.

CONSUMER AFFAIRS IN THE HOUSE

The House Commerce Committee's treatment of consumer issues reflects the reluctance of its chairman to delegate responsibility to either staff or subcommittees—in vivid contrast to the "new" Warren Magnuson in the Senate. There is no Michael Pertschuk on the House committee to help parcel out assignments, absorb the heat of disagreements, balance the equities between competing interests, make sure key issues can be won. Instead, about eight senior professional staff members work directly for Chairman Harley Staggers on all of the committee's issues and serve as his liaison to the various subcommittees. In contrast to the Senate, the House Commerce subcommittees have tight, jealously guarded jurisdictional lines through which each piece of legislation formally passes before consideration by the full committee. Although most of the legislative and oversight work is done by the subcommittees, each one is allocated only one professional staff member and one secretary (except for Staggers' own Subcommittee on Investigations, which is loaded with nine professional and four clerical staffers). The remaining administrative staff assists in running the full committee.

Because of the increasing independence of the House subcommittees, encouraged by the Democratic Caucus rules and the assertiveness of such subcommittee chairmen as John Moss and Paul Rogers, Staggers has tried (in violation of the caucus rules) to retain his control by a stingy allocation of staff, absolute veto power over the scheduling of hearings, and assignment of members to subcommittees. An outwardly congenial man, he is seldom able by force of personality to lead his committee, and thus resorts to procedural and mechanical devices to give him a measure of influence.

In the July 1973 *Progressive,* Robert Dietsch pictured Staggers as overwhelmed in the rough-and-tumble world of controversial legislation, a man with his circuits overloaded. Industry lobbyists hover around his committee and connect with members who will oppose and delay the committee's bills, many of which affect millions of households and businesses. The combination of industry activity and Staggers' passivity often spells doom for proconsumer legislation:

No one has ever accused Harley Staggers of being a crook, or even of being impolite. But few persons have ever judged Staggers to be a strong man, or one with enough force and intellectual determination to manage effectively the pile of legislation which comes his way, let alone his forty-three member Committee. Staggers is basically a passive individual who hates to get involved in a legislative hassle. When confronted with a decision, he prefers to duck and weave. . . .

Staggers' policy, apparently, is never to attack a consumer bill frontally. He stalls it; he likes to have any initiative on consumer and safety legislation come from the White House, not his committee staffers, and he likes to have the full Committee avoid straight up or down votes on a controversial bill, preferring to recommit it to a subcommittee. The public might think this means the measure will get further consideration, but any politician or lobbyist knows a recommittal usually means death.

Under House rules, committee members cannot vote by proxy,* so committee chairmen must see that members are present to vote. A strong chairman tells members—at least those of his party—to "be there," and they obey. Staggers does not operate that way, and as a result, the nineteen Republicans, who are better organized, carry more voting clout than their minority representation might indicate. Nor does Staggers permit his staff to keep a rein on the Democratic Committee members. . . .

. . . Adding to Representative Staggers' own disinclination to tackle controversial legislation is the conservative bent of the Committee itself. There are more than enough Democratic conservatives among the forty-three members to team

---

* Some committee rules permit proxies; some do not. Proxies are not used in the House Interstate and Foreign Commerce Committee.

with Republicans to defeat any measure. Moss's important [consumer] subcommittee, for example, includes five Democrats and four Republicans, but one of the Democrats is conservative W. S. (Bill) Stuckey of Georgia. Early this year, Moss tried to persuade his chairman to realign the subcommittee so that consumer bills would have a better chance of enactment. Staggers refused. Stuckey once said he enjoys being on the Moss Subcommittee because there he can stop "super-liberals" like Moss and Bob Eckhardt of Texas from voting out "socialistic legislation such as national no-fault auto insurance."

Moss for many years was best known for his authorship of the Freedom of Information Act of 1966, which he sponsored as chairman of the Subcommittee on Foreign Operations and Government Information of the Government Operations Committee.* It was enacted over the objections of many in government in large measure because of Moss's tough but low-key and persistent advocacy, a trait he has also displayed in handling consumer legislation.

Moss's Commerce and Finance Subcommittee has jurisdiction over much of the House Commerce Committee's consumer legislation, including auto safety, product safety, radiation safety, toy safety, poison prevention, flammable fabrics, warranties, cigarettes, advertising, fair packaging, the Federal Trade Commission, no-fault insurance, class-action law suits, food dating, and such disparate areas as tourism and the Securities and Exchange Commission. In the Ninety-second Congress, the subcommittee consisted of four Democrats and three Republicans: Moss, Bill Stuckey, Henry Helstoski, and Bob Eckhardt in the majority, and James Broyhill, John Ware, and John McCollister in the minority.

---

* This act requires federal government agencies to supply information requested by any person, regardless of the reasons for his request, unless such information falls within any of the nine narrow exceptions in the Act, such as trade secrets, personal information about an individual, or internal government policy memoranda.

Most of them had business backgrounds.* Moss and Eckhardt are strong proponents of legislation on behalf of consumers. Helstoski was generally favorable to consumers but often absent and merely acquiescent when present. Broyhill, Ware, and McCollister generally opposed strong consumer legislation—as did Stuckey on many occasions.

John Moss believes that federal regulation should fully protect American consumers, but the subcommittee majority disagrees, and Moss realizes that his views cannot prevail in the subcommittee without modification and compromise. While pushing for tough provisions, he is even-handed and fair with his colleagues and is usually receptive to reasonable compromise. Two of the four bills reported out of the subcommittee during the Ninety-second Congress saw the light of day only because of compromises worked out between Moss and Eckhardt and two Republican members: McCollister on the auto-cost-savings (bumper) bill, and Broyhill on the product-safety bill. Stuckey voted in the subcommittee against both compromises.

Bob Eckhardt, a former trial lawyer, is considered by many to be the most scholarly member of the Texas delegation and a sophisticated legislator. He enjoys the tough competition of mental gymnastics with his subcommittee colleagues, and his judicious handling of controversial matters makes him an extremely popular congressman. Not surprisingly, Eckhardt is often the subcommittee mediator; he was probably most responsible for breaking the logjam on the consumer product safety agency bill. He views the subcommittee with respect:

* Broyhill was formerly associated with Broyhill Furniture Factories of Lenoir, North Carolina; Ware is former president and chairman of various Pennsylvania utility companies; McCollister is former president of McCollister and Company; Samuel Young, who joined the subcommittee in the 93rd Congress, was vice president of American Hospital Supply Corporation (1965–66). On the Democratic side, Moss is a former businessman and real estate executive; Stuckey is a corporate officer of several family businesses now associated with Pet Milk; and Henry Helstoski was an advertising management consultant from 1962 to 1964 while serving as mayor of East Rutherford, N.J.

> It's not a plum for the special interests, so we get on the Republican side persons not so deeply partisan. For example, Mr. Broyhill is a good man; you can work with him across the aisle. Mr. Ware is a thinking man—a nice guy of substance and ability. Mr. McCollister is extremely conservative, and he brings the business side into our discussions; but we can compromise with him on the issues. So the subcommittee gets more substantively oriented minority members and no uncompromising ideologues.

Ranking subcommittee Republican Broyhill confirmed Eckhardt's view: "We have an excellent relationship. We've been able to disagree without being disagreeable." His views were echoed by his Republican colleague McCollister:

> It's a great subcommittee: I feel under no restraint whatsoever about participation in debate and offering amendments to bills under consideration. I really think our subcommittee should serve as a model for congressional committee operations.

And Moss commented, "Mr. Broyhill has been a most helpful ranking member. He's reasonable. He's never been an obstructionist."

The members' views toward the subcommittee have changed over the past few years. When most of the members were first appointed to Commerce, they did not list Commerce and Finance as their first choice among subcommittees, and some listed it last. The conservatives thought that consumer legislation held little interest for them; the liberals apparently did not at first realize the broad scope of the subcommittee's jurisdiction and its potential impact on everyday American life. Subsequently, the more conservative members have found that the subcommittee is a rallying point for business lobbyists who oppose most of the legislation under their jursidiction, and they have been urged to remain and battle for modifications to the consumer proposals. Not incidentally, such relationships generate significant campaign contributions.

In the Ninety-third Congress the subcommittee was enlarged by

two members: a moderate Democrat from Kentucky, John Breckinridge, and an uncompromising business-apologist Republican
from Illinois, Samuel Young. Thus the anticipation that the new
Congress would bring a more flexible balance in new appointments to the subcommittee was not realized. In the Ninety-third
Congress, only two significant bills, on toxic substances and auto-
safety defect recall, were reported out of the subcommittee by the
August 1973 recess. (Toxic substances was reported out by a
four-to-four vote when Stuckey was absent.)

Other frustrations—such as the insufficiency of staff for the
subcommittee and the inability to make long-range plans because
of Staggers' absolute control over the scheduling of all hearings
and executive sessions—have ripened into a confrontation between subcommittee chairman Moss and full-committee chairman Staggers. Moss has aimed his objections at some of Staggers'
methods that are in direct contradiction to the House Democratic
Caucus rules passed in 1973 and in some cases of the House
Commerce Committee's own rules for the Ninety-third Congress.
For example:

1. Both committee and Democratic Caucus rules require subcommittee chairmen to set subcommittee meeting dates after consultation with the committee chairman (to avoid conflicting
schedules). In practice, Staggers delays for weeks before permitting a meeting or hearing to be scheduled and sometimes requires
meetings to be changed after they have been approved. The effect
is to prevent subcommittee chairmen from making any long-range
plans for the orderly consideration of legislation or giving witnesses lead time in which to prepare testimony.

2. Democratic Caucus and House Commerce Committee rules
require that all legislation referred to a committee be further referred within two weeks to subcommittees unless members decide
by majority vote to consider the matter in the full committee. In
fact, Chairman Staggers, without vote by the full committee, often
delays weeks and months before referring controversial bills, or
those on which there is some question of jurisdiction, to subcommittee.

3. Democratic Caucus rules require Democratic Party members be represented on subcommittees in a proportion no less favorable than on the full committee, and that committee ratios be established to create a firm working majority on each subcommittee. The spirit—if not the letter—of caucus rules is violated in Moss's subcommittee. While the Democratic representation on the full committee (55.81 percent) is reflected in the subcommittee (55.55 percent), the fact that one of the Democrats, Representative Stuckey, consistently and proudly votes with the Republicans prevents a "firm working majority."

Stuckey claimed in 1972 that he was the compromiser on the subcommittee "because there are three liberals, three conservatives, and I'm the moderate in the middle." He was an announced opponent of class-action legislation prior to the Ninety-second Congress, when it was a priority item before the subcommittee. During the Ninety-second Congress Stuckey voted with the Republicans on a key vote to keep the consumer product safety agency in the Department of Health, Education and Welfare (HEW) rather than making it a separate independent agency. The bill was finally reported out when ranking Republican Broyhill agreed to a compromise (see below). It was Stuckey's opposition that was responsible for the low priority given the no-fault insurance bill in the Ninety-second Congress; subcommittee counsel Michael Lemov admitted, "We just didn't have the votes [in subcommittee] to pass it." The absence of a "firm working majority" on the subcommittee blocked a number of key consumer bills in the Ninety-second Congress, and the same prospects are in sight for the Ninety-third.

4. Democratic Caucus rules state that, subject to the overall control of a majority of the committee's Democratic Caucus, each subcommittee shall be authorized an adequate budget for the discharge of its responsibilities. House Commerce Committee rules state that the chairman shall authorize the expenditure of funds appropriated to the committee "for the reasonable expenses of the subcommittees in carrying out such subcommittees' assigned duties and responsibilities."

In January 1973 Moss submitted to Staggers a budget of about $100,000 for three professionals and two secretaries. His request was rejected by Staggers. The net result of running a subcommittee without a budget is that any expenditure of funds, whether to hire a secretary or consultant or take a trip, must be personally approved by Staggers.

Staggers agreed to amend the committee rules in 1971 to provide for one staff member for each subcommittee. That is all he had allocated to each of the four legislative subcommittees out of a total staff of forty-three,* until Moss and other members complained in the spring of 1973 about not having even a subcommittee secretary, and Staggers relented and gave Moss a secretary to assist his one professional staffer, Michael Lemov.

Moss is still quite dissatisfied with staff allocations. "The staff ought to be enlarged. It's so important to have sufficient staff to enable us to do an adequate legislative job." Broyhill agrees with Moss. "We need two, three *times* the staff we have today. It's ridiculous to cover our subject-matter jurisdiction without more staff help."

5. Although Democratic Caucus rules state that each member of a committee shall be entitled to membership on one subcommittee of his choice, House Commerce Committee rules confer upon the committee chairman the right to make and change subcommittee assignments. Staggers has adhered to the House Commerce rule in disregard of the Democratic Caucus rule.

In the early part of the Ninety-third Congress, when the rules of the House Commerce Committee were awaiting adoption by the Democratic majority, Moss and Paul Rogers went to Staggers and objected to the inconsistencies with the caucus rules. Staggers promised to give their objections consideration, but proceeded to ignore them for weeks. By mid-February 1973, when the committee rules still had not been adopted, Moss drafted a letter to

---

* Eight professional staff members are assigned to the various subcommittee areas at the full-committee level, but this dual system of appointment is inefficient and often does little to lift the burden on the subcommittee staff member who reports to the subcommittee chairman.

Staggers signed by twelve of the twenty-four Democrats on the committee (but not by Rogers) requesting the opportunity to discuss the committee rules and their relationship to the caucus rules at the next meeting of the committee's Democratic caucus. But, apparently fearing retribution from Chairman Staggers, only a few members appeared at the meeting to support Moss's position, and the inconsistent committee rules were adopted.*

Despite the shortage of staff, the lack of budget, the difficulty of scheduling hearings and meetings, and the lack of a firm working majority, the Commerce and Finance Subcommittee was active during the Ninety-second Congress. It held eight days of hearings on the no-fault insurance bill, six days on the Federal Trade Commission reform and consumer warranty protection bill, thirteen days on the consumer product safety agency bill, five days on the auto bumper bill, and twenty-six days on a study of the securities industry, as well as numerous days of executive sessions to discuss and mark up some of these bills. But the output in enacted legislation is less impressive: only bumpers and product safety survived.

Subcommittee counsel Mike Lemov is unhappy with the subcommittee's legislative progress. "We have a pile of bills ready right now for action, but we can't get to them because we don't have staff people available for them." Lemov listed areas needing study: advertising (including truth-in-advertising, documentation of claims, impact of advertising on the reader, viewer, or lis-

---

* In January 1975 the rules came back to haunt the chairman. The gross inconsistencies between the Commerce Committee rules and the Democratic Caucus rules were highlighted in a report prepared by public interest groups just before the election of committee chairmen by the caucus. Shortly thereafter Representative Moss challenged Staggers and led a successful move in the committee to adopt a tough new set of rules that significantly curtailed the power of the chairman and conformed with the caucus rules. Following that victory, Moss opposed Staggers for the chairmanship of the influential Investigations Subcommittee and won. Staggers thereafter decided not to chair a subcommittee. The Commerce and Finance (renamed Consumer Affairs and Finance) Subcommittee chair fell, on the basis of full-committee seniority, to Lionel Van Deerlin, a progressively inclined legislator, who, however, had left Commerce and Finance for the Communications and Power Subcommittee in 1965.

tener); investigation of travel agencies ("Every summer we have a flock of people stranded in Europe. Why?"); food content, nutritional value, and date labeling ("the most important area waiting for thorough investigation"); and international standards. Lemov said, "We need at least a year to completely investigate international standards; we just don't know the impact of measurements and standards used in foreign commerce upon the American economy. . . . We just can't go ahead and pass legislation as the administration would like us to do when there are so many unanswered questions."

In the consumer area, the Senate has been the leader and the House the obstructionist, contrary to what our forefathers would have expected when they created the two bodies. Because the full House committee is unwieldy and recalcitrant, the anticonsumer business lobby concentrates its efforts there. "They've given up on the Senate committee," mused House Commerce Committee staffer Charles Curtis. The anticonsumer pressures may be stacked on the House, but the shock waves are felt in the Senate. Senator Frank Moss, in particular, is frustrated by House inaction and negativism toward strong consumer bills passed by the Senate:

> We try to guess which consumer bills will have the best chance of passage in the House. It's as if we have our hands tied, and that's frustrating. Our strong bills are nearly always watered down, and if not watered down, they're held up.

THE CONSUMER PRODUCT SAFETY BILL

The lack of action is evidenced by the fact that only two consumer bills were passed by the Ninety-second Congress. The bumper bill authorized the secretary of transportation to set bumper standards for automobiles to reduce low-speed collision damage, and to set up a consumer information service which would provide data as to the comparative collision repair costs of various models of cars.

The story of the bill to create an independent Consumer Product Safety Commission is illustrative of previous problems and compromises affecting consumer legislation. Beginning with the ground-breaking National Traffic and Motor Vehicle Safety Act of 1966, Congress had followed a haphazard, piecemeal response to consumer product-safety problems. In rapid succession it passed the Child Protection Amendments of 1966, the Flammable Fabrics Act Amendments of 1967, the Wholesome Meat Act of 1967 and Wholesome Poultry Act of 1968, the Natural Gas Pipeline Safety Act of 1968, the Radiation Control for Health and Safety Act of 1968, the Child Protection and Toy Safety Act of 1969, and the Poison Prevention Packaging Act of 1970. Each law was directed at a specific consumer-product category that had received some public notoriety prior to legislative treatment, but even in combination these laws covered only a small portion of the multitude of products produced for American consumers. As Republican Senator Charles H. Percy (Ill.) observed:

> The folly of Federal regulation of consumer products is all too plain. Legislation in this area consists of a hodgepodge of unrelated statutes dealing with specific hazards in very narrow product categories.[9]

The House Commerce report on the product safety bill concluded:

> The technological revolution and ever-increasing public demand for consumer products has produced over the last several years thousands of new products whose applications are not easily understood by consumers and whose use may pose great potential for harm.[10]

Recognizing that a flood of new products was inundating the marketplace, Congress in 1967 authorized a two-year study to develop a systematic approach to product safety. It created the National Commission on Product Safety (NCPS), headed by Arnold B. Elkind, a New York lawyer, to "conduct a comprehensive study and investigation of the scope and adequacy of measures now employed to protect consumers against unreasonable risks of injuries which may be caused by household products."

Out of an original list of more than 350 product categories, the National Commission on Product Safety was able to investigate only 16, but it found within each category makes and models unreasonably hazardous to consumers. In addition, the commission identified 17 more product categories where investigation of consumer complaints was sorely needed. The investigated products, all identified as presenting unreasonable hazards to safety and health, were: color television sets, glass bottles, high-rise bicycles, rotary lawnmowers, toys, power tools, household chemicals, fireworks, hot water vaporizers, infant furniture, ladders, floor furnaces, architectural glass, protective headgear, unvented gas heaters, and wringer washing machines. The commission listened to hair-raising accounts of children and adults being killed or maimed by seemingly harmless household products.

As Chairman Elkind later testified before the Subcommittee on Commerce and Finance:

> The core of our learning was that a significant number of injuries and deaths each year could be avoided by channeling our technology toward the goal of hazard reduction in consumer products. . . . Our gut estimate was that [the] laissez-faire approach to consumer products costs the American public about 20 percent of the overall toll that the public pays in injuries or deaths for the privileges of enjoying consumer products. This translates into 6,000 lives, 22,000 cripples, 4 million injuries, and $1 billion in treasure that could be saved each year by an effective system for making products safe to use.[11]

The commission's final report was submitted to the President and Congress on June 30, 1970. It recommended a tough legislative response that would establish a permanent, independent consumer product safety agency with strong powers to set minimum safety standards and to pull safety-deficient products off the market. The commission found that:

Federal product safety legislation consists of a series of isolated acts treating specific hazards in narrow product categories. No Governmental agency possesses general authority
to ban products which harbor unreasonable risks or to require that consumer products conform to minimum safety
standards. Such limited Federal authority as does exist is scattered
among many agencies. Jurisdiction over a single category of
products may be shared by as many as four different departments or agencies. Moreover, where it exists, Federal product safety regulation is burdened by unnecessary procedural
obstacles, circumscribed investigative powers, inadequate
and ill-fitting sanctions, bureaucratic lassitude, timid administration, bargain-basement budgets, distorted priorities, and
misdirected technical resources.[12]

In his 1971 testimony before the House subcommittee, Elkind
responded to the persistent argument that businessmen and the
marketplace can adequately protect the American consumer:

In our report and studies we have analyzed the reasons why
competitive private industry cannot be expected to take the
initiatives essential to hazard reduction. In the 18 months
that have passed since the publication of our report, no one
has challenged our observation that the competitive marketing imperatives are eye appeal and cost as opposed to safety.
. . . The need for intervention into this problem area by the
Federal Government is generally acknowledged by all men
of good will who have considered product safety and its
implications to the consumer.[13]

Presented with documented information, Congress swung into
action, but not without considerable controversy over the scope of
the federal authority and the independence of the regulatory
agency.

The Senate Bill

Senators Warren Magnuson and Frank Moss drew upon the
final recommendations of the National Commission on Product

Safety for the bill they introduced in 1970 as the Consumer Safety Act. In the Ninety-second Congress the bill was reintroduced by the two senators on February 25, 1971, as S. 983 to create an independent consumer product safety agency. The administration response came two months later, when the Department of Health, Education and Welfare prepared an alternative bill (S. 1797). Perhaps the most controversial aspect of S. 1797 was its proposal for expanding the product-safety authority of the federal government for most consumer products but retaining that authority within HEW, the department responsible for several other health and consumer programs. During the hearings on product safety before the full Commerce Committee in July 1971, Chairman Magnuson cautioned:

> Unless the Administration can demonstrate otherwise, I am convinced that the new consumer safety administration must be made independent of HEW, directed by an administrator appointed for a set term of office and confirmed by the Senate, with separate commissioners responsible for food, drug and product safety.[14]

Presidential Special Assistant for Consumer Affairs Virginia Knauer made the case for locating all product-safety authority in HEW's subsidiary Food and Drug Administration (FDA):

> Within this organizational frame, undergirded by more specific legislative authority and reinforced by this administration's commitment to seek the necessary resources, we will be well prepared to serve the needs of the American consumer in the 1970's and beyond.[15]

Criticism of the administration proposal was swift. Elkind, testifying a few hours after Knauer, said, "I do not like the Administration's proposal, and that dislike is not arbitrary nor political but is grounded on the lessons which the Commission learned in the course of its work."[16] He called the administration proposal a "paper tiger," asserted that if its drafters read the commission's reports, "they have deliberately decided to build into the Consumer Product Safety Act many of the weaknesses which have afflicted previous efforts to legislate for consumer safety."[17] With some bitterness, he continued:

> The first step in creating a paralytic consumer protection function is to place it deep in the recesses of the already overburdened and unsuccessful Department of Health, Education and Welfare. . . . It is frustrating to find that the Administration desires to bury this new consumer activity with the very people who have such a poor track record . . . and there is every reason to assume that such a program would have a low profile, a low priority on appropriations, and a low assignment of manpower. . . . Congress will have again created a facade of a consumer protection program but not a reality.[18]

A second major difference between the Nixon approach and the Magnuson-Moss bill were the procedures for developing and adopting safety standards. The administration's bill allowed the regulated industries extensive opportunity to participate in and control the standard-setting process, while the Magnuson-Moss bill gave the government broad authority, with informal procedures, to develop standards without dependence on action or opposition by industry.

1. The administration bill authorized the agency to adopt an "existing" standard as a proposed safety standard rather than offering interested parties the opportunity to develop a new standard (the provision in the Magnuson-Moss legislation). With few exceptions, existing standards consist of voluntary industry standards, most of which have inadequate specifications for mandatory enforcement.

2. Under the Nixon bill the agency could proceed to develop a proposed product-safety standard only after (a) rejecting the option of using an existing standard and (b) not receiving a satisfactory outside offer to develop a proposed standard. The senators' bill permitted concurrent standard development.

3. The administration bill contained no time limits within which the standards had to be developed, while the Magnuson-

Moss proposal required speedy action under specific time periods, with extensions only for good cause.

4. The administration bill did not state whether the proposed standard developed by outside persons would have to be published by the agency as submitted or whether the agency could amend it before publication. The Magnuson-Moss bill specifically allowed the agency to merely consider the standard proposed by outside persons prior to publication of a proposal.

5. The administration bill required the secretary of HEW to consider "disruption or dislocation or competition" and "reasonable manufacturing and other commercial practices" in promulgating standards, often an impossibility for regulatory agencies because of the difficulty of getting factual information from the affected companies.

6. The Magnuson-Moss bill required informal administrative procedures to be used in issuance of standards, while the Nixon bill permitted a hearing to resolve any material issue of fact. The hearing process in such agencies as the Food and Drug Administration has been used over and over by industry to delay, sometimes for years, the issuance of a standard.

7. In order to declare a product a "banned hazardous consumer product" and cause its removal from interstate commerce, under the administration bill the agency would have to find that no feasible product-safety standard would adequately protect the public, and would have to promulgate its order just as though it were a safety standard. Under the Magnuson-Moss bill, if the agency found that a consumer product contained an identified hazard which presented an unreasonable risk of death or injury, and removal of the product from commerce was necessary to protect the public, the agency by informal regulation could declare the product banned. If the agency, before or during the preparation of such a regulation, found the product presented an imminent hazard, it could declare the product banned by publication of its order which would be in effect pending the completion of the rule-making procedure.

8. In the sections applicable to imminent hazards, the Nixon

bill permitted the agency to request the attorney general to file an action in district court, notwithstanding the existence of an applicable product-safety standard, and the court was given jurisdiction to declare the product imminently hazardous and grant temporary or permanent equitable relief, such as notification of purchasers, recall and replacement or repair, or seizure. The Magnuson-Moss bill permitted the agency to issue interim safety standards effective immediately with court review sustained only if the challenger established by clear and convincing proof that the agency's action was arbitrary.

A third issue dividing the White House and the senators was a Magnuson-Moss provision creating an independent consumer advocate to represent the general public in government product-safety proceedings. This provision duplicated the concept in a comprehensive consumer-advocate bill, S. 1177, which would have created a consumer protection agency to represent the views of consumers before federal regulatory agencies. The administration opposed S. 1177, and its product-safety bill did not include a consumer-advocate provision.

Fourth, the bills differed considerably on how much information the government should provide consumers about unsafe products. Both bills authorized government information retrieval about hazardous products and the injuries they cause. To collect this information the government, under the Magnuson-Moss bill, could conduct its own inspections of factories or other establishments, carry out investigations and testing, and extract information from contracted research and from industry studies. The Nixon bill did not authorize inspections and investigations.

The Nixon proposal also would have prohibited the disclosure of "trade secrets, formulas, processes, costs, methods of doing business or other competitive information not otherwise available to the general public." Ralph Nader pounced on this provision in his testimony before the committee:

> The Administration's bill would not only cover a huge area called trade secrets and commercial processes, but doesn't even begin to develop, first of all, definitions for what a

trade secret is, and second of all, procedures for challenging the assertion of trade secret or allied designations by the industry or by the company involved. This has led in prior laws to enormous secrecy that not only is unjustified, but is closed from challenge by consumers or petitioning groups. . . .

In short, under the present situation, a company can take a legitimate trade secret, put it into a great bin of material that has nothing to do with trade secrets, send it to the Government as they are required to by the law, and receive recognition that all of the information will be given trade secret recognition.[19]

The Magnuson-Moss bill emphasized public disclosure of as much information as possible, even including trade secrets, if necessary "to protect [the public] health, safety or economic well-being." In contrast, the Nixon bill required the safety agency to give the pertinent manufacturer an opportunity to comment for thirty days before the release of *any* information identifying him and would require a public retraction for release of any inaccurate information.

A fifth difference between the bills concerned the authority of consumers to redress injuries and to have defective products brought up to standard. The administration bill, to the amazement of consumers—who otherwise could find little to praise in the government's legislation—allowed any interested person to sue for enforcement of a safety standard thirty days after notice to the government and the defendant. The Magnuson-Moss bill did not contain such a provision, but it did allow treble damage suits by parties injured by reason of knowing or willful violation of a safety standard, regulation, or order; the administration bill did not contain such a provision.

As for assuring the public of the safety of their products, S. 983 required manufacturers to certify to distributors and dealers that their products conformed to all applicable safety standards and regulations; the administration bill did not require this. Finally, both bills provided for civil and criminal penalties for violations of the act. Magnuson-Moss allowed a maximum civil penalty of $2,000 for any violation, not to exceed $500,000, while the administration bill contained a $10,000 civil penalty per act, with no maximum for any "knowing" violation. The Magnuson-Moss criminal penalty for knowing or willful violation was $50,000 or 180 days in prison, or both. The Nixon bill included a penalty of $10,000 for each act, or imprisonment of one year, or both if the act was willful.

Industry lobbyists went on record at the hearings as favoring federal consumer-safety legislation, but they continually stressed the importance of retaining a large measure of industry participation and control in the standard-setting process, and of preventing the agency from releasing information embarrassing to companies that manufacture or sell consumer products. The National Association of Manufacturers, represented by Stanley Groner, told the Senate Commerce Committee in the hearings:

> U.S. manufacturers should be accorded every opportunity to remedy any problems through voluntary standards.
>
> We further ask for every procedural safeguard against precipitous or overzealous administration of this largely untried area of regulation. . . . There must be no one-man decision making affecting the interests of diverse consumers, employees, investors, taxpayers and others who comprise the whole public interest.
>
> The advantages of voluntary standards and the voluntary institutions and procedures that have existed for many years within the industrial system are so obvious and important as to warrant maximum legislative support.[20]

One knowledgeable industry group opposed the concept of voluntary standards: the Industrial Designers Society of America, a professional organization whose members are designers of consumer and other types of products. Spokesman Charles Mandelstam, the group's general counsel, testified that voluntary standards would not insure safe products:

As counsel for the Society, from time to time I have to advise members on how far they can push a client with respect to a safety factor in a product, and they ask me what is their responsibility if the product is not safe and a suit is brought. . . .

One sees again and again the pressure against a product safety improvement factor. It may just be inherent in the system of distribution that we have in the country. It may be too much to expect industry to police itself. And we are therefore very much in favor of doing it the way this bill does it.[21]

After eight days of intensive hearings in July 1971 on all versions of the bills, publication of several committee-print revisions of the bill as introduced and six days of executive-session deliberations with four roll-call votes (during February and March 1972), the committee, on March 24, 1972, ordered a clean bill reported in lieu of S. 983 and S. 1797. For eight months committee staffer Lynn Sutcliffe and others had pored over both bills, seeking to incorporate the strengths of each in the rewritten bill.

The bill reported out of the Commerce Committee on April 13, 1972, the Consumer Safety Act of 1972 (S. 3419), closely resembled the Magnuson-Moss version. The full extent of congressional dissatisfaction with the performance of the FDA was revealed. The new bill transferred all FDA functions to the new independent consumer safety agency. Members of the committee explained this decision. Senator Moss said:

We were frustrated. So many acts had been passed over to the F.D.A., but we never got anything out of them. F.D.A. lagged on the Flammable Fabrics Act. They didn't even set a standard for three years! And the F.D.A. was timid. They seemed to be afraid of tackling businesses. We just decided it wasn't best to place the consumer agency with that body.

Senator Cotton, an opponent of the move, admitted that it had a certain plausibility:

Well, the bill always had an independent product safety agency—I guess it was more a matter of deciding that logically you might as well bring the food and drug stuff over.

In response to this legislative pressure, HEW added $27 million to its FDA budget request for fiscal 1973 to permit greater activity on product safety. But it was too late to save the administration's position.

The control of standard-setting was retained by the agency and not delegated to the industry; a consumer counsel was included to ensure that the decision-makers would hear all sides; the agency was given authority to conduct inspections and investigations; and the information-disclosure provisions permitted release of trade-secret information if relevant in any proceeding or to protect the public health and safety, after opportunity for comment within fifteen days by the pertinent manufacturer. The public could (1) bring a suit for injunctive relief against the agency if individuals have by agency acts or omissions been exposed to unsafe products; (2) sue to enforce a safety standard or order a product banned or declared imminently hazardous; and (3) recover damages and attorney fees in case of injury by reason of knowing violation of a consumer-product-safety standard, regulation, or order (the treble damage provision was dropped).

The bill as reported dropped some key provisions from the original Senate bill and some of its later committee prints. The civil-penalty provisions were adopted from the Nixon bill, along with the requirement that there be a knowing violation for a civil penalty. The authority to declare a product imminently hazardous by a quick interim standard, as in the original Senate bill, was dropped in favor of the court-order provision in the administration bill. Taken from the Nixon bill was the authority to ban a product from interstate commerce with the same cumbersome procedures as used in developing a safety standard, instead of the informal rule-making procedures in the original Senate legislation. The requirement that the manufacturer certify compliance of a product with the safety standards was dropped, and the authority for the agency to hold hearings to resolve any issue of material fact during the development of safety standards was taken from the administration bill, as was the provision for a formal hearing under the Administrative Procedure Act before the agency could find a product defective.

Two important provisions from the committee prints developed by the staff were also dropped. One would have required the agency to submit its budget to Congress at the same time it was submitted to the White House. The other, a new and innovative provision, would have created a fiduciary duty on the agency employees to protect individuals from being exposed to unreasonable risks of injury associated with consumer products under the agency's jurisdiction. This duty would have been enforceable in a civil suit by any individual or class exposed to an unreasonable risk, and if violated the agency employee could be ordered to perform his duty, or he could be suspended or removed. As a further protection the United States would have been responsible for compensating individuals injured as a result of the breach.

Several new provisions were incorporated into S. 3419. A conflict-of-interest section prohibited a former agency employee from assisting any person, whether or not for compensation, in any transaction in which he had been involved personally (not collaterally) or in an official capacity within eighteen months after the transaction. The new agency was given authority equal to the attorney general to represent itself in civil or criminal penalty proceedings, or injunctive or imminently hazardous consumer-product actions. Such authority is jealously guarded by the Justice Department and seldom accorded to other agencies. Another provision, favored by consumer advocates, required any communication from a person (including a corporation) to the agency on a matter in rule-making or adjudication to be made part of the public file of the proceeding unless it would be entitled to protection under the information sections of the bill. In the section on judicial review, the committee bill permitted "any interested person"—not just "any person adversely affected"—to petition for review.

In addition, the bill as reported by the Commerce Committee contained a number of new concepts seldom found in federal law, including: agency authority to require by regulation that manufacturers follow certain quality-control procedures to insure compliance with safety standards; a prohibition against stockpiling of consumer products by a manufacturer between the time a final order is issued and the time it becomes effective; authorization for detailed safety-analysis studies of consumer products not subject to a consumer-product-safety standard in order to insure that manufacturers give adequate consideration to safety; a joint Scientific Committee of agency employees to assure an exchange of scientific information between various parts of the agency and to advise the agency director on scientific matters; a National Injury Information Clearinghouse to establish nationwide reporting centers to monitor accident occurrences; maintenance at the agency of a public-information room equipped with a copy machine.[22]

When the Commerce Committee voted on the bill on March 21, 1972, only Senator Cotton dissented. As the administration's spokesman, he maintained that the agency should rest within HEW; he feared that backers of the independent safety agency had been "blinded by the 'gold glitter' of what can be accomplished through the establishment of yet another independent agency." But Cotton characteristically made little effort to hold his fellow Republicans on the committee together in a voting bloc. He stated later:

> On the question of separating Food and Drug, I just thought it wasn't a good idea and that the case ought to be made. I pretty much carried it alone, though. Five of our minority members are up for reelection this year [1972], and it really would look bad for them to be opposing this thing. One of the first things I learned in politics was that it wouldn't work just to oppose things . . . there has to be something you're *for*. Now in this instance the Administration and I saw eye-to-eye. They probably lobbied the minority members, and

the whole committee for that matter—H.E.W. people came up, you know—more than I did, but I really wouldn't know. But I know what the realities are in a situation like this, and I didn't try to push anybody.

Industry reaction to S. 3419 was fierce. Winston Pickett, a lobbyist for General Electric, called committee staffer Sutcliffe a "wild man" when he saw one of the committee prints. After years of successfully cultivating the lower- and upper-echelon staff in the FDA and HEW, industry did not want to be confronted with a new and perhaps vigorous agency with a broad safety mission. But having learned in recent years that lobbying the State Commerce staff was not productive, industry lobbyists turned their attention to possible floor amendments and especially to the House Commerce Committee.

Since the bill as reported overlapped the jurisdictions of other Senate committees with responsibility for the existing agencies that would be part of the new agency, the bill was referred for sixty days to the Government Operations and Labor and Public Welfare committees for consideration and approval before being taken to the floor. (The Government Operations Committee held hearings, but took no further action on the bill.) Labor and Public Welfare reported out the bill on June 5, 1972, with several amendments. The title was changed from "Consumer Safety Agency" to "Food, Drug and Consumer Product Agency." The Agriculture Department's activities in veterinary; biological controls; meat, poultry, and egg inspection; and voluntary food-grading programs were transferred to the new agency, and the consumer-counsel provisions were deleted as unnecessarily duplicative of other legislation before the Senate (S. 1177, to establish a Consumer Production Agency).* The Labor and Public Welfare Committee report was approved unanimously, but with an attached supplemental statement from Senator Peter H. Dominick (R., Colo.) opposing, as Senator Cotton had opposed in the

---

* The consumer advocate provisions were deleted to separate the opponents of S. 1177 and Product Safety and avoid a compounded opposition to both bills.

Commerce Committee report, the administrative independence of the proposed agency.

The Senate debated S. 3419 on June 21, 1972. Commerce chairman Magnuson promptly accepted the changes made by the Labor and Public Welfare Committee, saying, "I congratulate the members of [the] Committee for their efforts in improving S. 3419." Immediately after Magnuson finished his opening speech, Senator Moss rose to propose an amendment to meat and poultry inspection within the Agriculture Department:

> It is with no great joy that I offer this amendment, because I fully support the action of the Committee on Labor and Public Welfare and the Committee on Government Operations in placing the authority of the Agriculture Department over food inspection in the Food, Drug, and Consumer Product Safety Agency. But to do so would involve the jurisdiction of another committee of this body and would involve recalling from the Department of Agriculture some of its jurisdiction. To do this would greatly delay the bill before us, while we discussed the matter in committee and held hearings and later had to come to the floor.[23]

Moss's amendment was offered to fulfill a previous commitment made by Magnuson to Senator Herman E. Talmadge (D., Ga.), chairman of the Senate Agriculture and Forestry Committee, to delete the agriculture-related amendments in the product safety bill in return for some amendments to the Agriculture Committee's pesticide bill (see Chapter 6). The Moss amendment was accepted by voice vote, but not without strenuous objection by Senator Abraham Ribicoff (D., Conn.), who went down swinging:

> I do hope that this will act as a warning to the responsible officials in the Department of Agriculture to clean up their own house and truly fulfill their mandate to provide the American housewife clean and wholesome meat and poultry.

With this untidy business out of the way, Senator Cotton took the floor to offer an amendment to make HEW the administrator of the act's provisions. Seeking to accomplish on the Senate floor what he could not do in the Commerce Committee, Cotton made a lengthy, elaborate statement (undoubtedly prepared by the White House). Cotton argued:

> Mr. President, I want to make it clear that this amendment which I am asking the Senate to consider is not a negative amendment. It sets up, in the Department of Health, Education, and Welfare, machinery which I insist is every bit as comprehensive and effective as this proposed independent agency.
>
> I, therefore, earnestly urge the Senate to favorably consider my amendment. I insist that it does not detract one ounce or one iota from the effectiveness of this meritorious measure to protect the consumer. Rather, it would separate within the department the whole health setup from education and welfare as practicably as it can; provide presidentially appointed leadership, and establish Offices of Food, Drugs, and Consumer Products, each headed by a director. Most important, it would not do violence to the experience and the know how that has been gained through all the years that we have been working on these problems. . . .
>
> I believe that if we want this bill to pass not only the Senate but the House of Representatives, and be signed by the President into law in the short time remaining in this session, my amendment would aid that effort very materially.[24]

The amendment was expected. Representatives of the pharmaceutical industry (regulated by HEW's Food and Drug Administration), mindful of their well-nurtured friends in HEW, had lobbied strenuously for it before Cotton introduced it.[25]

Senators Moss, Percy, and Joseph M. Montoya (D., N.M.) led a successful floor fight against the Cotton admendment, which was turned back on a vote of thirty-two to fifty-one. This vote again evidenced the cohesion of the Commerce Committee: only Senators Cotton and Spong among the committee members voted for the amendment.

Senator Edward J. Gurney (R., Fla.) then proposed to delete the authority of the agency to prosecute its own cases. This amendment was seen as an attempt to cripple the agency, and it was defeated thirty-one to fifty-one, with Senators Magnuson and Percy protesting loudly against it. Percy described the FDA's frustration when it had been faced with evidence of food contamination in need of immediate correction but without the power to go to court.

> You go to the U. S. Attorney—and they did. They did not go once or twice. They went several times. The FDA lawyer told the prosecutor of the conditions that were found, and his belief that a criminal action was clearly warranted. But the U. S. Attorney wrote that he did not feel that action was appropriate at that particular time. . . .
>
> What do you have to do to break the law in a food warehouse? This is not an isolated case. It has been documented many times over that these conditions exist. The hearings held before the Committee on Government Operations are filled with instances of this kind.
>
> I maintain that we must do something more than we are now doing if we intend merely to fulfill our public responsibility.[26]

Senator Cotton, still the administration spokesman, then offered an amendment to delete the new agency's authority to enforce criminal penalties:

> Mr. President, this amendment simply leaves everything in the bill. It leaves in the injunction authority. It leaves in the enforcement of civil penalties up to $10,000. It merely takes from the bill the authority for the attorneys of the new agency to prosecute criminally in the courts. This is all it does. It leaves everything else intact which, in my opinion, would give the new agency all the power it needs, including the situation outlined by the distinguished Senator from Illinois. But it does not start the precedent of having the attorneys employed by the various agencies becoming criminal prosecutors in the Federal courts.[27]

The debate was brief: Magnuson spoke exactly one sentence against it, and John Sherman Cooper (R., Ky.) said not much more in its favor. The proponents of a strong agency squeaked by, defeating the proposal forty-one to thirty-nine. On this closest of votes, the loyalty factor is the more remarkable. Magnuson kept all but three Commerce Committee members with him; the three defectors were Senators Cotton, Spong, and Stevens.

The other significant amendments adopted were those proposed by: Ribicoff, to provide twenty-five new positions in the Civil Service's highest salary positions (grades 16–18), for the new agency; Talmadge, to award manufacturers actual damages suffered as the result of an agency order banning a product as a hazardous substance if a court determined that the agency abused its discretion by making such an order; Gaylord Nelson (D., Wis.), to prohibit a manufacturer, distributor, or retailer of consumer products from suggesting new standards which would cover their products; and Thomas Eagleton (D., Mo.), to apply the provisions of the bill to design as well as manufacturing defects.

The Food, Drug and Consumer Product Agency Act was passed by the Senate on June 21, 1972, by a sixty-nine to ten vote, with Senator Cotton the lone Commerce Committee member voting no.

The House Bill

The early terms of debate in the House, as in the Senate, were set by the National Commission on Product Safety proposal for an independent agency (H.R. 8157, introduced by Commerce and Finance Subcommittee chairman John Moss, and the administration substitute (H.R. 8110), both introduced in May 1971. The central point of dispute was the provision in the Moss bill that an *independent* consumer product agency be established. Subcommittee consideration was extensive—thirteen days of hearings and eight executive sessions in the fall of 1971 and in early 1972. The junior Republican on the subcommittee, John McCollister, called this legislation "the best effort our subcommittee has made this past session":

We approached it from subject-matter areas, not by consideration of individual pieces of legislation before us. We covered all the subject-matter areas systematically contained in all the bills introduced on the subject. We took it issue by issue, with good give-and-take. No one was locked into a hard-set, inflexible position. There was a pervasive atmosphere of open-mindedness, cooperation and careful debate. We went about it to create a semi-formal administrative procedure act that we could be proud of.

But the deliberations were hardly as smooth as the congressman indicated, especially on the issue of agency independence. The subcommittee initially voted in May, 1972, four to three, with Representative Stuckey joining the Republicans, to keep the proposed agency in HEW. However, at this stage, Bob Eckhardt went to work to build a winning coalition of four subcommittee votes. As Eckhardt said, "We can compromise on the basis of the issues," and he began looking for the fourth vote. This is Eckhardt's account of what happened:

I said, "Maybe you guys don't understand the importance of this HEW thing. You're asking a cabinet official to make judicial decisions, to decide whether a product goes on the market or not. A cabinet post is a political one and the Administrator is likely to swing with the Administration. And he won't be accessible to Congress.

"An independent agency, on the other hand, can be called before this committee. What if a Democratic president were in office and you guys wanted to call the Administrator before this committee? You could do it if it were an independent agency, but you couldn't if it were a cabinet department."

McCollister was convinced by these arguments. He came back from the Republican huddle and said if we'd agree to delete the consumer advocate provision he'd vote for a separate agency. We quickly agreed.

Congressman Stuckey gave a more graphic description of the events behind closed doors:

> Eckhardt convinced McCollister. He told us that only an
> independent agency would be directly accountable to Con-
> gress. He looked at McCollister and said, "Just think if
> McGovern was elected and put his man in charge of the
> safety agency. . . . You couldn't do anything about it!"
>
> That swung McCollister quick. His eyes bugged right out
> and he popped out of his seat. . . . I think Eckhardt was just
> waiting to use that argument. He pulled it out of his bag at
> just the right time!

McCollister admits he was persuaded to switch his position by
three arguments: (1) HEW is not an efficient agency ("I worry
about an agency being buried in the bureaucracy"); (2) the
committee was creating a quasi-judicial agency whose decisions
should be independent; and (3) the agency should be responsible
and accountable to Congress. "I moved to reconsider the earlier
vote and my motion passed. . . . I was responsible for it." While
he may have been responsible for the motion, he was not responsible for the result; independence for the consumer product safety
agency had been rescued by Bob Eckhardt.

But there was an added problem in the House Interstate and
Foreign Commerce Committee: the transfer of the Food and
Drug Administration's responsibilities in the Senate bill to the
proposed product safety commission caused a territorial snag between two subcommittees.

On February 1, 1972, Representative Paul Rogers, chairman
of the Public Health and Environment Subcommittee, wrote a
letter to Moss about the Rogers subcommittee's potential loss of
jurisdiction over the FDA if the product safety bill transferred the
FDA activities to the proposed agency. On February 14, 1972,
Moss responded that his bill, H.R. 8157, conformed to the recommendations of the National Product Safety Commission in giving the proposed new agency jurisdiction over consumer products
subject to regulation by the FDA *only* to the extent hazards presented by such products are not subject to duly promulgated regulations under the Food, Drug and Cosmetic Act. Thus, to the
extent that the FDA failed to issue regulations protecting the

public from product hazards, the proposed new agency could do so. Moss concluded, "I do not believe that any of the Product Safety bills . . . would affect Subcommittee jurisdiction as it is presently defined in the rules of our Committee."

Rogers evidently was not satisfied with these assurances. Even if the Moss bill did not actually transfer the FDA functions to the new agency, the forthcoming conference of Senate and House members on the Senate and House versions of the bill could adopt the Senate bill with its FDA transfer provisions. Should the Senate bill prevail, "we could totally lose the jurisdiction," explained Health Subcommittee member James Hastings. Such a move was also vehemently opposed by the drug industry, which was not willing to tolerate any interference with its well-developed network of influence on FDA operations.

Rogers then took the initiative. On June 1, 1972, he introduced H.R. 15315, a bill to strengthen the FDA and thus defuse some of the criticism of its inadequate performance. Although the Moss product safety bill was approaching full-committee markup, Rogers scheduled hearings on his bill for June 9. House Commerce Committee chairman Harley Staggers, faced with a possible head-on clash between two strong-willed subcommittee chairmen, negotiated to report out the Moss bill and not the Rogers bill, but with the concession from Moss that neither the FDA nor responsibility for medical devices and radiation safety would be transferred to the new agency. The fuss raised by Rogers was a successful tactic in protecting his territory—although there is some question about whether it would have suffered any encroachment had the comprehensive bill been enacted. (Moss had promised that each subcommittee would retain its current jurisdiction.) The interest of consumers in having a vibrant agency responsible for regulating consumer products was the obvious loser.

Moss had little choice but to compromise on the issue. There were rumblings that Rogers would have argued against other provisions of the bill if he had been denied his request that food and drugs be excluded. Moss related why he had accepted the specific exclusion of food and drugs from his strong bill:

Why? Because it went beyond the jurisdiction of my sub-committee. That only leads to endless and unnecessary squabbling. I felt that the principle of a consumer product safety agency was so important that it must be enacted as quickly as possible. The FDA is showing improvement lately. Let's see if it performs well. Then, if need be we can transfer its functions at some later date. But for now that protection agency is the most important thing.

Congressman Eckhardt said of Moss's compromise, "He wanted to stay absolutely clear of jurisdictional problems. Rogers insisted and prevailed upon him. Moss is anxious to get the bill through, so he agreed."

Moss's staff counsel on the Commerce and Finance Subcommittee, Michael Lemov, agreed that Moss had few options; he didn't have enough votes to push the stronger bill out of his subcommittee, with the Stuckey-Republican coalition united against him, and he would surely lose the bill in the full committee if Rogers organized an opposing force.

After eight days in private executive session, the Commerce and Finance Subcommittee on May 16, 1972, unanimously reported a clean bill which represented an accommodation between the the two earlier versions. The fresh bill (H.R. 15003), now supported by the ranking Republican on the subcommittee, James Broyhill, was reported favorably on June 20, 1972, by the full committee, which held two more days of executive sessions, where many of the same issues were raised, debated, and resolved.

On the most crucial issue in the bill, the independence of the agency, the House committee agreed with the Senate and resisted White House and business pressures. The committee recognized that "an *independent* agency can better carry out the legislative and judicial functions contained in this bill with the cold neutrality that the public has a right to expect of regulatory agencies formed for its protection" (emphasis added).[28]

The House committee's bill differed in a number of minor and several major respects from the Senate-passed bill. While the Senate bill provided for a single administrator, the House bill created a five-member independent Consumer Product Safety Commission, with the members appointed by the president for seven-year terms. The rule-making sections were similar in granting interested persons the opportunity to recommend adoption of existing standards or to offer to develop a proposed standard. But although the Senate bill expressly prohibited a manufacturer, distributor, or retailer of a product that would be affected by the proposed standard from offering to develop the proposal, the House bill was silent on this issue. The Senate bill expressly permitted the agency to develop a proposed standard whether or not it had accepted outside offers to develop the same standard. The House bill prohibited such simultaneous development unless the offerer was determined not to be making satisfactory progress, although the agency could concurrently acquire technical capabilities necessary to properly evaluate the standards recommended.

The penalties differed considerably in the two bills. The Senate bill provided for civil penalties of $10,000 for knowing violations of the act ("knowing" defined to mean actual knowledge or presumed knowledge of a reasonable man), while the House committee bill provided $2,000 for each knowing violation with a maximum of $500,000 ("knowing" defined differently depending on the offense). For criminal penalties, the Senate bill included a misdemeanor penalty of $10,000 or one year in jail or both for willful violations, while the House bill permitted imposition of a $50,000 fine or one year in jail or both after a knowing and willful violation *and* after having received notice from the agency of noncompliance. The requirement of notice about noncompliance virtually nullified the House criminal-penalty provision by giving corporate and white-collar violators a second chance to repeat the same crime before imposition of the penalty. Few members of the generally conservative House Commerce Committee would have afforded a petty thief such an option.

The House committee bill also significantly restricted the availability of information to consumers about consumer products. It required confidentiality of all information that contained or related to a trade secret, except when relevant in any proceeding under the act. The emphasis in the Senate bill, in contrast, was on disclosure; it required release of all information unless it related to a trade secret or other confidential business information not indicating the presence of an unreasonable risk of injury or death, but with the key overriding exceptions that it may be disclosed if relevant in any proceeding under the act or to the public to protect the public health and safety.

One indication of independence for a regulatory agency is the freedom to go to court with the agency's own attorneys rather than having to persuade Justice Department attorneys to take the case. With a few exceptions the basic law for years gave litigation rights only to the Justice Department, which was authorized to represent the various government agencies. And for years the Federal Trade Commission, Food and Drug Administration, and others have been frustrated by the failure of the Justice Department to vigorously prosecute their cases in a timely manner. The Senate-passed product-safety bill gave this authority to both the new agency and the Justice Department, thus permitting the agency to initiate cases in its discretion but also to request Justice Department assistance as appropriate. The House committee bill gave the new agency self-representation in the case of imminent hazards, but did not provide for it enforcement of civil penalties or injunctions.

On June 20, 1972, the House committee by voice vote reported the bill. Seven Republican committee members (none of them on the Commerce and Finance Subcommittee)* dissented from the majority House committee report:

> The record shows that the FDA has compiled a record in the past 30 months that can be favorably compared with any other regulatory agency in the Federal Government. . . . The creation of a new commission will cost the taxpayers far more than leaving the product safety effort in an already organized and operating department of government. . . . The

* Samuel Devine, Ancher Nelsen, James Harvey, Clarence Brown, James Hastings, John Schmitz, and James Collins.

interest of the consumer will clearly be served best by strengthening the present organization [the FDA] as a key health and safety related agency within the Department of Health, Education and Welfare.[29]

Although unable to stop the House committee action on the bill, industry lobbyists did not despair. They revived one of the House's ancient blockades the Rules Committee,* by lobbying Rules committee members in an effort that stalled but did not defeat the bill. And they almost precipitated a constitutional crisis when an assistant to the Chief Justice of the United States was discovered, hand-in-glove with the drug industry, lobbying the speaker of the House. Syndicated columnist Jack Anderson charged on October 5, 1972, that Chief Justice Warren E. Burger had sent Rowland F. Kirks, chief administrative officer of the federal courts, to discuss the consumer bill with House Speaker Carl Albert (D., Okla.). Kirks was accompanied by Thomas Corcoran, a Washington attorney and one-time aide to President Franklin D. Roosevelt, who was representing several drug firms (all opposed to the legislation). According to Albert's office, Corcoran was spokesman for the two at a late-summer meeting where he contended that the bill would add significantly to the number of cases before federal courts.

At the time of Kirks's visit the House bill was locked up in the Rules Committee, where it had been held since late June by the arch-conservative chairman, William M. Colmer of Mississippi. A memorandum by Kirks complaining about the citizen-suit provisions had been sent to a number of House members with Corcoran's calling card. No copy was sent to the chief House sponsors.

On October 11, John Moss wrote Chief Justice Burger a letter raising basic questions about the propriety of Burger's actions and Kirks's role in approaching the speaker to obtain agreement for removal of certain judicial remedies from the bill. Moss indicated there was evidence to suggest that Kirks's lobbying delayed con-

* All legislation must be approved by the Rules Committee before going to the House floor.

sideration by the Rules Committee of the Commerce Committee request to bring the bill to the floor.

On October 13, Kirks said publicly that Burger was unaware of his visit to Albert's office, and added that he considered his visit a routine one to inform Congress of the impact of legislation upon the courts. Albert said that neither Kirks nor Corcoran represented themselves as being sent by Burger.

Also on October 13, Burger released a letter he had sent to Albert in which he declared that he had taken no position with regard to the consumer-product-safety bill. "However," Burger added, "I do have and always will have a strong view that when the Congress considers legislation that will add a substantial volume of cases in the federal courts, the Congress should also provide the means to handle those cases."[30] Although after the legislation had passed Burger stated categorically in a letter to Moss that he authorized no one associated with him to express an opinion on the bill, this had been far from clear at the height of the controversy.

Following loud complaints about the Rules Committee bottleneck, the bill was finally released in September and was sent to the floor. The compromises reached in the committee proceedings for the most part protected the bill from assault. Although Representatives William Springer and George A. Goodling (R., Pa.) spoke against the independent agency, no one offered an amendment to put the agency in HEW. An indication of the genuine satisfaction with the committee bill came from the floor remarks of James Broyhill:

> An independent commission can give more objective single-minded attention to consumer safety. An independent agency has undivided responsibility for product safety and can be more easily held responsible for any failures that occur. . . . And, significantly, an independent agency would combine existing fragmented programs which are currently dispersed through approximately 30 different federal organizations.[31]

Most of the nine amendments adopted on the floor were minor, but three did remove significant consumer protections in the bill. Representative David W. Dennis (R., Ind.) successfully deleted the authority for persons injured by a product not complying with the safety standards to sue for damages unless the amount of the claim amounted to at least $10,000. Dennis claimed his amendment was "a means of limiting this proliferating litigation to more important cases involving the real need for federal court remedy." Corcoran and Kirks had found their sponsor. Bob Eckhardt tried —unsuccessfully—to defend the consumers' right to sue:

> I am tired of hearing the argument that the rights of people, no matter how small they may be, must depend on whether or not we have established enough courts to defend those rights.[32]

Commerce Committee chairman Staggers successfully guided through an amendment to permit open-dating information to appear in coded form, thus depriving consumers of information where secret or unclear codes are used to indicate the age of a product.

Finally, Eckhardt, generally a consumer advocate, followed his trial-lawyer instincts (i.e., support of the advocacy process) and succeeded in removing the burden on manufacturers to notify owners of defects following expedited and relatively informal adjudication. The committee bill instead required rapid notice to owners but lengthy procedures before the manufacturers would be required to correct the defect. The Eckhardt amendment combined the two steps, permitting manufacturers to delay any notification until the case had been processed through lengthy procedures and a final determination made as to whether the manufacturer was required to repair the product.

The bill finally passed the House on September 20, 1972. To assure the germaneness of the Senate provisions not in the House bill, the House first passed H.R. 15003, substituted the items in this bill for the provisions of S. 3419, and then passed S. 3419 as so amended by a 319-to-50 vote.

In view of the differing House and Senate versions of this legislation, the bills were sent to conference, where the conferees haggled for days over the differences. The House conferees were spearheaded by ranking Commerce Republican William Springer, who was retiring from Congress and had plenty of time to obstinately refuse to accept the broad-scoped Senate provisions. Because of the press of time, the senators frequently acceded to Springer's demands, and the final compromise was closer to the narrower House version than to the Senate measure. Senate conferees also believed that President Nixon, who had long opposed S. 3419, might veto their stronger bill, so they reluctantly accepted the House demands. The conferees deleted the Senate provision transferring FDA out of HEW into the new agency. They also modified the Senate provision that permitted a private person to petition the agency to promulgate a safety standard for a product he considered dangerous. As adopted by the conference, the bill permitted the petitioner, if the agency failed to issue the regulation petitioned for, to appeal to the courts the agency's failure to act; if the courts found in favor of the citizen, the agency would be required to begin the rule-making procedure. The conferees also added a proviso that would not make this section of the act effective until three years after the bill was signed into law.

A little-noticed but significant provision included in the conference compromise was the requirement that whenever the commission submits a budget estimate or legislative recommendations to the president or Office of Management and Budget, it must concurrently submit a copy to Congress.* In complying with this unique requirement to inform Congress of theretofore tightly held information (until the president decides after review to send it, or a substitute, to the Congress) the chairman of the new Product Safety Commission, Richard O. Simpson, in 1973 issued a policy statement saying that the commission would supply Congress with copies of everything it sends to the OMB and invite members of Congress to all "hearings, briefings or discussions" with OMB.[33]

---

* Authority for concurrent submission of legislative positions and of the budget in annual reports was in the Senate-passed bill.

The OMB was furious. Its associate director for Human and Community Affairs, Paul H. O'Neill, wrote Simpson asserting that "hearings, briefings or discussions" were "comparable to closed executive sessions" of congressional committees where "confidentiality and a free exchange of ideas are absolutely essential." O'Neill claimed that "the statutory language does not embrace these negotiations, but deals instead with the actual submission of budget estimates or requests by the Commission." OMB asserted that invitations to these private sessions could be issued "solely" by OMB and information about them could be disseminated "only" by OMB. Senator Magnuson and Representative John Moss wrote to OMB Director Roy L. Ash reinforcing Simpson's interpretation of the legislation. With this strong backing Simpson has not budged from his policy, but Washington watchers snicker and, nodding their heads, suggest that OMB with its enormous power will win in the end, somehow.[34]

The House and Senate accepted the Conference Report just before the Congress adjourned in mid-October. On October 27, 1972, the Consumer Product Safety Commission Act was signed into law (PL 92-573) by President Nixon after considerable speculation that even in the heat of his reelection campaign he might veto the only significant consumer bill passed by the Ninety-second Congress.

3

Surface Transportation

· In late 1972 Jill Halyard went shopping for a new bicycle. None of the Arlington, Virginia stores had any in stock. They did not expect a shipment for at least three months, even though manufacturing firms within five hundred miles had ample inventories.

· Fred Porter could not get reservations for a passenger train ride into Chicago; the station manager put him on hold for twenty minutes. The train arrived forty minutes late. Its cars were thirty years old and rusted. Its heating system was defective in the freezing weather.

· A truck with two massive trailers was weaving back and forth unsteadily in front of Janet Schuck's car. It was going about 55 mph. She was afraid to pass it, but traffic was piling up behind her.

· A moving firm was two weeks late in picking up Larry La-

NOTE: This chapter was written by Robert Fellmeth and Jonathan Low.

trobe's furniture in Maryland for a move to Oregon in late 1971. Larry missed his first week of work, and his family had to spend three weeks in an Oregon motel waiting for their furniture. The driver demanded $550 in cash before he would complete the delivery. And to round off the family's nightmare, the firm had damaged the hi-fi set. The company refused to reimburse them for the damages, the delays, the inconveniences.

A public relations magazine for the transportation industry has admitted that "transportation is the hidden ingredient in everything we buy."[1] In 1970 freight costs alone amounted to $87 billion, or ten cents of every dollar spent in this country. Consumers pay from $3.4 to $5.6 billion each year in excessive transportation costs because of the nature of current regulation, according to experts.[2]

THE RUBE GOLDBERG GOVERNMENT

A massive tangle of red tape in the government agency that regulates most surface transportation—the Interstate Commerce Commission (ICC)—is partly responsible for our transportation ills. The ICC determines the distance carriers may go, the routes they must take, the commodities they may carry, and the rates they set. It protects monopoly carriers: shippers—those whose goods are carried—must accept ICC-authorized carriers unless they are very large manufacturers and can afford a private fleet. To get authority for a new carrier, shippers must offer the ICC evidence that an existing carrier has absolutely refused to carry their goods. Agency critics say that the indirect consumer costs—in missed deliveries, damaged merchandise, and inefficiency—of ICC's protection of monopoly carriers are incalculable.

Protected by government regulation from competition, carriers allegedly underutilize their equipment. About 40 percent of all regulated trucking mileage is without cargo to pay for the trip. The ICC may, for example, authorize a truck to carry undeveloped photographic paper in one direction, but not developed pictures in the other. The average boxcar is in motion about two and a quarter hours each day, and empty boxcars await the convenience of General Motors and other corporations for months.[3] Meanwhile, Midwestern farmers may have to use more expensive transportation or see their crops rot.

An August 1971 study by the Department of Agriculture found that instances of "deregulation" or competition lowered the cost of transportation significantly. It found that "small and out of the way buyers are able to be reached"; "the quality of service improves"; and the "in transit time is reduced by half [yet] rates do not fluctuate."[4]

Instead of encouraging competition in the surface-transportation industry, the ICC fosters huge carriers and conglomerates by rubber-stamping mergers. The average size of a trucking firm has more than doubled over the past decade, and thirty out of thirty-four rail-merger proposals have been approved by the ICC since the 1950s. The ICC permits truck, rail, and water carriers to band together in legal rate cartels called "rate bureaus." Unlike industries that are subject to federal antitrust laws, carriers are virtually unmonitored and may collusively set rates to protect one another. The ICC then enforces the rates that carriers have set [5]

While granting the privilege of monopoly powers to certain carriers, the ICC reportedly has failed to set and enforce commensurate standards on behalf of consumers. It does not vigorously enforce standards against violations of home moving regulations (estimating costs improperly, failing to pick up or deliver, and damaging goods) or violations of safety regulations (requiring drivers to work excessive hours or not repairing transportation equipment).* It has a potentially effective enforcement power: to suspend or revoke the operating authority of its seventeen thousand regulated carriers. But it has invoked this power just six times since 1935; all six cases involved only partial or minor suspensions.[6]

The ICC theoretically has an overlord: Congress. Under the Constitution, Congress has the power to legislate surface-transportation policy, "to regulate commerce with foreign nations, and

---

* Such repairs are now a responsibility of the Department of Transportation.

among the several states."[7] It has the power to fund programs through the transportation subcommittees of the Appropriations committees in both houses. And it oversees the administration of the laws that it passes by checking on agencies like the ICC that are delegated the responsibility of regulating surface-transportation carriers.

Since passage of the Interstate Commerce Act in 1887, Congress has exercised this jurisdiction, passing about two hundred amendments in the area. But the problems of surface-transportation monopoly, mergers, overcharges, and shoddy services have been largely unaffected by curative legislation.

The task of legislating, appropriating, and overseeing surface-transportation policy are fragmented among several congressional committees—highway policy under Public Works, urban mass transit under Banking, Housing, and Urban Affairs, and so forth. But the broadest jurisdiction has been claimed by the two Commerce subcommittees: the Senate Surface Transportation Subcommittee (with jurisdiction over interstate railroads, buses, trucks, some water carriers, and pipelines) and the House Subcommittee on Transportation and Aeronautics (with jurisdiction over these same areas as well as railway labor issues and civil aeronautics).* Such dispersions of authority contribute to Congress' failure to set cohesive national transportation policies and priorities. Each committee or subcommittee fights for its own territory and adjusts the details of regulations and policies already in effect. For example, the subcommittees of Commerce have spent much time considering whether freight forwarders should be given the status of carriers or shippers in paying certain freight rates, not whether collusive rate arrangements are improper or not. They dwell on whether or not water carriers should be allowed to carry commodities that are subject to regulation in the same shipment with bulk

---

* In the Senate, aviation is handled by a separate Commerce subcommittee, while railway labor is under the jurisdiction of the Labor and Public Welfare Committee. The Committee Reform Amendments of 1974 drastically altered House Commerce jurisdiction in this area. Most aviation and surface transportation matters (except railroads) were transferred to a reconstituted Public Works and Transportation Committee.

commodities that are subject to open competition, not whether regulation should exist in the first place and not what the results are.

In fact, no one is rearranging the fragmented pieces of this elaborate Rube Goldberg machine, with its complication for complication's sake. The two Commerce subcommittees are supposed to oversee the Interstate Commerce Commission, but there are many other agencies with regulatory functions in the transportation-Goldberg machine, with other committees overseeing them. Here are some examples of the hodgepodge of agency jurisdictions sanctioned by Congress:

Rail. The ICC has jurisdiction over all interstate rail transportation except intercity passenger service. Urban mass transit has been moved from the Department of Housing and Urban Development (HUD) to the Department of Transportation. DOT regulates all rail safety.

Water. The ICC regulates only inland and coastal carriers, except those transporting liquid-bulk and some dry-bulk commodities. While the ICC looks after United States–Canada and United States–Mexico *rail* transportation, the Federal Maritime Commission watches over international ocean shipping, except for some functions falling under the jurisdiction of the Maritime Administration in the Department of Commerce. Water-carrier safety, however, is under the jurisdiction of the U.S. Coast Guard. Meanwhile, the Army Corps of Engineers builds the canals and harbors.

Air. The ICC has no direct jurisdiction over air transportation. That job is divided between the Federal Aviation Administration within the Department of Transportation and an independent agency, the Civil Aeronautics Board.

Trucking. The ICC regulates most interstate trucking and busing, except firms carrying agricultural commodities. The National Highway Traffic Safety Administration within the DOT administers bus and truck safety as well as transportation of dangerous articles and explosives.

Pipelines. While the Federal Power Commission now regulates pipeline transportation of natural and artificial gas, the ICC has jurisdiction over all pipelines. And the DOT handles pipeline safety.

INFLUENCING THE LEGISLATIVE CLIMATE

The executive branch and the Congress might not be well enough organized to coordinate surface-transportation policy, but trade associations for railroads, truckers, bus companies, barge lines, and freight forwarders certainly are. Many associations represent the carriers in Washington: the National Association of Motor Bus Owners (NAMBO), the Freight Forwarders Institute (FFI), the American Waterways Operators (AWO), the American Trucking Associations (ATA), and the very active Association of American Railroads (AAR). In addition to these major associations, the carriers have the Industrial Trailer on Flat Car Association, the Western Railroad Traffic Association, and scores of rate bureaus in each region. Major carriers retain attorneys and lobbyists in Washington for added influence on government policymakers.

Shippers are also represented in Washington: the National Industrial Traffic League, the American Institute for Shippers, the National Grain Trade Council, occasionally the Grange, the American Farm Bureau Federation, the Midwest Coal Producers' Institute, the Small Shipments Association, the National Association of Railroad Passengers, and six transportation unions.* But all of the shippers' organizations together cannot equal the power and monetary commitment of any of the major carrier associations to influence surface-transportation policy. Indeed, although a shipper may want a better carrier for himself and hence better service or cheaper costs, he would prefer it if the other shippers he competes with have poor transportation service and high costs. And for typical shippers, such as manufacturers, transportation is but one

---

* These are the Congress of Railway Unions, the Brotherhood of Locomotive Engineers, the National Railway Labor Conference, the Teamsters, the Brotherhood of Maintenance of Way Employees, and the United Transportation Union.

cost. They cannot afford to commit political resources on one aspect of their cost. For the carriers, the whole operation is transportation and they organize appropriately. Carrier commitment includes the extensive hiring of former members of Congress, former Commerce committee staff, and former executive branch officials as active lobbyists.

In many ways, Congress has let itself be strongly influenced by the executive branch and organized surface-transportation carriers. One factor in this deference is Congress' lack of adequate staff. The executive branch has about two thousand professionals directly involved in transportation matters; about fifty of these are concerned with Congress' transportation subcommittees. A comprehensive count of the lobbying staffs working for the private industries is difficult to come by, but the Association of American Railroads alone has about twenty professionals involved in lobbying Congress, and this figure doubles if one counts the attorneys and lobbyists working for the individual railroads. The lobbying forces of trucking, barge, and bus interests are of equivalent strengths. Against this array during the Ninety-second Congress stood *two* staff members on the Senate Committee, Daniel O'Neal and John Cary, and *one* staff man on the House side—William Dixon, whose responsibilities also included aviation! These staffers received only sporadic aid from minority committee aides or legislative aides in the offices of individual members.

Where do overloaded staffers turn for information, consultation on legislation, drafts of legislation, witnesses at hearings, or supporting materials? They turn to the industry representatives or to the executive branch. The AAR alone can cull a lot of data for them from its departments of Economics and Finance, Management Systems, and Research and Operations. So far, subcommittee or committee staffers have compiled no major reports, provided little alternative information, conducted no detailed investigations, and raised few original issues for Congress' consideration.

The Washington-based carrier associations fully use their staff members to write, check over, and lobby legislation. In 1969 the AAR's legal department was staffed by William Malone, Jerry J.

Breithaupt, Jr., and six other attorneys. In the words of a description of AAR in *Modern Railroads*:

> The [AAR legal] department is charged with drafting legislation which the railroads plan to have introduced. It prepares and submits statements and oral testimony before Congressional Committees and handles various proceedings before federal agencies. On an informal basis it frequently presents the industry's position to individual members of Congress or to a Congressman's staff.[8]

Sometimes these associations sneak their legislation into Congress by delivering it to the ICC first, since the ICC sends a dozen or so bills to Congress each session. During congressional hearings on these bills, it becomes apparent that the commissioners are not always familiar with the legislation and sometimes cannot even say why it has been written. A former Senate staffer recalled one case where the Senate Commerce Committee actually became interested in an ICC bill—which so surprised the commissioners that they reread it and then withdrew it from consideration.

Many Americans are probably unaware that the industry gets privileged access to preliminary drafts, much less that they actually draft public laws. According to an AAR publication:

> The system for supporting or opposing legislation having a bearing on the industry is not necessarily complex on the surface, but by the time the decision stage is reached in Congress, it may have required that all the stops be pulled out. Take for instance a single measure—one that appears in the form of legislation the railroads did not institute. The legislative staff obtains copies of the bill (it goes without saying that these individuals often know of the legislation or have obtained copies of the bill before it is actually tossed in the hopper).[9]

The carriers do not stop here. They go on to lobby for the bills they want and against those they dislike. The AAR self-description in *Modern Railroads* also acknowledges the lobbying activities of its legislative department, even though some of its staffers have not registered as lobbyists:

This group is responsible for the "leg work." If an objection to a piece of legislation is desired or the industry thinks an amendment is necessary, this is the team that carries the ball. In a very strong sense, these men handle the industry public relations work in Congress. If it requires waiting around the Capitol until a late hour to support or oppose an amendment in late session, they are the people responsible. This small group generally knows the sentiment of a given Congressional group and can give a pretty thorough and quick analysis of the legislative climate a particular bill faces. They decide just how much assistance may be needed from state railroad organizations or from other sources that might be helpful.[10]

Association presidents are not above doing leg work on behalf of industry interests. According to the AAR publication, "President Thomas M. Goodfellow himself [is] no stranger to legislation under consideration. Mr. Goodfellow has made it a point to visit and become acquainted with nearly every member of Congress and top officials of the administration."

Members of Congress have not done their share to maintain checks and balances among the executive branch, the transportation industry, and Congress. A basic element of intimacy among these three institutions is job symbiosis. People move freely from one institution to another, acting first as a legislator, then as an executive administrator, and then as a corporate executive—or any other combination of these positions. Ten of the past twelve ICC commissioners have left the agency to become transportation-industry executives; most of them had previously been campaign or personal aides to members of Congress. On December 22, 1972, Senator Vance Hartke announced the appointment of former ICC commissioner John Bush as his personal expert staffer on Senate surface transportation matters. Allan R. Jones, once a legislative assistant to Senator William B. Spong who sat on the Commerce Committee and the Public Works Subcommittee on Roads, was hired by the American Trucking Associations in January 1973. Jones is in the ATA's Governmental Relations Unit and will probably lobby those he used to serve. Dan O'Neal, who headed the Senate Surface Transportation Subcommittee staff for five years, was appointed in January 1973 as an ICC commissioner. And recently defeated Senator Gordon Allott (R., Colo.) has been appointed to direct the ICC's long-promised "rate regulation" transportation study. One executive-branch official in antitrust admitted that Allott knew little about rates, adding, "Except for O'Neal, this interchange is like a wild merry-go-round of political hacks and incompetents between Congress, the executive, and private interests. Where is the check, the balance?"

Committee members further weaken their position as monitors of American transportation policy by accepting substantial campaign contributions and other favors.

Industry associations publish weekly or monthly newsletters in professional, glossy formats that have wide circulation. These publications often identify members whom the carriers judge worthy of support. Rather than directly endorsing a candidate or attacking an opponent, these articles usually feature members who have introduced favorable bills (often drafted by the association itself) or who have delivered a favorable speech (sometimes written by the association). The American Trucking Associations has a weekly radio program called "Guest Conductor." The guest conductor on this program is a member of Congress or a "key government official" who selects a favorite tune and explains the choice.

According to the *Interstate Commerce Omission*, a Nader report on the ICC, transportation associations contributed typically to the 1968 campaigns of select Commerce committee members:

> Members of the Senate Commerce Committee and the House Interstate and Foreign Commerce Committee have received large amounts of legal campaign contributions for many years from ICC-regulated industries and labor unions in these industries. In 1968, the Bus Industry Public Affairs Committee of Washington, D.C., James T. Corcoran, Secretary-Treasurer, gave Howard Cannon of Nevada $200;

Warren Magnuson of Washington, $200 [and five House members over $1,000].

The rail labor campaign fund, the Transportation Political Education League of Cleveland, Ohio, was also quite active in 1968. Among [Commerce Committee members] receiving contributions from this source were Nebraska Republican Glen Cunningham . . . $1,000; Maryland Democrat Samuel Friedel, second-ranking Democrat of the Commerce Committee, $500; California Democrat John E. Moss . . . $1,000. . . .

The American Trucking Associations, the Truck Operators Non-Partisan League . . . gave $73,456.50. . . . Reps. John Dingell (D-Mich.) of the Commerce Committee . . . $1,500 . . . Samuel N. Friedel (D-Md.) of the Commerce Committee, $1,000 . . . Brock Adams (D-Wash.) of the Commerce Committee . . . $500. . . .

Transportation Subcommittee Chairman Friedel received $1,000 in October, 1966; $250 in May, 1968; and $750 in April 1968.

Other Subcommittee members and the amounts they were given: Dingell (D-Mich.), $1,500 in May, 1968; Samuel Devine (R-Ohio), $1,000 in 1966. . . .

These members of the full Committee had also received campaign contributions from the truckers, each getting $500: Reps. Lionel Van Deerlin (D-Cal.), 1966; Fred Rooney (D-Pa.), 1966; John Murphy (D-N.Y.), May, 1968; Ancher Nelsen (R-Minn.), 1966; and James Harvey (R-Mich.), 1966.[11]

The regulated carriers also reach members by placing high-priced ads in the Democratic convention programs every four years. At $15,000 a page, the ads are yet another way for corporations to avoid breaking the federal law that prohibits their making direct contributions to political candidates. The 1964 Democratic convention program had five pages of railroad ads and sixteen trucker ads. In 1968 Southern Railroad used a two-page, $30,000 ad to make a direct appeal to members of Congress to expand the agricultural exemption to railroads and to give permission to use new, aluminum boxcars. Referring to these restrictions, the message ended with "the lawmakers of our country should have the courage to correct this sorry situation."[12]

A sample of 1970 contributions to two Transportation and Aeronautics Subcommittee members—J. J. Pickle and Brock Adams —reveals the extent to which transportation contributors try to affect whoever is making the transportation laws in Washington. Pickle received $250 from the REA Action Committee, $100 from the Bus Industry Political Affairs Committee, and $1,000 from the Truck Operators Non-Partisan League. Adams received $2,500 from the Transportation Political Education League, $1,000 from the president of Universal Airlines, $500 from the assistant vice president of the Southern Railroad, $500 from the chairman of the board of Trans International Airlines, $1,000 from the Seafarers Union, and $500 from the Railway Clerks.[13]

Especially prone to taking industry welfare is the chairman of the Senate Surface Transportation Subcommittee, Vance Hartke. During his 1972 campaign for the Democratic presidential nomination, Hartke solicited funds from the very industry representatives most affected by his subcommittee's legislation. One of his 1972 presidential campaign managers was an executive with the Freight Forwarders Institute, which is regulated by an agency that his subcommittee oversees, the ICC. According to reporter Robert Walters of the *Washington Star-News*, the select group buying tickets to Hartke's December 1972 dinner included the following:

> Among the railroad industry contributors were Civil Trust 80-Santa Fe Employees Good Government Fund, $1,000; The Fund for Effective Government, political action arm of the Union Pacific Corp., $250; the Burlington Northern Officers Voluntary Good Government Fund, $500; Anthony Haswell, chairman of the National Association of Railroad Passengers, $1,000; Charles R. Van Horn, Washington representative of the C&C-B&O Rail System, $125; William J. Taylor, government affairs vice president of IC Industries, the parent corporation of the Illinois Central Gulf Railroad, $125, and Richard P. Theile, a Washington representative of IC Industries.

The trucking industry was represented by Jerry Chambers, board chairman of Clipper Express, Chicago, $250; Charles W. Hulett, executive vice president of Mero Mayflower Transit Co., Indianapolis, $125; Robert L. Hiner, president of American Red Ball Transit Co., Indianapolis, $125; Denver Eyler, president of Penn Truck Lines, Inc., King of Prussia, Pa.; Maurice Tucker, treasurer of Tucker Freight Lines, Inc., South Bend, Ind., and others.

A number of well-known lawyers whose practices include extensive political work also contributed to the dinner.

Also donating were the Washington vice presidents of many of the nation's largest corporations, including William G. Greif, of Bristol Myers Co., $125; William G. Wythe, of U.S. Steel Corp., $250; and Claude C. Wild Jr., of Gulf Oil Co., $125.

Most of the largest contributions came from labor unions including the Railway Clerks Political League, $15,000; the Transportation Political Education League, the political arm of the United Transportation Union, $3,000; the United Steelworkers of America Political Action Fund, $1,500; and the Seafarers International Union political fund, $1,000.[14]

Many of these contributors had turned out for Hartke's 1969 Chicago fund-raising dinner during his bid against a strong opponent—Republican Richard Roudebush. Walters reported, "At that party . . . Senator Russell B. Long (D., La.), chairman of the Finance Committee, told the approximately 600 guests present: 'Vance Hartke will be the man to provide the leadership to see that your investments are protected.' "[15]

Hartke was still holding events to raise money after his 1972 campaign funds appeared to be sufficient to pay off his stated campaign expenses.* One of the two men organizing the campaign fund today is former Senator George Smathers, chief lobby-

---

* In the March 11, 1973, issue of the *Washington Star-News*, Bob Walters reported that Hartke spent just over $100,000 and collected over $111,000 from his three campaign committees during 1972. Walters also contended that Hartke did not maintain a careful accounting of his 1972 campaign expenses—intermixing senatorial and presidential campaigns, office, parking, and other expenses.

ist for the American Association of Railroads and ASTRO, a powerful organization of carriers trying to get Congress to pass the Surface Transportation Act. Hartke introduced the ASTRO bill in Congress (see page 168).

"GOVERNMENT BY PUBLICITY STUNT"

Seniority and membership transfer figures suggest that the House Subcommittee on Transportation and Aeronautics is considered an exceptionally desirable subcommittee by House Commerce members. The Senate Surface Transportation Subcommittee, without jurisdiction over aviation, ranks as only moderately desirable (see Table 2, Chapter 1). But members seem to desire seats on these committees for the leverage they gain on behalf of the transportation industries rather than as a means of finding long-term solutions to America's transportation carriage problems.

Both subcommittees suffer heavy absenteeism, making quorums difficult to come by. Senators face a particular problem: too many committee assignments. Hartke, for example, chairs one full committee and three subcommittees. Howard Cannon, the second-ranking Democrat, chairs four subcommittees and serves on four full committees, one joint committee, and six subcommittees. Next in line is Frank Moss, who chairs three subcommittees, is vice chairman of a fourth, and serves on three full committees, one special committee, one select committee, and fourteen subcommittees. Every other member of the Senate subcommittee faces the same problem to a certain degree.

Beyond the problem of heavy committee assignments is the Senate subcommittee's rural orientation—its members coming from such states as Indiana, Nevada, Utah, South Carolina, Louisiana, Tennessee, and Kansas. As a result, a relatively large number of subcommittee bills focus on rural transportation problems: tax or regulation exemptions for certain farm vehicles, the boxcar shortage, and track abandonment. In the early sixties the subcommittee refused to take up urban mass transit,* and a pattern of neglect with regard to urban transportation has persisted ever since. Of the more active House subcommittee members, only Brock Adams seems to give as much weight to surface transportation as to aviation issues. Among the relatively *inactive* House subcommittee members are included most of its urban representatives—Samuel Devine (Columbus), Ralph Metcalfe (Chicago), and Bertram Podell (Brooklyn).

Transportation policy-making, in short, does not appear to titillate members' political interests. One veteran transportation staff writer for a weekly news magazine commented, "Despite its significance, and condition, Congress takes a very casual approach to transportation." The members' approach is so casual that one lobbyist has said, "They have done practically nothing for years, so at the end of each session about all they can say is, 'We gave serious consideration to the following measures.' " As House Transportation and Aeronautics Subcommittee member Fletcher Thompson (R., Ga.) put it, transportation issues lack "political sex appeal." Even Adams, the subcommittee's most active member, believes that transportation is "an unrewarding thing." Only headlines on such matters as the spectacular mismanagement of the Penn Central seem to energize members. One staffer explained this sense of transportation policy as "government by publicity stunt":

> Look, what we've got here is the breakdown of pluralism—it doesn't work. Those organized around their interests don't clash to produce the public interest except now and then. And these guys [representatives] are not structured electorally or within the Congress to represent the consumer or general citizenry aggressively, if at all. For them, and because of the media, what we've got is government by publicity stunt. The members feel 10,000 eyelids close a minute with each mention of ICC or "rate regulation." No one gets elected President that way.

* As a result, jurisdiction passed to the Senate Banking and Currency Committee.[16]

Ineffective Chairmen—Too Unpredictable or Too Weak

Hartke, who chairs the Senate subcommittee, has an aggressive, unpredictable style. He may brashly take on industry witnesses at one moment and sponsor the industry bill with at least some enthusiasm the next. He has come into conflict with Magnuson on occasion. In fact, he assumed the Surface Transportation Subcommittee chairmanship only after Magnuson denied him the Aviation Subcommittee chairmanship to which, according to seniority, Hartke should have fallen heir. Since then, Hartke's freedom of movement has been restricted by Magnuson's continuing control over subcommittee funding and staffing. Hartke was allowed to appoint one committee aide, Karl O'Lessker, during the Ninety-second Congress, but O'Lessker had little freedom of movement in the face of long-time Magnuson staffer Daniel O'Neal. (O'Lessker was soon replaced, having fallen victim to one of the many internecine feuds among Hartke's aides.) Publicly Hartke maintains that he and Magnuson "proceed down the line pretty well." He has to be this politic, for as he admits, "the full committee acts as a clearinghouse" for legislation, so that Magnuson has the upper hand in the final proceedings.

In the House, Chairman John Jarman of Oklahoma has not been an active leader. "The man surely has a pace all his own," said J. J. Pickle in a valiant attempt to be charitable after his relatively noncontroversial bill on cargo safety had been held up in Jarman's subcommittee for months. Members of Congress and their staffs have described Jarman as a "phantom," an "enigma," and "an absolute zero." Jarman, who is careful not to offend anyone, has been called the "house establishment gentleman." His humility and languid approach furnish a marked contrast to Hartke's style. Jarman turns over questions at hearings to other subcommittee members, and he is even reluctant to use the gavel to cut off extraneous debate. Before he became Transportation and Aeronautics chairman in 1970, Jarman chaired the Public Health Subcommittee, where he seemed content to turn over most leadership functions to second-ranking Paul Rogers. Jarman, the third-ranking Democrat on House Commerce, made the move to Transportation and Aeronautics to gain experience: "As I move closer to the chairmanship of the full committee, I believe I should have background experience on all four of our subcommittees."* Like Hartke and Magnuson, Jarman and Staggers have their differences. Jarman admits that his move met with some opposition:

> Chairman Staggers did his best to get Congressman Macdonald, who has seniority . . . to take the Transportation and Aeronautics Subcommittee. Said subcommittee deals with many labor-management problems in the field of transportation (Mr. Staggers is railroad labor oriented and knows that I am management oriented.) When Mr. Macdonald chose to stay on the Communications and Power Subcommittee, my seniority gave me Transportation and Aeronautics.

As on the Senate side, the full-committee chairman has set up certain controls over the subcommittee. Jarman explained, "Though receptive to suggestions, Chairman Staggers exercises a one-man rule over the subcommittee agenda. Once the decision has been made to consider a particular bill, the subcommittee has little contact with Mr. Staggers." Jarman continued.

> I believe the subcommittee and its chairman should have a more active role in the selection of the subcommittee agenda. . . . I also believe the subcommittee should be the ball carriers on subcommittee bills when they are considered on the floor of the House. Chairman Staggers . . . obviously believes it is his responsibility to handle each bill on the House floor, even though he has not attended the hearings.

Actually, fifth-ranking Democrat Brock Adams runs most of the subcommittee's hearings. He is well-informed on the issues, although biased toward the transportation carriers' interests. His

---

* Stripped of most of his subcommittee jurisdiction by the Committee Reform Amendments of 1974, and disgruntled by what he called the "liberal takeover" of the House Democratic Caucus, Jarman became a Republican and left the Commerce Committee as the 94th Congress began.

appetite for work has earned the respect of the rest of the sub-committee members and the staff, who say that he not only makes them work hard but helps them do it.

THE DROPOUTS

Through hearings, investigations, and reports, the surface-transportation committees are supposed to oversee the regulations and the appointments of the regulators, those who administer the laws that Congress has passed. Upon discovery of nonfeasance or misapplication of the law, members of Congress should initiate corrective measures. But, whether from industry influence or indolence, they have not completed these oversight tasks with enough independence or vigor. The transportation industry, as a result, is relatively undetected and unconstrained in its efforts to secure agency decisions congenial with its interests. Congress' inaction benefits vested interests at the expense of the public interest.

Hearings

The congressional system allows for adversary proceedings, but hearings rarely take that form. During 1970 and 1971, even before the carriers' blitz of Congress in support of the Surface Transportation Act (described later in this chapter), representatives of groups that did not stand to profit from public policy were a minority at congressional hearings (see Table 12). The 9.1 percent of academicians testifying before Senate hearings in 1970 is a deceptive figure, for almost all of the witnesses were consultants with think tanks or other groups awaiting transportation-research contracts. The subcommittees mainly gathered their information from the two powers that they should be *checking*, the carriers and the executive branch, which together provided from 55 to 80 percent of the testimony.

This deficiency in getting testimony from outside experts is especially debilitating when members do not encourage witnesses

TABLE 12.

Affiliations of Witnesses, 1970–1971

A. House Subcommittee on Transportation and Aeronautics

Group	1970			1971		
	No. of witnesses	Pages of testimony	Percent	No. of witnesses	Pages of testimony	Percent
Carriers	39	487	38.8	23	409	30.6
Railroads	7	116	9.2	8	248	18.5
AAR	6	162	12.9	2	40	2.9
ATA	2	27	2.1	1	10	.7
Other associations	17	154	12.2	11	103	7.9
Other carriers	7	27	2.4	1	8	.6
Shippers	16	104	8.2	3	10	.7
Unions	17	91	7.2	9	122	9.8
Farmers	0	0	0	8	49	3.6
Executive branch	25	284	22.6	35	658	50.0
ICC	8	92	7.3	12	166	12.4
DOT	13	144	11.4	20	456	34.1
Other	4	48	3.9	3	46	3.5
Members of Congress	56	151	12.0	10	53	3.9
Local officials	7	60	4.7	3	25	1.8
Consumers or non-profit groups	3	30	2.3	0	0	0
Academicians	0	0	0	0	0	0
Citizens	1	8	.6	0	0	0
Other	4	40	3.1	0	0	0

TABLE 12. Affiliations of Witnesses, 1970–1971 (Cont'd)

B. Senate Subcommittee on Surface Transportation

Group	1970			1971		
	No. of witnesses	Pages of testimony	Percent	No. of witnesses	Pages of testimony	Percent
Carriers	37	565	31.4	20	343	36.7
Railroads	18	287	15.9	12	304	32.5
AAR	6	119	6.6	1	6	0
ATA	1	8	0	0	0	.0
Other associations	9	121	6.7	2	8	.8
Other carriers	3	30	2.2	5	25	3.4
Shippers	10	60	3.3	8	30	3.2
Unions	18	207	11.5	4	39	4.1
Farmers	5	14	.7	3	10	1.0
Executive branch	43	396	22.0	17	386	41.3
ICC	15	153	8.5	3	117	12.5
DOT	18	191	10.6	6	142	15.2
Other	10	52	2.9	8	127	13.6
Members of Congress	15	108	6.0	6	50	5.3
Local officials	25	167	9.3	0	0	0
Consumers or non-profit groups	10	92	5.1	2	56	6.0
Academicians	8	165	9.1	1	19	2.0
Citizens	2	20	1.1	0	0	0

to argue beyond the provisions that affect them directly. At the 1972 Surface Transportation Act hearings, no one argued against the $3 billion authorization in low-interest loans to carriers. A staff man summarized the situation: "There was no objection to it because no one is against it. The shippers don't give a damn; labor doesn't care. There is simply no one there." And the aggrieved taxpayers are not organized to come to Congress and argue against each provision that takes money out of their pockets. Many of them probably believe that their representatives and senators are doing this task for them. But in fact these very elected officials tend to invite vested interests to testify and to leave that testimony unquestioned.

Not only have few experts outside the administration or transportation industry been invited to testify, but members have held few intense hearings where industry and agencies have been held accountable for their requests and decisions. The House Interstate and Foreign Commerce Committee last held major ICC oversight hearings in 1958. Little came of them. In 1961 the Senate Commerce Committee commissioned a broad-scale style of transportation policy and appointed retired Air Force General Alexander Doyle to direct it. Congress ignored the Doyle report's major recommendations; it did not follow up with corrective legislation.

Vance Hartke's Senate Subcommittee on Surface Transportation held the next major oversight hearings in the summer of 1969. Only three senators bothered to attend these hearings,[17] which were the first in almost a decade. Most of those who did attend asked superficial questions, dealing mostly with issues raised in other hearings: passenger-train service, the boxcar shortage, and the collapse of the Penn Central.

Senator Hartke, however, succeeded in exposing the ICC's industry orientation, albeit without any followup. He called the eleven ICC commissioners to a long table in front of the subcommittee panel and did not permit them to consult with their staff members. He was testing rumors that the agency was run by the staff. The long silences that followed the chairman's sorties confirmed the rumor: only commissioners Lawrence K. Walrath and Rupert L. Murphy were able to answer many of Hartke's uncomplicated questions.

The exchanges that did take place revealed the commissioners' understanding of "consumer representation" before their regulatory agency. For example:

> SENATOR HARTKE: Who advises the commission what is reasonable from the consumer's standpoint?
>
> COMMISSIONER WALRATH: Fortunately for the consumers they have probably more adequate representation through associations before our agency than most.
>
> The National Industrial Traffic League, for example, represents not only large but small shippers and shippers that are representative of all types of shippers. In addition, they have—
>
> SENATOR HARTKE: But those are the shippers you are referring to?
>
> COMMISSIONER WALRATH: Yes.
>
> SENATOR HARTKE: Those are not consumers. You see, always you come back to these two groups of people, the carriers and the shippers. What disturbs me is that it appears that this process has gone on so long, in an atmosphere of adjudicating the rights between individuals, that the economics of the carrier become paramount and the consumer or the public generally has been lost sight of, not from any conscious misdoing, but as just the very nature of the apparatus and the way it works.[18]

Senators learned that the commissioners did not keep vital information on file at their agency and therefore did not know, when they approved a merger, just who was merging.

> SENATOR HARTKE: Does the Interstate Commerce Commission know who owns the railroads?
>
> COMMISSIONER [GEORGE M.] STAFFORD: Up to a point. They must file a certain number of them.
>
> SENATOR HARTKE: To be very candid and frank, do you know who owns the railroads? I didn't ask you what they filed. You are an expert in this. Let's not play games.

MR. STAFFORD: Commissioner [Kenneth H.] Tuggle is our expert in this.

MR. TUGGLE: I disclaim the title of expert. And I don't have to prove that, I suppose.

Singularly, we do not know who owns the railroads, because some of them have many thousands of stockholders. The requirement now is that they file the names of their thirty largest stockholders. However, historically over the past decades there have been so many proceedings for control and things of that kind that as far as many of the railroads are concerned, it is pretty well a matter of public record as to who controls them.

SENATOR HARTKE: Let me be very specific then. Does the Commission have available in its records today information which would inform the researcher of exactly who owns the Penn Central?

MR. TUGGLE: No, sir.[19]

The committee learned that a commissioner did not know that the ICC was given explicit and broad discovery powers to ascertain ownership under the Interstate Commerce Act, and that such powers were not used.

SENATOR HARTKE: Let's take the Penn Central merger case. The Interstate Commerce Commission was specifically requested to look into the complex patterns of ownership of the two carriers to determine who owned the two lines and what effect these patterns of ownership would have on the public interest. Isn't that correct?

. . . Let me ask you here, let's go back: Do you know whether or not, or did you look into the background of the ownership of the Penn Central, the Pennsylvania Railroad and the New York Central at that time, as was specifically requested?

MR. TUGGLE: I don't believe so.

SENATOR HARTKE: You did not.

MR. TUGGLE: No.

SENATOR HARTKE: You are certainly familiar with section 12 of the Interstate Commerce Act; are you not?

MR. TUGGLE: Well———[20]

After Hartke read section 12 to refresh Tuggle's memory, Tuggle explained that the law did not *require* the ICC to get this information. Hartke explained that the ICC's list of brokerage houses or other dummies holding ownership for unknown parties did not reveal who the real owners were. Hartke's cross-examination filled ten pages; the commissioners finally agreed to provide the actual names of anyone owning 1 percent or more of Penn Central stock.

Senator Hartke barked, but he never bit. The committee did not follow up on what it learned at these hearings. There is no requirement to *disclose* ownership, and that law was not amended. Congress did not seek to include sanctions for noncompliance or force compliance. And the subcommittee did not try systematically to obtain the information through court proceedings or its own subpoena powers. Without requiring the ICC to discover ownership and without including sanctions for failure to disclose, the ICC and the public cannot be sure who is really merging. Are controlling interests already controlling pipeline, air, or trucking networks for complete transportation monopoly? Are their interests with oil, food, or other interests the merged firm might favor in terms of service? For many reasons this information is basic, but while Senator Hartke's questions were well taken their total effect was to give some commissioners temporary indigestion.

Between 1969 and 1972, the House and Senate subcommittees held about thirty hearings (which were poorly attended by subcommittee members), a minimal oversight action since most of them were routine, superficial examinations in which the two subcommittees covered parallel ground (see Table 13). One hearing covered the constituent-related issue of passenger-train service; people who relied on rail transport had been pressuring their members of Congress to do something about threatened cuts in service. The surface-transportation subcommittees responded to the problem by offering a bill to set up a quasi-government railway corporation (Amtrak). None of the other hearings went into any kind of depth about consumer problems arising out of

TABLE 13.
Subject Matter of Hearings Before Transportation
Subcommittees, 1969–1972

A. House Subcommittee on Transportation and Aeronautics

Subject	Number of hearings	Pages of testimony	Days spent
Passenger-train service	2	730	9
Surface freight rates	1	288	6
Railroad safety and hazardous materials	1	285	4
Emergency rail services	3	1,332	11
Attorney's fees for property losses	1	123	2
Routine hearings*	8	99	79

B. Senate Subcommittee on Surface Transportation

The Federal Railroad Safety Act of 1969	1	430	5
Passenger train service	1	613	4
An advisory commission to study freight rates	1	154	3
Freight car shortages	1	1,046	11
Failing railroads	1	1,743	16
Routine hearings†	7	1,350	11

* These hearings considered: adding a labor representative to the National Railroad Adjustment Board; allowing certain transportation employees to avoid having wages withheld by more than one state; state property-tax discrepancies; a new thirteen-part accounting basis for motor-carrier annual reports; and two hearings on routine extension of high-speed ground transportation research for another year or more.

† These included perfunctory hearings on the following: the hours of service of railroad employees; an alternative and less crowded appeal route for litigants suing the ICC; high-speed ground transportation research extension; water-carrier commodity rules; the Nader ICC report; environmental considerations of new routes; and British advances in passenger service.

surface-transportation spending and regulatory decisions, nor did they raise any of the issues of concern to economists and academics expert in the area. At hearings on surface freight rates, members did not examine maximum rates, rate discrimination,*

* Rate discrimination is the charging of rates or prices well above cost in areas of monopoly or market power and at or below cost in other areas (usually those subject to competition).

lack of competition, violation of laws outlawing favors for big manufacturers, or other issues. Instead they looked into whether or not freight forwarders, who consolidate small shipments of freight and organize their transport, should be given a special break in rates when dealing with railroads. This was at the request of the freight forwarders, who are also regulated (i.e., protected from competition).

Appointments

The Senate Surface Transportation Subcommittee has turned the Senate's advice and consent powers into smiling and genuflecting rituals. It has abdicated their monitoring and screening procedures. It goes on confirming ICC commissioners who have no qualifications in regulation, transportation, law, or economics. Following perfunctory hearings on his appointment, Robert Gresham admitted: "[I do not consider myself] an expert in the regulation of surface transportation—if I said I was, I'd be telling a tale."

In only one recent case did the Senate hold up an appointment of an ICC official, and that for the appointee's political rather than professional qualifications. The ICC is supposed to have six members of one political party and five of the other. In 1971 President Nixon wanted to appoint Alfred MacFarland, a lawyer from Lebanon, Tennessee, to fill a Democratic slot on the commission. MacFarland's Democratic credentials were open to doubt. He acknowledged that he had voted for Richard Nixon in 1960 and 1968; he had turned against Democratic incumbent Senator Albert Gore with a vengeance and had headed the Democrats for William E. Brock III, the Republican candidate opposing Gore in the 1970 Tennessee senatorial campaign. McFarland's confirmation was held up briefly in token protest by the full Senate Commerce Committee to get a full allotment of real Democrats on the commission.

Spending

Congress has also abdicated its controls on ICC spending. By passing the Reorganization Act of 1970 Congress allowed the Office of Management and Budget, which is responsible to the president, to oversee the ICC budget. The OMB has taken up a new task, acting under no congressional authority, to "coordinate" all testimony, press releases, and other agency and executive-department policy statements. By clearing and cleansing all statements so that they are not contradictory, OMB hands Congress one point of view. Because of its weak information-gathering facilities and the fragmentation of appropriations and policy-making committees, Congress has not been equipped to challenge the estimates submitted by the OMB.

Congress has turned itself into a rubber stamp, approving the OMB's estimates on ICC or (at most) lowering them slightly (see Table 14).

TABLE 14.

Budget Statistics, Interstate Commerce Commission, 1967–1972
(thousands of dollars)

Year	ICC request to OMB	Level approved by OMB or president's budget	Appropriations or congressional action
1967	29,875	28,479	28,479
1968*	26,710	24,134	23,846
1969	25,765	24,813	24,660
1970	28,672	27,483	27,743
1971	31,275	28,442	28,424
1972	32,775	28,940	30,640

* ICC functions transferred to DOT amounted to about $4 million.

In only one major case did Congress actually increase funds beyond OMB requests. In 1972 it restored $2 million of $4 million that OMB cut from an ICC request. The OMB then challenged

Congress on even this by refusing to spend any money that was not OMB-approved. And Congress has done nothing about this usurpation of its constitutionally delegated spending powers: a bill that would have provided for the direct submission of ICC budgets to the Congress did not pass in 1972.

GIMME SHELTER

In 1972 the surface-transportation subcommittees addressed the deficiencies of the nation's transportation policies for the first time. But they came to the task by default rather than design. The administration and the transportation carriers handed them the materials to work with—two new pieces of legislation, which became catalysts for action. The story of how neither bill got to the floor of Congress by the end of the Ninety-second Congress is fascinating and instructive.

Stage One: Drafting Bills

The administration bills—the Transportation Regulatory Modernization Act and the Transportation Assistance Act, supported as a package by the Department of Transportation—grew out of growing challenges from consumer groups and academic critics to the ICC–transportation carriers alliance. The bills also provided the new-born Department of Transportation an opportunity to challenge its rival, the ICC. The first draft of the administration bill evolved from supportive recommendation of a Committee on Economic Policy subcommittee composed of representatives from the Departments of Commerce, Justice, Labor, and Transportation; the Council of Economic Advisers; the Office of Management and Budget; and the Office of Consumer Affairs. After this subcommittee reported in September 1970 that the ICC should undergo changes, the Departments of Transportation and Justice drafted legislation to implement its recommendations.

Work on the bills in the Department of Justice in late 1970 was concentrated in its Antitrust Division, where Joe Saunders drew up a first draft and Jack Pearce and Keith Clearwaters in consultation with Robert Calhoun (a DOT official who had previously served as legislative liaison for the ICC) revised and developed it into final form in early 1971.

The two DOT bills made basic changes in the transportation alliance between ICC and carriers:

· to make it easier for carriers to abandon unprofitable lines and runs if they wish;

· to make rate discrimination more difficult, explicitly outlawing rates below marginal cost or above 150 percent of total (fully allocated) cost, thus outlawing profiteering by carriers where there is monopoly power or predatory pricing *below* cost to drive competitors unfairly out of business;*

· to make it easier for a new carrier to compete for the carriage of commodities and to remove operating restrictions (such as the specifications of a carrier's routes or commodities), thus making it possible for a new trucking line to carry products where the old was inefficient or gave poor service and to allow existing carriers to carry anything and go anywhere for more efficiency and lower costs;

· to ban rate bureaus and all price-fixing;

· to appropriate $37 million to create a computerized system to keep track of the movement of rail cars and to authorize the guarantee of certain kinds of loans.

The Transportation Assistance Act included this latter provision, while the Transportation Regulatory Modernization Act included the measures to increase competition. The Departments of Commerce, Agriculture, Transportation, and Justice, along with the Council of Economic Advisers, all backed the bills, as did representatives of shippers, consumers, and virtually every major economist and academician who had ever studied or written on the

---

* Briefly, since truckers, railroads, and water carriers are each allowed to get together and set prices by collusive agreement, the railroads will set prices very high for products and in areas where trucking and water cannot compete and below cost where there is trucking or water competition.

ICC and transportation.* Senators Magnuson and Cotton introduced the bills as S. 2842 and S. 2841 in the Senate; Staggers and Springer introduced them as H.R. 11826 and H.R. 11824 in the House in 1971. In charge of the DOT bills was White House adviser Peter M. Flanigan, who contacted key Republican legislators for their views on the legislation. Springer reportedly told Flanigan that their chances of passage were about 30 percent. Given the opposition of organized interests, support by economists for "competition" had a small active constituency. Conservatives listen to the appeals of the carriers for protected profits and tend to forget their ethic, and liberals tend to eschew competition as a model entirely.

With this news Flanigan and Attorney General John N. Mitchell wanted to drop the project. They did not believe that the effort required to get the bills through Congress would be worth the political repercussions that might ensue. Eventually, however, Richard McClaren, chief of the Justice Department's Antitrust Division, prevailed upon Mitchell to continue to back the legislation. The last major holdout was Commerce Secretary Maurice H. Stans, who was finally won over by executive-branch consensus that the reform legislation should be introduced.

President Nixon endorsed the bills in 1971, but because they

---

* The most impressive list of independent experts backing the DOT statement and legislation includes: Walter Adams, Michigan State; Morris Adelman, Massachusetts Institute of Technology; Richard Caves, Harvard; Paul Cherington, Harvard; Ross Eckert, University of Southern California; Kenneth Elzinga, University of Virginia; Ann Friedlaender, Boston College; Richard Heflebower, Northwestern; George Hilton, University of California, Los Angeles; Hendrik S. Houthakker, Harvard; William Iulo, Washington State; Carl Kaysen, Institute for Advanced Study; William Jordan, American International University; Frank J. Kottke, Washington State; John Meyer, Yale; Leon Moses, Northwestern; Thomas G. Moore, Michigan State; James C. Nelson, Washington State; James R. Nelson, Amherst College; Walter Oil, University of Rochester; Merton J. Peck, Yale; Samuel Peltzman, University of California, Los Angeles; Charles Phillips, Washington and Lee; George Stigler, University of Chicago; Leonard Weiss, University of Wisconsin; Ernst Williams, Columbia; Oliver Williamson, University of Pennsylvania; George Wilson, University of Indiana.

were controversial, the DOT, not the White House, proposed them to Congress. Since it was an election year, the White House did not exert much pressure on behalf of the bills. But the time seemed relatively right given the bills' lack of political "juice," as one lobbyist explained. "Every ten years or so there is a major bill of some kind which promises reform. The current administration's proposal is directly related to an Eisenhower proposal of the late 1950s." The latter also proposed allowing truckers more freedom to carry what the market would bear, allowing new truckers and water carriers to compete at will, and allowing some competition in the setting of rates.

The carriers, meanwhile, not only developed a strategy to stop the DOT legislation in Congress; they drafted their own bill, the Surface Transportation Act, in order to get even more money from the government without incurring further regulations or competition. The bill was drafted by legal counsel for the Association of American Railroads, the American Trucking Associations, and the Water Transportation Association.

It was an elaborate set of gifts to industry. A consumer activist called it "the worst single piece of legislation ever drafted." Donald Graham, counsel for the National Counsel of Farmer Cooperatives, called the bill a "Christmas Tree Bill—Gimme, Gimme, Gimme." Among its provisions were:

Loans. The secretary of the Treasury was authorized to give out $5 billion in loans to carriers *gratis*, for the term "loan" has a unique definition in the bill. Buried in the last sentence of section 606 was: "As used herein, the term 'loan' shall include any extension of financial assistance, by loan or *otherwise*." To give the impression of institutional safeguards against direct influence-peddling in loan applications, the bill provided for two review boards and defined "conflict of interest." But the review boards, staffed by a few presidential appointees, would have no power at all. They would be strictly advisory. The only criterion for the extension of the loans was the secretary's view that "the public interest would be served," and a $750,000 ceiling on the loans to a single firm. There were no requirements about who would qualify. The government's rights as a creditor were not spelled out. There was no minimum interest rate; the act said only, "It shall be the general policy of the Secretary to establish reasonable rates, that, in the judgment of the Secretary, will take into account the cost, administrative expenses and other expenses, and a risk factor." And because the bill placed no limitation on how the money could be used, the loan could finance shrimp trawlers or land speculation. The provision's repayment schedule was also purposely hazy. It gave the borrower fifteen years to repay, but the first year would not begin until the construction project had been completed, a moment that could be put off indefinitely.

Rate Increases. The ICC was ordered to accept carrier rate increases automatically whenever a company showed an actual or probable cost increase.* There was no provision for rate *decreases* when there had been a decrease in costs. If the ICC found the justification for the increase to be spurious, it would have no power to require a refund. If six months of ICC inquiry should turn up a false claim to a cost increase, the carrier could simply declare another cost increase of even greater proportions; ICC inquiries could then go on indefinitely, while the carriers would never have to refund the overcharges.

Regulation of New Carriers. The two kinds of carriers that set prices by competition rather than ICC regulation—bulk commodities by water and truck and agricultural produce by truck— would be regulated. (This provision was proposed by the railroads, which foresaw that rates for barge and truck transport would probably go up in the new monopoly price-fixing environment of ICC "regulation"; the result would be more business for the rail carriers.)

Tax Subsidies. The railroads asked for a 10 percent investment tax credit to improve equipment; the credit would be reduced to 8

---

* Note, however, that a carrier's allegation of increased costs does not necessarily justify a rate increase for a monopoly power utility. Labor costs may go up 10 percent but the workforce may go down by the same amount or productivity per worker may go up by the same 10 percent as the wages do. Actual unit costs may not increase at all.

percent by 1973. The current five-year amortization of railroad rolling stock, which allows the owner to deduct the full price of a rail car as "depreciation" over the first five years of its life, would be expanded. The reason for the loophole originally was to stimulate the supply of boxcars which are sometimes in short supply at harvest. This bill permitted industry to use the break for all transportation equipment (despite the fact that the big problem in transportation generally is *underutilization* of existing equipment). These two provisions would cost the public $55 million in revenue. Under the present 7 percent tax investment credit, purchasers of railroad equipment save about $35 million. The proposed 10 percent credit would have increased this amount by another $35 million, while enactment of the proposed five-year amortization allowance would have decreased 1972 tax liabilities by about $20 million.[21]

The carriers' efforts to formulate and promote this bill were mobilized in a preexisting organization called America's Sound Transportation Review Organization (ASTRO). Transportation associations funded it handsomely and retained former Senator George Smathers, one of Hartke's 1972–1973 campaign finance managers, as counsel and chief lobbyist.

ASTRO was not accepted by the carriers when first formed around 1970 until they realized that they needed each other to stop bills that would require competition, such as the DOT bills. At first, ASTRO was mostly a railroad organization encouraged by the AAR and lobbyist George Smathers. As late as May 3, 1971, the American Trucking Associations had accused ASTRO of "waging a deliberate campaign of distortions, half-truths, and deceptions aimed at destroying federal regulation of transportation."[22] On June 15 the truckers added that ASTRO was planning a "raid on the Treasury."[23] These criticisms centered on railroad appeals for subsidies and favors.

But on September 2, 1971, ASTRO announced the new alliance of rail, trucking, and water carriers. Since carriers within each of these modes were legally price-fixing and politically organized, the only competition of sorts left was between these three modes, now combining politically. According to the 1971 Annual Report of the Association of American Railroads,

> Agreement on the measure [among ASTRO members] came after several weeks of talks involving representatives of the railroad, trucking, and regulated water carriers industries. It reflected an awareness that a program having the support of all three modes would have a far better chance of congressional passage than legislation designed to assist only one.

No longer bickering, they would all ask for what they wanted in the way of tax breaks, protection from competition, and direct subsidies through a Surface Transportation Act. A staffer on the House side noted that this was the first time that the transportation modes had gotten together on anything publicly. "They all want champagne," he said, adding, "they just usually disagree on the brand." Another staffer added, "They decided on Taxpayer and Consumer Bond."

ASTRO's principal asset was George Smathers. A former chairman of the Senate Surface Transportation Subcommittee, Smathers knew whom to see on Capitol Hill and how to be convincing. He had served two terms in the House of Representatives and eighteen years in the Senate, retiring in 1968. In 1969 he explained his retirement to a *Newsday* reporter: "A fellow with my background can make more money in thirty days out here than he can in fifteen years as a senator."[24] While on Capitol Hill, he had also engaged in money-making deals. He maintained ties with his Florida law firm of Smathers and Thompson, whose clients included Seaboard Airline Railroad, Pan American Airways, Standard Oil, Phillips Petroleum, Western Union, Union Carbide, Anheuser-Busch, and many insurance firms. He also had substantial bank holdings, numerous real estate interests, and a number of shares in Winn-Dixie grocery stores. In 1958, he had helped eliminate the 3 percent cargo tax (thus benefiting carriers such as the Seaboard Airline Railroad). In 1966 Smathers had worked to prevent the U.S. Post Office from delivering parcel post packages over a certain size; they would instead be carried by such firms as REA Express, 35,000 shares of which were owned by Seaboard. After retiring from Congress, Smathers formed the Washington law firm of Smathers and Merrigan. He picked up immediate business as a lobbyist for airlines, oil interests, shipbuilders and -owners, railroads, and ASTRO. He also maintains two Florida law firms today and has become director of Winn-Dixie stores, Aerodex (a defense contractor), Major Realty Corporation, Gulf and Western (a giant conglomerate), and several banks.

We obtained a copy of the minutes and of Smathers' working papers for the ASTRO negotiating meetings where the powerful carriers agreed to work together on a bill in the first place. The minutes reveal a general magnanimity, with the truckers allowing the railroads to get their grade crossings paid for from highway money and other benefits cited above. In drawing up plans to divide taxpayer monies to their own advantage, the various parties came to quick and fruitful agreement. They agreed especially on supporting the ICC, their friend. Typical of the minutes is this paragraph:

> The water carriers would like to have five years amortization of equipment for tax purposes, a special privilege the railroads now enjoy. This change was also favored by the motor carriers. In addition, the proposed legislation would eliminate the ten percent preference tax on railroads (and make other changes). These changes in the present law would be very beneficial to the tax-paying [*sic*] railroads.

Smathers' working papers include a handwritten pep talk with such phrases as "and in this form and with their support, this can and will pass." On another working paper, Smathers shrewdly identified the lobbying problems he faced:

1. Pacify shippers; Tolan mtg, on 30th,
2. Labor-Bill Johnson, Freshehan
2a. DOT
    1. may never come,
    2. no great weight anyway
3. Getting sponsors-cosponsors.

Smathers' analysis was astute, for Fred Tolan, representing Northwest shippers, did not come through for ASTRO. But Tolan was not a total loss; even though he testified on behalf of the DOT bill at the House hearings, he did argue that several provisions should be deferred.

Smathers' first move with Congress was to line up sponsors for the Surface Transportation Act. In the House he got Brock Adams, Dan Rostenkowski, and Pennsylvania's Fred Rooney to introduce the legislation. House cosponsors were Bill Stuckey, Lionel Van Deerlin, David Satterfield, William Roy, John Schmitz, Ray Blanton, Goodloe Byron, Tim Lee Carter, Henry Helstoski, Ralph Metcalfe, J. J. Pickle, and Bertram Podell.*

Vance Hartke introduced the ASTRO bill in the Senate as S. 2362. Hartke hailed the new alliance of carriers as he introduced the bill, remarking, "The transportation industry is its own worst enemy. There are so many differences among the railroads, the truckers, and the water carriers that we cannot make a start on solving the industry's problems. . . . [The industry] must lay aside its differences. . . . Now [they] have done what I asked."[25]

The next step for ASTRO, and Smathers, was to get Congress behind the carriers' bill. Smathers' lobbying style is quite effective: immense charm and apparent sincerity, bolstered by ties with old school chums in government, the access on a first-name basis to senior members of Congress, and the privilege of meeting in the intimate, private Senate cloakroom just before members vote on the floor. In 1971 *Newsday* profiled Smathers' technique:

> Always a master of cloakroom negotiations and behind-the-scenes dealings, Smathers knew the world of the Washington lawyer long before he became one. "But you don't sneak around, playing the footpad" [he said], "you know who can be helpful and you talk with them right out in the middle of Pennsylvania Avenue if that is convenient."[26]

---

* Five identical bills were introduced in October and November 1971: H.R. 11207, H.R. 11310, H.R. 11347, H.R. 11674, H.R. 11694.

Smathers had been successful on one of his first lobbying assignments—scuttling certain reforms in the 1969 Tax Reform Act on
behalf of his client, the American Horse Council.* Part of Smathers' success could be attributed to a forty-minute meeting with
President Nixon and to a list that he provided Nixon through the
classmate and political supporter to whom he introduced Nixon in
the 1960s, Charles G. (Bebe) Rebozo. This list contained the
names of American Horse Council members who had contributed
to Republican candidates—to the jangle of $6 million in coin.

The former senator used similar behind-the-scenes tactics to
energize members to accept ASTRO's bill. He took a positive
approach, not fighting the DOT bill and thereby calling attention
to it, but only supporting the industry bill.

Smathers used his personal access to senior members of Congress and persuaded others in ASTRO's favor through his knowledge of their districts and political philosophies. He had Commerce Committee chairman Magnuson's respect because he had
been a member of the Senate club, a part of an "in group" of
senators, and a friend of John F. Kennedy. Even Magnuson's own
staff members had trouble being heard over Smathers' voice. It
was months before Magnuson read with any care a memorandum
from transportation counsel Daniel O'Neal outlining some of the
flaws in the industry bill. Smathers recognized a fear of predatory
competition on the part of House subcommittee member Dan
Kuykendall (R., Tenn.) and directed arguments to play on that
fear. For example, Smathers warned the congressman:

> There are all sorts of problems with competition, people are
> driven heartlessly out of business, things are constantly mov-
> ing and invisible, the carriers can screw the little guy by
> giving favors to the big boys.[27]

With conservative J. J. Pickle, he could talk about the "chance to
do business like any other business" and the "need to modernize"

---

* The American Horse Council is an association of thoroughbred breeders,
many of whose prize three-year-olds travel each spring from Kentucky's
bluegrass stables to Churchill Downs outside Louisville.

to meet the needs of all business and commerce. And lobbying Magnuson, Hartke, and Adams, he appealed to the 1940s mindset that saw federal regulation as a panacea:

> What is needed is regulation, a watchdog for the people in Washington to check abuse, and government aid of purchase on a case by case basis where necessary to make sure those carriers keep on serving the little guy as well as the big boys.[28]

Smathers' lobbying style was also effective because 1970s brazenness supplemented the old-fashioned personal approach. The 1971 annual report of the AAR, for example, brashly trumpets ASTRO's campaign on behalf of the Surface Transportation Act:

> ASTRO's grass-roots organization was active throughout the year, reaching some 200,000 people through speeches given before groups ranging from local garden clubs to major national meetings. Numerous appearances also were made on radio and television, and more than six thousand contacts with the news media were reported.
>
> Additional millions of people got the message through distribution of some three million pieces of printed material.

Stage Two: Committee Work on the Competing Bills

Over the period November 1971 through May 1972 the Senate subcommittee held hearings on the DOT and ASTRO bills and variations of them;[29] the House held its hearings from March to May 1972.[30] But the industry lobby had apparently made its mark, for neither subcommittee gave the DOT bills a fair hearing. Partly at fault was the method of questioning, which did not encourage the supporters of the DOT bill to speak against the industry bill, and the selection of witnesses, which was biased in favor of carriers.

The bulk of the 1,300 pages of House testimony and exhibits weighed in favor of the transportation industry, as this breakdown of House witnesses shows:

Witness group	Pages of testimony	Percent
Departments of Transportation, Justice, Agriculture	151	11.7
Academicians	48	3.7
Shippers	214	16.5
Farmers	105	8.1
Union	32	2.4
Carriers	521	40.2
Other	126	9.7

The 3,000 pages on the Senate side followed a similar pattern, but the figures do not reveal the whole story. Farmers, for example, limited their arguments to two provisions under discussion: the one putting agricultural goods under ICC control and the other allowing rail lines to be abandoned easily. Aside from the 15 percent contributed by the academicians and administration witnesses, there was only sporadic testimony for the DOT proposals.

Neither subcommittee provided the academicians with a copy of the Surface Transportation Act, so they came prepared to support the DOT bills and not to criticize another bill. The carriers, on the other hand, were well prepared to speak on both bills. In addition, the large shipping firms joined the carriers' side. Large logging companies and the giant Coal Institute, for example, testified against a DOT provision outlawing predatory pricing (where rates are below the actual cost of carrying goods) to drive others out of business. Generally, only the small shipping companies joined administration and academic witnesses in supporting the DOT reform measures. A tally of all the testimony and evidence that spoke directly to the issues shows that about three times more was presented on behalf of the industry bill and against the DOT than vice versa.

To make matters worse, House subcommittee members further ensured a biased presentation by treating with hostility any academicians and economists who supported the DOT measures. Their objections were based on the industry line, which had already been formally discredited by experts outside the transportation industry. For example, subcommittee members were not exactly gracious to Harvard professor Hendrik Houthakker. They berated him for serving on the Council of Economic Advisers from 1969–1971, when the U.S. budget went $70 billion in the red (Congress had passed this budget). They also attacked another academician as biased merely because he testified at the request of the Department of Agriculture. But they did not charge subcommittee witness L. Waters of Indiana University's Business School with bias, even though he was a *paid* consultant for the American Trucking Associations.

Brock Adams praised the testimony of Jerry White of Inland Freight Traffic Service, although his testimony on rate bureaus was clearly open to question. White had been negotiating with various rate bureaus on behalf of shippers and therefore had a special interest in speaking against the provision in the DOT bill that would wipe out rate bureaus. In denying that rate bureaus were cartels (arrangements by which carriers get together in a systematic fashion to fix prices by agreement rather than by competition), White acknowledged that they were "vehicles" in which carriers could negotiate rates collusively:

> The bureaus themselves have certainly no power whatsoever to do anything in the rate-making field. They are simply a vehicle by which the carriers are allowed to sit down in the so-called "smoke-filled room" and decide in concert amongst themselves what they are going to do.[31]

Adams commented to White, "First I want to say yours is an excellent statement. I guess it is because I agree with most of the things that you say."

While the academicians tried to substantiate their conclusions through a hostile screen, the carriers were presenting distorted and falsified evidence without challenge. Members asked few penetrating questions despite the fact that industry testimony was self-serving. After four executives from carriers that transport frozen food had testified against the DOT bill, the subcommittee gushed:

> MR. ADAMS. Thank you, gentlemen. I particularly appreciated the factual manner in which you have presented your

specific examples. Obviously, there are controversial points in the bill.

MR. DINGELL. I have nothing except to compliment our witnesses for the forceful presentation they have given.

MR. ADAMS. Mr. Harvey?

MR. HARVEY. I would like to commend the gentlemen. They delivered quite a message here today.[32]

The subcommittee members participating in the hearings exhibited substantial ignorance about articles cited, evidence presented, and even transportation and economic terms used. Adams, the most knowledgeable, and Dan Kuykendall, who did most of the questioning, had plenty of opportunities to show that they did not understand basic transportation lingo. Although he had been on the subcommittee for five years, Kuykendall had not learned what "marginal costs" in transportation were all about. Not having mastered this fundamental concept, Kuykendall was forced to respond to a fairly clear explanation of the term by John Ingram, the federal railroad administrator of DOT speaking on behalf of the DOT bill, with these words: "Would you yield and let me give a specific? I am just getting deeper and deeper into this quicksand of this quite intelligent sounding professional language, most of which I do not understand."[33]

Unable to argue with expertise in transportation matters, Kuykendall had to fall back upon his personal experience. As a former shipper of food products, Kuykendall knew about a competitor who had engaged in predatory pricing—going below cost until others are driven out of business and then raising prices for profits as a monopoly. Since Kuykendall misinterpreted "marginal costs," he misunderstood the meaning of the provision and was hostile to the DOT bill. Industry representatives who knew of his fear of "destructive" competition keyed their pitch to him. The ATA filled three hundred pages of House hearings—distorting facts, quoting out of context, and using data with apparent dishonesty in their presentations and rebuttals. But the subcommittee members asked no questions in challenge.

At the Senate hearings, Hartke, who ran the show, was biased

toward the carriers and out of touch with the independent authorities on surface transportation—Dr. Walter Miklius, Dr. George
Wilson, and Dr. Ann Friedlaender. Hartke allowed lobbyist
Smathers to go off the record to discuss a matter during the hearings and warmly welcomed the carrier officials. But he seemed to
have difficulty hearing what the experts had to say, and continually
brought up extraneous issues. Hartke took these witnesses to task
for not possessing precise and detailed studies about the effects of
public policies, and seemed to berate them simply for being academics:

> You ought to get out of that atmosphere and come to the
> Midwest where we have problems. I am being lighthearted
> with you, but I am serious. You people come in here as ex-
> perts, you are paid good money, I presume, for being ex-
> perts. How many classes do you teach a day?
> DR. MIKLIUS. One.
> SENATOR HARTKE. One per semester, right?
> DR. MIKLIUS. Right.
> SENATOR HARTKE. How many hours a week?
> DR. MIKLIUS. Three hours. But this is because——
> SENATOR HARTKE. You have plenty of time; you could
> have gone into this work. I am going to tell you, sir, that I
> am not very impressed. I have accommodated you, and you
> will get your plane at 1:30. I guess you will be glad to get
> back to that Hawaii.
> DR. MIKLIUS. I am director of economic research, sir, and I
> have an appointment I am serving.
> SENATOR HARTKE. I want you to know this testimony
> hasn't helped us very much.
> DR. MIKLIUS. I am sorry.[34]

And he dismissed Dr. Friedlaender and then Dr. Wilson:

> DR. FRIEDLAENDER. The real issue we are talking about is
> in some sense whether society will be better off if we relax or
> increase regulation or maintain it as it is. I have done quite a
> lot of work, Professors Wilson and Miklius, and a lot of
> economists have done a lot of work indicating that if we

deregulated there would be a fairly substantial social savings.

SENATOR HARTKE. What would happen to the workers?

DR. FRIEDLAENDER. That is what I want to come to. You commented on specific interest groups who will claim they will get hurt by deregulation and the question is really—no one knows what will happen really. I think that I, as an economist, can say that costs will drop, rates will drop, the shippers will be better off, the consumers will be better off. What happens to the truckers that you were talking about—that is something that I don't know. But I think that clearly some people will be hurt by this. The real issue is whether the community as a whole, the gains to the community are great enough to offset the losses to specific groups.

SENATOR HARTKE. Can I stop you a moment and just come back and show you the parallel which you people in academia just seem to completely intentionally ignore or don't understand. In this thing, unless there is somebody who can consume, there isn't anything for the consumer to have. That means you have to have a decent standard of living for these people. . . .

What you are saying is that deregulation really takes it out of the hide of that worker.

DR. FRIEDLAENDER. Senator Hartke, what I think is probably the people who will be hurt most by deregulation are the truckers who are on the high value, high density lines, the major shipment lines.

One of the interesting things about Mr. Flott's testimony, I thought was that he essentially said that rails didn't have a comparative advantage and if we deregulated or if we relaxed regulation very little would happen to the truckers, anyhow. . . .

SENATOR HARTKE. . . . I will guarantee you, and there is no testimony to the contrary in these hearings yet, but what the average wage of that [unregulated] trucker, for example, and that carrier of agricultural products, that his average wage even working at no overtime is little better than $3 an hour. Now is that what you want to do, reduce the entire transportation work force to a $3 an hour wage?

DR. FRIEDLAENDER. I just don't see that happening.

SENATOR HARTKE. Why not? In every exempt field that is
exactly what is happening. Where has that not happened?
DR. WILSON. Can I respond to that, Senator? I think in the
exempt sector they are owner-operators.
SENATOR HARTKE. They are workers.
DR. WILSON. Small entrepreneurs.
SENATOR HARTKE. Okay, go ahead.
DR. WILSON. If the results of this bill, if enacted, are along
the lines we think, then it seems productivity will rise and
there has been a close correlation between productivity and
wages in the industries. So rather than seeing the standard of
living drop, I would envisage it rising if the consequences are
correct.
SENATOR HARTKE. Let me ask you, you say they are owner-
operators. What do they make a year?
DR. WILSON. I don't know.
SENATOR HARTKE. You came here as an expert, George.
Go back to school.
DR. WILSON. I intend to this afternoon.
SENATOR HARTKE. I mean—. . .
SENATOR HARTKE. Well, I am really shocked that you
come in here as experts in this field and didn't give one
thought to what happens to a workingman in this field, and
that you are going to go ahead and make a major contribution toward going ahead at this time and saying that this bill
is good.[35]

In contrast, the carriers who testified before Hartke's committee received a warm reception. On March 28, 1972, George
Smathers chatted with his former Senate colleagues, and along
with other ASTRO witnesses, filled the hearings with ninety-five
pages of statements and exhibits. Subcommittee members did not
ask industry representatives a single question about the bill on
this day or later in the hearings. They asked only perfunctory
questions of the American Trucking Associations and never challenged their evidence or materials. But if they had read the evidence provided by Professor Thomas Gale Moore, as they should
have, they would have recognized the ATA's distortions. As it

was, Moore had to insert his rebuttal into the hearings, and the committee members never responded to his charges:

> Their [the ATA's] critique [of the DOT] amounts to a considerable quoting out of context, some misunderstanding of what I was saying, some irrelevant exaggeration and two insignificant mathematical errors. . . .
>
> I do not want to take up the committee's time with a detailed rebuttal of Mr. Flott's comments on my paper. I am tempted to say that the best rebuttal is to ask the Committee to read my work. . . . Then the out-of-context quotes will be clear, the exaggerations apparent. For example, on page three and again on page nineteen they quote me as saying "deregulation of trucking by itself might lead to new misallocations and to new costs on the economy" without indicating that I was setting up a hypothesis to be examined and later I found that the gains would clearly outweigh any losses.[36]

Economists, transportation experts, consumer advocates, organizations of small shipping firms, environmental leaders, and concerned congressional staffers supported the DOT bills, but their voices were weak against the strong beam coming from George Smathers and the powerful carriers he represented—ASTRO. The organizations representing small shipping firms had much smaller lobbying budgets, and fewer contacts inside Congress than ASTRO. They also pursued the misdirected strategy of supporting the administration bill without telling members what was wrong with the industry bill, point by point. Groups like the National Institute of Transportation (NIT) also lost some congressional leverage by taking their cues from a White House that had not actively sought support for its bill. Further, they lost the support of executives from the large shipping companies who tended to think along the same lines as the carriers—that the cost of the tax subsidies and other provisions of the Surface Transportation Act could be passed on to consumers. It soon became apparent that only one side of the story was being heard, and that was Smathers' side.

Stage Three: Biding Your Time

At the end of the House and Senate hearings in May 1972, the three bills rested until August executive sessions. The Senate held two subcommittee executive sessions in June, but only Hartke and James Pearson showed up for the first one, and only Hartke for the second. Three of the most important pieces of transportation legislation in the Ninety-second Congress did not have much status yet.

In the meantime, the carriers drummed up public support for their proposals. Pearson's office disclosed that the senator had received three thousand pieces of mail on the Surface Transportation Act in the first three weeks of July. Lobbyists and railroad employees, such as workers for the Reading Railroad that had recently gone into receivership, had generated the bulk of these letters.

Senator Frank Church exposed one of ASTRO's more interesting maneuvers: the Union Pacific Railroad offered the prize of a $100 savings bond to the employee who persuaded the most people to write members of Congress in support of ASTRO's proposals. The railroad also urged employees to endorse tax subsidies such as the low-interest loan provisions totaling up to $600 million a year over an eleven-year period. The employees as taxpayers would eventually have to help make up this lost federal revenue.

Especially effective in the Smathers-ASTRO campaign were television ads that directly lobbied for the bill. Over one hundred times in a three-month period in 1971, NBC's Washington affiliate broadcast two ads lobbying for the ASTRO bill. Before beginning to lobby the public through these ads, Astronaut Wally Schirra could be seen on TV holding out a glass of clean water and asking America to thank her railroads for providing it (by carrying the fluoride that purifies water). Starting in 1971, Washington metropolitan residents, of course including members of Congress, heard and saw Schirra this way, making a direct political appeal:

1. Schirra in outer space:

The future of transportation. From up here it appears pretty good. Down there on earth, people worry about it. Because America's railroads, trucks and regulated water carriers can't produce the money needed to modernize for the future, *their* future . . . is in doubt. Nobody asked for it, but this is everybody's problem. Because if America can't deliver the goods, we'll all pay the price, *higher* prices, for fewer goods. But there's hope yet. The Surface Transportation Act now in Congress. It calls for loans and guarantees to assure funds needed for improvements—such as new locomotives and freight cars. *Loans*, not subsidies, to be repaid in full, *with interest*. And in the end we'll all be repaid. We'll go on getting the goods we want . . . at prices we can pay. Who needs the Surface Transportation Act? We all do.

2. Schirra holding a toy train:

It would cost only a penny and a half to run this toy electric train a mile. While it's going, think about this: a *real* train can move a *ton* of goods a mile . . . for about the same penny and a half. Our economy pretty much runs on railroads. But railroads—and trucks and regulated water carriers, too—have run into a problem. Because they can't produce the money needed to modernize for the future . . . their future is in doubt. That's why they support the Surface Transportation Act now in Congress. It calls for up-to-date regulations that would allow more freedom to adjust rates to a changing economy. *And* more freedom to abandon unprofitable services chewing up funds needed if America is to deliver the goods. Or else we'll all pay the price: higher prices for fewer goods. Who needs the Surface Transportation Act? We all do.

The Washington NBC affiliate broadcast this ad despite a September 1970 NBC directive that controversial ads were not permissible.*

* A group of businessmen offering to purchase time to present their case against the Vietnam war had been denied access under the directive. Allstate Insurance Company likewise was prevented for a while from purchasing air time for an ad supporting air bags.

At the 1972 Democratic convention in Miami Beach, ASTRO funded a lavish setting of free drinks and sandwiches for politicians and newsmen. When Congress went back into session in the steamy Washington of mid-July, outside pressures to consider the transportation bills had grown intensely, but quietly. Smathers continued his rounds, concentrating on Magnuson, whose support was crucial for the bill's passage.

During June and July of 1972, DOT officials and House subcommittee members could not seem to come to any kind of understanding. Some DOT representatives complained privately that House subcommittee members did not understand their legislation and, what was worse, were not trying to understand it. And subcommittee members charged that DOT should have written their explanation of the bill more simply.

Brock Adams, meanwhile, had prepared a compromise bill, and he prevailed upon Chairmen Jarman and Staggers to take up this bill in six days of executive sessions in August 1972. Although strongly resembling the carriers' bill, it also: provided $3 billion in insured loan guarantees to railroads, outlawed below-cost pricing, eased procedures for publication of bulk water rates, allowed direct congressional review of the ICC budget (bypassing OMB), and lowered rates for recyclable commodities. These provisions did not address the basic issues of increased competition raised by the DOT Regulatory Modernization Act; rather they perpetuated the tradition of market protection and liberal subsidies to the transportation industry.

The DOT bills got short shrift in executive session, with Adams explaining that the committee felt "closer" philosophically to his version. Deputy Assistant Secretary of Transportation Robert Binder, who had testified on behalf of the DOT bills at the May hearings, indicated that he would not back Adams' "inadequate" bill. According to Binder, the final administration version (described above) of the Regulatory Modernization Act already represented a great compromise.

Binder evidently was not aware that his subordinates at DOT's Federal Railroad Administration (FRA), sympathetic to the railroad position and to ASTRO, were actively encouraging support for Adams' compromise over the DOT bill at the same time as he opposed it. The carriers had been pushing with the FRA's blessing for federal aid without regulation. Secretary Volpe allegedly told the carriers that the price of financial aid would be regulatory reform, as provided for in the administration bill. One observer said of the carriers, "If the government sets up this latter day Reconstruction Finance Corporation, it'll never see its money again."

Hartke too, began to move; the full Senate committee held executive session in the second week of August. By this time, Senator Philip Hart led the opposition—small shipping firms and consumer advocates—against the carriers' bill. Jack Pearce, who had formed an organization of small shippers called COMET and had helped draft the DOT bills, worked with Senate staff members in coordinating their supporters. When Magnuson finally got around to reading the Surface Transportation Act and O'Neal's memo against it, he realized how one-sided Smathers' presentation had been. In Senate executive sessions, then, the carriers' bill was gutted. The loan-guarantees provision was reduced to $3 billion, and staffers O'Neal and Cary were delegated the responsibility of writing in extensive controls. The bill's opponents estimated that they had curbed "90 percent" of the bill's abuses by the time of the final Commerce Committee vote.

The committee reported out the newly revised Surface Transportation Act on September 15, 1972, with these provisions: a twenty-eight-month moratorium on rail line abandonment where there is opposition to it, federal matching grants of $50 million to pay up to 70 percent of the upkeep of lines that might otherwise be abandoned, and a limit on dividend increases (not beyond 2 percent) for the carriers receiving the federally guaranteed loans. These provisions curb some of the obvious abuses possible with the ASTRO bill, but do not address the issues in DOT's procompetition measure.

When the Ninety-second Congress adjourned, no floor action had been taken in either house on these transportation bills, although (including one each on rate bureaus, carrier rates, and recycled solid wastes) the Senate Commerce Committee had initiated several studies that could be used in the next session.

Stage Four: Starting Over

Brock Adams has continued his efforts to turn out a compromise bill based on the industry version. On the other side, supporting the DOT bills, have been environmental leaders like Rafe Pomerance and Burt Blackwelder of the Environmental Policy Center, officials of the Consumer Federation of America, Consumers Union, COMET, and others. But many of the economists in the Department of Transportation who had supported the DOT bills have left. The administration is shifting focus, along with the committees, to the issue of northeastern railroad bankruptcy, especially the Penn Central.*

In 1974 both the DOT Regulatory Modernization Act and the industry Surface Transportation Act remained buried, still failing to emerge from either full committee. However, a very mild reform attempt, the Transportation Improvements Act, was reported by the House Commerce Committee. House approval came on December 10, too late in the session for a conference to work out differences with the Senate-passed bill (which provided a loan

---

* The new Secretary of the Department of Transportation, Claude Brinegar, has suggested a reorganization bill that would give enormous monopoly power to private interests and that would allow a new railroad to cut off service to areas relying on it, regardless of external costs. A new ICC plan wisely allows a phased abandonment of unprofitable lines and opportunity for new carriers to provide abandoned service with limited public subsidies but adds an unregulated subsidy system to railroads, generally for tracks. Adams' proposal would facilitate federal purchase of rail rights-of-way and charging user taxes. Such a provision might reduce the hassle of interconnecting arrangements for trips along the tracks owned by different railroads. It also puts the rail mode on an equal footing with trucking since it would no longer have to pay property taxes on its right-of-way. And the public could charge user taxes on track suitable for high-speed transport, schedule runs of many more competing railroads, and decide where tracks should and should not be abandoned or extended—according to public interest criteria the rail market may not provide. These new ideas, however, are not being seriously pushed, whatever their respective merits. No action is expected aside from extended subsidies into 1975.

guarantee program for the railroads but no regulatory reform). A modest attempt to produce some competition, the Improvements Act would have allowed carriers to vary prices up to 7 percent without ICC involvement and reduced the antitrust immunity of the railroad rate-fixing bureaus. The bill did little to increase competition among truckers; kept the system of operating restrictions so abhorred by shippers, consumers, and economists; and would have only marginally affected the areas it did cover.

Now pending and more certain of attention is the Regional Rail Reorganization Act, which passed the Senate in January 1975. It authorizes $250 million for additional funding to carriers now in reorganization (for example, the Penn Central). The entire issue of regulation, oversight of the ICC, rates, and competition is shelved, and will likely remain so. In 1975 the Departments of Justice and Transportation were working on two mild bills to be introduced *seriatim*. One would provide for slightly increased competition in rail, the second would do the same in trucking. Officials are not optimistic. This departmental team is not likely to win unless the focus shifts to the basic issue of transportation policy instead of piecemeal legislation increasing tax subsidies for carriers. George Smathers and the AAR are still in business.

Associations such as the AAR are proud of molding a highly elaborate "system for dealing with the government and with Congress which can be looked upon as highly effective."[37] They are not ashamed to say that a lot of their public relations events are ultimately aimed at Congress: "AAR's effort is aimed at creating the best atmosphere [a public sympathetic to AAR's aims] in which the individual railroads can sell their product or the industry can go to Congress and the state legislatures for what they need." They have gone so far as to consider public relations as a kind of weaponry: "[Mr. Schultz] describes one of the PR departments' primary jobs as 'making bullets for PR people on the railroads to fire their individual campaign to win over the public. . . . Maybe 30 caliber bullets are passé,' he jokes. 'We may need ICBMs.'"

4

Aviation

Civil aviation as it exists today is the creation of Congress. In theory, Congress monitors the industry for the public good through legislation and oversight of aviation's regulatory agencies. In practice, Congress is a shorthanded, shortsighted middleman through which lobby groups compete among themselves and with the executive branch for subsidies and regulatory favors. Congress is a sometimes active but rarely independent or creative partner among these powers, often reluctant to act at all when faced by intransigent and conflicting pressures.

The centers of congressional debate over civil aviation are the House and Senate Commerce committees. Other congressional committees occasionally contribute aviation legislation, and the Appropriations committees annually consider funding of aviation programs. But the major authority rests in the Commerce committees. This involvement dates from 1926, when Congress placed aviation under the Department of Commerce's regulation, and 1938 and 1958, when the modern regulatory structure for

NOTE: This chapter was written by Andrew Weiner.

aviation was erected by legislation originating in the Commerce committees. When aviation crises are perceived, the Commerce committees react. When Congress produces a new grant or subsidy program for aviation, the legislation usually emerges from the Commerce committees. When Congress fails to act on aviation, it is especially the fault of the Commerce committees. Because of Congress' central role on aviation, the lapse in scrutiny by the Commerce committees often means no government action at all.

Civil aviation, which includes all nonmilitary facets of aviation on the United States and international problems which impinge on domestic aviators, certainly provides sufficient matter for congressional attention. Civil aviation's components include the commercial air carriers (including scheduled trunk lines such as TWA, local service or "feeder" airlines such as Ozark, and supplemental or charter airlines) and what is known as general or private aviation (pleasure and business aviation, air taxis, crop dusters, etc. —more than 100,000, or 98 percent, of civil aircraft).[1]

All of civil aviation, but commercial aviation especially, has developed in response to congressional programs of subsidy and enfranchisement. The Civil Aeronautics Act of 1938, for example, legitimized sixteen existing commercial outfits as first-level trunk airlines; no new ones have been added since then. Inflated federal payments to the airlines for airmail services served as an important "means of subsidizing the development of air transportation in the United States."[2] A direct subsidy program replaced airmail subsidies in 1953.

Pressures from smaller communities, the members of Congress serving them, and the first-level airlines that wished to abandon less profitable, less traveled routes, led to the creation in 1944 of a program whereby second-level, local service or "feeder" airlines were certified to assume lower-volume routes. The local service airlines were subsidized yearly in an expanding program that has already disbursed over $1 billion.[3]

The feeder airlines followed the trunks in seeking to abandon their more isolated routes, despite the fact that they were created and subsidized to serve those routes. Congress encouraged this trend in 1950 and 1957 by underwriting the purchase of larger aircraft that were uneconomical for the routes served by the feeder airlines. By 1966 the federal government had guaranteed some $38 million in loans for the purchase of forty-seven aircraft —none of which had a capacity of less than thirty-six passengers.[4] Some local service airlines that purchased larger-capacity airplanes could not fill them. To stay operative, they had to request more federal subsidies, to increase fares, or to abandon the less-traveled routes.

The subsidy program could have encouraged the carriers to purchase smaller aircraft. But neither the administrative agency nor Congress exercised its authority to this end. On the contrary, loosened restrictions on the routing and scheduling of local service airlines have allowed them, in effect, to achieve trunk-line status.[5] While in some cases this has had the virtue of increasing competition and reducing the need for subsidies, it has not resulted in the lowering of fares and it has discouraged the expansion of local service and in some cases has actually reduced it. Congress is thus again confronted with a shortage of air service in smaller communities. Bills to create and subsidize a *third* level of airlines from the air-taxi "commuter" lines that have begun to fill the vacuum left by the feeder airlines have been prominent in recent Congresses.

The industry has been decisively shaped not only by the structure of airline subsidies but also by the regulatory agencies which Congress (again, through Commerce committee legislation) has established and empowered: the Civil Aeronautics Board (CAB), an independent agency established in 1938, and the Federal Aviation Administration (FAA), which was established in 1958 and placed in the new Department of Transportation in 1967. The CAB is comprised of five members appointed by the president for six-year terms and regulates the economic side of the airways. It assigns rates and routes, certifies air carriers, authorizes mergers, and administers a subsidy program for local-service air carriers. The FAA regulates aviation safety. It controls commercial air traffic flow with about 15,000 air traffic controllers (who are civil servants). The air-traffic-control system encompasses over 500,-000 miles of telephone, telegraph, and microwave communications, over 300 airport towers, and additional hundreds of flight service stations that provide weather and route information, search and rescue operations, and radio communications. The FAA also administers airport development programs. Virtually every phase of airlines management and aviation planning falls within the scope of the CAB and FAA.

Each segment of the aviation industry has developed organizations to influence Congress, the CAB, and the FAA. These organizations battle for federal subsidies for such items as air-traffic-control facilities and personnel, radar, approach lighting, weather and route information, search and rescue operations, radio communications, and airport construction grants. They also fight for a maximum share of the aviation market, favorable regulatory treatment, and the greatest use of existing aviation facilities at the least possible cost.

THE COMMITTEES AND THE "SUPER-MODE"

The Senate Aviation Subcommittee, established in 1955, was first chaired by A. S. "Mike" Monroney, to whom full-committee chairman Magnuson gave a relatively free hand in developing aviation policy. When Monroney was defeated in 1968, the member in line for his chairmanship was Vance Hartke, an erratic legislator whom aviation industry leaders viewed with suspicion. Magnuson's solution was to claim the Aviation Subcommittee chairmanship for himself. In 1971, however, with Hartke safely ensconced as chairman of the Surface Transportation Subcommittee, Magnuson turned the Aviation Subcommittee chair over to the member next in line, Howard Cannon, in whom he and the industry had greater confidence. In the House, a Transportation and Aeronautics Subcommittee was established in 1959, replacing an earlier Transportation and Communications Subcommittee. John Jarman succeeded to the chairmanship in 1971, after the defeat of Samuel Friedel (D., Md.). The House and Senate subcommittees differ in temperament, energy, and expertise. But in one essential matter they are identical: only a handful of members understand aviation and determine aviation policy.

In the Senate, only Senators Magnuson, Cannon, Pearson, and Cotton follow aviation closely. Other members are anything but indifferent to aviation; on the contrary, the sense is widespread that, as former chief counsel Gerald Grinstein put it, "Aviation is the 'super-mode.' . . . [The] philosophy is, hell, build all the airports you can." But Aviation Subcommittee staff member Robert Ginther observes:

> Most of the work is done by Cannon, Magnuson, and Pearson, sometimes assisted by Cotton and Baker. . . . Magnuson and Cannon don't clash on priorities, although they sometimes have furious arguments over tactics. . . . In general, however, the senators won't buck Magnuson or Cannon.

Senator Pearson, ranking Republican on the subcommittee during the Ninety-second Congress, reports that the other members of the Commerce Committee usually accept the work of this small contingent:

> We're just not formal here on Commerce. There might be subcommittee executive sessions, but when there's a rush, the committee can go along with no hands on the handlebars when it wants to. . . . Subcommittee bills don't get changed much when they come to the full committee. We're more preoccupied with telling the other members how the bill will affect their constituencies. But people respect Cannon's and my expertise. . . . We both have the confidence of the committee. It's not that we don't have differences, but we settle them between ourselves.

On the House subcommittee during the Ninety-second Congress, only four of the twelve members were considered reasonably knowledgeable about aviation—John Dingell, Brock Adams, Dan Kuykendall, and Fletcher Thompson. Except for Dingell, these congressmen did not have enough seniority to participate in the conference between the Senate and the House, the last stage of most major bills. None of them had major aviation initiatives to their credit, though Dingell and Adams were leaders in other policy areas.

The House subcommittee's leaders are less knowledgeable than their Senate counterparts, and hardly dynamic. The chairman of the subcommittee, John Jarman, has been characterized by a Republican member as no more than "a good timekeeper." Nor is full-committee chairman Staggers a leader in aviation matters. A Johnson-era Department of Transportation official called him "a kindly gentleman, very interested in his district and little else . . . his only aviation interests being [the needs of] his district." The official continued, "Jarman has little input . . . [is] not dynamic, not having an overriding interest in aviation. . . . The House staff does a lot of work, almost in a vacuum." Congressman Podell substantiates this assessment. Transportation and Aeronautics was his third choice among the five Commerce subcommittees. Why? "If a subcommittee's got an exciting chairman, things begin to move. John Jarman's not a sexy chairman, although he's a sexy guy. A good chairman can *make* a subcommittee."*

Staggers controls the subcommittee agenda. He may not have his priorities clearly set, and committee discussions may be free-wheeling, but he does not yield the right to set the schedule. He has to be courted on a particular bill and can be exceedingly coy. A lobbyist for the airlines commented, "Harley won't ever say no. Sometimes he'll say see the clerk; and the clerk will show you a packed calendar. Sometimes the promises don't come through." Another lobbyist explains how Staggers forms priorities: "If you want a hearing before this committee you have to work on it. There are many competing pressures, and it's often a question of who's going to be the successful nag."

---

* Podell, it should be added, played an insignificant legislative role on the subcommittee after his assignment to it. But his alleged activities in seeking to influence CAB and FAA deliberations regarding an airline route to the Bahamas in exchange for $41,350 resulted in his indictment in 1973 on charges of conspiracy, bribery, perjury, and conflict of interest.

The House subcommittee is more swamped and frantic than the Senate subcommittee. One major reason is the scope of its jurisdiction. The Subcommittee on Transportation and Aeronautics handles not only aviation, as does Cannon's subcommittee, but railroads, trucks, buses, and inland waterways as well. Its work is further complicated by the tendency of its members to dwell upon and argue over details. House members have few competing subcommittee assignments to divert them, but this often seems to lead not to greater efficiency but to a tendency to wrangle over legislative minutiae. The lack of decisive leadership, of course, exacerbates the problem. Says Podell, "If someone asks unanimous consent to ask what time it is, someone is sure to object."

Commerce committee members in both houses agree that the Senate committee shows more activity and initiative in aviation matters. One Senate aide is explicit: "I can recall no major aviation legislation sponsored and initiated by the House Interstate and Foreign Commerce Committee. . . . House members never really sponsored more than token proposals." Even when House Commerce reports out a bill before its Senate counterpart, it generally reworks legislation initiated elsewhere.

Not even persistent leadership can be effective without sufficient committee staff, and both aviation subcommittees are inadequately staffed. The Transportation and Aeronautics staff, dealing with three modes of transportation (railroads, civil aviation, and inland waterways) and an army of lobbyists and bureaucrats, consists of only two professionals, Walter Graham and William Dixon. Graham, who was hired pursuant to Staggers' agreement with his subcommittee chairman to increase the professional staff in 1971, has been largely diverted from subcommittee work by Jarman. Dixon, the full-committee aide assigned to aviation, has been described as "completely overcommitted in terms of problems."

On the Senate side, the shortage of personnel is somewhat less drastic. The Aviation Subcommittee has one professional staff member, Robert Ginther, to handle all its business. Harold

Baynton, assigned to the full committee, is occasionally active on behalf of Cannon. Minority staffers Art Pankopf, the chief minority counsel, and John Kirtland, aide to Pearson, spend some time on aviation matters. But Ginther has to do most of the work himself.

Without sufficient staff, neither subcommittee can match the investigative and the analytical capabilities of its wards—civil aviation carriers and their regulatory agencies. The members and their staffs therefore have difficulty assessing airline needs and the public interest. Statistical and technical materials that pour in from the air carriers and agencies need extensive critical analysis. For example, the major carriers' organization, the Air Transport Association (ATA), alone introduced forty-seven pages of complex statistical and technical material in its two appearances before the Senate's 1969 hearings on the Airport and Airways Development Act, and the FAA submitted fifty-one pages detailing its projections for aviation growth.[6] The committee members and their staffs are not in a position to analyze their material; yet they base most of their decisions and legislative actions on such information.

Despite these frustrations, many members still seek assignment to the aviation subcommittees; as Table 2 (Chapter 1) shows, they rank first in "desirability" on both the House and Senate Commerce committees. Senator Pearson explains, "Aviation has a glamor and every state has airports—that is why the subcommittee's so popular." Staff member Ginther adds:

> I suspect the members want to associate with the work of the subcommittee for political reasons. Others have particular interests that they pursue at intervals. Senator Spong, for example, is bugged about Washington National [Airport].

And a CAB official commented, "It's obvious that when a congressman on a committee related to our agency wants something, say a congressman on Commerce, his request gets more serious attention than another congressman's." In short, the desire to acquire or improve aviation facilities for their districts is often a major motive of aviation subcommittee members. Few, however, become further involved.

Some of the most important subcommittee members have compelling reasons to take a prominent role in legislation affecting the aviation industry. The economic base of Pearson's state is aircraft manufacture; 56 percent of America's commercial aircraft are built there. Washington, Magnuson's state, is the home of Boeing. Jarman's congressional district includes the Altus and Tinker Air Force bases, the Oklahoma City Air Station, and an FAA Aeronautical Center. Fletcher Thompson had operated a small but profitable firm that specialized in aviation law and had represented small airline companies in suits and FAA hearings. Thompson has also served as a past vice president of the National Aviation Trades Association and director of Lawyer-Pilots Bar Association.

Many Commerce members also receive campaign contributions from transportation industry and labor groups. The Transportation Communication Division of the Brotherhood of Railway, Airline, and Steamship Clerks made the following contributions to aviation subcommittee members in the 1970 campaign: Hart, $1,410; Hartke, $3,300; Moss, $1,700; Stevens, $500; Dingell, $1,600; Murphy, $1,000; Adams, $2,500; Skubitz, $600; and Thompson, $800. Representative Devine received a $400 contribution to his 1972 primary fight from Charles F. McErlean, a Chicagoan who is executive vice president and general manager of United Airlines. And Brock Adams received $2,000 from airline-industry executives for the 1972 general election.*

It should come as no surprise, then, that these members actively *promote* the "super-mode." Senator Cannon has intoned that "general aviation . . . offers a real prospect of bringing [the United States] together into an air transportation system whose advantages are equally shared by city, town, and countryside

---

* G. A. Cramer, of Trans-International Airlines, gave $500; G. L. Hickerson, president and director of Universal Airlines, $1,000; and H. J. Korth, chairman and president of Saturn Airways, $500.

alike."⁷ According to the 1972 Congress Project profile of Cannon, the Nevada senator

> has received $11,850 in honoraria the last four years, much of it from speaking engagements before aviation groups. In 1971 he reported that he had received $2,750 from his speaking engagements: $1,250 from the Airport Operators Council; $1,000 from the Aircraft Owners and Pilots Association; and $500 from the Hughes Air West Executive Club.⁸

Senator Magnuson is equally effusive about civil aviation: "I don't think anyone would disagree that we have the best private enterprise commercial air system in the world."⁹ Magnuson's personal and political ties to aviation are strong. In 1971 he introduced a bill that, according to Robert Ginther, "originated with [the ATA] and Boeing. . . . It was a case of a special interest wanting a bill." (The bill, which would have forced the military to send half its cargo by civilian airlines, was opposed by the Armed Services Committee and was narrowly defeated on the Senate floor.) Magnuson is also well known for his defense of the supersonic transport project, for which Boeing had the contract.

Campaign contributions and home-district interests are not the only motivations of aviation-subcommittee members. Many members are genuinely fascinated with aviation. Cannon, Pearson, Thompson, Moss, and Stevens were pilots or served in the Air Force or the Army Air Corps in World War II. Several committee members are licensed pilots, and obviously all are frequent passengers on airlines and private jets. When these men act to promote civil aviation, their position is usually emotionally honest as well as pragmatic. This is not to say that it is designed to promote rational or balanced transportation development.

THE LOBBIES

Perhaps the largest single factor in aviation matters is the aviation lobby. Various groups furnish the Commerce committees with legislation and information, and while they are fragmented and often in conflict, their collective impact is enormous.* According to a Senate Commerce staff man:

> Lobbyists are in and out of here all the time, using the phones, etc. . . . Lobbyists do provide many of our bills. Three recent bills pertaining to supplemental air carriers came from NACA [The National Air Carrier Association] and from World Airlines [a supplemental outfit]. The bill to shift military cargo from military to civilian airlines came from the ATA and Boeing. The bill to set up a class of

---

* The following list, though partial, illustrates the range of aviation trade associations in Washington trying to influence members of Congress:

The Air Transport Association (ATA), representing virtually all trunk and local-service airlines in the United States.

The National Air Carrier Association (NACA), representing the supplemental (charter) airlines.

The Aircraft Owners and Pilots Association (AOPA), an especially vocal organization with over 150,000 members, most of whom are nonprofessional pilots. In 1969, it boasted a membership comprising 22 percent of all active pilots and 76 percent of all active general-aviation aircraft.

The National Business Aircraft Association (NBAA), representing corporate aircraft and their owners.

The National Aviation Trader Association (NATA), composed of many commercial sales and service businesses involved with general aviation.

The Airport Operators Council International (AOCI), a nonprofit trade association of the public agencies that own or operate principal American airports.

The National Association of State Aviation Officials (NASAO), composed of state agencies related to civil aviation.

The Professional Air Traffic Controller Organization (PATCO), and the Air Traffic Control Association (ATCA), two organizations representing controllers.

The Air Line Pilots Association (ALPA), representing commercial pilots.

The American Association of Airport Executives (AAAE).

The Aviation Progress Committee, representing principal manufacturers of aircraft.

The National Association of Government Employees, representing FAA air controllers and electrical technicians.

The Aerospace Industries Association of America.

The commercial airlines also maintain their own staffs in Washington and/or retain attorneys in Washington law firms. Legal fees filed with the CAB alone totaled almost $3 million in 1970.

limited air carriers came from the National Air Transportation Conference [the air taxi lobby].

Senate chairman Cannon is in frequent communication with lobbyists and industry groups and welcomes their views. His contacts range from "three or four times a month" with the Air Line Pilots Association (ALPA) to "once every four or five months" with the Air Transport Association. According to Charles Spence of the Aircraft Owners and Pilots Association (AOPA), Cannon often invites industry comment on pending legislation: "Cannon is a very reasonable type of person, always eager to hear our views. He listens and his staff is very receptive." Cannon told a Congress Project profile writer: "I use lobbies frequently. They're helpful in presenting the views of various phases of an industry. We'd find it much more difficult to go out and try to look up their various positions on issues."

The aviation lobby is far from monolithic. In fact, one thing that Commerce committee members can safely assume when dealing with lobbyists is that every proposal by one part of the industry will incite another industry group. Commercial and general aviation are in conflict on airport development priorities and on the distribution of the burden of "user" taxes; scheduled and charter airlines differ on the regulation of charter service; the various "levels" of scheduled carriers fight over who is to be regulated and subsidized. Naturally, all this breeds a certain caution among aviation's advocates. According to a lobbyist with fifteen years' experience on Capitol Hill:

> Cannon puts the burden on the groups to resolve their differences. Sometimes when aviation groups approach him he says he won't go ahead until they clear the road a little. . . . I have heard that there are situations where Cannon has refused to consider legislation when groups come to him with contradictory purposes.

The only interested parties *not* normally sought out by the Commerce committees or represented in Congress are consumers. Passengers and other portions of the public—those who cannot afford air travel, for example—are hardly ever heard or contacted for information by the aviation subcommittees. Congressional hearings—to say nothing of less public channels of information-gathering—are heavily biased toward organized industry groups. Hearings have the tone of quarrelsome family reunions where lobbyists counter lobbyists or agency officials who are also promoting the industry. Dr. K. G. J. Pillai, executive director of the Aviation Consumer Action Project, a public-interest group in Washington, reports that his group gets second-class treatment. For example, since witnesses are placed in a pecking order, his group, along with other nonindustry, nongovernment voices, has been placed at the end of a day or at the end of the hearings, when press corps, media, and members are no longer listening.

OVERSIGHT: THE PRICE OF NEGLECT

Congress' basic attitude toward the aviation industry is that of a patron and promoter. Commerce committee leaders, regarding the industry as *constituents*, refrain from any public exposure of industry shortcomings and engage in large-scale investigations only during times of crisis. Cannon, for example, was stimulated by the 1970–1971 airline-industry recession to hold hearings on "The State of the Air Transport Industry." But the Aviation Subcommittee has yet to issue either a transcript or a report of those hearings. Committee sources say this failure is deliberate: "Cannon felt that a committee report might weaken the investment posture of the industry. Rather than issue a critical report, he let the matter ride."

House Commerce declines to hold oversight hearings on aviation matters. Its commitment to oversight has actually decreased in recent years. It used to open each Congress with a general review of agencies under its jurisdiction, but under Staggers even these superficial panels have been discontinued. Says a committee source, "We've just given them up, I'm not sure why. Perhaps we just don't have the time."

When FAA or CAB witnesses are called before the Commerce committees to testify on one bill or another, they are generally, as Senator Pearson puts it, "taken in many different directions." They can expect questioning about constituent problems and issues of the moment that are unrelated to the bill on which they are testifying. Often a member will use their appearance to highlight a particular grievance, typically a widely publicized issue or problem. For example, Vance Hartke appeared at the hearings on the Airport and Airways Development Act of 1970 only to badger witnesses on the inadequacies of the air-traffic-control system.

The effectiveness of such tangential questioning is doubtful. Occasionally regulatory policies will be affected; as a CAB official admitted, "As a regulatory agency and arm of Congress, we don't like to be chastized by Congress." But too often committee members lack the will or capacity to press their questions or to effectively follow up. A former Senate aide deprecates oversight as it normally takes place:

> There is no substitute for detailed oversight. The claim that separate oversight hearings are unnecessary because an FAA or CAB witness at a [legislative] hearing might be grilled on other matters is true, but irrelevant. Most of the time these are questions on an issue that has suddenly gained national attention. The senator gets the questions from his men, doesn't really know enough to pursue them, and never follows them up after a hearing. . . . The mail flow between the committees and the FAA and the CAB handles mostly constituent problems, not substantive matters.

Congress' neglect is especially serious because of the cozy relationship that the agencies themselves maintain with the industry. A conflict of interest in fact lies at the heart of aviation regulation. The Federal Aviation Act of 1958 directed the CAB and the FAA to work for "the promotion, the encouragement, and the development of civil aeronautics." At the same time, the agencies are instructed to police and, if necessary, reprimand the industry. The contradiction between regulating and promoting has seriously affected the way agencies approach the industry.

A striking example was uncovered by Congressman John Moss, who published in the *Congressional Record* a list of seventy-two private meetings between CAB officials and airline representatives that took place between November 1969 and October 1971. In his letter of transmittal to Moss, CAB chairman Secor D. Browne had written, "I think we simply must keep in contact with all persons interested in air transportation who wish to meet with us. This is part of our statutory duty, as I see it, for to understand the industry is essential if we are *to regulate and promote it*" (emphasis added). These meetings with industry representatives behind closed doors violate the spirit, if not the letter, of the Administrative Procedure Act under which the CAB operates. They preceded CAB decisions on merger cases and were considered by Moss to be *ex parte* meetings.* Browne denied that any *ex parte* meetings took place and tried to justify meeting privately with aviation representatives: "We recognize the necessity of operating in the fish bowl [of public meetings], but to refuse all meetings except those in a court room would be truly harmful to the Board as an institution."[9]

The FAA, too, has a reputation for being pro-aviation. One of the most experienced bureaucrats at the FAA revealed: "I'm an aviation man. My first objective is the promotion and expansion of civil aviation. If it weren't I shouldn't have the job. I'm a salesman for aviation, and a damn good one." Another FAA official, who works closely with Congress, explained that "the FAA has a gung-ho, pro-aviation attitude, a high esprit-de-corps, a sort of Chamber of Commerce attitude." It is important to note that Congress accepts the projections of the hardly impartial FAA for aviation growth at face value and uses them in figuring federal subsidy requirements.

---

* *Ex parte* meetings are discussions in adjudicatory proceedings where one or several parties (but not all parties) meet privately with a judge, commissioner, or examiner to discuss a pending matter.

SPORADIC LAWMAKING

The Commerce committees seriously consider few pieces of aviation ,egislation each session. Some of the factors responsible have already been mentioned: the competition among powerful industry groups and the stake most of them have in the *status quo* make inaction an attractive refuge for committee leaders. There is a limit to the time each member, even if he is in the leadership, will devote to committee work. Committee staff members are too harried to research all bills suggested to the committees or to develop ideas initiated by committee members.

Public attention is an overriding determinant of congressional action. After a major disaster, a strike, or a well-publicized industry crisis, civil aviation enters the public and media consciousness. Especially where the issue in question is reasonably simple, Congress will act. As more industry groups are involved, however, or an issue becomes more complex, congressional inertia increases, so that the intensity of the pressures for action must also rise to prompt hearings and legislation. During the Ninety-second Congress, for example, only three aviation bills processed by the Commerce committees became law. Relatively controversial and complex proposals did not in general fare well: bills to restrict presidential authority in rewarding international air-carrier routes, to require collision-avoidance systems for general aviation airplanes, to create third-level airlines from air taxis, and to liberalize the conditions under which charter flights could operate—all could not get past the hearing stage in either house.* A Senate-passed bill to control sonic booms by prohibiting SST flights over the continental United States died in the House committee. The bills that got

* In 1973, provoked by restrictive CAB rulings, the Senate committee reported a bill aimed at making airline holiday package tours cheaper and more flexible. On this issue, Cannon and Magnuson were uncharacteristically defiant of the scheduled airlines, who feared increased competition from the charters. But the scheduled airlines enlisted the support of all Commerce Republicans except Griffin for an opposition report and kept the bill off the agenda of the House committee. In the Senate it was never brought to a floor vote.

farther along were generally less controversial: an antihijacking measure (on which, however, the House and Senate conferees could not agree), a bill to forbid "head taxes" by local airports on arriving or departing passengers and to raise the federal share of airport construction subsidies for smaller airports (eventually vetoed by President Nixon), and a bill pushed by the CAB and the domestic airlines (and finally agreed to by the State Department) to permit the CAB to veto the rates to and from the United States set by foreign carriers.

The agenda of the aviation subcommittees is thus severely restricted, and its successful legislative endeavors fewer yet. The three aviation bills which became law during the Ninety-second Congress were all modest in scope and significance: the bill regulating foreign carrier rates, a bill prohibiting the diversion of Airport and Airways Trust Fund monies from their designated purposes (termed by Senate participants as the House subcommittee's only legislative initiative in recent memory), and a routine extension of the loan-guarantee program for the purchase of aircraft by local-service airlines.

The Airport and Airways Development Act

Major aviation legislation is processed by the Commerce committees only about once every decade. The last such bill was the Airport and Airways Development Act of 1970, which established the aviation trust fund and launched a new program of federal assistance for airport construction and for the development of traffic-control systems. Although this bill showed Congress' power to promote the industry, it also showed how such an initiative could actually intensify Congress' dependence on its industry clients and on the executive branch.

A major component of the federal role in civil aviation has been the subsidizing of aviation facilities. The first major aviation legislation, the Air Commerce Act of 1926, committed the government to the construction and operation of the federal airways system, which has provided air control and flight support facilities for civil aviation. The Federal Airport Act of 1946 created a matching grant program for airport construction, called the "Federal-Aid Airport Program" (FAAP). These funds were expended from general Treasury revenues. Users of the airports and airways—the air carriers, passengers, and general aviation—were never taxed through user taxes at rates sufficient to offset the costs of these services to the Treasury.

Different factions of civil aviation have continued to fight over the division of limited federal subsidy funds. This struggle exists because, while the air carriers and general aviation overlap in their use of aviation facilities, their facilities requirements are quite divergent. Less than 10 percent of all civil aviation airports have even one scheduled air carrier flight.[10] Many general aviation craft never enter the federal airways system; they use nonsubsidized airports and thus receive no benefit from federal expenditures. General aviation organizations have sought federal support for facilities particular to general aviation needs: separate facilities at airports shared with air carriers, "reliever" airports in urban areas reserved to general aviation, and airports in nonurban areas. General aviation has supported its funding demands by documenting a large expansion of general aviation travel: from 84,000 craft in 1963 to 124,000 in 1969, with an increase to 200,000 expected by 1979.[11] During this period, larger and more sophisticated general aviation planes have increased their per capita demand on the federal airways system and on airport facilities.

On the other hand, the air carriers experienced an even larger expansion during the 1960s. FAA statistics documented a rise in annual air carrier passenger miles from 54.2 to 119.4 billion miles in the 1963-1969 period, and predicted almost a doubling by 1974 and tripling by 1979.[12]* Furthermore, many air carrier airports were unequipped for the jumbo jets introduced by the airlines in the 1960s. Smaller airports with infrequent air carrier traffic were effectively forced to choose between expensive mod-

---

* These projections, which the Commerce committees accepted as fact and used as the basis for setting expenditure levels, did not consider such variables as alternate modes of transportation or adverse economic conditions, and thus may prove to have been quite erroneous.

ernization to accommodate the larger jets and traffic volumes, or the loss of scheduled service. For all air carrier airports, modernization of terminal facilities was needed to process the additional passenger traffic. Modernization was expensive, amounting to more than half of all projected construction costs at even the smallest air carrier airports.[13] However, the smaller airports competed for funds with the "large hub" airports, which in only twenty-four metropolitan regions emplaned 69 percent of all air carrier passengers.[14] Costs for "hub" airport modernization dwarfed those costs projected for smaller air carrier airports, and were required largely for terminal facilities.[15]

Competition for funds among regions, and among state and local governments, have further complicated federal subsidization. Airports are universally sought as effective stimuli for economic development. Urban states, with expensive subsidy needs concentrated in a few metropolitan airports, compete with rural states. Urban regions within each state compete with rural areas and small cities. In the former contest, the legislative formula for distributing grant monies among states is the crucial issue. In the latter, urban jurisdictions have sought the right to apply directly to the federal government for funds, a position supported by the air carriers. State governments, in which general aviation and rural areas have a larger influence, have sought control over the distribution of all federal aviation grants within their limits.

Finally, congressional funding habits have interfered with the effective functioning of the federal construction grant program, and of the federal airways system. First, airport construction is an expensive and multiyear undertaking, but federal subsidization has not been securable for the length of an individual project, because Congress would not guarantee multiyear funding levels for any program, and refused to authorize multiyear obligational authority for funding particular projects. Second, authorization levels set by the Commerce committees do not bind the House and Senate Appropriations committees, whose annual appropriations bills have frequently cut subsidy funds below the level authorized.

In fact, the Appropriations committees reduced FAAP appropriations during the 1960s, although applications for FAAP construction grants was reaching record levels. In 1969, $75 million was authorized for FAAP, $70 million appropriated, and $392 million requested.[16] The committees also refused to expand the federal airways system as traffic increased. This position was approved by the Johnson and Nixon administrations, and was provoked by the aviation industry's successful battle against additional user taxes to finance additional aviation subsidies. Such taxes had been recommended by every postwar president,[17] but aviation industry organizations had blocked congressional enactment. General aviation was particularly adamant, contending that federal airport and airway facilities were designed to accommodate the largest planes of the air carriers, and were oversized, overengineered, and overpriced for the needs of general aviation.[18] Further, such expenses as passenger terminal modernization were seen as exclusively benefiting the air carriers. In response, however, the Appropriations committees cut aviation spending, and the Bureau of the Budget "repeatedly enforced reduction on the FAA's planned expenditures" for FAAP and the federal airways system.[19]

This stalemate resulted in a serious deterioration of aviation safety, speed, and comfort during the 1960s. Public and media attention focused on passenger delays, on flights "stacked up" waiting to land, on air controllers who complained of overwork and understaffing, and on space rationing for general aviation at air carrier airports. A political response by Congress was not long in coming. The Aviation Subcommittee of Senate Commerce, under Senator Mike Monroney, and the House Government Operations Committee, prompted by Representative Jack Brooks, held separate sets of hearings on airport congestion during the Ninetieth Congress (1967–68). (The House Commerce Committee was to take no action until 1969.) Monroney gathered statistics from the FAA and from industry groups indicating that there were "serious problems of congestion" at many airports, but that these were "overshadowed by the threat of strangulation . . . based on predicted growth of air traffic and radical changes in aircraft technology . . . in the next ten years."[20] Monroney then attempted to reconcile the interests of the air carriers, general aviation, and the administration in a single bill.

General aviation was highly suspicious of any legislation. Its representatives, the Airline Owners and Pilots Association and the National Business Aircraft Association, recognized that existing programs gave general aviation substantial subsidies, but that only the air carriers paid user taxes (through passenger ticket taxes). The AOPA and the NBAA feared that new subsidy programs would lead to new user taxes, and that general aviation might lose its current benefits if it refused to pay its share of those taxes. In 1967, they did not feel their prerogatives to be in enough danger to risk new user taxes.

The Johnson administration and the air carriers, represented by the Air Transport Association, had reached an unofficial agreement that new taxes could be traded off for increased federal spending on aviation. In 1966 the administration proposed higher passenger taxes and a levy of 4 cents a gallon on general aviation fuel. By 1967 this proposal had become roughly acceptable to the ATA. Feeling outflanked, the general aviation organizations counterproposed an across-the-board tax on aviation fuel. This levy would have fallen most heavily on the air carriers, whose fleet consumed more fuel per mile than general aviation aircraft.

The air carriers differed with the administration on the structure of the new spending program. The administration demanded that expenditures be offset by user tax revenues; the ATA agreed, but insisted that these funds be kept sacrosanct after the fashion of the highway trust fund. However, as a former DOT official states, "The Bureau of the Budget and the Office of Management and Budget were opposed to trust funds in principle. They saw the way the Highway Trust Fund tied down revenues, and didn't want to repeat that 'mistake.'" Instead, the administration proposed legislation creating a $1 billion loan guarantee program for large airports, and a $100 million matching grant program for smaller airports; new user taxes would offset the costs of these programs.

The air carriers, however, refused to agree to new taxes unless the programs using those revenues were insulated from executive and congressional budget cutting through a trust fund mechanism. Their own bill, introduced by Senator Randolph, proposed an "Aviation Development Trust Fund" from which multiyear grants would be made for up to 75 percent of airport improvement costs. A federal loan guarantee program was also proposed.

Monroney introduced his own compromise bill, combining elements of the administration and the air carrier proposals, but the Senate passed none of the bills, and the House took no action of any kind. General aviation preferred inaction to user taxes. The administration would not accept the trust fund concept. Monroney was distracted by an election challenge (which ultimately unseated him and forced him into a new profession as an aviation lobbyist), and the ATA faltered before the opposition. The Ninetieth Congress therefore ended in 1968 without an aviation bill.

By mid-1969 an aviation crisis had clearly arrived. For the second straight summer, air traffic controllers protested a lack of personnel and modern equipment by a work slowdown. This exacerbated overcrowding and delays for air carrier passengers. General aviation also had its faith in the status quo jolted when, in June, the nation's five busiest air carrier airports established quotas and high landing fees to discourage general aviation traffic.[21] It was in this atmosphere that the Nixon administration and the air carriers developed new legislative proposals. The House and Senate Commerce committees prepared to process the bills. House Commerce chairman Harley Staggers, meaning to be optimistic, said, "If we put half of the effort on trying to solve this problem that we put on getting those boys on the moon, we will solve this problem pretty easily."[22]

The Senate Commerce Committee, whose Aviation Subcommittee was now chaired by Senator Magnuson, with Senator Cannon as vice-chairman, acted first. In May 1969, Senators Cannon, Pearson, and Baker were dispatched to the general aviation manufacturing center of America, Wichita, Kansas, to hold a hearing on the role of general aviation and to generate general aviation support for legislation. The administration bill was submitted to Congress on June 16. On June 17 the Senate Commerce Committee began an introductory set of hearings on the aviation "crisis" at which a procession of federal agencies and aviation lobbyists presented extensive analyses of the need for additional government subsidies. Absent from this and all subsequent hearings were witnesses from other modes of transportation, and witnesses who might claim that aviation traffic need not or should not expand as rapidly as the FAA and the industry predicted. A second set of Senate Commerce hearings was held in July to discuss specific legislative proposals. The House Commerce Committee met in July for its own hearings on proposed legislation. Whereas Senate Commerce worked through its Aviation Subcommittee, House Commerce chairman Staggers preferred to hold the hearings at the full-committee level as a way of expediting and controlling the negotiations.

The Commerce committees had been presented with three different proposals: an administration bill (S. 2437), an industry bill (S. 2651), and the Monroney bill from 1968, reintroduced as S. 1637. The administration bill rejected the trust fund structure but, as a compromise with the air carriers, offered a "designated account" in the Treasury, composed of user tax revenues and used only to defray costs incurred in the airport and airways programs. The concept of a designated account was new to the federal structure, and even the Treasury expressed uncertainty as to the practical difference between it and a trust fund. The ATA suspected that the administration would use the difference to divert monies in the account to purposes other than construction grants. According to Senator Pearson, industry groups "expressed great reservations about the user taxes, believing that no matter how we could construct the trust fund, there would always be means to divert funds from it. We had to promise them that the trust fund would be inviolable."

The administration and the air carriers disagreed about whether construction grants would be available for "comfort" as well as "safety;" that is, whether trust fund monies could be spent on terminal modernization, hangars, and parking lots. General aviation, rural members of Congress, and the administration, afraid the "large hub" airports and the air carriers would get most of the grants, opposed spending for "comfort." Senator Cotton, the ranking Republican on the Senate Commerce Committee, and Representative Springer, the ranking Republican on House Commerce, led the fight to prohibit aid for facilities "beyond the gate." Proponents of aid for terminals, hangars, and parking lots, including Senators Cannon and Pearson, argued that any prohibition would be inequitable, since commercial airline passengers would pay most of the user taxes, and since most of their needs involved the so-called "comfort" facilities.

Meanwhile, the air carriers and the airport operators sought and achieved a marriage of convenience with general aviation so that an industry-wide bill could be presented against that of the administration. An industry lobbyist remembers that the "ATA and AOCI [the airport operators' association] did bring the AOPI into their coalition by promising general aviation a free ride. The industry figured it needed a united front to get a good bill passed." The industry again submitted a bill through Senator Randolph, proposing a user tax only on passenger tickets while promising annual grants of $50 million for general aviation airports. User taxes would be placed in a trust fund whose proceeds could subsidize airport development, including the "comfort" facilities.

All three bills established construction grant programs, with set-asides for general aviation. According to the administration and Monroney bills, surplus revenues from user taxes would be used to defray the operation and maintenance costs of the federal airways system, while the industry bill exclusively reserved the trust fund for airport construction subsidies. The administration and Monroney bills also authorized the modernization of the federal airways system. The industry bill, alone of the three, authorized multiyear funding commitments for individual construction projects. In contrast, the administration bill provided for annual appropriations and authorized funds for the entire program for only two years.

The hoped-for industry unity, important if its bill was to prevail over that of the administration, quickly fell apart. Actually, it had never been complete; business aviation interests (through the NBAA) had refused to participate in the initial compromise. The rest of general aviation had felt that it could support an airport construction bill, but not one for modernization of the federal airways system, where the air carriers and general aviation had sharply conflicting interests. However, the air carriers recognized that Congress wanted a joint airport/airways bill, and that it would not accept a partial proposal. Senator Randolph was thus asked to introduce an industry airways bill, to complement the airport subsidy bill already before the Commerce committees. At this, the general aviation organization (the AOPI) withdrew from the industry coalition. This act, and the administration's characterization of the industry bills as inflationary, persuaded the House Commerce leadership to choose the administration bill as its working text.

At the executive sessions of the full House Commerce Committee, a conservative majority managed to preserve most of the restrictive provisions of the administrative bill. The committee reported a bill that declared that no less than $2.5 billion should be authorized over the next ten years for airport construction grants, and $250 million annually for airways modernization. The bill itself authorized funds for only three years. Construction grants could not be used for terminals, nor was there authority for multi-year obligations to individual projects. Twenty-five million dollars was set aside for general aviation. Although the Ways and Means Committee would draft the user tax provisions, the Commerce bill stated that user tax proceeds would be placed in an aviation trust fund. The Ways and Means Committee then met and proposed a user tax package of increased passenger and air freight taxes, and a seven-cents-per-gallon general aviation fuel tax. The combined bill passed the House without major amendment on November 6, with a vote of 337 to 6, after less than one day of debate.

The Senate Commerce leadership, unlike the House Commerce leadership, sought to achieve a coherent set of objectives. These objectives were established in consultation with the air carriers. Staff man Ginther says, "We asked the industry for suggestions. . . . The industry especially wanted the multiyear obligational authority and terminal aid; Senator Magnuson wanted a long-term program." Although he was nominally the subcommittee chairman, Magnuson trusted the drafting of a Senate version to Senators Cannon and Pearson, who met as the Aviation Subcommittee with Ginther and a staff man for Senator Cotton. The four men selected the administration bill as their starting point. The Monroney bill was rejected because it had lost the support of an industry assured of a more generous proposal. The industry bill was opposed by general aviation and was regarded as perhaps too generous and long-term a commitment (thirty years). Further, the House had chosen the administration bills. Finally, Cannon and Pearson had to balance the needs of the air carriers and "large hub" airports, which they recognized, against the demands of general aviation and rural areas, which they represented. They perceived, correctly, that they could liberalize the administration bill sufficiently for their purposes.

Obtaining Magnuson's approval, Cannon and Pearson presented a bill to the full committee that satisfied the leadership's criteria. Compared to the House bill, it was generous: $3.1 billion was projected for a decade-long airport construction grant program, and a concurrent airways modernization program was created. The trust fund structure was adopted, aid for terminal areas was permitted, and multiyear obligations of up to five years were authorized. Funds were authorized for each of the following ten years (compared to three years in the House bill). An innovative proposal was adopted that set annual minimum expenditures under the program. Says Ginther, "There were not enough assurances that the executive felt a commitment to development. We were afraid the executive would use the money for housekeeping." The full Senate Commerce Committee approved the bill after only forty-five minutes of debate, during which a solid majority defeated amendments to delete aid to terminals and to give states more control over grants.

The Commerce Committee reported the bill on December 5. The Senate Finance Committee ratified the tax provisions of the House, with minor alterations, and a complete bill reached the

Senate floor in February 1970, where it met vociferous, but ultimately ineffective, opposition from general aviation, which objected to taxes on general aviation fuel. Senator Long, chairman
of the Senate Finance Committee, rejected these arguments:

> I would think that when you get down to where general
> aviation is paying less than 9 percent of the total user taxes,
> and more than 80 percent of the operations of the airports
> are for general aviation, the commercial operators are perhaps
> the ones paying the disproportionate share.[23]

Minor amendments kept the Senate debate going for three days,
until, toward the end, a chant of "Vote, vote!" broke out from
senators on the floor, and an impatient Magnuson threw Len
Bickwit, a staffer on Hart's Environment Subcommittee, off the
floor for too zealously pressing an amendment. In the end, the
bill passed unanimously.

A delegation of House Commerce leaders, from which most
of the more liberal and knowledgeable committee members were
excluded, met with the Senate Commerce leadership in four
heated conferences and produced the final bill. Since the House
and Senate bills agreed on the trust fund structure, most user
taxes, and separate programs of airport construction grants and airways modernization, these were easily agreed to. Important con-
cessions were made by each side: aid to terminal areas was deleted;
a ten-year program was created, with authorizations for five years,
but at a lower total level than in the Senate bill. The annual minimum expenditure provision was kept, as was the multiyear obligational authority. Both houses passed the conference committee
bill, and the President signed it on May 21, 1970.

Passage of the act did not end the controversy over airport funding. In 1972, Congress learned that the FAA was not spending the
minimum amounts from the aviation trust fund required by the
act, and was using trust fund monies for the maintenance and operation of the federal airways system. Their pride insulted and
their credibility with the air carriers threatened, the Commerce
committees obtained amendments to the act to close any conceiv-

able loopholes allowing diversion of funds from purposes other than construction grants.* Another set of amendments, initiated by the Senate Commerce leadership, raised the airport aid authorization and increased the federal share of the matching formula; the President vetoed this bill in 1972 but in 1973, faced with overwhelming votes in both houses, gave it his approval.

The history of the Airport and Airways Development Act demonstrates several features of Congress' role in civil aviation. A few members of Congress and their aides arbitrate the future of the industry. Largely satisfied with the present system of subsidies and anticompetitive regulation, they usually need a substantial sense of crisis before they will act. When they do act, they are heavily dependent upon industry-generated information and executive branch proposals. They are overwhelmingly promotional in their orientation but still take few independent initiatives. As Senator Pearson puts it: "I don't think the Aviation Subcommittee sets priorities so much as priorities come to us and we respond to them." The aviation consumer is rarely heard in the halls of Congress— whether at hearings or in congressional offices—and a single-mode bias precludes any consideration of a balanced transportation policy. Legislators active in aviation affairs are constrained by the necessity of tiptoeing among contending industry interests, but when the "super-mode" can pull its factions together, it can generally get what it wants.

* An outsider might ask why the users of the federal airways system should not have to pay its maintenance and operation costs to the Treasury.

5

Communications

Telecommunications is a $19-billion-a-year industry that is regulated by the federal government. In recent years struggles for control over telecommunications policy have been raging among the communications subcommittees of the House and Senate Commerce committees, the nation's broadcasters, the Federal Communications Commission, and the White House Office of Telecommunications Policy. As we shall see, these four are not evenly matched in terms of dedication, power, and resources.

Telecommunications is within the jurisdiction of the Senate Commerce Subcommittee on Communications and the House Commerce Subcommittee on Communications and Power. It is from these subcommittees that legislation in the communications area can be expected to emanate, and it is here that oversight of the agency established by Congress to regulate communications—the Federal Communications Commission—should be carried out. But, as we shall see, the record of Congress is very scanty; it has to a large extent abdicated its responsibilities in the communi-

NOTE: This chapter was written by John Paris.

212

cations field, permitting the FCC to operate with very little control by Congress and allowing the initiative for legislation and policy-making to pass to the White House. One reason is lack of effective leadership; another is grossly inadequate staff resources and expertise. But perhaps the most important reason is the broadcasting industry itself—the industry that Congress has passed laws to regulate and that the FCC is charged with overseeing on a day-to-day basis.

Broadcasters control the very lifeline of most politicians—media exposure—and the need for a good broadcast image is a basic factor in Congress' approach to broadcast policy-making. From the president to the newest alderman, every politician knows and respects the power of television coverage to influence his or her political future. Major candidates now spend roughly 60 percent of all campaign expenditures for radio and TV.[1] In addition, to build an image as an effective and concerned legislator, the incumbent member of Congress depends on television news spots, interviews, panel discussions, and the free airing of film clips.

Broadcasters have organized very effectively to maximize their political leverage. They are represented in Washington by numerous trade associations and lobbyists, the largest of which is the National Association of Broadcasters (NAB), a trade organization with more than four thousand member radio and television stations. According to the *National Journal*, the NAB had a budget of $3 million in 1970 and a staff of about a hundred. Some FCC commissioners, Robert G. Wells, for example, were active members of NAB before appointment to the regulatory agency. The NAB has organized the Future of Broadcasting Committee (FOB), a lobbying effort, to press its views directly on every member of Congress.[2] "No one group of lobbyists in Washington could even approach this power," boasted one FOB spokesman.[3] And the NAB has abandoned its long-held policy of political neutrality by collecting a war chest for distribution to its political friends on Capitol Hill.[4]

The broadcasters also devote considerable time and resources to courting the Federal Communications Commission, which is supposed to regulate the communications industry. The FCC was created in 1934 to regulate interstate and foreign commerce in radio and wire communications and to serve "the public convenience, interest, and necessity." Its seven commissioners, appointed by the president for seven-year terms, are answerable to Congress for the powers delegated under the Radio Act of 1927 and the Communications Act of 1934. The FCC is directed by law to provide Congress with communications policy advice and long-range planning proposals.

Senate Communications Subcommittee chairman John Pastore dismisses as myth the notions of commission independence and congressional control:

> Once you have decided on a plan in the FCC, it becomes the administration plan. . . . You men [the FCC commissioners] are appointed by the President. . . . It has often been said that you are an arm of the Congress . . . but that is only a fiction.[5]

The FCC is no better equipped to provide long-range planning proposals than is Congress itself. It has but one man in its planning office, Ken Goodwin, who devotes half his time to review and coordination of the commission's activities. Former chairman of the FCC Dean Burch acknowledges that he raided the planning-office budget when he needed money for other FCC projects.

The void in congressional initiative and FCC independence is willingly filled by an ever-growing executive branch, which sees in the congressional morass an opportunity to increase its control over communications policy. The Office of Telecommunications Policy (OTP) is the instrument the administration has used to achieve its own political goals in the name of communications advice.

The OTP was established in 1970 by President Nixon to work in many of the same areas as the FCC but to be responsible to the White House. He explained:

We live in a time when the technology of telecommunications is undergoing rapid change which will dramatically affect the whole of our society. It has long been recognized that the executive branch of the Federal government should be better equipped to deal with the issues which arise from telecommunications growth.[6]

Chairman Dean Burch of the FCC, appointed by President Nixon in 1969 (and a staunch public defender of the President after he left the agency in 1974 for a White House position) professed unconcern at the threat posed to the commission by OTP: "We have consistently favored a strong, centralized entity to deal with telecommunications issues within the Executive." Considerably more skeptical, however, was Clarence Brown (R., Ohio) of the House Communications and Power Subcommittee, who in 1970 commented prophetically:

> The method by which the [White House could influence the FCC] is establish this Office, give it the muscle of direct association with the Presidency and the executive branch, provide it with the wherewithal to do the scientific research or evaluate the scientific research that is being done so that it speaks with scientific authority in this area, deny the FCC some of the resources through the [Office of Management and Budget] to provide similar scientific research or the accumulation of scientific research, and pretty soon you have muscle in the Office of Telecommunications and the FCC becomes a function of the OTP.[7]

By 1972 the OTP had a staff of sixty-five, forty-four of whom were professionals, and a budget of $3 million. While congressional staffers try to think amid the babble of overcrowded rooms, with senior committee counsels talking over the noise of two assistants and several secretaries, OTP staffers are comfortably ensconced in suites in the Executive Office of the President. Brian Lamb, assistant to OTP director Clay T. Whitehead, has a spacious office that is better equipped than those of all but the most senior members of Congress. Even *his* assistant, Helen Hall, has a private office that would be the envy of the Senate Commerce

Committee's chief counsel. Since its inception, then, OTP has had the means to influence decisions in the telecommunications area. Director Clay Whitehead has left little doubt that it also has the will: "The White House has no qualms about seeking to influence the [Federal Communications] Commission or other so-called independent agencies."[8] One reason the White House has been able to succeed at this is the void in leadership elsewhere in the communications field.

THE SENATE COMMUNICATIONS SUBCOMMITTEE

John Pastore is in a position to do something about America's telecommunications policy. He is chairman of two committees with jurisdiction over communications: the Senate Commerce Subcommittee on Communications (with jurisdiction over telephone, telegraph, radio, and television communications, and the FCC) and the Senate Appropriations subcommittee that controls the FCC budget.

Pastore enjoys a reputation as a scrappy debater and an energetic worker. But when it comes to legislating communications policy, he is often content to do little. His subcommittee reported only six bills during the Ninety-second Congress; two concerned the regulation of campaign broadcasting, two renewed authorizations for public broadcasting, and two made minor statutory revisions. The subcommittee's review of the fairness doctrine, cable television policy, broadcast advertising, sports programing, and overall telecommunications policy did not result in specific legislation.

One reason for the subcommittee's poor record is that Pastore allows media-oriented public hearings to take the place of actual legislative activity. Of the seven hearings held during 1971 and 1972, only three centered around legislation—and their subject was election reform. Two were confirmation hearings on Nixon appointees. Hearings on television violence and cable television were treated merely as opportunities for discussion; no legislation was actually pending.

Pastore is frequently criticized for waiting for the White House and the FCC to act rather than originating his own legislative proposals. OTP's Brian Lamb has acknowledged that criticism: "Check and see how often Pastore comments, 'I am waiting for the administration's proposal.' It occurs over and over again. There is not even the expectation that Congress should initiate proposals on its own." As a result of the members' passivity in the area of communications policy-making, the administration formulates most of the legislation that comes to the subcommittee. According to minority counsel Ward White, "The committee reacts, rather than acts. It waits until an issue develops and the administration sends down some proposal to resolve it."

That Pastore does not get very much legislation through his subcommittee thus is not a sign of weakness, laziness, or inexpertness. It is a sign of his willingness to replace the public legislative process—where he could be held accountable—with behind-the-scenes maneuvers that defer to the executive branch and the broadcast industry. Former FCC commissioner Nicholas Johnson describes the subcommittee chairman's style as "rule by indirection." Johnson would like to have extensive hearings on communications issues, development of white papers, and a wide discussion of policy, culminating in legislation. "Pastore prefers to work things out through [majority counsel Nicholas] Zapple and then express his views informally," Johnson commented.

People are not in Washington very long before they discover that Pastore is the man to see in the communications field. But to get to see Pastore, one must first visit Nicholas Zapple, his communications counsel. Former FCC chairman Dean Burch has warned, "If you try to get to Pastore first, Zapple will run interference." It is not surprising that with a senator's very demanding schedule, including fourteen subcommittee assignments, Pastore willingly defers to his communications counsel on most communications matters. With twenty-five years of experience on the committee, Zapple is able to keep Pastore well-advised—"probably more advised than Pastore would want," as Burch quips, referring to Zapple's tendency to submit overdetailed analyses of issues under discussion.

Drawing on his expertise and his relationship with Pastore—described by one critical observer as "Edgar Bergen and Charlie McCarthy, with Zapple pulling the strings"—the communications counsel has been able to carve out his own little fiefdom in the Senate. Rather than reporting to chief counsel Michael Pertschuk, director of the Commerce Committee staff, Zapple goes directly to Pastore and full-committee chairman Warren Magnuson. The relationship between Zapple and Pertschuk is described by Ward White in terms of cold-war strategy: "They don't get along, but they manage to stay out of each other's way—there is a sort of a mutual coexistence."

In contrast to Pertschuk and many other staff members, Zapple is attuned to the older committee style of concern for business interests. He has a reputation among communications lawyers and lobbyists for never missing a convention, a dinner, or a business luncheon. As one communications lawyer remarked somewhat waggishly, "Nick must have some sort of a record on Capitol Hill for consecutive times being taken to lunch." Needless to say, the comfortable relationship built up over years of social interaction with members of the broadcast industry does not work to the detriment of the industry.

Zapple's Republican counterpart, Ward White, does not possess Zapple's experience or knowledge of communications. Senator Baker hired White in October 1971 from Senator Robert Dole's (R., Kans.) staff. As minority counsel, White must work closely with Zapple's office, since the majority party controls the flow of subcommittee business. White claims that Zapple is open to his ideas. But in talking with White, one gets the impression that Zapple tolerates rather than consults him. Communications material that is automatically sent to the chairman does not reach the minority counsel. White admits that "Zapple doesn't volunteer any information. The only things that I get are what I go over and ask for."

The relationship between Zapple and White is not indicative of problems within the subcommittee, for Communications is generally not marked by partisanship. Pastore's attitude toward communications legislation is usually not challenged by any of the ten other subcommittee members. According to minority counsel White, ranking subcommittee Republican Howard Baker of Tennessee is the "only one on the Republican side who takes an interest in communications."

Pastore's subcommittee does not have the benefits of partisan competition and debate. Pastore and Baker tend to support the same interests (some specialists allege that they both uncritically favor the broadcasting industry). In addition, Pastore's cautious approach to legislative initiative coincides with the minority party's strategy. As minority counsel White put it, "Pastore's conservative attitude is not very different from our approach on communications issues." Even when Pastore managed the Public Broadcasting Act of 1972, which was strongly opposed by the administration, he was criticized by the White House for trying to dispense with the bill quickly, not for advocating a partisan position. Pastore did sponsor a campaign-financing reform bill in the Ninety-first Congress that was ultimately vetoed by Nixon, but he publicly separated himself from the bill, attributing its initiation to the National Committee for an Effective Congress. Pastore introduced another campaign-financing bill (S. 382) in the Ninety-second Congress; it was eventually enacted. The bill called for retention of the "equal time" requirement of the Communications Act of 1934; limited media spending by presidential and congressional candidates; required broadcasters to sell advertising to candidates at the lowest rate prior to primaries and elections; required the public disclosure of the names, addresses, and occupations of campaign contributors of over $100; and repealed the Corrupt Practices Act of 1925.

The License-Renewal Bill

The 1969 case of broadcast-license renewal illustrates that Pastore's propensity for accepting drafts of bills from industry, his deference to the executive branch, and his delays in taking decisive action have been instrumental in the formulation of policies that favor the broadcast industry.

In early 1969, the broadcast industry was thrown into turmoil by an FCC decision to invoke a provision in the Communications Act of 1934. To encourage competition and diversity in the media, the FCC denied a renewal application to Boston's WHDH on the ground that the station owner, the Herald Traveler Corporation, had a monopoly on communications media by controlling two radio stations and two newspapers in the same city. This action marked the first time in its thirty-five-year existence that the FCC had denied a renewal application except in the case of technical defects or misrepresentations to the commission.[9]

Instead of automatically accepting an application for renewal in the WHDH case, the FCC offered the license to a broadcaster who gave a promise of better service. It acted under a clause requiring that "the commission must determine from among the applicants which of them will, if licensed, best serve the public." Uncomfortable with the unexpected exertion of the FCC's statutory power to oversee broadcast performance, the broadcasters' powerful trade association, the National Association of Broadcasters, proposed an amendment to the Communications Act that would grant an automatic renewal of a broadcast license unless there was proof the licensee was not operating in the public interest. To be certain that nothing was left to chance, the NAB sent John Pastore the "precise legal language" it wanted enacted.[10] Except for the change of several words, Pastore introduced the bill (S. 2004) exactly as dictated by the broadcasters. Pastore's acknowledged intent was to protect broadcasters from the threat of losing their license because of their political views—which seemed to him a possibility in the light of attacks on the media by Vice President Spiro T. Agnew, among others. Pastore wanted, he said, "to remove the sword of Damocles from the heads of licensees at renewal time." Some 35 senators cosponsored Pastore's bill, and about 120 representatives supported similar legislation in 80 House bills on license renewal.

Even with such widespread congressional support, Pastore's bill ran into serious snags in Congress. Witnesses at the Senate hearings on the bill, for example, brought out glaring problems that politically sensitive members could not get around. Citizens groups testified that the bill was racist because, by granting present license owners virtually perpetual tenure, it would exclude minorities from access to media ownership, and that the bill was inimical to community efforts to improve television programing. Some experts criticized industry programing practices and the broadcasters' unresponsiveness to the needs of important and sizable segments of the television audience.

When it became too politically unpopular to support Pastore's bill, the scene shifted from Congress to the even more nebulous and manipulable bureaucracy, the FCC. In this instance Pastore did not have to depend upon Zapple to carry his message to the commissioners; publicity over S. 2004 made his sentiments clear to everyone. The commission readily followed Pastore's lead, in the process gracefully shielding him from the line of fire. Without following the rule-making proceedings required under the Administrative Procedure Act, the FCC issued a policy statement compromising its previous position. "A licensee with a record of 'substantial service' to the community," the commission stated, "without serious deficiencies, will be entitled to renewal notwithstanding promise of superior performance by a challenger."[11]

The broadcast industry had placed considerable pressure on the FCC for the compromise policy, as Commissioner Nicholas Johnson underscored in his dissent from the statement. Congress and the commission, he said, are almost powerless in their attempts to control America's "other government—the mass media." Then he lamented, "The industry's power is such that it will succeed one way or the other" in whatever it seeks. The commission really had no open options in the case, Johnson wrote. "It is not at all clear to me that more than they have done would have been politically possible, or could have withstood political appeal. . . . With frustration and sorrow, I dissent."[12]

Once the FCC had taken the politically sensitive issue into its domain, the Senate quietly "deferred in favor of the commission's 'compromise.' "[13] But Judge J. Skelly Wright of the Court of Appeals for the District of Columbia Circuit subsequently struck down the FCC policy statement in *Citizens Communications Center* v. *Federal Communications Commission*. The judge commented, "In effect, the policy statement administratively 'enacts' what the Pastore bill sought to do."[14]

The broadcasters continued to press the goals that they put into the Pastore bill—to legitimize automatic renewal procedures. They sought and received lavish encouragement for changes in the license process from President Nixon during a June 22, 1972, cabinet-room meeting on broadcast problems. And in March 1973 the OTP introduced a bill to lengthen the term of broadcast licenses and to protect them from FCC hearings unless challengers established that the stations had failed to operate in the public interest.* Subcommittee chairman Pastore has become more cautious since his attempts on behalf of the broadcasters were used against him in his 1970 reelection campaign. In 1974 he brought a bill to the floor that spelled out and strengthened the "presumptions" in favor of license holders, but he strongly defended the existing three-year license term. He was reversed on the floor ("The word is already around that the industry has sixty votes," he said. "Stopping this amendment is going to be like stopping the wind"[15]); only three Commerce Committee members voted with him against a five-year term.

In spite of such industry successes, the House and Senate never ironed out the differences in their license-renewal bills in 1974. But even if new legislation is not passed, the broadcasters may achieve most of their objectives. They were given a scare by the original WHDH decision. But their post-decision influence on the Congress and the commission have proven that there is little danger to their continued stability and power. Former FCC chairman Burch implied as much when he stated, "The commission will not

---

* While publicly criticizing and even threatening broadcasters—with charges of bias in news coverage, for example—the Nixon administration quietly pushed these bills, which the NAB had sought for years.

follow the WHDH opinion."[16] In Nicholas Johnson's words, "The broadcasters will see to it that the one fluke decision in thirty-eight years will not be repeated in the next thirty-eight years."[17]

"Something Needs to be Done"

It should not be assumed that Senator Pastore and the subcommittee are a one-way conduit for the broadcasters' demands. On some issues the senator has taken ostensibly strong positions for reform and change in the industry. Over the years he has been increasingly concerned with the incidence of violence on television and its effect on children. The subcommittee itself has made several attempts to reduce the amount of violence portrayed over the air waves. But here, too, it has been the informal style of the chairman rather than any legislative effort that has marked the subcommittee's involvement. No bills on the subject have been considered or reported.

The first round against television violence began in 1969, when Pastore sought to have the industry practice self-regulation with regard to the portrayal of sex and violence. That move, which resulted in little improvement, coincided with Pastore's introduction of S. 2004, the industry-designed license-renewal bill. Though counsel Nick Zapple describes a "deal" theory as "hogwash," the fact that both issues were handled in the same set of hearings could not have escaped the broadcasters' notice.

Pastore's concern over children's programing also led to the commissioning in 1970 of a report by the surgeon general on the relationship between television violence and antisocial behavior in children. That report, which took two years to complete, established a causal relationship between televised violence and aggressive behavior in children. Rather than using that data as the basis of substantive legislation setting guidelines or norms for the protection of younger viewers, Pastore reverted to his informal style of sitting down with representatives of the industry "to work things out." This method of "working things out" was translated by the industry as another business conference designed to protect its highly profitable programing. To effect that result, it sought a clarification of guidelines from the government, knowing that such a study would delay the implementation of any restrictions on its program content.

The industry has been successful with the tactic. It took two years for the surgeon general to conduct his study. After it was completed in 1972, HEW Secretary Elliot L. Richardson informed Senator Pastore that a meaningful television-violence profile was still another two to four years away. The FCC's planning director, Ken Goodwin, commented in an unusually frank statement:

> The *Surgeon General's Report* came out much stronger than anyone anticipated. It was hoped that it would be weak, but Jesse Steinfeld refused to do that. A very strong report came out. All that happened was Pastore's comment that "something needs to be done about violence on television." Yet he didn't do anything. He had the broadcasters right where he could have done something effective, but he let them off the hook. They can still do what they want. The most that will happen is that they will be a bit more careful.[18]

THE HOUSE COMMUNICATIONS SUBCOMMITTEE WATCHDOG

The House Communications and Power Subcommittee has a different profile from its Senate counterpart: it has wider jurisdiction, including interstate electric power, petroleum and natural-gas policy; most of its members have no other major committee assignments; committee chairman Staggers and Torbert Macdonald, chairman of the subcommittee, set a more crowded subcommittee agenda; and the members are slightly more selective in accepting broadcast-industry arguments. House subcommittee members have nonetheless failed to define a decisive congressional role in the communications field.

Part of the subcommittee's failure lies with Macdonald, who

has lost a lot of the fighting spirit he had as a Harvard football captain and PT boat commander. He frequently defers to the full-committee chairman even when he does not agree with him. This was the case during Staggers' famous attempt to cite CBS and its president, Dr. Frank Stanton, for contempt of Congress after the network had refused to provide the Commerce Committee with the outtakes (film not used) of its program "The Selling of the Pentagon." Macdonald claims that he did not approve of Staggers' action, yet, in his own words, "I voted down the line with Staggers on the citation." Fully aware of the chilling effect the probe would have on broadcasters, Macdonald willingly abdicated his responsibility to protect broadcast programing from political pressure. Macdonald commented, "Every guy is entitled to a blind spot. Staggers has his. He asked me to support him, so I did." When George McGovern tried to get the House to approve a Senate bill allowing for the suspension of the equal-time provisions of the 1934 Communications Act, Staggers sat on the bill because of his personal pique at the House leadership's failure to support the CBS citation. Macdonald again supported Staggers, explaining that "Staggers has a bitch against the leadership. Let him have it. Nixon would probably veto the bill anyway."

Macdonald rarely takes the initiative even when important issues confront his subcommittee. His behavior during the cable television controversy was typical of his inaction. According to an industry lawyer:

> Macdonald knew for months that Whitehead was having secret meetings at OTP with members of the various interests on cable and copyright problems. Yet he did nothing. He would rather wait until the White House had effected its will and blunderbuss about it in a later hearing when he can sound good, than face the task of formulating an alternative proposal. He could have trimmed Whitehead's sail and probably ended the negotiations with a sharp intervention. Yet he refused to do so. He would rather wait and then rant and rave about the expanding bureaucracy and White House power.

One of Macdonald's former committee aides, Martin Kuhn, confirmed the chairman's lack of initiative. Kuhn, former editor of *Broadcasting* magazine, was hired by the Commerce Committee at $20,000 a year as a communications specialist. Incredible as it may seem, Kuhn relates that during the entire year and a half he worked for the subcommittee he and Macdonald never got together to plan areas of responsibility or to mark out a legislative program. "Torby didn't have any plans in mind and didn't know what he wanted me to do," Kuhn explained. So Kuhn spent his time "keeping up with the field," until he decided that "what Macdonald wanted was a PR man to do some work for him in the district." Since that prospect did not interest him, Kuhn resigned. Though quick to defend Macdonald's integrity, Kuhn stressed the chairman's inactivity: "The congressman is not beholden to any broadcaster, but he does not choose to be effective."

A former congressional aide who prefers to remain anonymous testified to Macdonald's weak leadership:

> Unlike Zapple and Pastore, Macdonald tries to be objective. But he doesn't show any initiative. He always waits for Pastore to have his hearings, then he does something. He could get any bill he wants, but he is too lazy.

For example, Macdonald has refused to use his committee's jurisdiction over the FCC to request confidential FCC files on broadcasters' profits. Subcommittee member Robert Tiernan (D., R.I.), who has proposed that the subcommittee request the documents, believes that such financial disclosure would be one of the best ways to reverse the industry's failure to live up to the public-interest commitment required in the original license-renewal law. When asked to respond to the issue of industry disclosure, Macdonald replied, "I don't know why that should be done." The chairman dismissed the idea that such information would indicate the stations' capacity for public-service programing in license-renewal challenges before the FCC with a disinterested "Nah, that's not necessary."

Part of the blame for the subcommittee's inactivity lies with the subcommittee members. Many of them have not gained expertise in communications and have not challenged or prodded the chairman. Democrats Fred Rooney (Pa.) and Goodloe Byron (Md.) take no active role in subcommittee affairs: Rooney can be depended upon to vote with the majority when his vote is needed; otherwise, he emphasizes his state's interests in state utilities commissions and lets the rest of the subcommittee's business go. In the Ninety-second Congress Byron honored the freshman code of silence by refusing to comment on any controversial issues before the committee.

Democrats Lionel Van Deerlin (Calif.) and Robert Tiernan are active subcommittee members, but neither has been successful in challenging the chairman. Candid but not aggressive, Van Deerlin, a former news broadcaster, has not openly challenged the lackluster leadership to implement his ideas about improving the subcommittee. Tiernan activated a communications task force in 1971 under the sponsorship of the Democratic Study Group, a coalition of liberal House Democrats, after some of his bills— such as one to establish a permanent trust fund for public broadcasting through a tax on new television sets—were ignored by Macdonald and Staggers. That independent move so infuriated Macdonald that he threatened to kick Tiernan off the subcommittee. In 1973 Tiernan left of his own volition; convinced that little was likely to happen under Staggers and Macdonald, he sought and received an appointment to the Appropriations Committee. His slot on Communications and Power was filled by the relatively inactive and conservative John Murphy (D., N.Y.).

Ranking Republican Hastings Keith, who retired in 1972,* was not an effective member of the subcommittee. Sometimes his statements and questions embarrassed his colleagues. During hearings on the FCC in 1971, for example, Keith persisted in raising questions about the commission's handling of the WHDH license-renewal case, then on appeal before the courts and the

---

* Fearing defeat in the 1972 election, Keith voluntarily left Congress after fourteen years' service.

commission and therefore not an appropriate subject for discussion. Repeated warnings from his colleagues and the FCC's Dean Burch did not deter him. Keith's limitations allowed Clarence Brown, the second-ranking Republican, to exercise minority leadership. A somewhat vain and ambitious man, Brown early became the Nixon administration's spokesman on the subcommittee. Despite the fact that the hard-working and articulate Brown is a former broadcaster, he was not committed to staying on the subcommittee. In fact, he sought a transfer to Ways and Means in 1973. When that failed he decided to stay on the Communications and Power Subcommittee and fell heir to Keith's ranking Republican slot.

The second-ranking Republican is now James Collins, a multimillionaire from Texas. In 1972 Collins was so busy running a tough reelection campaign after his administrative aide was convicted on a salary-kickback charge that he did not have much time for communications issues. When the Texan did speak, it was, in Lionel Van Deerlin's words, "as the only industry representative on the subcommittee." The remaining Republican member, freshman Louis Frey, Jr., of Florida, did not have an opportunity to do much in the Ninety-second Congress, although his firm stand against the administration's political pressure on the public broadcasting bill increased his stature with subcommittee members.

Even if Macdonald were receptive to outside suggestions, the overburdened professional staff of the Commerce Committee has neither the time nor the inclination to bring issues to the subcommittee chairman's attention. The staff's self-perception militates against new ideas being raised from within its ranks: as former Commerce Committee staff director Jim Menger stated, "The House staff does not think up ideas for the committee. It only responds to the felt needs of the members."

The subcommittee majority receives a portion of the services of Robert Guthrie, one of five professional staff members on the full committee, and Richard Krolik, a former NBC broadcaster and Time-Life cable manager who succeeded Martin Kuhn as Macdonald's subcommittee man. Until the Ninety-second Congress, the minority had been served only by Lewis Berry, a counsel who had responsibility for *all* of the Commerce subcommittees. In 1972 Berry obtained two additional lawyers for his staff, one of whom, Bennett Schram, devoted half his time to communications policy.

Guthrie, the senior communications staffer, is admired as an honest, industrious, and knowledgeable counsel. His effectiveness is hampered, however, by a heavy workload. In OTP staff member Brian Lamb's words, "Guthrie is a very good man, but he has ninety-five different issues to contend with." Another problem is that Guthrie has trouble getting Macdonald's attention. Tiernan perceives some "intimidation" in the relationship, but the result of Macdonald's erratic behavior is more often simply to leave Guthrie in the lurch, uncertain of the chairman's intentions and unable to implement what in his view are the subcommittee's obligations.

Dick Krolik, to whom Macdonald is more inclined to turn than to Guthrie, is on the committee payroll, but his desk is in Macdonald's office. He was hired by and is responsible to Macdonald. His slot was first made available by Staggers' 1971 agreement with his restless subcommittee chairmen, whereby each would make one staff appointment. No job description or requirement was specified for the new position, and the lack of defined duties drove the slot's first occupant, Martin Kuhn, off the committee. Macdonald dismissed as nonsense Tiernan's suggestion that the subcommittee should follow the Education and Labor Committee's rule for specific job qualifications: "Christ, what the hell do you want—five-foot-eight, blue eyes, a Harvard degree?" As the disillusioned Kuhn commented, "The chairman could have used the man for his personal chauffeur if he wanted to."

The subcommittee's staff was hardly a match for OTP forces, with its forty-four professionals, when the 1972 public broadcasting bill was introduced by Macdonald and Tiernan. And although Macdonald fought valiantly for public broadcasting, he was no match for the forces arrayed against him.

JAPANESE WATER COLORS AND FRENCH COOKING: THE FATE OF PUBLIC BROADCASTING

A major power struggle erupted in the Ninety-second Congress between Torbert Macdonald and Clay Whitehead over the proposed two-year authorization of funds for the Corporation for Public Broadcasting (CPB). Macdonald, a strong supporter of an independent public broadcasting system, sought to strengthen and insulate it from political control. The White House, sensitive to any independent source of criticism, wanted to weaken, if not dismantle, the burgeoning national network. Whitehead was particularly critical of the Washington, D.C., public television news organization, the National Public Affairs Center for Television (NPACT). The resulting clash was bitter and unyielding. The White House won the first round, but the clash continued in the Ninety-third Congress.

The Corporation for Public Broadcasting, with fifteen board members appointed by the president, was established by the Public Broadcasting Act of 1967 to control the flow of federal funds to a maximum of two hundred television stations and five hundred radio stations. The 1967 act also provided for the Public Broadcasting Service (PBS), which represents station managers and distributes programs to supplement local programing. The legislation provided annual appropriations until a long-range financing plan could be developed. The issue between the administration and Congress in 1972 was twofold: should the CPB continue to receive annual appropriations, or should a long range plan be formulated; and how much power should the managing board have over programing and policy-making? The administration position was to minimize the role of CPB, while Congress tended to favor increased, long-range funding of CPB.

In the short time that it had operated, the CPB had developed into a strong competitor to the major networks in news analysis.

It was here that the Nixon administration focused its attacks, even before the issue came before Congress in 1972.

The opening round of the administration's assaults on public broadcasting news programs began in October 1971, when OTP director Clay Whitehead cautioned a National Association of Educational Broadcasters convention in Miami that the educational stations were becoming too centralized and that their news programs were being formulated "by people with essentially similar outlooks." Whitehead attacked control of the media by the "Eastern establishment" and warned broadcasters that such programing would be an open invitation to political scrutiny.* If local stations did not heed his advice by withdrawing their support from CPB's centralizing policies, Whitehead threatened, "permanent financing of public broadcasting will always be somewhere off in the distant future."[19]

Some three months later, in a radio panel discussion on "Politics and Public Broadcasting,"[20] the White House telecommunications director repeated his demand. This time he raised the question whether public television should be carrying public affairs and news commentary at all. Commercial networks adequately cover these areas, Whitehead argued, and he indicated that public television could avoid the criticism it was experiencing if it would abandon controversial programing and news analysis. He concluded his remarks with the heavy-handed threat that "the public television people will have to decide how much of that kind of activity they want to do." The implication was clear: either stop the news analysis that offended the administration or forfeit the possibility of federal funds.

At hearings on freedom of the press before Senator Sam Ervin's Judiciary Subcommittee on Constitutional Rights in early February 1972, the OTP director made the rather remarkable statement—all the more incredible since it was made in the con-

---

* All of this predated, of course, Whitehead's postelection attack on "ideological plugola" in the networks. In 1971 he chose to argue that the presence of network news and public affairs programing made it unnecessary for public television to involve itself in these areas.

text of First Amendment rights—that "no citizen who feels strongly about one or another side of a matter of current public controversy enjoys watching the other side presented."[21] In order to protect the sensitivities of such citizens, Whitehead proposed that public television should be kept "above" faction and controversy. Which, in the words of one House staffer, "would be to reduce public television to showing Japanese water colors and French cooking."

In early 1972, there were two major proposals before the Congress for CPB appropriations. Torbert Macdonald introduced a bill (H.R. 11807) to provide for CPB funding for five years, increasing from $65 million in 1973 to a high of $160 million in 1977. Local public stations were to receive 30 percent of the funds, but CPB would retain control of fund distribution. The administration, on the other hand, proposed that CPB should receive $30 million in 1973, with an additional $15 million allotted directly to the local stations. The House Communications and Power Subcommittee began hearings on the legislation in February 1972.[22] Chairman Macdonald left little doubt as to his antagonism toward the White House Office of Telecommunications Policy and his disapproval of the informal, though constant, communications between OTP and FCC chairman Dean Burch. Macdonald resented what he took to be the political intrusions of the White House into the exclusive domain of Congress and its agency arm, the FCC, in such critical policy areas as cable television, public broadcasting, and license renewal. He set out to cut both Whitehead and his agency down to size: he berated Burch for abdicating his responsibilities to "that nebulous organization downtown [OTP]."[23] Macdonald apparently lashed out at Burch because he was upset by secret White House meetings on cable television, which Burch had attended. He and Tiernan asked Whitehead whether or not presidential adviser Peter Flanigan was behind the administration's growing power in the telecommunications field. When Whitehead artfully dodged Macdonald's questions—which were designed to determine the chain of command between Whitehead and the President—Macdonald's pique reached such proportions that he shouted, "Do you understand that your funds come from the Congress, that the Congress pays your salary?"[24] Although Macdonald's questioning was a legitimate method of eliciting information about OTP, its delivery in the flush of a hot temper lost the chairman some respect.

Other subcommittee members participating in the hearings attacked public broadcasting. While Macdonald, Tiernan, and others were testing OTP's role in the future of the Corporation for Public Broadcasting, Representatives James Collins and William Springer (an *ex-officio* member of the subcommittee as the ranking Republican on the full committee) focused on what they considered to be the failings of public broadcasting since 1967— news analysis and programing. Springer was particularly angry about the salaries being paid to newscasters Sander Vanocur ($85,000), and Robert MacNeil ($65,000). He attacked Vanocur's liberal leanings as they had been expressed in a speech at Duke University, where Vanocur said, "Nixon lies all the time, lies are his version of truth."[25] Springer criticized the former NBC commentator's "psychological frame of mind" and wondered whether Vanocur could abide by the corporation's rules of "strict adherence to objectivity and balance."[26] Another opponent of CPB was Clarence Brown, who in December 1971 had inserted these words against "The Advocates" and "The Great American Dream Machine" into the *Congressional Record*:

> What has already appeared has convinced many that education—in the public broadcasting context—is really a code word for propaganda. It is bad enough that this kind of reactionary, radical hot air goes out over the air waves, but should it be subsidized with hard-earned taxpayer money?[27]

On April 11, 1972, the full committee by a nearly unanimous vote reported out a bill (H.R. 13918) for a two-year funding program for CPB. The bill called for CPB to receive $65 million in 1973 and $90 million in 1974 with 30 percent earmarked for local public radio and television stations.

Extensive attacks on the House floor against CPB's news events failed to shake the conviction of members that, despite occasional lapses and mistakes, public television had provided a unique and valuable contribution to the nation's educational efforts. Among the dissenters was Commerce Committee member Sam Devine, who wanted to restrict programing:

> One would not be concerned with so great a proportion of cultural and public affairs programs . . . if the production entity had a reputation for balanced and objective programing. Key officials and employees of NET have had a record of biased, leftist, and left-leaning programing, and have openly acknowledged their biases.[28]

James Collins compared the corporation's public affairs programs with Russian propaganda agencies. So far as he was concerned, no funds should ever be spent "developing a *Pravda* as an official government TV news propaganda source."[29]

Due to deft handling by subcommittee members Lionel Van Deerlin and Robert Tiernan, both vigorous supporters of public television, the Macdonald bill managed to ward off crippling amendments and passed the House on June 1, 1972, by a vote of twenty-five to sixty-nine.[30]

The Senate Commerce Committee, with a minimum of debate, passed on June 20 a bill similar to the House bill. The committee felt Congress was "once again" called upon to authorize funding for CPB because neither the Johnson nor the Nixon administrations had developed the long-range funding plan called for by Congress.

In late June, the Macdonald bill came to the Senate floor, where Senator Pastore wanted it to pass without amendment. Senator Baker, however, pressed an amendment to limit the authorization to one year at $45 million, claiming that this apparently unfriendly amendment might actually help public television by heightening pressure on the White House to present its frequently promised, but as yet undelivered, plan for long-range financing. Baker then proceeded to air his own complaints—

against CPB's screening of a ballet containing fleeting nudity, Sander Vanocur's salary, and the antiadministration views presented on a five-hour WNET-TV program on Vietnam. But Baker's arguments did not prove persuasive to a majority of his colleagues; his amendment was defeated, fifty-eight to twenty-six.[31]

Just before the final vote was taken on the two-year authorization, Senator Lowell Weicker, the independent-minded Republican from Connecticut, took the floor to state that the central issue in the White House opposition to the authorization was not the duration of the funding, the question of salaries, or the problems of a national television network. In his opinion, Baker was expressing the President's displeasure with some of the political views public television had broadcast. In Weicker's words, "The administration does not like federally financed criticism."[32] Baker heatedly rejected Weicker's interpretation of his motives, but Weicker refused to retract the charge.

The Senate passed the House version of the Macdonald bill on June 22, 1972, by a vote of eighty-two to one.

On the very day that Pastore was guiding the Macdonald bill safely through the Senate, Macdonald was setting in motion a plan that would ultimately backfire and destroy his bill. On the House floor, Macdonald proposed an amendment to an appropriations bill that would have cut OTP's funding by two-thirds, from $3 to $1 million dollars for fiscal 1973. Macdonald criticized OTP as little more than "the administration's tool for muzzling the media and controlling the FCC."[33] That day he proudly boasted that the administration's attempt to transform public broadcasting into a localized, innocuous, impotent service had failed miserably in Congress.

The proposed cut in the OTP budget, designed to bring the agency to its knees, or at least to chasten its "czar," failed 188–148. Yet Macdonald's staff thought that the support from more than a third of the House would stun OTP into the realization that Congress would not sit idly by while the White House tried to dismantle public broadcasting.

If OTP was stunned, Congress was shocked. Eight days later,

despite its overwhelming approval by both House and Senate, Macdonald's public broadcasting bill was vetoed by President Nixon. Macdonald was shocked. Senator Pastore pointed an accusing finger at "someone down at the White House who is carrying a chip on his shoulder against public TV." Lionel Van Deerlin attributed the veto to "a petulant and petty President who is unable to tolerate any independent sources of criticism." The chairman of the full House Commerce Committee, Harley Staggers, was equally upset by the unanticipated move because, as he put it, public broadcasting is not properly "a political matter."

Brian Lamb, Whitehead's assistant at OTP, asserts that the "shoddy treatment" accorded administration views in Congress, not simply opposition to public broadcasting, precipitated the veto. According to Lamb, the Senate gave only a cursory glance to the President's position, because Pastore was more interested in getting the bill through the Senate without amendments than in listening to the administration's objections. Worse still, to his mind, was the response in the House, where Macdonald used the February 1972 public broadcasting hearings as a forum to insult and humiliate Whitehead. Besides demeaning Whitehead's qualifications and competence in communications, Macdonald continually questioned the right of the President's chief communications adviser to speak for the administration. OTP viewed the entire episode as a direct slap at the President. When Macdonald proposed cutting OTP's budget, the administration decided to fight back; Whitehead asserted that a new agency could not sit back and suffer repeated assaults from its detractors without losing its credibility and effectiveness.

If the veto served notice that OTP was beyond congressional criticism, its more immediate effect was to seriously weaken public broadcasting. Because of the veto, CPB-announced plans for a new national children's series had to be scrapped, public affairs programing suffered cutbacks, and pending requests from twelve new television stations to join the network had to be shelved. The veto also demoralized the corporation, leading to the resignation of CPB's chairman, president, vice president, and director of television in the summer of 1972. The "general state of alarm" at CPB was reflected in President John Macy's parting comment that President Nixon's reelection would be "the death blow to public television as I envision it."[34]

Congress saw the "handwriting on the wall," and bowed to the President's wishes. In July and August, the Senate and the House passed S. 3824 to provide $45 million in 1973 to the Corporation for Public Broadcasting. The President's request for $15 million to be earmarked for local public stations, though, was not included in the bill. Representative Macdonald, sponsor of the earlier five-year CPB authorization, urged support of S. 3824

> without further delay, and without amendments that would nit-pick and quibble and serve only to make the public broadcasting people more insecure and frightened of vague and formless threats to their existence.[35]

The President signed the bill (PL 92–411) on August 29, 1972.

While passage of the post-veto bill represented a clear victory for the administration, it guaranteed a continuation of the struggle of which it was the product. As the Ninety-third Congress began, Pastore and Macdonald, with CPB and PBS support, introduced modest authorization bills providing $140 million for two years. Whitehead testified that the figure should be cut to $45 million for one year and that CPB should only be funded on a year-to-year basis until its "basic problems" were worked out. The President, however, his political stock seriously eroded by the Watergate scandal, signed the two-year authorization on August 6, 1973. By this time, Senator Baker and Representative Brown, ranking Republicans on the Communications Subcommittee, had been able to reduce the authorization by $10 million by invoking the specter of a veto.[36]

The White House meanwhile has increased its efforts to compromise CPB independence through political appointments and OTP pressure. Former Representative Thomas Curtis, appointed

CPB chairman by President Nixon in 1972, supported administration-backed moves whereby CPB took over many programing functions previously controlled by the station licensees through PBS, and then proceeded to discontinue a large number of public-affairs programs. Even Curtis, however, in March 1973 displayed an independence of mind of which the men in the Nixon White House were wary:

> There are people in the White House who feel that you can't do public affairs objectively and with balance and therefore [they would] throw the baby out with the bathwater. . . . I happen to think that one can argue objectively for a point of view and do it with objectivity and balance.[37]

What Curtis meant is perhaps best exemplified in a comment special consultant to the president Patrick J. Buchanan made before a Dick Cavett television audience at about the same time:

> If you look at public television, you find you've got Sander Vanocur and Robert MacNeil, the first of whom, Sander Vanocur, is a notorious Kennedy psychopath, in my judgment, and Robert MacNeil, who is anti-administration. You have Elizabeth Drew—she personally is definitely not pro-Administration, I would say anti-Administration. "Washington Week in Review" is unbalanced against us, and you have Bill Moyers, who is unbalanced against the Administration.
>
> And then for a fig leaf, William Buckley's program. So they [Congress] sent down there a $165 million package [public broadcasting bill], voted 82-to-1, out of the Senate, thinking that Richard Nixon would therefore have to sign it, he couldn't possibly have the courage to veto something like that. And Mr. Nixon, I'm delighted to say, hit the ball about 450 feet down the right field foul line, right into the stands, and now you've got a different situation in public television. You've got a new board on the Corporation for Public Broadcasting, you've got a new awareness that people are concerned about balance. And all this Administration

has ever asked on that or on network television frankly, is a fair shake.

But Curtis and the White House differed, as it turned out, on what a "fair shake" required. Curtis led in the development of a compromise plan on programing whereby CPB would continue to determine how federal funds were expended, local licensees would retain control over scheduling, and a joint CPB–PBS panel would pass on programs contested for "balance and objectivity." Ralph Rogers, who as PBS board chairman represented the local stations, relates what happened then:

> We pursued this plan for three months, and we had a complete agreement worked out, and a majority of the [CPB] board were in favor of this agreement, and then, all of a sudden, something happened. The question is what happened. I suspect it was Mr. Whitehead who happened.[38]

Specifically, White House pressures led to a ten-to-four decision by the CPB board to defer action on the compromise plan. This prompted Curtis' resignation in April 1973 and revealed once again the transparency of concern for "localism" professed in the President's 1972 veto message:

> With its latest coup, the Administration has, in effect, let it be known that its goal is not a decentralized Public Broadcasting System, but one that is submissive to the will—and thus to the disguised central control—of the Office of Telecommunications.[39]

Curtis, PBS's Rogers mused, is "a fine gentleman and an outstanding Republican" who would be unlikely to resign "unless he felt that there had been improper influence." As matters stand, he added, local stations "don't know whether negotiating with the [CPB] board is negotiating with an independent group or negotiating with Mr. Whitehead."[40] His expressed puzzlement was in part rhetorical, however, for the White House's quest for control was becoming increasingly evident, as was the administration's immediate purpose: to eliminate the transmission of public affairs programs via the PBS network.* It was a scheme public television's professed congressional supporters decried, but were doing little to stop.

OTP'S WIRE-CLIPPING SERVICE

Sherlock Holmes, in a famous case, calls Watson's attention to the curious activity of a watchdog during the night of a murder. When Watson points out that the dog did nothing on that night, Holmes replied, "That, sir, was the curious activity." Congress has engaged in a similar curious activity during "the night of the cable television murder." From all that can be learned, Congress did not have a direct hand in the formulation of the policy to determine the course of cable's development in the coming decades. No member was involved in negotiations and no staffer contributed to the deliberations. However, the role of the Senate Communications Subcommittee was important at one juncture: Senator Pastore opened the door to executive and industry intervention, giving presidentially appointed officials the opportunity to reverse the FCC's proposed policy toward the expansion of cable TV. Watchdog Congress not only let the intruder in without a bark; it opened the door.

The potential of community antennae, or cable, television (CATV) is a great unknown to most Americans. It was born some twenty years ago in Landsford, Pennsylvania, when a TV salesman installed an antenna atop a nearby mountain and ran a cable down into the valley to provide local reception. Cable can carry television programs from great distances into areas that

---

* Developments in 1974 raised further questions as to whether even a "tamed" CPB could satisfy the administration. Whitehead, preparing to leave OTP, prepared a long-promised bill providing long-range financing for CPB. Nixon at first rejected the bill, intimating that he wanted to phase out federal funding of the CPB system, but in July he reversed himself and sent the bill forward. The Senate Commerce Committee increased OTP's authorization figures and reported the bill, but after its re-referral to the Senate Appropriations Committee it died, partly because of disputes between CPB and PBS over the distribution of funds.

have been unable to receive over-the-air signals. By 1970 the National Cable Television Association (NCTA) estimated that the 2,500 cable systems in the United States served 5.4 million homes, or approximately 9 percent of the nation's 60 million television households. The profits realized from that relatively small market amounted to some $300 million per year.[41] If the nation were fully wired for cable, marketable communications services and products would yield an estimated $40 to $60 billion annually.[42]

At present, the system provides little more than sharp reception and diversified programing from distant stations. But with two-way terminal connections, cable could offer a wide array of communications services. Instead of the four to ten stations possible with very-high-frequency (VHF) transmission, eighty or more channels could provide low-cost, all-day educational programing and community dialogue; police and emergency services; burglar alarms and surveillance services; shopping by wire; instant credit and bank transfers; electronic mail; and newspaper facsimile delivery. Home terminals could also permit viewer response and two-way communication. Minicomputers could even allow nearly instantaneous connection between the home and a doctor's office. Patients wearing a special vest could have their body temperature, blood pressure, respiration, and heartbeats monitored by their physicians without ever leaving home. Moreover, cable can relay information with startling speed. A facsimile of *Gone With the Wind*, for example, could be transmitted in about twenty seconds. The Bible would take a little longer—about half a minute.[43] If viewers paid to see first-run movies, local athletic contests, community players and events without commercials, advertising monies would not be needed for production. As OTP director Clay Whitehead said in a July 1971 speech to the NCTA:

> I think it is safe to say that we all view the development of cable as the most important single policy issue on the communications front—perhaps one of the most significant domestic issues of this decade.[44]

The vast potential of cable TV, due to the relatively simple . task of delivering off-the-air signals, has been stifled, however, by copyright owners* and by broadcasters, who perceive cable as a threat to their viewing audience and advertising profits. Broadcasters and copyright owners have been lobbying Congress and the FCC to stop the expansion of cable systems into their markets. The FCC responded with several rulings in 1966 and 1968 which put a virtual freeze on further cable.† In 1971 the NAB made Pastore one of its targets in their campaign against cable. The senator received letters from thirty-five colleagues who urged him to hold hearings "in order that the Federal Communications Commission be given proper congressional guidance and direction" on the future of cable TV.⁴⁵ James Eastland, chairman of the Judiciary Committee, majority leader Mike Mansfield, former Republican national chairman Robert Dole, and former Vice

---

* Copyright owners, such as movie and television producers, had become involved in the cable squabble in 1968, when the Supreme Court ruled in the *Fortnightly* case that cable operators need not pay copyright fees for the retransmission of programs picked off the air.⁴⁶ The court's decision hinged on its determination that a retransmitted broadcast signal is not a "performance" within the meaning of the 1909 Copyright Act, and hence is not granted the privilege of monopoly-power protection. From the copyright owner's view, the decision legalized cable's "piracy" of television programing.

The copyright holders' attorney, Louis Nizer, took their case to Congress. He succeeded in getting the House Judiciary Committee to report out a bill protecting the copyright interests against CATV. However, the Judiciary Committee became embroiled in a jurisdictional dispute with the Commerce Committee over control of CATV legislation. The section concerning CATV was then stricken from the bill. Since then, Senator McClellan's pro-cable Copyright Subcommittee has been trying to devise new copyright legislation. So far it has been unable to report out a satisfactory proposal.

† In the *Southwestern Cable* case, the Supreme Court affirmed FCC's regulatory jurisdiction over cable. In the FCC's 1966 *Second Report and Order*, the agency declared that no cable system could import signals into the top one hundred population centers without authorization from local stations or proof to the FCC that importation would not adversely affect local broadcasters.⁴⁷ The commission changed the rules in December 1968 to a flat ban on all cable importations in the largest markets, unless local stations granted prior retransmission consent.⁴⁸

President Hubert Humphrey were among those induced by the NAB to write to Pastore.

Pastore responded to the widespread interest with hearings in July 1971. At the hearings FCC chairman Dean Burch reported on a recently completed study of cable that included feasibility studies by the Rand Corporation, experiments, evaluation of alternative proposals, and a series of public panel hearings.[49] Burch said the FCC would be ready by August to present Congress with a proposal for future cable development—"not to please broadcasters; not to please cable, but because we believe it is our obligation in the public interest."[50]

As the hearings came to a close, Pastore asked Burch "as a courtesy" if he would "informally sit down with our committee to talk the thing out for a while to see what we can do" when the commission finalized its proposed cable policy. FCC commissioner Robert Bartley shook his head and warned, "It sounds like delay to me." There would be no delay, Pastore answered: "Within twenty-four hours after you agree among yourselves, we will sit down with you. Do you call that delay?"[51] "Dangerous precedent," is what House Commerce minority counsel Lewis Berry called it. In his view, "Pastore's action was an open invitation for the interests to rewrite the rules."[52] Powerful pressures might have made for a "rewriting" in any case, but Pastore's move certainly facilitated the process.

On August 5 the FCC completed its deliberations. But the commission chose not to promulgate its decision in the customary form of a "rule and order." Instead, Burch responded to Pastore's resquest and took what he admitted was the "extraordinary step of coming to Congress with a Letter of Intent."[53] In his letter to the chairmen of the Communications subcommittees, Burch wrote:

> Ample opportunity has been afforded to all interested parties to present their views on the subject. The policies put forward here result from an intensive study of the issues, a balancing of all the equities, and represent our best judgment on the regulatory course that should be followed.[54]

The FCC proposed to end the freeze on cable development "so that the public may receive its benefits without, at the same time, jeopardizing the basic structure of over-the-air television."[55] For this purpose, it devised a formula that would allow cable systems in the largest one hundred markets to import two out-of-market signals in addition to the local signals carried to provide "minimum" service.* Cable systems in smaller areas would be restricted to the three network stations and one independent station required for "minimum" service. The rationale behind the restrictive regulatory scheme was that broadcasters in the smaller markets were likely to suffer a severe loss of profit from cable's competition and needed protection.[56]

Instead of calling a meeting of his subcommittee and FCC commissioners to discuss the proposed policy with the commission, Senator Pastore inserted the FCC's Letter of Intent into the *Congressional Record* with a request that all interested members respond to it.

"The broadcasters and copyright owners were nearly beside themselves when they saw the published letter," reports Burch's assistant, Chuck Lichtenstein. "They vowed to do everything possible to stop the proposed cable expansion." For the broadcast-industry lobbyists, "everything possible" amounted to a great deal. Burch's assistant conceded that "with their political muscle the broadcasters and their allies could very easily block us in the Congress and then nibble the policy to death." In the Senate Commerce Committee minority counsel's words, "The interests came in here screaming, 'Save us, save us!'" Dean Burch himself recounted that he had been "importuned by copyright owners, who came pleading that their interests had been ignored in the proposed rules" (although they had participated extensively in the lengthy FCC proceedings).

The broadcasters and copyright owners then turned to the White House and OTP director Whitehead. The broadcasters had good reason to believe that White House involvement would re-

* Three network and three independent stations were required in markets 1–50, three networks and two independents in 51–100.

sult in policy shifts favorable to them. Despite Spiro Agnew's attacks on news programing, the Nixon administration had spent much of its time wooing the broadcasters. With the help of Washington-wise lawyer Louis Nizer and former Lyndon Johnson aide Jack Valenti, Whitehead arranged secret bargaining sessions in mid-November 1971 with a handful of financially interested parties (broadcasters, cable operators, and copyright owners) for the purpose of rewriting cable policy. Whitehead explained that the executive branch was involved in the negotiations because the participants "did not feel it was appropriate to involve members of the FCC in trying to work out an agreement."[57]

Having suffered the pangs of both lobbyist attacks and White House pressure, "Dean Burch concluded that there had to be negotiations to settle the differences that arose over the Letter of Intent."[58] Burch attended the secret White House meeting in November 1971, even though as an FCC commissioner he was bound by the Administrative Procedure Act, which requires that all rule-making and adjudication processes be open to the public.

The "consensus" agreement reached by the White House, broadcasters, copyright owners, cable operators, and FCC chairman Burch favored cable obstructionists and turned out to be costly to the public. The copyright owners exacted a guarantee of monopoly-power exclusivity, "for the run of the contract," for all programs in the top fifty markets and of two years' exclusivity in markets fifty-one to one hundred. In other words, the right of a program supplier to sell, and of a station to buy, an "exclusive" right to a given program in a given market area was extended to guarantee not only that another local station would not carry the program but also that a cable system could not import the program from an out-of-market station. As Nicholas Johnson explained in his dissent from the FCC's later approval of the agreement:

> Translated into concrete examples, based on current programming and currently existing contractual arrangements a cable system in Charlotte, North Carolina, the forty-second market, would have to black out over 16 hours a day

of programming from WTCG–TV, Atlanta, Georgia, if it chose to import that station. . . . Obviously, we can expect to find a rush to exclusive contracts in the future to permit local stations to take advantage of this FCC-sanctioned anticompetitive device.[59]

FCC studies show that this exclusivity arrangement will increase owner profits by at least 40 percent.* The major broadcasters will also profit from the arrangement since they are guaranteed retention of a captive audience.

The broadcasters likewise were spared competition by a changed definition of the "viewing standard." The agreement raised to 2 percent (from 1 percent in the Letter of Intent) the number of viewers who must *already* view a station outside a thirty-five-mile radius in order for it to be placed on a cable system as a "local" station. In effect, this reduced by approximately one-half the number of such stations that could be carried without counting against a cable system's quota of out-of-market signals.

Finally, severe limits were placed on a cable system's right to import signals from the top twenty-five markets, that is, from the most desirable stations. "It would appear," the Letter of Intent had stated, "that the minimum number of distant signals that might reasonably open the way for cable development is two additional signals not available in the community."[61] In the final decision, however, it was provided that a cable system could reach out only to the *two closest* among the top twenty-five cities. Only when exclusivity arrangements required the system to black out one or both of these signals could a system go nationwide for programing.

These industry-induced changes did not merely modify the policy in the FCC Letter of Intent; they reversed it. The basic thrust

---

* A study by Harbridge House, Inc., attempted to calculate the loss of revenues to program producers resulting from the loss of first-run exclusivity. The study assumed, as the best estimate available, that loss of exclusivity reduces the value of a first-run film by 40 percent and even more in the case of series programs.[60]

of the FCC's original plan had been to encourage cable development throughout the nation while protecting the smaller, more vulnerable broadcasters; the industry-devised rules do just the opposite. The result is most aptly described by former FCC planning director Ken Goodwin:

> The only ones who gain from this are the copyright owners and the major broadcasters. The cable people and the FCC went along because otherwise the cable freeze would have continued indefinitely. They were willing to take some thaw and development over the prospect of no development whatsoever. . . . It was the public who got left out.

The interests of small broadcasters and independent ultra-high-frequency (UHF) stations, on the other hand, were ignored in these back-stairs deals. Although they were the most vulnerable to economic injury from cable expansion, they were neither represented at the negotiations nor protected on the copyright issue, as were the top markets. Since they lacked economic and political clout at the secret negotiations, they were sacrificed by the NAB to the cable owners in order to effect a consensus agreement.

Where Was the Donnybrook?

The White House denies that its role in the affair was anything other than that of "a neutral observer, responsible to the public interest, in working out an agreement that would be in the public interest." In February 1972, Clay Whitehead explained to the House Communications and Power Subcommittee that he had organized the trilateral discussions among the broadcasters, copyright, and cable interests because "these people wanted to reach an agreement among themselves, thinking that would be best for themselves and the public." Brian Lamb, Whitehead's assistant, went one step further, to argue that the president's appointed representatives, rather than the elected officials of Congress, best represent the public interest:

> The August 5th Letter of Intent produced an explosive situation on the Hill. The broadcasters and the copyright people

were not going to allow the FCC's policy to go into effect without some sort of royalties and market protection. The issue threatened to embroil the Congress in an insoluble problem that would postpone cable expansion for years. Our involvement avoided an open donnybrook on the Hill between the competing interests. The consensus allowed the offended parties to negotiate a mutually agreeable settlement that would protect their economic interests and open the way for some cable development. For cable it was either the consensus or nothing. OTP was the most appropriate agency to mediate the differences because we represent the President. It is he alone who is elected by all of the people. So, even better than the Congress, he is able to represent the public interest.

The 1972 agreement was not viewed by OTP as an optimal solution; on the contrary, OTP officials portrayed it as an interim settlement that would permit them to formulate a more adequate plan for cable deregulation and development. But the agreement was likely to define the relationships among the interested parties for many years, and OTP, in carrying out and defending the negotiations, proved itself willing to define the "public interest" as nothing more substantive than "what the economic forces will agree to." Commerce Committee staff members seemed to use a similar definition. Minority counsel Ward White, for example, explained that the Senate Commerce Committee's role is "to resolve conflicts among the economic interests." He justified the privately arranged consensus agreement by stating:

A decision had to be made. *That* was the public interest. Oh, I know there should be public hearings, but nothing would ever get done if you had to have more public hearings. Sometimes decisions have to be made. Burch is to be commended for pushing the compromise along. Right or wrong he had to make a decision.

Burch defended his role before the Senate Communications Subcommittee:

I met individually with representatives of the copyright, the cable, and the broadcasters. I got nowhere. . . . Thereafter, Mr. Whitehead did have further meetings with the three groups and a document which was the skeleton of the so-called consensus agreement emerged. I will say that at all times I knew what was in the document and I knew the evolution of the passages in the document. Ultimately, at the time the industries were asked to accede to this agreement, I spoke individually to members of that industry and pointed up what I thought were the shortcomings of the document and the long suits of the document. During all the time we were discussing this so-called consensus agreement, I pointed up to the parties involved that failing agreement of any sort the Commission would proceed with its August 5 letter, as we indicated to you.[62]

The FCC chairman viewed his role in the negotiations as an attempt to unplug congressional blockage of cable development: "We tried to put people in a position where no one gains from blocking the compromise."[63] In Burch's rationale, negotiations gave "the broadcasters and the copyright owners enough gain so that it was to their advantage to let the compromise go through." He did not explain why these negotiations could not be in public and why they were not held at the FCC instead of the White House.

Burch entered into closed session with industry spokesmen, acceded to their rewrite of the commission's rules, and then presented their version to the commission on February 2, 1972, on a take-it-or-leave-it basis.* Burch claims that the cable policy reflected FCC findings.[65] OTP staffers and other FCC commissioners provide a different scenario: political power brokers carved out the policy at the White House to suit the economic interests of the existing industries. The FCC chairman then pre-

---

* FCC Commissioner Robert E. Lee, a strong supporter of the independent UHF system, condemned the entire procedure whereby FCC commissioners were handed a "consensus" agreement to vote on as "most regrettable, unfair, and perhaps in violation of the legal requirements of the Administrative Procedures Act."[64]

sented the industry-dictated results to independent regulatory commissioners, not for their individual evaluation and discussion, but as a *fait accompli*. Commissioners Charlotte Reid, Richard Wiley, and Robert T. Bartley went along with the chairman, but not without explaining, in Wiley's words, that "the choice realistically confronting the Commission was this particular program— or none at all."[66]

Burch's definition of public interest seemed to be similar to that held by White and the OTP. When it was suggested in the House subcommittee hearings that cable would be free to develop if it were not for the FCC's protectionist attitude toward broadcasters, Burch replied, "Well, we are concerned with the health of the *existing* industry. It was that industry we were set up *to regulate and promote*" (emphasis added). At the Senate hearings Burch told the members of the Communications Subcommittee that cable was a complex problem "because it involves emotions as much as it does facts and data." Senator Pastore shot back the peppery comment: "You left out one ingredient. It involves a lot of money, too."[67] What the negotiations had sought was control of the "gold."* The allotment was determined in the White House on the basis of power and political considerations. As Burch later explained, "Very frankly, we roll logs here. That is the way things are done in this town." The logrolling, he admitted, is not done for the public's benefit. "What the lobbyists want is to protect their own economic self-interest, not the citizen's right."

The Justice Department, which describes itself as "the executive agency charged with responsibility for protecting the public interest," did not share the White House's interpretations of the public interest. The Justice Department's statement filed with the FCC in September 1969 had noted, "It is not the purpose of public policy to protect the highly profitable broadcast industry from potential competition, particularly at the expense of diversity for the viewing public." The Justice Department had recommended instead a situation in which "the commission actively fosters competition

---

* This fulfills Nicholas Johnson's wry version of the Golden Rule: "Them that has the gold makes the rule."

among communications media and prevents private agreements from restricting CATV's future."[68]

But the FCC did not follow this advice. Instead, Chairman Burch justified negotiating with private interests by saying that "the affected parties have the wisdom that is necessary to formulate a plan for the future." Chuck Lichtenstein explained why the FCC did not follow the Justice Department's advice: "It is nice to be above the battle and be able to issue sweeping statements on public policy. The Justice Department doesn't seem to live with the political reality of the situation." The political reality, according to one of Whitehead's staffers, had more to do with private political advantage than with public policy: "The administration didn't care how the cable issue was settled. Its main goal was to keep the broadcasters happy during the election year."

Nicholas Johnson highlighted the breakdown of effective public control of policy formulation:

> In future years, when students of law or government wish to study the decision-making process at its worst, when they look for examples of industry domination of government, when they look for Presidential interference in the operation of an agency responsible to Congress, they will look to the FCC handling of the never-ending saga of cable television as a classic study. It is unfortunate, if not fatal, that the decision must be described in these terms, for of the national communications policy questions before us, none is more important to the country's future than cable television.[69]

6

Health and Environment

For Chairman Paul Rogers and his colleagues on the House Public Health and Environment Subcommittee it is more than a matter of historical curiosity that the main function of the Public Health Service in its early years was to provide health care for merchant seamen. It is because of this fact that most health legislation in the House originally fell and continues to fall under the jurisdiction of the Interstate and Foreign Commerce Committee. In the Senate such matters are generally handled by the Labor and Public Welfare Committee.* The related area of environmental protection is handled in large part by the Commerce committees in both houses. The addition of "and Environment" to the name of

NOTE: This chapter was written by David E. Price.

* A critical exception is health insurance, which, because it is tied to the social security tax, is handled by the Ways and Means Committee in the House and the Finance Committee in the Senate. In 1974 the House broadened Commerce's responsibility for health-care programs not financed by payroll taxes.

the House Public Health Subcommittee in the Ninety-second Congress reflected the increased importance of this issue area, though not a major shift in the subcommittee's preoccupations. A Senate Commerce Subcommittee on Environment was formed in 1969; Philip Hart has served since then as chairman and Frank Moss as co-chairman.

THE POLITICS OF HEALTH

When Harley Staggers was asked to name the House Commerce Committee's proudest accomplishments, he invariably catalogued the health measures processed in recent years. The list is indeed rather impressive, and members often portray Paul Rogers' Public Health and Environment Subcommittee as "the most active and productive in the House." During the Ninety-second Congress the subcommittee reported bills aimed at the expansion of health manpower and nurse-training aid, the establishment of a federal drug abuse office and treatment program, an attack on sickle-cell anemia, a major research effort on cancer, stepped-up heart and lung research, the establishment of health maintenance organizations, and the formation of a National Institute of Aging within the National Institutes of Health. Members credit much of this legislation to Paul Rogers, who has been able to pull together a smoothly functioning subcommittee and to gain from the chairman a relatively free hand in developing a legislative program.

Rogers and his subcommittee are not usually the source of major policy innovations, and as Chapter 1 (see Table 8) shows, they frequently kill health bills which come to them from Edward Kennedy's Health Subcommittee and the Senate. Still, health stands out as the area of House Commerce's greatest productivity. The committee reported twenty bills in the area in the Ninety-second Congress—this represented more than one-third of its total output—and steered all of them to House passage. That the Rogers subcommittee often processes legislation coming from the Senate or the executive with efficiency and dispatch is especially impressive in light of the sluggishness of Interstate and Foreign

Commerce in other areas. Moreover, the legislative reformulations and refinements put forward by the subcommittee are often of considerable originality and scope.

Members often describe Rogers and John Moss, chairman of the Commerce and Finance Subcommittee until 1975, as the two activists among the House Commerce subcommittee chairmen. But Rogers is placed in a class by himself as a tactician. "I really don't know how Moss's record would compare," said one staff man, "but he is an 'idealist' in a different sense than Rogers. He hates to compromise and will often dig in on relatively inconsequential points. Rogers is much better at bargaining and persuading people to go along." A glance at Rogers' record suggests that this flexibility is not an unmixed blessing. At times he might have been better advised to "dig in"—as in his handling of the Radiation Control Act of 1968.

When it was revealed in 1967 that General Electric had found it necessary to recall ninety thousand color television sets that leaked x-radiation in excess of levels generally accepted as safe, Rogers seized the issue. He berated HEW's National Center for Radiological Health and introduced legislation providing for the development and administration of standards for radiation emissions from electronic products. Senator E. L. Bartlett (D., Alaska) and others with long-standing credentials in the area were disturbed by what they perceived as Rogers' sensationalism and his reluctance to open up the potentially more important (and more controversial) matter of the x-radiation dangers related to medical and dental equipment and practice. After the Senate passed a rigorous bill, it became clear that Rogers intended to stand by the weaker, industry-approved House version in conference. Rogers withheld his approval until provisions in the Senate bill for defective-product seizure, on-site plant inspection, worker protection, and the development of advisory standards for the licensing of x-ray technicians were dropped from the compromise measure. "Your conferees met, struggled, and won," Ancher Nelsen, ranking Republican on the Public Health Subcommittee, announced to the House.[1] But those seeking a strong radiation-protection bill were inclined to view the performance in considerably less heroic terms.

Rogers' ambition and industry have made him a uniquely productive Commerce member. It is widely believed that he aspires to the Senate and, indeed, he has increasingly sought to play the kind of entrepreneurial role that has become associated with senators seeking media exposure and national recognition for policy leadership. Although Rogers has remained overshadowed by Senate Health Subcommittee chairman Kennedy in this regard, given the formidability of such competition and the frequent inhospitability of the House to such efforts, Rogers has done rather well for himself.[2] The Conquest of Cancer Act of 1971 and the subcommittee-reported proposal of 1972 to underwrite the formation of health maintenance organizations are two illustrations of the impact of Rogers and his subcommittee and the conditions under which they operate.

Cancer Research: The House Leaves its Mark

House members were not prominent among those initially attempting in 1970 to instigate an increased federal effort in cancer research. The prime movers were Mary Lasker, a philanthropist whose contacts in the world of science are extensive and whose lobbying on behalf of increased medical research has been unstinting; Ralph Yarborough (D., Tex.), Edward Kennedy, and other long-time Senate champions of Lasker causes; and President Nixon, who knew an appealing issue when he saw one and hoped to gain the initiative. The effort in many ways harked back to the machinations of the medical research partisans whom Elizabeth Drew dubbed "Washington's noble conspirators." During the fifties and sixties Mary Lasker, NIH Director James Shannon, House Labor-HEW Appropriations Subcommittee Chairman John Fogarty and Senator Lister Hill, chairman of both the Labor and Public Welfare Committee and the Labor-HEW Appropriations Subcommittee, functioned as a "highly polished quartet," bringing a parade of evangelistic medical researchers before congressional committees and systematically stepping up the health appropriations requests of Democratic and Republican presidents alike.[3]

The last major research authorization prior to the Conquest of Cancer Act was the Heart Disease, Cancer, and Stroke Amendments of 1965.[4] Lasker's strategy in that instance had been to secure the appointment of a presidential commission, whose proposal for the establishment of regional research and treatment "complexes" became the basis for an administration bill. The Senate, which usually took the initiative in such matters, acted first; it modified the administration bill to insure NIH administration and control, a primary focus on research, and the strengthening of existing medical schools and hospitals as opposed to the construction of new facilities. The House Interstate and Foreign Commerce Committee under Oren Harris was quite hostile to the bill; it cut back authorization figures drastically and collaborated with the American Medical Association in devising a series of amendments designed to give practicing physicians a decisive role in the operation of the program.

The 1971 cancer episode was striking for both the continuities and discontinuities it displayed with this earlier effort. Lasker's energies remained unflagging and her political and scientific connections unsurpassed. Yarborough and Kennedy could not match Senator Hill's monopoly of the health area, but they considered themselves his heirs as promoters of medical research. There was also a continuity in strategy: Lasker, working in close concert with the American Cancer Society, again utilized a study commission to launch her crusade, although with Nixon in the White House she was less certain of the executive branch's reliability and turned instead to her Senate allies to set up the commission. More significant differences were apparent with respect to other participants in the earlier battles. The House Commerce Committee had a less conservative chairman, and a vigorous partisan of health research at the helm of the Public Health Subcommittee; if this promised to make the House's role less negative and obstructive, it also promised greater energy and assertiveness. Equally striking was the fall of NIH from the favored position it had always enjoyed under Fogarty and Hill. Partisans of stepped-up research were in fact prepared to bypass NIH in order to assure adequate funding and energetic administration for the cancer program. The change had less to do with new faces on Capitol Hill than with the perceived loss of NIH's independence and political clout. Director James Shannon and other resourceful administrators either left or were forced out, one Labor and Public Welfare staff member explained, and OMB and HEW were largely successful in their attempts to assert budgetary and administrative control over the agency. To leave the cancer program within NIH's National Cancer Institute thus seemed to invite bureaucratic routinization and trade-offs with other research efforts.

The Senate in 1970 unanimously approved a Yarborough resolution authorizing the Labor and Public Welfare Committee to study the most expeditious means of advancing the attack on cancer. The committee subsequently formed a Panel of Consultants on the Conquest of Cancer, consisting mainly of Lasker allies and past or present American Cancer Society board members. After four months of deliberation the panel made its report, which recommended an increase in federal spending on cancer research from the 1970 level of $234 million to $400 million in 1972, and a rise by annual increments to a total of $1 billion by 1976. The panel also recommended that in recognition of the urgency of finding a cure for cancer, the National Cancer Institute should be replaced by a new superagency, which would be independent of NIH and whose director would report directly to the president.[5] When the Ninety-second Congress convened, Edward Kennedy, who fell heir to the Health Subcommittee upon Ralph Yarborough's defeat, joined with ranking Labor and Public Welfare Republican Jacob Javits in introducing a bill based on the panel's recommendation.

President Nixon, meanwhile, sensed an issue in the making. In his 1971 State of the Union Message he called for a "total national commitment" to the search for a cure for cancer and announced that he would ask for an additional $100 million to launch the campaign. The administration expressed misgivings about the administrative scheme proposed in the Senate bill, however. "From both a scientific and a managerial standpoint," Surgeon General Jesse Steinfeld told the Senate subcommittee in March, "we believe that the formation of a separate authority outside NIH and HEW would be a serious mistake."*

Representative Rogers shared these misgivings. He was by no means always a partisan of administrative coherence and consolidation. In fact, one of the charges most often leveled against him was that he was all too willing to wreak administrative havoc for the sake of making a legislative splash (as with his proposal to form a separate Institute of Aging) or of maximizing his subcommittee's opportunities for oversight and review (as with his pet proposal for a separate Department of Health). But in the case of cancer research he decided that it was a bad idea to begin a process that might in the end lead to the dismantling of NIH; he correctly anticipated that similar efforts to give special priority to other diseases would follow.

In addition, what one HEW official dubbed the "trade-mark factor"—the sense that there should be a distinctive House "mark" on the bill—was at work. This consideration was especially important for Rogers because the cancer legislation was the first major bill processed by the subcommittee under his chairmanship. He wanted to be identified with cancer research, but with the field already so crowded it was not easy to carve out a distinctive role. The question of how the research effort should be organized and administered thus gave him an important opening. On September 15, 1971—two months after the Senate passed the Kennedy bill—Rogers offered a bill "to strengthen the National Cancer Institute and the National Institutes of Health in order to conquer cancer and the other major killer diseases as soon as possible."

Although the provision for a new agency in the Senate bill was

---

* The administration did at this point contemplate a plan, however, whereby a new Bureau of Cancer Research would be placed under a director having the status of deputy director of NIH and the NCI would be "elevated into the bureau."[6]

evidence of the decline of NIH's independence and political potency, Rogers' move and the support it received demonstrated the special loyalty the Institutes still commanded among legislators. As one high HEW official reflected:

> You have to think of these policy areas as *communities*: there are complex personal networks that grow up around them. Nobody would need to say explicitly to a Hill or a Kennedy that "this will hurt NIH." They pick it up. So I wouldn't doubt that that's what happened here. [Is Rogers well-connected at NIH?] Yes, very.

Rogers' move was encouraged and supported by the American Hospital Association, the American Medical Association, and the Association of American Medical Colleges. But it provoked the resentment and distrust of Lasker and her allies; a series of newspaper attacks and public protests followed, leaving Rogers with something of a siege mentality about the whole episode. The pressure was increased by the administration's decision to "tilt" in favor of the Senate bill, a move that infuriated Rogers ("We counted up six different positions the administration had taken," remarked Health Subcommittee aide Stephan Lawton).

The shift in the administration's position was dictated at the White House, where it was decided that to take exception to the Senate reorganization proposal would risk appearances of petty politics and of a less than total commitment to the attack on cancer. When House hearings were held in September, HEW Secretary Elliot L. Richardson had therefore changed his tune considerably. Stressing the importance of the additional provisions for administrative coordination that had been written into the Kennedy bill, he pronounced the new bill, S. 1828, the one best suited to give cancer research new prominence and the desired degree of executive direction. At his elbow was the director of the National Cancer Institute, who gamely, if somewhat wryly, agreed.[7]

Rogers prevailed in the end, partly because of the number of elements in the medical and research communities that came to the defense of NIH, partly because the administration vacillated in its commitment to the independent-agency idea. Also important, however, was Rogers' success in "lining his ducks up"—a maneuver at which House Commerce members generally acknowledge him to be extraordinarily skilled. He succeeded in unifying his subcommittee and later the House conferees around his proposal that the new cancer program remain within the National Cancer Institute. Republican subcommittee member Tim Lee Carter, of Kentucky, a physician who had his own ideas but also portrayed himself "to some extent" as a partisan of the administration, left little doubt as to his own preference for "shaking things up" at NIH. But the ranking Republican subcommittee member, Ancher Nelsen, chose to play the kind of mediating role that he portrayed as his usual lot in committee life: "trying to work out a compromise." He proposed the creation of a presidentially appointed panel to "provide a direct channel of communication between the President and the Director of the National Cancer Institute and . . . act as overseers to monitor" the program.[8] This was an idea that Rogers, according to Nelsen, "seized on immediately." The subcommittee bill also made the NCI director an associate director of NIH and gave him authority to submit his annual budget request directly to the president. It was a compromise the subcommittee could vote to report unanimously. The Senate bill, offered by Brock Adams in full committee, was defeated 4 to 24, while the Commerce Committee version passed the House 350 to 5 on November 15, 1971.

The solid House support, as well as his own expertise and strength of conviction, served Rogers well at the conference stage. The congressional session was drawing to a close. The administration, anxious to get a law on the books and satisfied that the House bill would give the president adequate means of administrative control, chose, as an HEW official put it, "not to weigh in heavily for the Senate version." The conference thus produced a bill that Rogers could with justification term "a substantial victory for the House of Representatives"[9]—a result he personally could view with considerable satisfaction. The episode had created misgivings about Rogers among Lasker forces and in certain elements of the research community, but he had finished the course with an enhanced reputation as a careful legislative crafts-man, a friend of NIH, and a power to be reckoned with in the health field—not bad for a little-known congressman completing his first year as chairman of the Public Health and Environment Subcommittee.

Delay and Default: The Failure of HMO Legislation

Health maintenance organizations are medical facilities that provide comprehensive health care to subscribers who pay a fixed premium in advance. Increasing numbers of consumers have found in these group health organizations a partial solution to soaring medical costs and an attractive alternative to piecemeal insurance programs. Some doctors have found in such plans, which nor-mally entail group practice, welcome opportunities for collegial-ity, professionalization, and the stabilization of their practice. But organized medicine has tended to see in HMOs, particularly if they are subsidized by government, a threat to the fee-for-service physician.

The Nixon administration perceived the HMO, at least for a time, as a delivery mechanism that could cut rising Medicare costs and as a constructive legislative idea that might partially counter the comprehensive national health insurance proposals being advanced by Democrats. Faced with the President's ad-vocacy, the potential popularity of the HMO idea and the advan-tages to be gained from leaving one's "mark" on a national plan, and the jurisdictional facts of life which largely shut them out of the health insurance area, members of the Health subcommittees came to regard the development of a proposal underwriting the nationwide establishment of HMOs as one of the major legislative tasks confronting them in the second session of the Ninety-second Congress.

The HMO idea had percolated in HEW during the first two years of the Nixon administration.[10] Encouraged by the favor-able reception given by the House Ways and Means and Senate

Finance committees to a 1970 proposal to authorize contracts with HMOs under Medicare and Medicaid, the administration included the HMO option in its proposed National Health Insurance Partnership Act of 1971 and sent up a separate proposal providing federal support, mainly through insured loans, for the formation of HMOs. Meanwhile, Senator Kennedy included a device similar to the HMO in his comprehensive national health insurance proposal. His Health Subcommittee then began a long series of hearings and markup sessions that culminated, on July 21, 1972, in the reporting of an HMO bill far more ambitious than the administration's proposal.

Rogers was slow to move. His circumspection here and in the related and more highly visible area of national health insurance may be attributed to his native caution and to his reluctance to provoke a direct confrontation with organized medicine or the Ways and Means Committee. But Dr. William Roy, a freshman congressman with an activist orientation relatively rare in those ranks, took up the slack. Roy, whose experience as a practicing physician gave him a unique grasp of the HMO question, worked on his alternative to the administration bill during most of his first year in Congress and introduced it on November 11, 1971. Whereas the administration had relied primarily on loan guarantees, Roy provided for federal grants that would cover a broad list of functions involved in the establishment and development of an HMO. He also prohibited assistance to profit-making organizations, specified in much greater detail than did the administration what services an HMO must deliver, and mandated a "meaningful role" for consumers in HMO policy-making.

Rogers was not accustomed to such activism in the lower reaches of his subcommittee, but, according to Roy, he proved encouraging and cooperative. In fact, Rogers persuaded six other subcommittee members to join in cosponsoring Roy's bill, bringing along three reluctant Republicans (Nelsen, Carter, and Hastings) by agreeing that he and Roy, in turn, would cosponsor the administration's HMO bill. It was an ingenious maneuver, for it combined a supportive gesture to Roy with a reinforcement of subcommittee solidarity and a guarantee that the processing of the Roy bill would be a collective venture in which Rogers would have a decisive hand.

Working mainly from the administration's projections, Roy came up with an authorization figure of approximately $1.1 billion over three years. Rogers persuaded Roy to remove this rather formidable figure from his bill before it was introduced and expressed the tentativeness of his endorsement to a reporter: "Dr. Roy devoted a lot of time to HMOs. We see it as a mechanism that probably can be developed, but to what extent we will have to go into in hearings."[11] Rogers' Health and Environment Subcommittee held twelve days of hearings between April 11 and May 18, 1972. The markup was an even more protracted process; the subcommittee bill was not reported until late September.

The issue was more controversial than most of those handled by the Health Subcommittee. The hearings left little doubt as to the hostility of the American Medical Association to the HMO idea. To make the HMOs anything more than a "limited, experimental" program, AMA witnesses claimed, would threaten the "pluralistic" nature of the health-care system, compromise the freedoms of patients and doctors alike, and possibly represent a major step toward "depersonalized, assembly-line medicine."[12] Subcommittee member John Schmitz of California, who soon was to bolt the Republican party to run for president on the American Independent ticket, was heartened by the AMA testimony:

> I see you are arguing for the defeat of all of these [HMO proposals]. It seems like the good old days of the AMA, doesn't it, before some slick PR man convinced you you had to change your image, to be for things instead of always against things. . . . But I am glad this is a flashback—I hope not a temporary one—to the better days of the AMA.[13]

Schmitz's compliments, according to a subcommittee staff member, produced self-congratulatory smiles among the less politically sophisticated of the AMA witnesses, pained winces among the others. His antics also prompted this tongue-in-cheek exchange among his fellow members:

> MR. ROGERS. I think it is pretty evident that those who oppose most legislation have their foot in the door in this committee—an effective foot.
> MR. NELSEN. An articulate foot.
> MR. ROY. Foot and mouth both.

But if Rogers and his colleagues were not inclined to take Schmitz entirely seriously, the same could not be said of their reaction to the AMA's misgivings, as the markup made clear.

Rogers made his own contribution to the partisan disputes that came to surround the HMO issue, attacking HEW for funding some one hundred experimental HMOs under existing authority but in advance of specific congressional authorization. Kennedy's role also became increasingly controversial. Irritated administration officials labeled his actions irresponsible and politically opportunistic:

> We wanted Kennedy to go ahead and mark up the HMO bill, while what he wanted to do was to go all over the country and keep on holding hearings—but of course that had nothing to do with the *legislative* process. *Now* the Senate has written such a bloated bill . . . so the whole thing may be in jeopardy.

The Kennedy bill authorized $5.1 billion over three years; Roy admitted that it "would be laughed off the House floor." The bill predictably served as a red flag for the AMA. The Senate approved it on September 20, 1972, by a 60–14 vote and with hardly a stir. But the AMA had long since turned its attention to the impending House subcommittee markup—and to the Nixon administration.

Members of the House Commerce Committee were, of course, all up for reelection, and the AMA contributed to the campaigns of nine of them.[14] Dr. Malcolm C. Todd, chairman of the Physicians' Committee to Reelect the President and a member of the AMA House of Delegates, publicly claimed credit for causing "some backtracking on the part of the White House."[15] During markup of the House bill administration officials reversed themselves on the crucial matter of preemption of state laws that restrict HMO development—thus electing, in effect, to give state medical societies veto power over the program in many communities. The administration also joined with the AMA in insisting on a limitation on HMO proliferation in terms of either the units or dollars authorized; the HMOs which President Nixon in March had declared should be "everywhere available" and had described as a "central feature of my national health strategy" had become, by the time the Republican National Platform was drafted in August, merely "innovative experiments."[16] But, as Roy said, the most important shift on the administration's part was the decreased "intensity" of its interest and support; this contributed significantly to the delays and misgivings that ultimately spelled defeat.

All of this, of course, meant that Rogers' characteristic quest for a consensual outcome was likely to produce a considerably diluted bill. According to one member, the fact that Deputy Assistant HEW Secretary John Zapp was, in accord with Commerce Committee custom, allowed to stay in the committee room during markup almost certainly made for the raising of many problems which the subcommittee Republicans, on their own, would not have had the knowledge and/or the inclination to develop.

Rogers delayed in taking up the bill and moved very deliberately in working it through his subcommittee—a method that reflected, it is fair to conclude, not only his devotion to careful and consensual procedures but also his reluctance to offend those wary of the entire HMO concept. Rogers' search for unanimity produced a preemption clause which eliminated specified kinds of state restrictions: the requirement that an HMO must secure medical society approval, for example, or that a certain percentage of physicians must serve on all HMO governing boards. But the states were left free to enact other sorts of restrictions and, in any case, the preemption clause applied only to HMOs receiving federal assistance. More serious, in Roy's view, was the subcommittee's failure to reach agreement on a meaningful "quality control" device; this failure, in fact, made him somewhat reluctant to push for the complete preemption of state regulation. The Senate bill had combined its general preemption of state statutes restricting HMO operation and development with the institution of an independent Commission on Quality Health Care Assurance to develop national health-care standards. The House subcommittee bill merely authorized the HEW secretary to bring civil action against HMOs that failed to provide the services or follow the operation procedures specified in the bill, and it provided for no regulation whatsoever of HMO's not receiving federal assistance.*

On September 21, 1972, the subcommittee voted seven-to-nothing (with Republican James Hastings and conservative Democrat David Satterfield abstaining) to report the bill, which was but a shadow of Roy's original proposal. The total authorization, $345 million over five years, was of pilot-project dimensions when compared to the Kennedy bill or even the earlier administration projections. Demonstration grants for special projects were included, but only for a maximum of sixteen HMOs for the purpose of enrolling the indigent, twenty HMOs in rural, medically underserviced areas (the Senate bill had authorized $360 million for rural "Health Service Organizations" alone), and eight HMOs for the purpose of enrolling high-risk individuals. Roy, although troubled by the absence of regulatory machinery in the bill, managed to be philosophical about the program's modest dimensions:

> I don't basically object to the experimental nature of the program. I'm not sure myself that we want whole chunks of the present delivery system replaced immediately by HMOs. But we will stimulate their formation. And the medical so-

---

* The public testimony of the AMA stressed its opposition to a control commission and to the subsidization of the premiums of low-income individuals.[17] The House subcommittee omitted the former from its bill; the latter was limited to a few demonstration projects in 1972 and dropped entirely in the 1973 version.

cieties won't like it, but they'll be forced to develop their
own counterproposals and try them out. All that will move
us ahead.

His aide, Brian Biles, added:

We actually consider that provision [sixteen HMOs subsidized for enrolling the indigent] a victory. The conservatives
didn't want that in at all. We had to compromise down from
thirty, but the principle is there.

Full-committee chairman Harley Staggers was as wary of the
HMO bill as Rogers. The passage of the Senate bill and the
prospect of a conference agreement that might go beyond the
House bill's experimental dimensions accentuated the fears of
the AMA, the administration, and dubious House Commerce
members, who pressured Staggers to let the subcommittee bill lan-
guish.[18] The fact that Congress was about to adjourn gave him a
perfect excuse, and the full committee never took up the bill.

The House passed an HMO bill during the first session of the
Ninety-third Congress, but only after the subcommittee, and then
the full committee, watered down the already minimal 1972 legislation still further. Bowing to the objections of the administration,
organized medicine, and committee Republicans, the full committee accepted a "compromise" worked out by Roy and Republican
James Hastings. The authorization was reduced to $240 million
over five years; the special programs for the indigent, for medically underserviced areas, and for high-risk individuals were deleted entirely; and *all* provisions were removed for the preemption
of restrictive state statutes. Meanwhile, the Senate passed a bill
considerably more modest than its 1972 measure but still significantly stronger than the House bill (authorizing $805 million
over three years and retaining state preemption and the Commission on Quality Health Care Assurance). The least-common-
denominator character of the House bill, Rogers' and Staggers'
well-known intransigence in conference, and the threat of a presidential veto combined to produce a conference settlement that

favored the House. The final version, signed by the President on December 29, 1973, authorized $325 million over five years; the funding timetable and the omission of operating subsidies left little doubt that the House concept of a one-shot, experimental program had prevailed. No assistance was provided for low-income or high-risk individuals, and earmarked assistance for medically underserviced areas was reduced to token dimensions. The Commission on Quality Health Care Assurance was dropped in favor of vague requirements that HMOs set up machinery to monitor themselves and that HEW study the matter. And the Senate's state preemption clause was dropped in favor of a narrower provision resembling the one contained in the House subcommittee's 1972 bill.

"We may reach a point on that subcommittee," Roy mused as the Ninety-third Congress began, "where you can't get *complete* consensus on *everything*. It's hard to know what price you might pay for that—sometimes you forestall a worse loss in full committee or on the floor by getting things ironed out in subcommittee." Indeed, it is difficult to know what obstacles might develop; there is certainly no denying that Rogers has achieved a remarkably high batting average in committee and on the floor, for which many members credit his skill and persistence in seeking an acceptable middle ground. The Health Subcommittee could have reported a stronger HMO bill than it did in 1972, although Democrats David Satterfield and Richardson Preyer and all four Republicans displayed varying degrees of ambivalence. But the opposition was more formidable at the full-committee level: there Republican detractors might well have been joined by such Democrats as Stuckey, Satterfield, Jarman, Blanton, Pickle, and Byron. Liberal majorities are not easy to come by on the Interstate and Foreign Commerce Committee. Rogers' and Staggers' caution can be partly understood in these terms. But caution and compromise can also exact a heavy toll, as the content of the subcommittee's 1972 and 1973 HMO bills and their final disposition attest. Nor is it at all clear that the opposition and dissension that Rogers and Staggers strove so mightily to avoid would have materialized or, if it had, would have resulted in defeat. This is particularly true in the health area, where, despite the clout of the AMA, legislators are particularly wary of acquiring a pecunious or partisan image. As Roy remarked in some amazement:

> Not only Jim Pearson but also Bob Dole [Republican sena-
> tors from his state, the latter quite conservative] voted for
> that *Kennedy* bill on the Senate floor without batting an eye.
> When you consider the trouble we were having over here
> [with a much more modest bill], I find that incredible. Of
> course it's easier to oppose health bills in committee, where
> there's not much publicity.

The public, bipartisan appeal of health issues surely helps explain Rogers' desire to identify himself with this area, but it is not a resource he fully exploits in handling his subcommittee. There, in fact, he relies on informal procedures, closed sessions, and personal agreements (only one formal vote was taken during the entire HMO markup in 1972). If Rogers is truly interested in strong legislation (which was never entirely clear on the HMO bill) he might indeed find that holding out for "*complete* consensus on *everything*" is too high a price to pay. If Rogers is content to stay in the realm of research and reorganization proposals, he may be able both to attain favorable public recognition and to keep the various partisans with whom he must deal reasonably pacified. But if he and his subcommittee wish to have a meaningful impact on the quality, cost, and delivery of health care as it affects millions of Americans, consensus and compromise might have to give way as supreme virtues. Increased legislative boldness and independence, a reduced deference to groups and colleagues who would obstruct, and an opening up of congressional deliberations to the scrutiny of the public whose well-being is at stake—these are the directions in which House Commerce Committee operations must move if public interest and support are to be mobilized, the sabotage attempts of the AMA and the White House are to be neutralized, and meaningful health-care-delivery legislation is to go on the books.

ENVIRONMENTAL POLITICS

Environmental affairs play a distinctly secondary role to health matters in the preoccupations and output of the House subcommittee, although it concerned itself extensively with air pollution, drinking-water pollution, and noise control during the Ninety-second Congress. It is the Senate Commerce Committee which, although its jurisdiction is more limited (excluding, for example, air pollution), has organized more effectively to develop an independent policy role. The assumption of initiatives in environmental affairs is a conspicuous goal of the Senate committee and its staff leadership.

Senate Commerce's involvement in environmental affairs has followed close on the heels of its ventures into consumer policy and has assumed a similar pattern in many ways. A separate Environment Subcommittee has been formed with activists Philip Hart and Frank Moss at the helm. Chief counsel Michael Pertschuk is quite interested in the area, and he has recruited and worked closely with energetic aides. Environmental issues, like consumer affairs, afford wide opportunity for legislative involvement due to heightened public interest, the relatively undeveloped state of the law, and a lack of creativity on the part of the executive branch. And whatever the intensity of the opposition that might arise to specific proposals, the interest groups operating in these areas are not as monolithic, entrenched, and locked into their positions as those with which the committee must deal in, for example, communications and transportation.

The Senate Environment Subcommittee took up an impressive range of proposals during the Ninety-second Congress, including the regulation of toxic chemical substances, pesticide control, drinking-water pollution, noise control, and citizens' rights to sue on environmental matters. But the environmental affairs agenda is considerably less extensive than that in consumer affairs, despite the parallels between the two areas, and the record of final successes falls shorter yet. The pesticide and noise-control measures became law in 1972, but in drastically weakened form (see below); the drinking-water and toxic substances measures died in the House and in conference, respectively; and the citizens' suit bill was never taken up by the full committee.

A number of conditions, in fact, constrain and inhibit the Senate Commerce Committee as it strives to make its impact on environmental policy. First, there is the problem of reconciling the newer policy concerns with the more traditional ties and commitments of the Commerce Committee. Rising environmental concerns do seem to have made a genuine impact, not only on the general distribution of the committee's energy and resources, but also on how it does business in other areas. Sometimes the committee proclaims such concerns in a largely specious fashion—as when the retention of its Pacific Northwest holdings by the El Paso Natural Gas Company is defended as a "consumer protection measure" or a requirement that oil imports be transported aboard U.S.-flag tankers (see Chapter 7) is justified in terms of the lesser peril these vessels pose to the marine environment.[19] But the committee's new priorities have been evident in the prominence of environmental-protection measures on the merchant marine agenda and the development and defense of a strong anti-dumping bill in the oceanography area.

Despite the currents of creativity and reform in certain sectors of the Senate Commerce Committee, the more inclusive public interests often remain unarticulated and undefended as the committee goes about "business as usual" in such areas as aviation, surface transportation, and communications. The committee, for example, failed to write even minimal environmental-protection standards into its coastal-zone-management bill (see Chapter 7); such concerns are peripheral and sometimes inimical to the promotional interests with which many members approach maritime policy.

The most revealing single incident during the Ninety-second Congress was the committee's action on the aircraft-noise-abatement section of the Environmental Noise Control Act.[20] Debate centered on which agency—the Environmental Protection Agency

(EPA) or the Federal Aviation Administration—should have enforcement authority. There was room for honest disagreement as to EPA's capacity to set and enforce standards in this area and on how responsibly the FAA had carried out its existing regulatory mandates. But there was no question at all that the aircraft industry and the airlines strongly preferred FAA administration. This the Rogers subcommittee bill, passed by the House on February 29, 1972, provided, giving the EPA administrator review but not veto authority. On the Senate side the bill was initially sent to the Public Works Committee, but with the Commerce Committee retaining the right to ask for re-referral. As it became known that the Public Works Committee was considering EPA administration, Senators Magnuson and Cannon, chairmen of the full Commerce Committee and of Commerce's Aviation Subcommittee, respectively, sent a sharply worded letter to Public Works chairman Jennings Randolph, "strongly recommend[ing] that the Public Works Committee reserve to the judgment of the Commerce Committee any proposed restructuring of the regulatory framework for the U.S. air transport system."

Environmentalist groups were dismayed, not only because of the substance of the Commerce Committee's position, but also because the threatened request for re-referral would almost surely kill the chances for final passage as the Ninety-second Congress rushed to adjournment. The Environment Subcommittee, which had held extensive hearings on noise control, in the end had little input; as one aide put it, "On the major administrative question, we've been preempted by Cannon." The Commerce Committee's initial plan was to offer the House language on aircraft regulation as a committee amendment to the Public Works Committee bill on the Senate floor. But after an aide to Senator John Tunney, chief sponsor of the bill, worked out further adjustments in language with Aviation Subcommittee aide Robert Ginther, Senators Cannon, Magnuson, and Pearson "reluctantly agreed" to go along, although insisting that "the basic objection to the Tunney bill still remains."[21] The Public Works Committee settled for a complex scheme of divided administration and Commerce agreed not to request re-referral. By this course the committee avoided the wrath of the environmentalists, but more important was the fact that the Air Transport Association was now also urging them to allow the bill to go through. Both the House Interstate and Foreign Commerce and Senate Public Works versions contained compromises favorable to industry on such questions as whether the states would be allowed to issue standards stricter than those issued at the federal level and whether past models would have to be "retro-fitted" so as to make them meet current standards. The ATA was content to see the bill passed as a means of preventing the reopening of these questions.[22]

It is hardly surprising that environmentalist members and aides should run afoul of the longer-standing pro-industry orientations of the other subcommittees and members. Environment Subcommittee aide Leonard Bickwit's handling of subcommittee chairman Hart's environmental amendment to the Airport and Airways Development Act taught him this lesson soon after he joined the Commerce staff and almost got him fired. Magnuson's basic ambivalences were also revealed in the little-noticed removal of "Energy and" from the title and the jurisdiction of the Environment Subcommittee as the Ninety-second Congress began. As a staff man explained:

> From the beginning Magnuson made it clear that he wanted to keep energy issues related to the Pacific Northwest in the full committee. Hart felt, by the end of the Ninety-first Congress, that if he wasn't going to have clear jurisdiction over all power issues then energy ought not to be in the subcommittee title, because he was not in a position to deliver.

Another aide elaborated:

> Power was removed quietly from the Hart subcommittee's jurisdiction at the beginning of this Congress. Hart didn't object. This was precipitated by nothing in particular, but I suppose that [it was] anticipated that in a new and unpre-

dictable area like this, Hart might tilt to the environmentalist side to Magnuson's disadvantage.

A young, activist aide in the Pertschuk mold, Henry Lippek, works on power matters at the full-committee level. The committee has thus far not distinguished itself in this area; major questions as to long-range energy needs, alternative energy sources, technological and manpower requirements of the energy industry, and new means of energy conservation have barely been broached. The work that has been done on power-plant siting legislation and energy research and development proposals, for example, has shown considerable sensitivity to environmental concerns. Still, Magnuson is not willing to give the Environment Subcommittee a free hand.

The competing jurisdictional claims of other committees constitute a second major constraint on those who would make the Commerce Committee a center for the generation of environmental policy. This is a much more serious problem in environmental than in consumer affairs, and it continues to be a major factor in restricting the committee's role. The most frequent conflict is with Public Works, although the policy differences between the two committees are frequently not great (the aircraft-noise episode was not altogether typical). What is at stake is often simply the pride and prerogatives of congressional chieftains. Environmentalist groups and the EPA, according to a Commerce aide, "get very frustrated at the way legislation gets bottled up up here with all sorts of petty squabbling. Often I'd have to agree with them . . . it's a political struggle pure and simple, and the bills come out pretty much the same way regardless."

The most striking case of conflicting jurisdictions during the Ninety-second Congress, however, involved the Agriculture Committee—and the policy consequences were anything but trivial. The Agriculture Committee agreed to refer the Pesticide Control Act to Commerce only after Commerce agreed to drop sections of the Product Safety Act that would have removed meat and poultry inspection programs from the Department of Agriculture. It was what Senator Cotton called a "Yankee bargain," for Commerce Committee members knew that the meat and poultry sections had no chance of survival in any event. As Pertschuk explained:

> The . . . transfer of inspection functions from Agriculture . . . was foredoomed from the start, because of the certain knowledge that both the Senate and House Agriculture committees would successfully insist upon referral of the bills, thereby bringing down the whole legislative effort.

The Agriculture Committee soon came to regret its agreement to re-refer its pesticide bill to the Commerce Committee. The fifteen amendments proposed by Commerce included language making it easier for EPA to challenge the "registration" of a pesticide, removing the anticompetitive requirement that each applicant must develop his own test data, increasing penalties under the act, providing for citizen suits, protecting the right of local governments to regulate the sale or use of pesticides beyond the terms of the federal statute, expediting suspension procedures for harmful pesticides, and broadening EPA's inspection prerogatives.

Most of Commerce's work on the pesticides bill was done under the aegis of Environment Subcommittee chairman Hart. The prime mover was subcommittee aide Leonard Bickwit, one of Pertschuk's recent recruits. "What we've done will change the way this problem is looked at from now on," Bickwit reflected. Perhaps so—but the subcommittee faced formidable obstacles in the short run. Agriculture issued a stinging point-by-point rebuttal of Commerce's actions. Magnuson had little taste for a showdown on the floor and the protests of apple growers in Washington had left him lukewarm towards Hart's efforts. Hart and Bickwit had no choice but to rework their bill before it went to the floor; the strength of Agriculture's jurisdictional claims and the indifference of the administration (whose earlier version of the bill had been roughly treated by the Agriculture committees in both houses) weakened their position further. The committee invited representatives of the National Agricultural Chemicals Association

(NACA) in for negotiations; this seemed more expeditious, Bickwit told a reporter wryly, than negotiating with the industry indirectly through the medium of the Agriculture Committee:

> The industry was talking as though they owned the [Agriculture] committee. We were distinctly under the impression that no bill was going to come out that didn't have industry approval. . . . The administration seemed to be able to accept that with more composure than we did. . . . The industry set the rules; the administration agreed to play by them.[23]

Given these circumstances, Hart and Bickwit did remarkably well; the bill offered up for Senate approval on September 26, 1972, contained some two-thirds of their amendments in modified form. But the bill approved in conference was considerably weaker: most of the surviving Commerce Committee amendments were dropped or altered and a House provision for the indemnification of any manufacturer whose product was removed from the market was added.

Both the noise-control and pesticide episodes illustrate a third constraint operating on Senate environmentalists: the organizational strength and resources of the interests threatened by environmental initiatives. There are some scattered *supportive* groups, however, and it is with them that subcommittee chairman Hart has taken what he regards as one of his most promising steps—instigating cooperation among previously disparate, sometimes hostile, labor, environmental, and urban organizations. Hart has been one of the Commerce Committee's most important members as it has moved into environmental and consumer affairs; his energetic advocacy of the Fair Packaging and Labeling Act, finally passed in 1966, was a key element in the committee's transition. But those closest to Hart have detected a flagging of his interest and involvement in Commerce Committee matters in recent years. He is overextended in his responsibilities—his chairmanship of Judiciary's Antitrust Subcommittee remains a demanding assignment—and his identification as a key legislator and "good guy" among consumer and environmental advocates has made for an exhausting barrage of requests and entreaties. Moreover, his own priorities have shifted somewhat: one effect of his 1970 campaign was reportedly to impress upon him the priority that problems of poverty and urban decay must have among the nation's social goals in the immediate future. Hart has therefore been selective and somewhat subdued and sporadic in his Environment Subcommittee pursuits, but he has taken a particular interest in *relating* environmental and urban problems. His instigation in 1971 of the Urban Environment Conference was aimed not only at a mutual strengthening of the groups called together, but also at influencing the agenda of the environmentalists. In mid-1972 Bickwit could cautiously claim some success in altering perceptions: "The environmentalists were pretty aloof at first . . . but some of them have shown considerable sensitivity to the groups representing the poor who criticize their priorities." Common efforts began on some specific problems—lead in gasoline, highway policy, and industry's use of antipollution requirements as a pretext for worker layoffs and transfers—but as 1973 wore on with little apparent motion, another Hart staffer was forced to conclude that "it's not going to amount to much." Hart and Magnuson have joined in publicizing the health hazards of leaded gasoline, but Hart's direct involvement in the Urban Environment Conference has not continued; he saw his role as initially catalytic, then supportive.

A number of factors thus limit the Environment Subcommittee's independence and impact: the checks exercised both within the Commerce Committee and by competing committees, the resources and points of leverage available to threatened interests, the inattentiveness, preoccupations, and lack of interest of the members (Bickwit listed only Hart, Spong, and Hollings as even moderately active among the subcommittee's members in 1972). But the subcommittee is highly favored by the chief counsel and others plotting the course of the full committee. It also has in Magnuson and Hart leaders who often are willing to sponsor and support the initiatives of their aides. One such effort during the

Ninety-second Congress was the rewriting of the pesticides bill. Another, in which Bickwit took particular pride but to which he perhaps devoted efforts disproportionate to the chances for success (the bill was never reported by the full committee) was the Environmental Protection Act—a bill empowering the courts to overturn federal agency actions on substantive as well as procedural grounds and granting citizens the right to sue for the enforcement of environmental statutes and for the enjoinment of "unreasonable" conduct in areas not covered by statute.[24] During the Ninety-third Congress the subcommittee turned its attention increasingly to measures designed to encourage recycling and materials conservation through product standards, disposal taxes, and the prohibition of discriminatory freight rates. The fate of many of these initiatives leaves little doubt as to the obstacles and difficulties environmental legislation will continue to meet. But the subcommittee nonetheless serves as a valuable additional access point for environmental advocates, and in time it might—through the publicizing of problems and abuses, the germination of path-breaking proposals, and strategic attempts to add safeguards and otherwise to modify bills coming through the committee or the Senate—have an appreciable policy impact.

7

Maritime
Affairs and
Oceanography

If Warren Magnuson's role as champion of the consumer was initially adopted only in the face of political difficulties, threatened preemptions, and staff instigation, his involvement in maritime affairs furnishes a contrast. The shipping and fishing industries are important to his state, where they wield considerable influence and control sizable campaign chests. Shipping and fishing matters have concerned Magnuson since he first came to Congress in 1937, and as he has gained in seniority, he has become increasingly prominent as a legislative champion of the two industries. During the 1960s Magnuson found it necessary to move into new areas by virtue of his tenuous electoral situation and his broadened responsibilities on both the Commerce and Appropriations committees, but he was anxious to retain his reputation as the

NOTE: This chapter was written by David E. Price.

279

foremost congressional figure in fishing and shipping, as well as in the related and burgeoning area of oceanography. These are areas, therefore, where committee decentralization has lagged—Magnuson retained the chairmanship of the Merchant Marine and Fisheries Subcommittee until 1966—and where members and aides of an activist bent must be particularly cognizant of the chairman's interests and prerogatives.[1]

THE CARE AND FEEDING OF THE MARITIME INDUSTRY

There is no area of its jurisdiction where the Commerce Committee has responded more faithfully and less imaginatively to the expressed interests of a powerful lobby than it has in relation to the United States merchant marine. Even here there are some signs of change: that Magnuson may be willing to loosen his grip on the policy area is suggested by the increasingly prominent role of Merchant Marine Subcommittee chairman Russell Long.* Meanwhile, new currents of consumer and environmental awareness in the committee as a whole (and several disastrous oil spills and tanker collisions) have made for the addition of matters such as ship safety, marine traffic control, and tanker construction and operation standards to the maritime agenda. But the main thrust of the committee's efforts are still in what is euphemistically termed the "promotional" realm, and Long does not perceptibly differ from Magnuson in his tendency to service uncritically the industry's demands. Operators in the states Long and Magnuson represent receive a major share of the Maritime Administration's construction and operating subsidies; the totals for fiscal 1971

---

* Fisheries policy, coupled with merchant marine policy when Magnuson headed the subcommittee, was placed under the jurisdiction of the new Oceanography Subcommittee in 1970. All of these areas are handled in the House not by the Commerce Committee, but by a separate Merchant Marine and Fisheries Committee.

and 1972 were $216.1 million for Louisiana and $26.9 million for Washington, which together constituted 27 percent of the national total.[2] To keep these funds flowing is foremost among the concerns Long and Magnuson bring to the leadership of the Merchant Marine Subcommittee.

The most recent statutory landmark is the Merchant Marine Act of 1970, which greatly expanded the federal effort to stimulate shipbuilding through direct subsidies. The Nixon administration, in sending the legislation forward, attempted to split the difference between what the President's advisers said national defense and economic considerations actually required and what Congress, solicitous for the maritime industry, might otherwise have been expected to pass.[3] This legislation followed years of agitation by the industry and its congressional champions for a "new maritime policy" that would arrest the alleged decline in quality and efficiency of the U.S. merchant fleet. From time to time senators grumbled about the parochial and short-sighted approach to transportation policy taken by the industry and its executive patrons (the fight to keep the subsidy-granting Maritime Administration out of the Department of Transportation was a notable example). But promoters of a "new maritime policy" in Congress were largely uncritical of the industry, and they wanted anything but a truly refurbished program that would tie maritime policy more closely to demonstrable national needs and establish realistic criteria of economic feasibility. What they wanted was much simpler: more money. This the Nixon bill, approved by the Senate Commerce and House Merchant Marine and Fisheries committees with few changes, provided: direct subsidies for shipbuilding were to double over the next decade, and the number of merchant vessels built annually was to increase from ten to thirty. Construction and operating sudsidies were extended to previously unsubsidized bulk carriers, and shipbuilders as well as owners were authorized to apply for subsidies.

The Commerce Committee authorized over $500 million to get the "new" program under way early in the Ninety-second Con-

gress, but processed no legislation comparable in scope to the
1970 act.[4] There were, however, a number of bills that demonstrated the committee's continuing solicitude for the industry, two
of which have been chosen for analysis here. The first, H.R.
11589, authorized the foreign sale of five prematurely retired U.S.-
flag passenger vessels. These vessels had been constructed with
the aid of $91 million in construction-differential subsidies,
whereby the government pays the difference between U.S. construction costs and those of competitive foreign shipyards. Such
ships may not be sold and transferred to foreign registry without
specific statutory authority. The government had also invested a
total of $297 million in operating-differential subsidies (the dif-
ference between U.S. and foreign-flag wages and other operating
costs) in order to make the ships competitive internationally.
Despite annual subsidies of approximately $40 million, these pas-
senger vessels lost some $10 million a year, and one by one they
were laid up.

Their owners, claiming they simply could not compete with the
airlines and with foreign-flag cruise vessels, naturally were anxious to unload them. The House Merchant Marine and Fisheries
Committee took the lead in processing the request. Several days
of hearings were held in 1971 during which administration witnesses "generally corroborated the testimony of the passenger
vessel operators."[5] Senate Commerce leaders were anxious to
complete action on the House bill by the end of the year, before
the expiration of Moore-McCormack's contract to sell its two
ships to Holland-America Lines for $20.5 million. But the oppo-
sition of maritime labor and of Senator Ernest Hollings of South
Carolina, the only dissenting member of the Commerce Committee but one who proved quite vocal and persistent, helped delay
action until mid-1972.

Industry lobbying was intense and effective—and, as a *Washington Post* article revealed, the process of persuasion involved
several conflicts of interest.[6] Former Commerce Committee chief
counsel Gerald Grinstein was hired by the ship owners to work in

Washington on behalf of the bill.* Two former executives of
Grace Lines, one of the affected companies, took leading roles in
formulating the administration's position from within the Maritime Administration. Maritime labor led the opposition. The
unions convincingly claimed that the Maritime Administration
and the industry had broken faith with the American taxpayer.
The operators, they argued, had made only the weakest efforts to
improve services, cut costs, and keep the ships in operation. But it
was difficult for Congress to dispute the argument of the bill's
proponents that to reactivate the ships would simply be to soak
the taxpayer further. The Senate committee concluded that reacti-
vation would require some $80 million in annual operating
subsidies—approximately $900 per passenger on a fourteen-day
cruise, or about $21,000 per year per person employed.[7] Con-
gress might act either to bail out the owners or to reinstitute a few
jobs: either way the taxpayer could not win. But of course the
taxpayer was not the one for whom the maritime program was
designed in the first place. Magnuson, Long, and others were fond
of stressing the shared interests Americans had in a strong merchant marine—mainly in terms of national defense. But the President's advisers admitted that, at most, one-third of the subsidies
authorized in the administration's new maritime program could be
justified on that basis.[8]

Congress finally decided to enable the owners and the government to cut their losses. Long took the bill to the floor for the
Commerce Committee on May 2, 1972. He could barely conceal
his irritation as Hollings persisted in decrying the "breach of
contract" that was being perpetrated with respect to the American
taxpayer. Hollings' South Carolina labor ties were related to his

* The Commerce Committee's present chief counsel, Michael Pertschuk,
notes that Grinstein "did not accept the client or the assignment until he
had received [Merchant Marine Subcommittee aide] Manny Rouvelas'
judgment that unlike most maritime legislation the [passenger vessel bill]
was in the public interest. This of course does not remove the conflict of
roles . . . [but] Jerry has rather scrupulously avoided lobbying before the
committee both before and after the passenger vessel debacle."

opposition, but his doggedness revealed a genuine personal conviction as well. He managed to pull together thirty votes in an unsuccessful attempt to block sale pending a study of the matter by the General Accounting Office. That amendment having failed, final passage came by voice vote.

The Senate committee's leaders fared less well on a second bill, and in fact were subjected to a rare rebuff on the Senate floor. Three months after the passage of the cruise-ship bill, the Senate took up fiscal 1973 maritime authorizations (H.R. 13324). No senator challenged the authorization level, but the Commerce Committee added an amendment that raised some hackles: a proposed requirement that at least 50 percent of oil imports under quota, with the exception of certain kinds of fuel oil, must be carried abroad U.S.-flag vessels. Once again, the Senate Committee gave national defense as the primary reason for the provision; the nation was pictured as being on the verge of "complete dependence on others for transportation of our oil imports." The 1970 Merchant Marine Act, the committee noted, had "recognized the need to build and operate tankers and bulk carriers" and had provided "construction and operating subsidies intended to make U.S.-flag vessels competitive." A crucial stone, however, had been left unturned: "It did not provide *cargoes* to *fill* those vessels, which is a prerequisite to having those ships built." (emphasis added). The 1970 act left oil importers free to build or utilize foreign-flag vessels, "thus avoiding U.S. wages and taxes and frustrating national policy."[9]

The success that promotional maritime legislation ordinarily enjoys is not solely attributable to the strengths of its lobby and its congressional champions, though these are formidable enough. Also of considerable importance is the fact that shipping is a "distributive" interest, the policy preferences of which can be implemented "more or less in isolation from other [interests] and from any general rule."[10] Like many distributive interests, shipping is regionally based; legislators from maritime states often assume particular responsibility for its well-being, and their way is smoothed by the patterns of logrolling and "mutual noninterference" that have grown up around distributive interests in Congress. This is not to say that a countervailing consumer-taxpayer interest does not exist; but it is not organized and articulated in such a way as to furnish effective competition. Members of Congress thus tend to *think* of merchant marine subsidies as a costless enterprise—benefiting a localized industry with special needs but spreading the costs in such a way as to hurt no one (very much). But the conventional logic of distributive politics ran into a snag on the oil-import bill. The reason was not that the long-suffering taxpayer/consumer finally found a voice, although New England legislators—who were particularly concerned about rising oil prices—did join the opposition. The reason was that the interests of the carriers in this instance came into conflict with those of another distributive interest, and one with even more power working in its favor: oil. And the oil industry did not want to pay higher prices for shipping its products in U.S.-flag vessels or to be forced to deal with the shipbuilding and maritime unions. For once, the game of "mutual noninterference" could not be sustained.

The shipping interests had no reason to doubt the amenability of Chairman Edward Garmatz (D., Md.) and most members of the House Merchant Marine and Fisheries Committee to their objectives.* But they rightly anticipated trouble in the Rules Committee, where, as one lobbyist put it, "the oil people had done their work well." The industry thus decided to go to the Senate first, where Long and Magnuson proved willing to take up the cudgels. That this would be Long's position was not clearly predictable, for in the past he had taken a back seat to no one in his championing of the oil industry, which plays a major role in Louisiana politics. Pastore's incredulity on the floor was understandable:

---

* The House Committee, by virtue of the narrowness of its jurisdiction, has tended mainly to attract members from maritime districts. The industry has long recognized that it benefits from this arrangement; the 1974 battle to keep the committee from being absorbed into a more inclusive transportation committee, where the maritime industry would have to compete more directly with other modes for favorable treatment, may be understood in these terms.

> MR. MAGNUSON: The oil people . . . do not want the
> bill.
>
> MR. PASTORE: Oh, I do not know about that. If they did
> not want the bill, the Senator from Louisiana would not be
> handling it.[11]

The oil importers whose profits would be reduced by the proposed amendment were a somewhat different grouping than those domestic companies to whom Long was ordinarily so deferential. But there was considerable overlap, and Long had to alter some of his long-standing commitments. "Humble, especially, worked on Long," recalled one lobbyist. "But SIU [Seafarers International Union] and maritime management had gotten to him first." The amendment provoked little debate or overt opposition in the Commerce Committee, and it was reported on June 7, 1972, with only Norris Cotton and Robert Griffin filing opposing views.

Long's was not the only reversal of roles the episode produced. Opposition on the floor was led by Cotton and other New England senators dubious of the committee's claim that the increased cost of importing oil would not be passed on to the consumer.[12] Cotton could not resist goading the committee leadership:

> There has been more legislation to protect the consumer that has originated from the Committee on Commerce than from any other committee. Much of it has been at the instigation of the able chairman, the Senator from Washington. . . . It is rather shocking to me, therefore, Mr. President, to find this language attached to [this] bill. . . . The Federal Office of Consumer Affairs . . . is opposing the amendment. And only today—and I never really expected to get any help from this gentleman—I have heard that Ralph Nader is opposed to this amendment, and for once I am on the side of the angels.[13]

Cotton was as anxious as Long to disavow any connections with the oil lobby: "The oil companies . . . can take care of themselves. We are interested in the consumer." The oil industry, in fact, viewed the support Cotton mustered with mixed feelings, for it revealed the depth of consumer hostility to the industry-supported quota system itself. As Senator Edmund S. Muskie (D., Me.) contended, the quota system and the high domestic prices it fostered would be "further entrenched" by making the maritime industry its direct beneficiary.[14] Cotton was also helped by the administration's efforts opposing the amendment. The Defense Department, according to a Senate aide, was initially sympathetic to the position of the maritime industry, but State, Commerce, and Interior were consistent in their opposition. Agriculture Secretary Earl Butz and others in his department became increasingly active as the bill advanced in the Senate; they reportedly convinced many Midwestern senators that the cargo-preference provisions would result in higher prices for petroleum products for farmers.

The upshot was a rare reversal for the Commerce Committee on the Senate floor, where on July 26 the Senate struck the cargo-preference provision from the maritime authorization by a thirty-three to forty-one vote. The Commerce Committee members present backed the Magnuson-Long position nine to six, with self-styled consumer champions such as Hart, Hartke, and Moss going along with the chairman. But a coalition of farm-state, oil-state, and New England senators, together with a few additional administration stalwarts, carried the day. The episode is instructive both as an example of the sort of proposal that is likely to be put forward by promoters of the merchant marine and as an illustration of the rather rare combination of factors that might occasionally make for their defeat.* But it can unfortunately offer little more than momentary comfort to those who are skeptical about the prospect of the common good arising from "noninterference" among distributive interests.

* The promoters of the merchant marine came closer to success in 1974, when a slightly more modest cargo preference bill (affecting 30 percent of oil imports) cleared both houses and was stopped only by a presidential veto. The inflationary potential was even more evident in this bill than it had been in 1972, but the political stock of the administration and of the oil companies had fallen because of Watergate and the energy crisis.

OCEANOGRAPHY AND ITS FRIENDS

The collection of research, development, environmental-protection, and governmental reorganization proposals that have come to be designated "oceanography" policy affect many of the same interests and regions as shipping policy and have many of the same congressional champions. But the Senate Commerce Committee has handled oceanography more imaginatively than merchant marine policy, partly because the policy area is much more in flux and the interested groups less monolithic and entrenched.

Governmental involvement in oceanography has grown phenomenally in recent years; federal expeditures in marine science have multiplied by a factor of at least twenty-five since the late fifties.* This increase is indicative of a growing recognition of the economic, military, and scientific importance of the exploration of the oceans and the development of their resources. But the figures also reflect a substantial promotional effort by partisans of stepped-up efforts in the Senate Commerce Committee and the House Merchant Marine and Fisheries Committee, under whose jurisdictions oceanography, like maritime policy generally, falls.[15]

A landmark twelve-volume report produced by the National Academy of Sciences Committee on Oceanography (NASCO) in 1959 served as a rallying point for advocates of increased funding inside and outside the Congress. Senator Warren Magnuson, attracted by oceanography's economic potential and by the ship and shore facility construction envisioned by NASCO, became an advocate of the NAS committee's ambitious funding recommendations ($2.8 billion for the decade). He also advocated governmental reorganization as a means of coordinating and giving

* Edward Wenk, Jr., estimates expenditures at $24.1 million for fiscal 1958, $658 million for fiscal 1973. *The Politics of the Ocean* (Seattle: Univ. of Washington Press, 1972), pp. 43, 121. On the comparability of the two figures, see p. 531 (fn. 8).

impetus to the federal oceanographic effort, which at that point was scattered among some twenty-two agencies. The Marine Resources and Engineering Development Act of 1966 was the culmination of several years of effort by Magnuson, sometimes in cooperation but often in competition and conflict with House Oceanography Subcommittee chairman Alton Lennon (D., N.C.), to develop mechanisms to coordinate existing programs and to project the course the nation should take in the area in the next decade. The act authorized the formation of a cabinet-level National Council on Marine Resources and Engineering Development to coordinate federal programs and a Commission on Marine Science, Engineering and Resources to plan the course of future federal activity.[16]

The commission, chaired by Julius Stratton of the Ford Foundation, produced in 1969 a "Plan for National Action" which, like the NASCO report in the previous decade, provided oceanography advocates with a ready-made agenda and an authoritative store of information with which to make their case. Major recommendations included improved management of the nation's coastal zones, new programs for the development and utilization of marine resources, and increased efforts in marine science and ocean exploration. Recommended funding increases in these areas approached 10 percent annually, with the yearly total reaching the $1 billion mark by 1980. The report aimed at comprehensiveness but gave clear priority to questions of economic development. The ordering of the introductory discussion was indicative: "New and expanded ocean industries offer some of the Nation's most inviting opportunities for economic growth. . . . Vital though marine economic development is, it must be *tempered* by other [i.e., environmental and ecological] considerations."[17]

On the organizational questions that had preoccupied congressional advocates during the sixties, the commission took a relatively bold position: neither the President's Office of Science and Technology nor the cabinet-level council established by the 1966 legislation would suffice:

> Federal councils are limited in their power to act and cannot fully compensate for fundamental shortcomings in the organization of operating agencies. Nor can a President's staff, for long, be the active proponent of a national ocean program which may be in competition with other urgent national programs. . . . The Commission recommends the creation of a major new civilian agency, which might be called the National Oceanic and Atmospheric Agency, to be the principal instrumentality within the Federal Government for administration of the Nation's civil marine and atmospheric programs.[18]

In addition to preparing a formal report, the commission drafted legislation to implement its objectives. The main recipients of these proposals were Magnuson and Lennon, though commission members proceeded with some circumspection in the hope that, in the event of a Nixon victory, their recommendations would not be solely identified with Democrats. One such draft provided for the establishment of an independent National Oceanic and Atmospheric Agency (NOAA).[19]

During the early sixties the Senate had proved much more willing than the House to entertain far-reaching organizational schemes in oceanography. The House had resisted even the notion of a cabinet-level council; Magnuson considered it a major victory to get the council as well as a study commission included in the 1966 legislation. But in 1969 it was Lennon and his subcommittee that took the lead in holding hearings on the NOAA proposal and other recommendations of the Stratton commission.

Not until late 1969 did Magnuson begin to follow up the commission report. Magnuson's natural tendency to coast a bit after his 1968 victory was in this instance reinforced by concern over his wife's health, and the time that he did spend in his office was increasingly absorbed by appropriations matters (he became chairman of the Labor–HEW Appropriations Subcommittee in 1969). Magnuson and his staff were anxious to keep the chairman identified with oceanography, but as a means of focusing attention and producing legislation they decided to create a new

Oceanography Subcommittee with Ernest Hollings, an active committee member who had displayed an interest in the area, as chairman. Crane Miller, a Stratton commission staff member with considerable expertise, was appointed subcommittee counsel. The first order of business was the holding of extensive hearings on two Stratton commission proposals that were to dominate the subcommittee agenda for the ensuing months: the NOAA reorganization proposal and a bill establishing a program for the management and development of the nation's coastal zones. "Magnuson's staff decided the coastal zone bill had the better chance," one participant recalled wryly, "so they put his name on that one. That left NOAA for Hollings."

It was indeed easily predictable that the executive would strongly resist the idea of a new, independent agency devoted to oceanographic affairs, with all the organizational upheaval and reordered priorities that would entail. But the Stratton commission's organizational recommendations were not made entirely in vain. On two of them—the establishment of a nongovernmental National Advisory Committee for the Oceans and the temporary continuation of the National Council on Marine Resources and Engineering Development—Congress acted independently.[20] And the administration's own reorganization efforts enabled NOAA proponents to get half a loaf. The President's Reorganization Plan No. 4 of 1970 consolidated Weather Bureau, Coast and Geodetic Survey, Environmental Data Service, Bureau of Commercial Fisheries, Sea Grant, Lake Survey, Navy Oceanographic Data and Instrumentation Centers, and other scattered functions in a new National Oceanic and Atmospheric Administration within the Department of Commerce. Congressional champions of oceanography had little direct influence on the reorganization decision, although the realization that more drastic proposals might otherwise be advanced in Congress represented a substantial incentive for the administration to develop its own plan.

The formation of NOAA has resulted in a measure of program coordination and has given congressional advocates a valuable source of information and point of access. But as the coastal zone episode (discussed below) shows, NOAA has operated under severe political and budgetary constraints; certainly it has been in no position to undertake large-scale efforts at program development. Congressional champions of oceanography have thus come to feel the need for a planning and promotional effort comparable to that provided at earlier junctures by NASCO and the Stratton commission. This time the device they have chosen is a congressional study group. Senators Magnuson and Hollings, pointing to congressional and executive "inaction" on a number of the "farsighted recommendations" of the Stratton commission, in 1974 secured passage of a resolution authorizing the conduct of a comprehensive "Ocean Policy Study" by the Committee on Commerce, with members from other committees with relevant jurisdictions also participating. Hearings were promptly begun on "the energy potential of the . . . outer continental shelf; the environmental, economic and social impact of major OCS development . . . [and] the status of state land and water use programs."[21] The result almost certainly will be a fresh spate of resource development, environmental protection, governmental reorganization, and funding proposals and, not incidentally, a reinforcement of the preeminence of the Senate Commerce Committee in the oceanography policy arena.

Congress, The States, and The Coastal Zone

The second and more promising of the bills heading the new Oceanography Subcommittee's agenda in 1970, a measure providing "encouragement and assistance [to the] States in preparing and implementing management programs to preserve, protect, develop, and whenever possible restore the resources of the coastal zone,"[22] began to move forward late in the Ninety-first Congress. The coastal-zone bill, introduced by Magnuson in the Senate and Lennon in the House, was largely drafted within the Stratton commission. The commission in this area as elsewhere laid heavy stress on economic development: "Any plan for the use of the coastal zone must seek to accommodate heavy industry . . . also must provide for additional transportation and power generating facilities"; the main concern was that future development be "orderly" and that "rational management" be attained.[23] The states, the commission acknowledged, had given marine matters "low priority," had diffused responsibility among agencies, and had failed to develop and implement long-range plans. Yet the commission apparently considered it politically necessary to make the states the focal point of the new program, which was to authorize federal grants-in-aid for the institution of management programs. The federal yoke was to be light indeed; the commission stated that states could not "and, of course, should not" be compelled to respond to the federal incentives, and no specific criteria for acceptable plans or performance were suggested.[24]

The Hollings subcommittee held extensive hearings on the coastal-zone bill and prepared legislation that also included portions of a bill, introduced by Senator Joseph Tydings (D., Md.), which provided federal assistance for state acquisition, development, and operation of estuarine sanctuaries. But time pressures caught the proponents short as the Ninety-first Congress rushed to adjournment, and the early months of 1971 saw the development of jurisdictional tangles within Congress and executive opposition from outside that threatened to kill the bill.

The administration gave its approval to the coastal-zone proposal in 1970. But the Senate Interior and Insular Affairs Committee was meanwhile developing its own "land use" bill, which would give the states incentives and means to develop comprehensive conservation and land-management plans. The potential jurisdictional conflict was obvious, and the administration made it acute with the introduction of its own land-use bill at the beginning of the Ninety-second Congress. This proposal, unlike Senator Henry M. Jackson's (D., Wash.) Interior Committee bill, identified coastal zones and estuaries as areas of critical concern, required that state land-use programs adequately inventory such areas, and made grants conditional on the recipient state's restricting activities that threatened the aesthetic and ecological values of wetlands. "This proposal," the President announced, "will replace and expand my proposal submitted to the last Congress for coastal zone management, while still giving priority attention to this area of the country which is especially sensitive to development pressures." Russell Train, Chairman of the Council on Environmental Quality (CEQ), headed the administration witnesses testifying as the Hollings Subcommittee began a new round of hearings in 1971. His recommendation was that the coastal-zone bill be abandoned in favor of the administration's more comprehensive land-use bill, which had been referred to the Interior committees.[25]

This shift naturally did not please Commerce Committee members. To their natural jealousy of their jurisdiction was added the quite accurate perception that the predilections of the House Interior Committee were such that the President, by submitting the entire land-use package to their tender mercies, was in effect inviting the shelving of the matter.[26] At the same time, Magnuson and Senate Interior chairman Henry Jackson, his colleague from Washington, had no desire gratuitously to offend one another. Jackson had earlier tailored his bill to play down coastal-zone management, and Magnuson's tendency, similarly, was to move ahead with the coastal-zone bill but to alter its provisions—by "fuzzing" the definition of the coastal zone and adding language regarding administrative coordination—in such a fashion as to minimize the intrusion into Interior's bailiwick.*

Hollings, however, moved prematurely: having secured an "order to report" the Magnuson bill from the committee, he proceeded to send it to the floor before the jurisdictional conflicts were fully resolved. Three "holds" were therefore placed on the

---

* Magnuson's conciliatory approach paid off in 1973 when the new coastal-zone program was experiencing funding difficulties. The Interior Committee wrote into its land-use bill (S. 268), and Jackson and Magnuson defended on the floor, an anti-impoundment provision requiring that the administration must make funds available for the coastal-zone program (which it had opposed) proportional to those made available for the land-use program (which, at the time, it favored).[27] The land-use issue later became ensnarled in impeachment politics; the administration largely abandoned its bill and in 1974 it was killed in the House. Land-use proponents thus, in retrospect, saw it as fortuitous that Hollings and Magnuson had moved ahead independently on the coastal-zone front in 1972.

bill immediately by Public Works, Interior, and Banking, Housing and Urban Affairs—creating a situation that eventually required re-referral for further refinements and delayed floor consideration until April 1972. "I guess to some extent I played the impetuous junior senator on that," Hollings admitted. "I talked with my chairman and we decided we'd better pull back." In the end, however, the Senate passed the bill unanimously. Hollings accepted several floor amendments designed to clarify the relationship of the bill to programs under the jurisdiction of the Public Works Committee, and then proposed a final amendment of his own.

> The intent . . . is to call [the bill] the "Magnuson Coastal Zone Management Act of 1972." . . . Some 12 years ago he started in this particular field. . . . It was the Senator from Washington who gave us the leadership, spreading oil on troubled waters, and we finally got a bill.[28]

The coastal-zone bill did not excite pressures nearly as intense as those generated by a bill restricting ocean dumping with which it shared the Oceanography Subcommittee's attention during the Ninety-second Congress and which dredging and other interests made a concerted effort to modify. One reason for this was that the coastal-zone bill's champions chose in advance to follow what was in many ways the path of least resistance. Opposition from city and county governmental units threatened for a time, but adjustments in language and enlistment of the support of the Council of State Governments served to defuse the threat. Both subcommittee aide Crane Miller and chief counsel Pertschuk, who processed the bill with minimal care after difficulties with Hollings led to Miller's dismissal, had misgivings about the extent to which the bill gave the states a "blank check." Miller in fact drafted a long list of environmental and other criteria that states would have to meet before qualifying for assistance. But the perspective finally adopted was, as Miller put it, that "we are now where water quality legislation was in the mid-fifties." If this implied that program standards and enforcement machinery were to follow, it had the more tangible and salient effect of "not alarming these municipalities *too* much" and minimizing Commerce's intrusion into the jurisdictional bailiwicks of the Interior and Public Works committees. What such laxity might cost—and whether tougher standards will indeed be developed—remains to be seen.*

The pro-industry proclivities of the House Merchant Marine and Fisheries Committee, which had been blatantly demonstrated during the ocean dumping episode,† were less evident in the coastal-zone case. The Senate's minimal language prohibiting land and water uses that "have a direct, significant, and adverse impact on the coastal waters" was softened further. On the other hand, the House committee authorized federally administered management programs for the area *outside* the coastal zone (beyond the three-mile limit of the territorial sea) but within the twelve-mile limit of the contiguous zone, and provided civil penalties for the violation of regulations under these programs.[31] This amendment proved to be an important one, for it aroused fears among oil and gas interests that were anxious to retain the Department of the Interior's control over offshore leases. Pressures from these industries and their executive patrons—in addition to a desire on the part of the administration and House Interior Committee

---

* Jonathan Ela of the Sierra Club suggested as a minimum that no new landfill should be permitted in estuarine areas of high productivity, that development projects should be required to meet strict pollution standards, and that development of public lands currently devoted to public use and recreation should be prohibited.[29]

† The House version of the ocean dumping bill (H.R. 9727) placed dredge spoil disposal under the control of the Army Corps of Engineers rather than the Environmental Protection Agency. The administration and the Senate Commerce Committee favored EPA administration, while the Corps was favored by the American Association of Port Authorities, the American Institute of Merchant Shipping, and, most vociferously, the American Dredging Company, represented by Washington lawyer Robert Losch. Participants generally portrayed Edward Garmatz, chairman of the Merchant Marine and Fisheries Committee, and Oceanography Subcommittee chairman Alton Lennon as long-standing allies of the Corps; several described Garmatz, in addition, as in the "hip pocket" of the dredgers, "Bob Losch's representative in the House," and so forth.[30]

chairman Wayne Aspinall (D., Colo.) not to compromise the administrative arrangements of the comprehensive land-use bill—spelled trouble for the Merchant Marine Committee's proposal in the Rules Committee and on the House floor.

Aspinall finally consented to let the bill come to the floor, but once it got there (on August 2, 1972) he lined up votes behind an amendment transferring the administration of the proposed program from Commerce's NOAA to the Department of the Interior. The amendment's sponsor, Republican Representative John Kyl (Ia.), claimed that the proposal was "prepared by the administration" and waved what he claimed was a letter from the Council on Environmental Quality in the air to prove it. The amendment passed easily, 261–112, with Interior Committee members for it by a 32–1 margin and Merchant Marine and Fisheries Committee members against it, 6 to 27.[32] As Hollings observed, "It's Interior that's got all the clout on the House side. Merchant Marine is simply no match."

It soon became clear that the administration's house was badly out of order. Lennon had received a letter from the Commerce Department which suggested that with minor changes the committee-reported coastal-zone bill would be acceptable, and he thought he had an understanding with Commerce officials that the White House, despite its preference for a comprehensive land-use bill, would not oppose the coastal-zone measure or ask for Interior Department jurisdiction. But administrative jealousies and solicitude for the oil industry led some second-level Interior and CEQ officials to pass the word that the bill was not acceptable to the administration unless the Interior Department was given control over the new programs. It was on this basis that Kyl claimed to have an "official letter" in support of his amendment. "We later found out," said a House staff member, "that Kyl's 'letter' was information he had obtained over the phone from CEQ and that Chairman Train had to sit down that night and write something."[33] Train subsequently admitted that he had not signed the letter until 7:00 P.M. on August 2. He implied, however, that the Commerce Department had misrepresented the administration's position and claimed that Kyl had been given a "preliminary draft" orally. (Kyl, however, had claimed to have a *copy* of the letter—and when Train's letter came it did not square with his "quotations.")[34] A rather dubious performance—but it served to confirm that the administration's ranks had indeed closed. NOAA officials, who naturally favored the Merchant Marine Committee bill, were discouraged but hardly surprised:

> The basic fact is that this administration is just not marine-oriented, just like the last one wasn't. . . . They *always* tend to look at things from the land out, while we look from the sea in. They've always preferred a comprehensive bill, but we thought they had agreed not to object to House adoption of the Senate bill. On that there *was* a reversal. . . . Yes, Interior wants the authority, but, no, they're not equipped to handle it. In fact it would be a real disaster if the coastal-zone program were placed over there right now. . . . We're going to argue with the administration on this; I don't know how well we'll do.

In the end, however, Hollings prevailed on the jurisdictional question. His way was smoothed in conference by virtue of the fact that the House conferees were drawn from the Merchant Marine and Fisheries Committee and thus were amenable to abandoning the House amendment and returning the program to the Commerce Department's NOAA. He also had the benefit of a unified delegation; the subcommittee's ranking Republican, Ted Stevens, "didn't waver," according to one aide, "though [Secretary of the Interior Rogers] Morton came to see him." In order to make their "concession" on the administrative question viable, the House conferees had to make a second concession, which prompted more genuine regrets: they dropped the contiguous-zone management program that had alarmed the oil industry and had made them anxious to see the Interior Department in charge. "That program was good politics on the East Coast and in California," remarked John Hussey, who succeeded to Miller's staff slot on the Senate subcommittee in mid-1972 and handled the coastal-zone bill in its latter stages, "but the House conferees were willing to sacrifice it. They weren't as concerned about this as they were simply to get the basic program going."

The administration weighed in heavily in favor of Interior Department jurisdiction. Pressures intensified as the conference bill was reported on October 5 in the midst of Congress' rush for adjournment. Senate approval of the conference report was a foregone conclusion, but the House battle precipitated what Hussey called "the most intensive lobbying effort I've ever seen." Senate and House committee members and aides perceived the administration's opposition as monolithic. "NOAA wasn't in a position to help," remarked one House Merchant Marine staff member. "I just don't think there was anything they could do." "I find it difficult to believe," wrote Lennon to Secretary Morton,

> that the Department of the Interior has such a narrow, selfish viewpoint that it would attempt to scuttle vital legislation simply because it has not been favored with the total responsibility which it sought. . . . I certainly will not support the rumored initiative of the Department of the Interior in attempting to kill the coastal zone legislation by supporting a motion to recommit the Conference Report, since that will be the result should such a motion prevail.[35]

Hollings was, however, able to play one high card quite effectively; both in conference and thereafter he let it be known that he would hold up the ocean-dumping bill, a matter of high priority with the administration and several key House participants, until a coastal-zone bill with NOAA administration was approved. And he was instrumental in persuading the oil industry to put out the word (though not until the day of the House vote) that the dropping of the House's contiguous-zone provisions in conference had resulted in a bill they could live with. The House thus approved the bill on October 6, and despite indications that the Interior Department was seeking a veto, the President gave it his signature.

The battle for an effective coastal-zone program is far from over. The budget submitted by the President in 1973 contained not one penny for this purpose, and it was only by threatening to hold up the administration's bill providing for the development of deep-water ports that Hollings and Magnuson were able to induce the administration to desist in its efforts in 1973 to get a bill out of the House Interior Committee that would, in effect, absorb the coastal-zone program into the projected land-use program. Even if the coastal-zone program is funded, important guidelines and priorities remain to be set. But the coastal-zone episode does point up a policy area where Congress has been able to have an unusually independent, and sometimes creative, policy impact. Hollings' efforts and their success are in part attributable to certain characteristics of the Senate Commerce Committee: an ethos that encourages such ventures, the relatively wide dispersal of authority and resources, the "marine-oriented" tradition and sympathies of the committee, the bipartisan unity that makes for strength on the floor and in conference. These advantages and strengths were almost offset, of course, by the industry and administration and House opposition that arose. But the fact that the oceanography area has *not* been generally "crowded" by the proposals and pressures of established advocates (in contrast, for example, to the related area of shipping) and that the administration has *not* been "marine-oriented," has generally left a certain slack which congressional advocates have found it possible and profitable to take up.

8

Investigations
and Oversight

On October 18, 1968, President Lyndon B. Johnson signed the Radiation Control for Health and Safety Act (PL 90–602). For all too many of the measure's supporters, inside and outside Congress, that was the end of the matter. But in reality it was only the beginning of the effort to establish a program that would effectively protect the American public.

The radiation-control program began with a basically flawed statute. Representative Paul Rogers and the House Commerce Committee had effectively gutted the provisions that would have given the regulating authority adequate powers for plant inspection and for the seizure of defective products (see Chapter 6). The bill's most important defect was its failure to deal with the problem of training and certifying the personnel who operate medical and dental x-ray equipment. Medical diagnosis and therapy is the source of more than 90 percent of all exposure to man-

NOTE: This chapter was written by David E. Price.

made ionizing radiation in the United States. The development of safer *equipment* will avail little if those using the equipment are not trained and motivated to reduce patient exposure to as low a level as is practicable.[1] Senator E. L. Bartlett (D., Alaska) and some of his colleagues sought to stimulate the development of licensing standards via the 1968 legislation, but even these minimal provisions were dropped at the insistence of the House conferees.

PASS IT AND FORGET IT?

If the content of the bill showed Congress to be ineffectual and compromised in its legislative performance, the subsequent fate of the radiation-control program has pointed up equally grave deficiencies in congressional oversight. This is not to say the program has been a complete failure. On the contrary, the Bureau of Radiological Health (BRH), located since 1971 in HEW's Food and Drug Administration, has made some promising beginnings despite low levels of funding and the absence of executive, congressional, and public attentiveness and support. The bureau moved quickly to promulgate a performance standard for television receivers, the product that had first excited public and congressional alarm. Standards for microwave ovens, cold cathode gas discharge tubes, and diagnostic x-ray systems have followed. The bureau has recognized the overriding urgency of the medical x-ray problem, and under authority of some ambiguous language in the 1968 act has developed training materials and drawn up model state legislation for certifying medical and dental users of ionizing radiation.[2]

Still, the bureau's performance displays critical weaknesses and failures. The "development and enforcement of standards for diagnostic x-ray equipment" has been listed as the bureau's first priority in its annual reports since 1970, but the enforcement of these standards, first published on August 15, 1972, was postponed until August 1, 1974. The bureau granted a year's delay in its original compliance deadline on the strength of objections from the manufacturers of x-ray equipment, even though it acknowledged that the manufacturers had been tardy in their planning efforts. The bureau even implied that the need of manufacturers to unload their inventories of substandard equipment constituted a justification for delay.[3]

The bureau's overseers in Congress must bear some responsibility for such laxity. They are also responsible, in large part, for the agency's perennial shortage of resources. Personnel levels have remained constant since 1970 (at approximately 375 persons, including clerical staff) and funding for fiscal 1974 leveled off at $12.4 million. The thirty-eight "compliance investigations" conducted in 1972 and the size of the compliance staffs (forty man-years for general compliance, thirty-two projected for diagnostic x-ray systems) needs to be viewed alongside the estimated exposed populations for the devices in question: 130 million people in a *single* year for diagnostic x-rays, 100 million for microwave ovens, thousands of workers and scientists for laser devices, and thousands of fetuses and newborn children for ultrasonic and light devices.[4] In many of these areas, the extent of risk and the appropriate standards for control are still unknown. And the bureau has lagged in its work in the laser, ultraviolet, and ultrasonic areas.

Bureau officials warn against attributing these lags solely to deficiencies in funds and personnel, asserting that these are matters of inherent complexity and difficulty. But as one of them puts it:

> The shortage of funds does prevent us from moving in several areas at once, like light and ultrasonic. Of course, a case can be made against an agency like this growing *too* fast, getting overcommitted. [How much in the way of additional funding would you say the bureau could use productively?] Oh, something in the neighborhood of an $18 million total, maybe 150 more people. That would be a sound baseline. Now there are shortages and compliance difficulties.

The bureau has, however, been constrained to play the part of the "good soldier" within the administration; it has not sought increased funding, new laws, or greater control over the industry it regulates. "We can discharge our responsibility," BRH Director John Villforth assured the Senate Commerce Committee in 1973. "I think that when one looks at the total priorities that the FDA is faced with, we have received excellent support."[5] The bureau has not responded to its mandate in the 1968 act to recommend such legislation as is needed to strengthen the radiation-control program. "That tells its own story too," acknowledged one official, drawing a comparison with the executive's control over the BRH budget. Bureau officials choose to paint a generally rosy picture of industry cooperation and compliance; they believe that no further authority is needed for inspection or seizure or sanctions. It is more difficult for them to claim success in getting user standards adopted by the states—only four states require the training and certification of radiological technologists, and only California requires instruction in health physics in medical schools—but here too the bureau has held its peace.* In the 1972 annual report the bureau finally sent up its first legislative recommendation: that the statutory requirement for the annual report itself be repealed![7]

The weakness of the bureau is in part attributable to the absence of external support and surveillance and pressure. Many of the people who vocally supported the passage of the 1968 act seem largely to have lost interest. Nor has Congress remained involved or informed. Paul Rogers geared up cursory oversight hearings in 1969, but the House Commerce Committee has done nothing in the area since then. The Senate Commerce Committee did nothing until the Ninety-second Congress, when a young staff man began to make contacts preliminary to oversight hearings; BRH and other experts in the area became mistrustful, however, because it seemed to them "he was just looking for something

---

* "The Department [of HEW]," BRH Director Villforth testified in 1973, "has not yet determined the best course of action in this regard and I think this is under study right now within the Department."[6]

sensational." Finally, early in the Ninety-third Congress, with a new staff man and a new member, John Tunney, who was willing to take the lead, the Senate Committee held three days of oversight hearings.

Not much activity has ensued, although Magnuson has been instrumental in getting BRH to step up its monitoring of the detection devices being used in airports and office buildings. Despite the obvious deficiencies in the 1968 statute, members of the Commerce committees have not pressed for amendments. Bills to accredit schools for training radiological technologists and to provide minimum standards for their licensing have been sponsored in the Ninety-third Congress by Senator Jennings Randolph and Representative Edward Koch (D., N.Y.) but neither is a Commerce Committee member. Senate Health Subcommittee chairman Edward Kennedy resisted attempts to refer the Randolph bill to the Commerce Committee, but included it in his subcommittee's ill-fated medical manpower package in 1974. The licensing bill and a second Koch bill, providing for the retroactive application of the 1974 BRH standard to *all* x-ray machines in use, have received few indications of support and only vague promises of consideration from Rogers and his House subcommittee. Surely this pattern of neglect is partly attributable to the low visibility of the policy area, the low incentives of members to undertake painstaking legislative and oversight work. But as Georgia Tech's K. Z. Morgan suggests with reference to the problem of medical school training, other forces may also be at work:

> Our country still awaits . . . a leader like the late Senator Bartlett who will, in spite of expected opposition from the American Medical Association, American Dental Association, and the American College of Radiologists bring about the passage of legislation which strikes at the problem of excessive exposure of the population from medical sources by requiring education, training, and certification of all doctors who prescribe or apply ionizing medication to their patients.[8]

In any case, the subsequent history of the 1968 act reveals what is an all-too-familiar pattern of behavior among lawmakers: pass it and forget it. Earlier chapters have pointed up the erratic and fragmentary character of the scrutiny the Commerce committees give the ICC, CAB, and FCC—regulatory agencies created by and supposedly responsible to the Congress. When hearings *are* held in these areas, where most committee members have a strong "promotional" orientation, there is generally a pro-industry bias to the witness list, superficial questioning, and inadequate followup. What the radiation case suggests is that the situation is not necessarily different in areas like health and consumer protection, where the Commerce committees have obtained a more activist image and a greater reputation for independence. The picture is somewhat mixed: the Rogers subcommittee, for example, has given more conscientious scrutiny to medical research and manpower programs than to radiation protection or the food and drug area generally. In the Senate, the reporting requirements made of the FTC and the continuing interest of Senator Moss have made for relatively effective oversight and a periodic prodding of the agencies in the area of smoking and health. Senator Hart, likewise, has retained an interest in the fair-packaging area—although the oversight hearings he has chaired from time to time must have convinced him that his labors have largely gone for naught.* Chief counsel Pertschuk points to auto safety—an area where public and hence senatorial interest has remained relatively high—as the area where the Senate committee has what is "probably our best record in oversight":

> Shortly after the act's passage and on at least annual intervals, we have scheduled full-scale reviews of the agencies' activities including outside (critical, of course) witnesses. Hartke has borne the primary burden, although Stevenson has filled in lately. Sometimes the oversight has been in conjunction with proposed amendments to the law or new

* The FDA and FTC announced in the Senate committee's 1970 oversight hearings that they were devoting *thirteen* and *nine* man-years, respectively, to the *nationwide* implementation of the Fair Packaging and Labeling Act.

authorizations, but essentially we brought [Highway Traffic Safety Administration Director Douglas] Toms and his predecessor on the mat, for well-informed grillings.

A number of Senate Commerce members and aides, aware of the overall inadequacy and irregularity of their oversight efforts, have recently made some promising innovations in this area. It has become clear that committee decentralization is not the answer; while the formation of new subcommittees and the dispersal of resources formerly controlled by the chairman have made for heightened legislative activity down through the ranks, there has been little apparent impact on the quality of oversight. It is a realization of this, in part, that has led committee chairman Warren Magnuson and his top aides to experiment, albeit cautiously, with the idea of a separate investigative staff. A special staff contingent numbering five and assigned to the full committee was assembled in 1971 under the direction of veteran investigator Donald Gray. Their original mandate was broadly to investigate the "effects of organized crime on interstate and foreign commerce"; ten days of hearings were scheduled during the Ninety-second Congress, "oriented," as one investigator put it, "toward the consumer and what mob pressures are doing to legitimate businesses." But as the inquiry lost focus and faltered because of member timidity and disinterest, chief counsel Michael Pertschuk began to envision a different role for the investigative unit. They might, he explained, "serve as 'floating' staff in aid of subcommittee oversight activities," not "going off on their own frolics and detours" but at the same time enabling the subcommittees to undertake investigations for which they might otherwise have little motivation or capability. The investigative staff's new role was formalized by Magnuson in a memorandum to his members on October 10, 1973:

> The principal staff investigators, Don Gray and Jim Kelly, have been reorganized as a staff investigative unit functioning as legislative oversight specialists in support of the subcommittees. The investigative work which Don and Jim per-

formed in Senator Cannon's oversight investigation into efforts to undermine the independence of the [National Transportation Safety Board] is an example of the kind of use to which the investigative unit will increasingly be put. This upgrading of the Committee's oversight capacity is particularly appropriate in the light of the Resolution introduced by Senator Humphrey to establish a select committee on regulatory commissions, a proposal which would supercede the clear legislative jurisdiction and responsibility of this Committee.

Early indications are that this redeployment of staff resources might significantly raise the caliber of Senate Commerce oversight. Gray's and Kelly's investigation of White House interference with the National Transportation Safety Board, alluded to in Magnuson's memo, moved the Aviation Subcommittee into a new area and resulted in legislation to restructure the NTSB as an independent agency. The temporary assignment of three investigative staff members to the special committee investigating Watergate and related matters should lead the Commerce Committee to confront more squarely the relationships between campaign contributions and regulatory decisions. Perhaps most important, however, is the increased capability the investigative staff have given the committee to scrutinize presidential nominees to the regulatory commissions and other agencies. The Magnuson-engineered defeat of FPC nominee Robert Morris in 1973 (see Chapter 2) signaled an apparent readiness on the part of the committee and the Senate to examine nominees more thoroughly and critically; extensive staff work is essential if the background of these candidates is to be adequately examined and sufficiently probing questions are to be explored with them in preparation for, and during, confirmation hearings.

Stepped-up activity in these areas still falls far short, of course, of the comprehensive oversight responsibilities with which the Senate Commerce Committee is charged. The most obvious need is for more frequent and more extensive investigations of the implementation of the landmark statutes enacted by the committee and of the overall priorities and performance of the agencies and commissions under its jurisdiction. Such inquiries now occur infrequently, generally occupy one or two days of public hearings, and usually come across to all concerned as perfunctory, low-priority affairs. Here too, staff changes—the development of the special investigative unit, and also the heightened activism and improved coordination across subcommittee lines fostered by the evolution of Pertschuk's and Sutcliffe's roles (see Chapter 1)—can furnish an important impetus to intensified committee efforts. But the low level of member interest and participation on the legislative subcommittees suggests that more drastic organizational expedients may be necessary if the situation is greatly to improve. An option that deserves consideration is the formation of a separate subcommittee with oversight responsibility. That this likewise is no panacea is suggested, however, by the performance of the House Commerce Subcommittee on Investigations—to whose operations we now turn.

THE HOUSE INVESTIGATIONS SUBCOMMITTEE

The House Interstate and Foreign Commerce Committee has intermittently received widespread public attention by virtue of the work of the Special Subcommittee on Investigations and its immediate predecessors.* The special subcommittee's original purpose was to examine the rule-making and enforcement activities of the regulatory commissions in light of their legislative mandates. However, under Oren Harris, who took over the subcommittee in 1958 after its stormy first year† and presided over both the subcommittee and the full committee until his retirement in 1966, the subcommittee mainly sniffed out scandals: industrialist Bernard Goldfine's connections with presidential assistant Sher-

---

* The Special Subcommittee on Legislative Oversight (85th and 86th Congresses) and the Special Subcommittee on Regulatory Agencies (87th).[9]
† The subcommittee's initial probes into alleged FCC misconduct resulted in the resignation of Commissioner Richard Mack, the firing of subcommittee chief counsel Bernard Schwartz, and Representative Morgan Moulder's replacement by Harris as subcommittee chairman.[10]

man Adams, the rigging of television quiz shows, "payola" in the music industry, and the accuracy and influence of radio and television audience ratings.

When Harley Staggers succeeded to the chairmanship of the Interstate and Foreign Commerce Committee in 1966, he elected, like Harris before him, to chair the Investigations Subcommittee as well. In fact, he sought to reinvigorate the subcommittee, whose funds and staffing had recently declined (see Table 15). Funding levels began to rise considerably under his chairmanship, and Robert Lishman, who had served as chief counsel during the subcommittee's earlier heyday, was rehired. But Staggers could not match Harris' competence and control; the subcommittee became a focal point of controversy within the Commerce Committee and eventually—with its attempt in 1971 to return a contempt citation against CBS in connection with its investigation of the television documentary "The Selling of the Pentagon"—in the full House as well.

TABLE 15.

Selected Indicators of Activity, House Subcommittee on Investigations, 85th–92nd Congress

	Congress							
	85	86	87	88	89	90	91	92
Days of public hearings	68	53	9	31	7	13	16	15
Number of members	11	9	9	9	9	12	16	5
Salaries and operating expenditures (thousands of dollars)	292	512	224	226	not available	397	462	652
Professional staff members	14	17	5	4	7	10	11	9

SOURCE: On staffing and funding, Daniel Manelli, Chief Counsel, Special Subcommittee on Investigations.

When Staggers took over in 1966, he immediately came under pressure from subcommittee chairmen and other members who wanted a stronger hand in investigations. Communications and Power chairman Torbert Macdonald in particular felt preempted by the Investigations Subcommittee's concentration on broadcasting matters; others simply wanted to loosen up the committee and enhance their own role. By 1969 the entire senior half of the full committee, including the chairman and ranking minority member of every legislative subcommittee, had been granted seats on the Investigations Subcommittee (see Table 15). But Staggers' attempts to control the subcommittee agenda and his monopoly of the staff for projects of his own choosing quickly led to disillusionment. There were surprisingly few strong objections when, in 1971, Staggers promulgated a rule limiting Commerce members to one subcommittee and reduced the investigations unit to five. "We've got too much of this business of people being on several subcommittees, not being able to handle the work on any adequately," Staggers said in defending his action. "So we made the one-subcommittee rule to strengthen the legislative subcommittees." But a former staff member made a more candid assessment: "Staggers simply had his belly full of the activists on the subcommittee who were always quarreling and pushing him—Moss, Dingell, Rogers, etc." Moss and Rogers, meanwhile, decided to concentrate on pressing for increased autonomy and resources for the legislative subcommittees; Staggers was thus left with what he regarded as a "manageable" Investigations Subcommittee, but the role of its members was not likely to be a vigorous one.

Commerce Committee members have shied away from the subcommittee in recent years, as both its small size and the low seniority of its members attest. William Springer, and then Sam Devine, have been willing to take the ranking Republican slots, since as ranking minority members of the full committee they could retain their voting privileges on the legislative subcommittees. But the other minority position was filled by Richard Shoup (Mont.) in the Ninety-second Congress and Norman Lent (N.Y.) in the Ninety-third, committee freshmen in both instances. Ray Blanton of Tennessee, an inactive legislator rendered all the more so by his unsuccessful attempt to unseat Senator Howard Baker in 1972, filled one of the Democratic slots during the Ninety-second Congress; his place was taken in the Ninety-third by twentieth-ranking Democrat Charles J. Carney of Ohio. The other Democratic member, J. J. Pickle, was a reasonably active legislator whom Staggers asked to return to the subcommittee after the 1971 reorganization to give it a more senior status. Pickle accepted, although he knew that labor pressures to get him off the Transportation and Aeronautics Subcommittee had also figured in Staggers' calculations. Pickle soon came to regret the move. He found no meaningful role to play on the Investigations Subcommittee, and in his absence his Transportation and Aeronautics projects floundered. In mid-1972 Pickle expressed his determination to rejoin his old subcommittee, but Staggers convinced him to stay on Investigations in the Ninety-third Congress. In 1975 Pickle left the Commerce Committee altogether, transferring to Ways and Means.

Pickle was not the only Commerce member impatient with the subcommittee's operations; one normally mild-mannered Democrat referred to it scornfully as "Staggers' little toy." The metaphor suggests both exclusiveness of control and triviality of activity:

> If John Moss were chairman of the Investigations Subcommittee, it would be the best one in town.* He would really do a terrific job, but under Staggers nothing is going to happen. . . . He wanted me on that subcommittee, but I refused. Poor J. J. Pickle is on it, [which means he] does not have *any* subcommittee. . . . It is a waste. Harley just dreams of bringing CBS to its knees, but that will never happen.

And a former staff member reflected:

> Harris knew how to run an investigative operation, how to get interest and attendance. You had to educate him, but once you'd done that there was no problem. Once you got him in it, he would go all the way. Staggers just basically

* In 1975 Moss was in fact elected by the committee's Democratic caucus to replace Staggers as head of the Investigations Subcommittee. Staggers' ouster—said to have been precipitated by the members' accumulated discontents and by the influx of eleven, predominantly liberal, new majority members—was approved by a one-vote margin after six ballots.

hates controversy. He *never* goes all the way—except maybe
on CBS, and there he was wrong.

Members admit to knowing little about what the Investigations
Subcommittee's sizable staff does, but they often suspect the
worst: "About all they do is sit up there looking at pictures of a
[supposedly staged] pot party at some university and old clips of
CBS trying to get into Haiti with some gun runners." Even one
senior Commerce staff member professes ignorance as to "what
goes on up there with all of that staff." And a minority aide
remarked, "The subcommittee doesn't produce much. . . . Its
energies might better be used on oversight functions. . . . But
things won't change as long as Staggers is in charge. It evidently
runs the way he wants it to."

How justified are such criticisms? They do not, after all, come
from purely disinterested sources. Members and aides alike naturally look with envy at the relatively large chunk of the Commerce staff (ten out of twenty-six committee professionals in
1974) and budget the Investigations Subcommittee absorbs. It is
not surprising that the leaders of the legislative subcommittees
feel that increased authority and resources should be delegated in
their direction. The cynical characterizations that Commerce
members tend to give of the Investigations Subcommittee—
together with the ready suggestion that the investigations function
should be spun off to the legislative subcommittees—thus can
hardly be taken at face value. It is important to assess objectively
the range of the subcommittee's activity, as well as the sorts of
oversight it does *not* generally undertake.[11]

From Staggers' accession to the chairmanship in 1966 through
the Ninety-second Congress, the subcommittee's agenda reflected
a preoccupation: deception in "the presentation of purportedly
bona fide news and news documentaries via radio and television."[12]

During the Ninety-first Congress, the subcommittee investigated a Chicago station's documentary, "Pot Party at a University," television reporting of the 1969 Democratic National

Convention, and CBS's coverage of "Project Nassau," an attempted Haitian invasion. Five of the subcommittee's nine professional staff members during the Ninety-second Congress concerned themselves full or part time with television news staging and editing practices; new heights of publicity and controversy were reached as Staggers attempted in 1971 to subpoena CBS President Frank Stanton to relinquish the outtakes of "The Selling of the Pentagon," so as to permit the committee to assess the editorial techniques utilized.[13] Many Commerce members disapproved of the chairman's efforts but most found it politic to support him; the full committee backed the subcommittee's call for a contempt citation, 25 to 13. But a combination of broadcasting industry pressures and the concern of members to tread cautiously "at the borderline between congressional power and First Amendment rights"[14] brought Staggers a defeat on the House floor, where members effectively scuttled his plan by a vote of 226 to 181 on July 13, 1971. Despite this major setback—which Staggers has been slow to forget or forgive*—the subcommittee continued to devote a large percentage of its resources to the investigation of news programing practices. Three days of hearings in May 1972 were devoted to alleged incidents of news staging or rigging, with testimony taken from TV technicians and others concerning incidents in which they had been involved. But a degree of sensitivity to public and congressional criticism was reflected in the subcommittee's apparent decision to de-emphasize this line of inquiry during the Ninety-third Congress.

To this disproportionate emphasis on news presentations the Investigations Subcommittee has added sporadic inquiries into other areas of Commerce Committee jurisdiction. By virtue of their scrutiny of the Securities and Exchange Commission (SEC) and possible securities-law violations, the subcommittee got in-

---

* House Democratic leaders found Staggers uncooperative when they later tried to expedite a bill to waive equal-time requirements so as to permit televised debates in the 1972 campaign, and several members of the Commerce Committee's Health and Environment and Commerce and Finance subcommittees still perceive resentment over their "disloyalty" to be the cause of the chairman's lackadaisical handling of their projects.

volved in a matter that received wide publicity in 1972 and 1973, but was hardly resolved. The Nixon administration had dismissed an antitrust suit against the International Telephone and Telegraph Corporation, and Staggers says that the subcommittee

> received definite and strong allegations that certain docu
> ments in the possession of the SEC detailed numerous con-
> tacts between [ITT] and high government officials seeking
> to obtain preferred treatment for the corporation under the
> law. Moreover, these allegations if supported would raise
> serious questions about the policies and procedures of the
> SEC itself.[15]

But the subcommittee's inquiry was hampered by the SEC's actions. At first the SEC refused to let subcommittee personnel investigate the files, and then it transferred them to the Department of Justice, where they would effectively be beyond the power of subpoena. As Investigations Subcommittee chief counsel Daniel Manelli puts it, the episode "is illustrative of the growing difficulty the Congress seems to be having in obtaining sufficient information to exercise its proper legislative oversight function." But the episode may signify a good deal more, for SEC Chairman William Casey admitted that he consulted with the White House before transferring the documents to Justice one month before the 1972 presidential election. Casey's assistant, Charles Whiteman, further acknowledged that he had pulled some documents that were "politically sensitive" from the thirty-two boxes of papers and had kept them under lock and key. Certainly such pre-election "prudence" (Casey's term) appears to have been a very dubious virtue.[16] In any case, the subcommittee held scattered hearings on the matter during 1973, taking testimony from former SEC Chairmen Casey and G. Bradford Cook and former Counsel to the President John W. Dean III.

The subcommittee's inquiries are seldom as well-publicized as the ITT matter, but they often have a similar *ad hoc* quality. The subcommittee held hearings on the collapse of the Penn Central Railroad in 1970 and issued a report, "Inadequacies of Protections for Investors in Penn Central and other ICC-Regulated Companies," in 1971. This report provided the basis for the introduction of corrective legislation by Chairman Staggers in the Ninety-second and Ninety-third Congresses. According to chief counsel Manelli, the legislation was slow to move "primarily" because of "the dilatory way in which the Office of Management and Budget cleared the comments from the SEC."* But in 1973 the ICC, "reacting to the possibility of tightened legislation in this area . . . on its own initiative increased the degree of investor protection which it affords those members of the public purchasing securities issued by ICC-regulated companies."[17]

Four staff members spent a major part of their time in 1970 and 1971 on the ICC study and a related staff study analyzing SEC records of broker-dealer liquidations and assessing the protections investors had in such circumstances. In addition, two staff men spent a good part of 1972 and 1973 on the freight-car-shortage problem, some staff worked on hearings that explored an apparently irregular ICC action in processing a rail acquisition application, and in 1973 a staff survey of the quality of Amtrak services was begun. Otherwise, the transportation areas and agencies in need of oversight have been largely ignored. Two widely publicized incidents—the exposure of Delta Airlines passengers to radioactive materials being shipped aboard scheduled flights, and the crash in France of a DC-10 that had been shown to have a defective door design—prompted subcommittee inquiries in 1974 into a hitherto neglected area, the FAA's aviation safety programs and policies.

The Investigations Subcommittee staff sometimes assists in the work of the legislative subcommittees; the primary recent examples are the Health Subcommittee's investigation in the Ninety-second Congress of the closing of Public Health Service hospitals and the Communications Subcommittee's inquiry concerning television blackouts of sports events during the Ninety-third. The

---

* The comments of the ICC were forwarded directly to the chairman, however. And in any case it is hardly plausible (or necessary) that the committee be entirely at the mercy of OMB in this matter.

investigations staff completed a study of drug abuse in organized sports in 1973, and Staggers, concerned that public hearings might encourage drug experimentation among young people, sought and received informal "assurances of intensified self-regulation"[18] on the part of the commissioners of the major professional sports leagues. The staff also continued an inquiry, begun in the Ninety-second Congress, into certain Food and Drug Administration management practices. And the explosion of a liquid natural gas storage tank on Staten Island in 1973 led to hearings on the enforcement activities of the Federal Power Commission and the Office of Pipeline Safety. But in health, communications, and power, as in transportation, the subcommittee's activity does not add up to a systematic oversight role. Nor has the assistance received by the legislative subcommittees been sufficient to offset a widespread feeling among their members that they would be better served by a dispersal of the staff resources controlled by Staggers and Manelli.

The work of the Investigations Subcommittee betrays a tendency to concentrate on individual cases and aberrations as opposed to *patterns* of institutional behavior. One staff member, asked in a 1972 interview to highlight the subcommittee's activities, dwelt at length on the exposure of the false testimony of the secretary of the ICC regarding his reimbursement of a trade association that had picked up his hotel tab. The FBI was called in to confirm that the check had not been written on the date alleged, and the secretary had little choice but to resign. It was an ugly incident, and perhaps was indicative of larger patterns, but as one legislative subcommittee aide noted, "Only the small fish get fried."

In another drawn-out case, the subcommittee investigated Federal Communications Commission license-renewal methods by dwelling upon an Indianapolis situation. The FCC had renewed the license of Star Stations Inc., including stations WIFE–AM and WIFE–FM in Indianapolis, despite findings of fraudulent advertising and promotions. Again, securing information from an agency was a problem; FCC Chairman Rosel Hyde was eventually voted in contempt by the full committee. The subcommittee succeeded in airing the issue and in stimulating a more critical commission review. The subcommittee issued a critical report in 1970 and received a measure of vindication in 1975, when the FCC denied license renewals for five Star-affiliated stations. One staff member has continued to spend considerable time on license renewals. But the broader dimensions of the problem are only hinted at by such piecemeal inquiries.

A third case in point is the investigation of FCC monitoring of employees' telephone calls, the subject of two-day subcommittee hearings in the Ninety-second Congress and of a report in early 1973. The subcommittee issued a stinging reprimand:

> The FCC has argued that since it had some indication of a security leak, its actions were reasonable and the secret telephone monitoring was thereby justified. . . . It should be self-evident, however, that any agency action dealing with improper leaks must be in accordance with the law and sensitive to the fundamental Constitutional rights and personal dignity of its employees. . . . The FCC has assured the Subcommittee that it will not engage in secret telephone monitoring in the future. It is imperative that it keep that pledge.[19]

But, again, the subcommittee showed little inclination to follow up beyond the single case.*

What does all this imply regarding the overall performance of the Investigations Subcommittee? Clearly the indictments of ineptitude and sloth which some Interstate and Foreign Commerce Committee members draw are exaggerated. At the same time, however, the subcommittee's activities do not add up to a comprehensive oversight role, or even to a systematic and effective sampling of major problem areas under Commerce Committee jurisdiction. Several observations may be made in summary:

1. The subcommittee has been hobbled by the exclusiveness of

---

* Routine assurances from other agencies that they do not engage in "secret telephone monitoring" were gathered but not probed by the subcommittee.

Staggers' control. By forbidding dual subcommittee memberships and by making the Investigations Subcommittee inhospitable to member initiatives, Staggers has weakened the subcommittee in terms of membership and participation. And the staff, apparently performing as the chairman wishes, have remained limited in their self-image and in their willingness to assume initiative and authority. Staggers' replacement by the more energetic and creative John Moss augurs well for the subcommittee's future. But it remains to be seen whether Moss will undertake the measures—recruiting a more distinguished cross-section of Commerce members for subcommittee service, for example, giving them free rein when they get there, and fostering more independent and aggressive staff operations—that will be needed to invigorate the Investigations Subcommittee.

2. The subcommittee's overall level of production is low relative to the share of full-committee funds and personnel it absorbs. This is not to deny that Manelli and several of his colleagues are well-meaning, hard-working, and relatively competent, or that printed output is an imperfect indicator of committee activity (Manelli stresses the importance of staff inquiries and member communications that do not show up in such statistics). But the subcommittee is, after all, dealing with matters of grave *public* concern; a two-year total (for the Ninety-second Congress) of fifteen days of public hearings on five separate matters seems woefully inadequate for a subcommittee responsible for the oversight of the Interstate and Foreign Commerce Committee's entire terrain. Other indicators of subcommittee output for the Ninety-second Congress—three reports, two published staff studies—are hardly more impressive. Moreover, by any standard one would wish to apply, the involvement of subcommittee *members* has been minimal. "I would like to give a brief explanation of our committee members," Staggers said somewhat plaintively during the hearings on television news rigging:

> Mr. Pickle has an operation of some kind this morning and will not be here. Mr. Blanton is in Tennessee and is unavail-

> able, and we are trying to get in touch with Mr. Springer so
> we will have at least three here. If not, Mr. Shoup and
> myself are here, and we will go ahead and not hold anybody
> up.[20]

The staff's level of productivity also seems generally low, even
when one matches men with projects in the way we have attempted and discounts for the short-term demands that inevitably
crowd in.

3. The subcommittee's agenda displays imbalance in terms of
the chairman's preoccupations, seems almost random in other
respects, and, in general, displays a preference for investigation of
individual cases as opposed to larger patterns of agency conduct.
Deceptive news presentations are not a trivial problem, but surely
one must ask whether the likely marginal returns justified the
devotion of so large a proportion of subcommittee resources to
what became a rather repetitive series of investigations—to say
nothing of the apprehensions excited by Staggers' apparent insensitivity to the First Amendment questions his inquiries raised.
The subcommittee's other work has shed light on a number of
problems with the regulatory agencies, pointing up instances of
improper behavior and needs for altered agency procedures. Important questions have been pressed with respect to governmental
secrecy. But it is not apparent that any clear priorities have been
established or any systematic sampling processes developed.
Problems rather seem to be dealt with as a crisis arises or as they
otherwise "come to the subcommittee's attention," with a clear
bias toward alleged instances of personal or agency malfeasance
and, too often, a failure to pursue broader policy questions.* The

* Manelli claimed that Staggers, having recently launched "a systematic
review of the SEC's enforcement program going back three years," had
"committed the subcommittee to conduct similar reviews of all of the major
regulatory agencies under its jurisdiction. . . . It is obvious to me that the
chairman is well aware of the need for intensified legislative oversight on
a systematic basis."[21] As of January 1975 the plans and priorities of the new
chairman, John Moss, include investigations in the following areas: "Energy:
natural gas reserves and withholding; effect of vertical integration in the oil
and gas industries; Federal Energy Administration—conflicts of interest;

subcommittee's piecemeal agenda and scattered efforts, its preoccupation with questions of personal morality and official corruption, and its apparent definition of its role in terms more of police functions (four aides are former FBI agents) than of broader forms of critical oversight—all this hardly adds up to the "review and study, on a continuing basis, [of] the application, administration, and execution of those laws . . . within the [Committee's] jurisdiction" with which the Subcommittee on Investigations is charged.[23]

Does this mean, then, that the counsel of those who advocate an abolition of the subcommittee and a dispersal of its functions and resources to the legislative subcommittees should be heeded? Not necessarily. The disappointing oversight record of the Senate Commerce subcommittees offers a cautionary note in this regard; it is significant that a recentralization of investigative staff functions is under way there. But there is no area of House Commerce Committee operations that cries out more obviously for refurbishing and reform. We will consider in the final chapter what some of the alternatives and prospects are.

Federal Energy Administration—implementation of petroleum price controls and of the Emergency Petroleum Allocation Act. Food: vertical and horizontal integration in the food industry. Environment/Consumer Safety: proposed moratorium on safety and environmental regulations; automobile passive restraint systems—cost and effectiveness. Health: nursing home abuses; Food and Drug Administration—food additives; health care costs; adequacy of national health care standards. General: independent regulatory agencies, their performance and independence; Northeast Rail Reorganization Act oversight; government resources allocated to the promotion of competition."[22]

9

The Committees
and the Future:
Mechanisms
for Change

The behavior of the House and Senate Commerce committees is
not a chance phenomenon. The patterns we have observed are
deeply rooted: in persistent norms, structures, and leadership
practices; in recruitment patterns and in the priorities and perceived "necessities" that recruits bring with them; in virtually
irresistible group and constituency pressures and the intractable
powers of the executive branch. In the face of this, mere moralis-
tic exhortation seems impotent, if not irresponsible. It should not
be supposed, however, that this is a closed system. On the contrary, a substantial minority of the members of the Commerce
committees, through their own skill and purposefulness, have

NOTE: This chapter was written by David E. Price.

322

made the best of their situation and have developed constructive and creative roles for themselves. Committee members clearly are faced with "slack" as well as fixity, opportunities as well as obstacles. It is our purpose in this final section to point up some of those opportunities and to discuss certain ways in which, in our view, the effectiveness of the House and Senate Commerce committees might be enhanced.

Recruitment. Both the low levels of legislative involvement on the committees and the parochial or "promotional" nature of much that is proposed reveal the prevalence on House and Senate Commerce of orientations toward district service and/or the defense of interests with a stake in the *status quo*, particularly in communications and transportation policy. One of the fortunate effects of media and population growth (and electoral competition) has been to force broader concerns and a more assertive policy role on Warren Magnuson and some of his colleagues. But both the House and Senate committees badly need new blood. The addition of Senators Tunney and Stevenson—urban-state progressives with incentives for and inclinations toward policy leadership—to the Senate committee in 1973 has already made a marked impact on the committee's level of activity, and several of the new members added to the House committee in 1975 appear similarly promising. Still, the chairmen and party leaders should make a far more concerted effort to recruit and appoint members with sufficient energy, experience, and independence to cut through the comfortable patterns of accommodation that too often substitute for effective lawmaking and oversight on both committees.

Leadership. Magnuson's growing permissiveness with his members, his increasing willingness to stake out bold positions in consumer and environmental policy, and his capacities for persuasion and conciliation are impressive marks of leadership, although tendencies to retrenchment and disengagement on his part render the Senate committee's policy role somewhat tenuous and unstable. The House committee's leadership problems are much more severe. Chairman Staggers is well-meaning and kind-hearted, but under duress he can be vindictive and obstructive. A crowded agenda and a querulous membership frustrate and threaten him; he has neither the taste nor the ability for strong and effective leadership. Staggers, from West Virginia's safe second district, was elevated to his position purely as a result of the seniority system; his difficulties point up the desirability of altering the process of selecting committee chairmen. The House committee, and probably the committee system in general, would be well-served by a rule setting a limited term for the chairmanship or establishing a rotation system. At a minimum, procedures should be established whereby the party caucuses would consciously *choose* the chairman and ranking minority member from designated *groups* of nominees.[1] Hoary precedents were broken in 1975 as both the Democratic Steering Committee (responsible for nominations) and the full caucus chose to remove several chairmen who were considered especially arbitrary or autocratic. The result may be to increase the responsiveness and accountability of even those chairmen who were not directly challenged.* But such challenges will probably prove a blunt instrument, irregularly applied, until a system of multiple nominations is instituted.

Legislative Subcommittees. The relative advantages and disadvantages committee decentralization offers should be considered carefully. Presently, systems of fragmented authority in both the executive and legislative branches set up destructive conflicts and deadlocks and make impossible a rational, coordinated approach to critical problem areas such as transportation, health care, and the environment. However, at certain *stages* of policy formation—when one's concern is to publicize pressing problems, to float new proposals, to gain access for disadvantaged or excluded groups—decentralization and overlapping jurisdictions have considerable advantages. Magnuson's devolution of Com-

---

* Staggers received a relatively large number of negative votes in caucus (54) but no Commerce member chose to mount a challenge and his seat was never really in danger. One constraining factor was that Staggers' most likely replacement, under the canons of seniority, was Torbert Macdonald, who had often been ineffective as a subcommittee chairman.

merce Committee authority and resources via an expanded sub-committee structure has had a positive impact in this respect, multiplying the leverage-points at which advocates might make their voices heard, while retaining the capacity of the full committee to coordinate and integrate. Subcommittee proliferation has also multiplied the incentives and resources that encourage and enable less senior members to have a policy impact, though the multiple memberships it necessitates have also badly overextended some senators.

The experience of the Senate Commerce Committee—and the manifest incapacity of the House Interstate and Foreign Commerce Committee to deal expeditiously with its agenda—suggests that an increase in the number of subcommittees on the House committee would be well advised. The subcommittee reorganization that took place at the beginning of the Ninety-fourth Congress made for a net gain of one subcommittee, splitting off energy and power from the Communications Subcommittee. But this leaves environmental policy the stepchild of the Rogers subcommittee, a group "choked," as a committee aide puts it, by its huge jurisdiction. It also preserves, for the most part, the muddled Commerce and Finance Subcommittee jurisdiction.* Organizing a separate subcommittee on the environment, and perhaps one dealing exclusively with consumer affairs, would seem a promising means of giving these critical areas the single-minded attention they deserve. If such subcommittee reorganization were coupled with loosening of a chairman's grip on committee authority and resources—as seems likely in light of the 1975 rules changes and the altered balance of forces on the committee—it could greatly increase the productivity and expedite the procedures of the committee as a whole.

The modification of the one-subcommittee membership rule, effected by Commerce Democrats in 1975, is necessary to the functioning of any expanded subcommittee system. But the member-

---

* Preliminary membership bids suggested that the renamed "Consumer Protection and Finance" subcommittee would continue to rank low among the priorities of Commerce members. Health-Environment and Energy-Power seemed to be the top choices.

ship limit should remain at *two*; with forty-three members, the House Commerce Committee can avoid the overextension the Senate committee has suffered.

The effectiveness of any reconstituted subcommittee system will also depend on whether the committee caucus asserts itself in the selection of subcommittee chairmen. (Although the Senate committee has suffered less from moribund subcommittee leadership, it too needs to develop procedures that enable the members to make deliberate leadership choices.) The rules adopted by the House committee in 1975, following guidelines laid down by the House Democratic Caucus, permit majority members to bid for subcommittee chairmanships in the order of their full committee seniority; if the majority caucus (voting by secret ballot) rejects a bid, a vote will be taken on the next most senior member who chooses to bid for that chairmanship. It is possible to conceive of procedures that would give less weight to seniority *per se* and more to experience on the subcommittee one wishes to lead—for example, choosing from among the *three* most senior subcommittee members —but if the members use the new rules to make conscious leadership choices, they will be taking an important step in the right direction.

Investigations and Oversight. Whatever its other advantages, subcommittee proliferation on the Senate Commerce Committee has not made for noticeably improved oversight. Even when opportunities and resources are made available, members often have few incentives to undertake the protracted, often tedious, and rarely headline-worthy process of monitoring the performance of the executive and independent agencies. This is a problem of which some Senate committee members and aides are aware, and their effort to expand the responsibilities of the special investigative staff unit to include oversight functions and the closer scrutiny of nominees is a promising experiment. If the legislative subcommittees do not effectively utilize this new resource, it might be necessary to consider the appointment of a special investigations subcommittee. The disinterest and overextension of many senators might also require the elevation of the staff's role to that of hearing examiners, although the resulting gains in expertise and in the capacity to press hard questions would have to be weighed against the losses in publicity value and political clout that might result if the senators themselves were less directly involved.

The idea of a special investigative unit in the Senate committee might be questioned in light of the widespread criticism of the House Subcommittee on Investigations. The House subcommittee is hardly fulfilling its mandate for continuous and comprehensive oversight. But it is not clear that the favored remedy of most Interstate and Foreign Commerce subcommittee chairmen and of many other members and aides—namely, abolishing the Investigations Subcommittee and dispersing its authority and resources to the legislative subcommittees—would greatly improve the situation. It is hard to imagine officials of the ICC or CAB or FCC losing much sleep over the prospect of increased scrutiny by Communications and Power or Transportation and Aeronautics as those subcommittees have been constituted. Nor do the results of decentralization in the Senate committee offer much encouragement as far as oversight is concerned. The preferred course is thus not to abolish the Investigations Subcommitttee but to strengthen it.

The replacement of Harley Staggers by John Moss as Investigations Subcommittee chairman is an important first step. Quite apart from the merits of the individuals involved, it is important that the investigations unit have a chairman who is head of neither the full committee nor a legislative subcommittee, and thus can give undivided attention to oversight work. But Moss has his work cut out for him. Ideally, the Investigations Subcommittee would integrate and give focus to the full committee's oversight work, drawing on the expertise of the legislative subcommittees but giving special priority to the kinds of inquiry they find it all too easy to ignore. This would require, in the first place, recruiting energetic and influential members, including experienced members from the legislative subcommittees, for Investigations Subcommittee work—and insuring their involvement and staying power by opening up productive roles for them once they get there. Such recruitment will be facilitated by the rescission of the prohibition of dual subcommittee service, but preliminary membership bids in the Ninety-fourth Congress still resulted in an investigations unit primarily populated by freshmen.

Beyond this, there is a need for a major shift in Investigations Subcommittee perspectives and preoccupations, away from the sorts of inquiries and exposures detailed in Chapter 8 and toward the broad mandate for oversight. There should be a selective review of the enforcement of key regulatory statutes and of their impact on the consumer. Staff teams might be assigned to the various agencies under the committee's jurisdiction, with responsibility for continuous and concentrated scrutiny. Certainly this would require increased member involvement and a higher level of staff industry and initiative.

If a refurbishing of the Investigations Subcommittee along these lines is *not* undertaken, the frequently heard proposal for the abolition of the subcommittee and the dispersal of its functions might indeed be the most desirable short-term solution. But on both the House and Senate Commerce committees the oversight function is in poor repair, and it is doubtful that it will ever receive adequate attention and resources without the presence of a separate staff contingent and/or subcommittee whose *prime* responsibility is investigations and oversight.

Staff. The activist, "entrepreneurial" staff norms that have been so crucial to the evolving policy role of the Senate Commerce Committee could not be transferred intact to the House committee. Service-oriented, "promotional" styles still hold sway in many parts of the Senate committee; in the less visible, relatively conservative, and more specialized House committee, aides of the Pertschuk stamp would find even rockier soil in which to flourish. The House staff could nonetheless take a lesson from their Senate counterparts: careful, even-handed, competent service has its virtues, but even more important can be the staff's role in ferreting out policy gaps and stimulating member initiatives. Interstate and Foreign Commerce members are not, for the most part, active legislators or vigilant overseers themselves, but neither do they have as restrictive a notion of how the staff should operate as many of their aides seem to assume. A more creative and catalytic staff role is feasible, and the committee's policy-making capacity and impact would be well served by it.

In general, the staff's orientation—the *way* information is gathered and recommendations are presented—is a more important determinant of the quality and impact of staff services than its mere size or even its technical competence. The usual calls for "more" and "better" staffs promise little in isolation. But in the case of House Commerce, the shortage and maldistribution of staff resources are indeed serious problems. The chronic overextension of full-committee aides such as Robert Guthrie (communications and consumer affairs) and William Dixon (transportation) has been only partially alleviated by the addition in 1973 of two new full-committee staff slots in consumer and environmental affairs. The relatively inefficient Investigations Subcommittee has received a disproportionate share of staff resources. And the shortage of staff at the subcommittee level remains acute. The problem has been exacerbated, to be sure, by Jarman's and Macdonald's misuse of their subcommittee aides for personal staff work. But the Health-Environment and Commerce-Finance subcommittees badly need more staff help, they are entitled to it under the caucus rules, and they should get it.* The Senate committee is more adequately staffed in terms of numbers, though here too committee aides are all too often siphoned off for personal staff work.

The Policy-Making Environment. While the resources and capacities of the groups and agencies operating in a given policy area are largely beyond the control of the legislators who must contend with them, Commerce committee members should not be portrayed as being at the mercy of their environment. Legislators

---

* In early 1975 it appeared that the subcommittee chairmen, having demonstrated their strength and improved their position through numerous rules changes, would also press successfully for a greater share of the committee's staff resources.

in fact have considerable freedom—and opportunities, often, for political profit—in appealing over the heads of dominant groups to a diffuse but mobilizable public sentiment. Mutually reinforcing relationships could be formed, moreover, with the public broadcasters and their supporters, fledgling consumer and environmental groups, and executive agencies such as NOAA and EPA. If the complexities of the policy-making environment offer pitfalls and obstacles, they also afford opportunities for maneuver and alliance. Too often the Commerce committees settle into comfortable patterns of accommodation or "promotion," abandoning their independence to dominant industry groups and the executive branch; the path to greater influence and responsibility lies in recognizing the alternative possibilities.

An examination of the policy-making environment is also instructive for those interested outsiders who wish to move the committees in new directions. Stances independent of the preferred positions of dominant groups are easier for legislators to take if it is clear that countervailing group and public support will be forthcoming—and if vigilant citizens are ready to expose and publicize accommodations that contravene the broader public interest. It is not enough simply to urge independence and integrity on legislators dealing with, say, communications or transportation policy. The established interests, well-financed and relatively tightly organized, have well-developed means of manipulating the negative and positive incentives that induce a legislator to do their bidding. The "public-interest" groups have different resources— less cohesion but a broader popular base, less money but more publicity potential—and they too must learn to manipulate incentives, to alter the legislator's perception of and relation to his environment. Consumer and environmental advocates have in recent years learned important lessons about doing their homework and paying attention to legislative and administrative detail, about utilizing the media to dramatize their case, about targeting and concentrating their campaign activity. The importance of building and acting upon those lessons becomes apparent when one recognizes the nature of the forces that are otherwise likely to dominate the legislator's field of vision.

These recommendations hardly exhaust the list that might be distilled from a study of the Commerce committees. Staggers' and Rogers' methods of accommodating their Republican members, for example, have a great deal to do with the internal sluggishness of the House Commerce Committee. Intercommittee rivalry and stereotyping are responsible to a large extent for the Commerce committees' pattern of diluted and obstructed conference reports. In these and similar instances, the remedies that creative leadership might invoke are fairly obvious. The concern here has been to highlight the conditions of increased committee independence, competence, and creativity and to focus on the structural and organizational factors, some of them immediately remediable, which impair the committees' effective functioning. But in conclusion it is important to reiterate a theme that has run throughout this study: whatever problems the House and Senate Commerce committees may have, they still offer a promising field of action for the creative and enterprising legislator. This is not to belittle the importance of the constraining factors that have been discussed, nor is it to assert that legislative effectiveness is simply a matter of resoluteness and good will. It is rather to note that there is considerable "slack" in the system. Both committees *already* afford more resources and freedom of movement for effective lawmaking and oversight than their members effectively utilize. Several ways in which both committees might be made more conducive to such endeavors have been suggested. But the roles and responsibilities that the House and Senate Commerce committees assume are in the end largely attributable to the energy, integrity, and vision of the individuals who sit around the table.

Notes

CHAPTER 1. THE POLITICS OF COMMERCE

1. See the historical sketches in U. S., Congress, Senate, Committee on Commerce, *History, Membership, and Jurisdiction of the Senate Committee on Commerce from 1816–1966,* 89th Cong. (June 24, 1966); and U. S., Congress, House, Committee on Interstate and Foreign Commerce, "Compilation of Activity Reports Together with Historical Data Concerning the Committee," 92nd Cong. (Apr. 1971).
2. George Goodwin, Jr., *The Little Legislatures: Committees of Congress* (Amherst: Univ. of Massachusetts Press, 1970), pp. 114–116. The rankings cover the period 1949–1968. We have omitted the anomalous case of the House Committee on Un-American Activities from tabulation.
3. Charles S. Bullock III, "The Influence of State Party Delegations on House Committee Assignments," *Midwest Journal of Political Science* XV (Aug. 1971), pp. 533, 540 541. On the House committee's reluctance to regulate cigarette advertising, see David E. Price, *Who Makes the Laws?* (Cambridge: Schenkman, 1972), pp. 37–49, 347–348 (n. 31).
4. See "Warren G. Magnuson," *Citizens Look at Congress,* Ralph Nader Congress Project (Washington: Grossman Publishers, 1972), pp. 4–9; and Price, *Who Makes the Laws?,* pp. 29, 77–79.
5. "Magnuson," *Citizens Look at Congress,* p. 10.
6. Data from U. S. Dept. of Commerce, "EDA Directory of Approved Projects," June 30, 1971. Computations by Murray Solomon.
7. Computed from data in Michael Barone, *et al., The Almanac of American Politics* (Boston: Gambit, 1972), pp. 878, 1010.
8. See David E. Price, "Professionals and 'Entrepreneurs': Staff Orientations and Policy Making on Three Senate Committees," *Journal of*

Politics XXXIII (May 1971), pp. 316–336; and Price, *Who Makes the Laws?*, pp. 29, 67–69, 99–104, 329–331.

9. Price, *Who Makes the Laws?*, p. 101.
10. Ibid., pp. 67–69.
11. The term "neutral competence" is taken from Herbert Kaufman, "Emerging Conflicts in the Doctrines of Public Administration," *American Political Science Review* L (Dec. 1956), p. 1060; see also Price, "Professionals and 'Entrepreneurs.'"
12. For a more detailed discussion, see Price, *Who Makes the Laws?*, pp. 82–90.
13. Ibid., pp. 87–90.
14. *The Federalist*, No. 62.

CHAPTER 2.   CONSUMER PROTECTION

1. Introduction of Senator Warren Magnuson at the Consumer Federation of America Dinner, May 7, 1973.
2. *Congressional Record*, June 13, 1973, p. S.11094. References are to the daily edition, unless otherwise noted.
3. Ibid., p. S.11110.
4. Seattle, Washington, *Post-Intelligencer*, June 13, 1973.
5. May 18, 1973 press release by Senators Warren Magnuson and Frank Moss and Representative John Moss.
6. Speech at the Ralph Nader Conference, "Verdicts on Lawyers," Washington, Aug. 4, 1973.
7. *Congressional Record*, June 21, 1972, p. S.9932.
8. Ibid., pp. S.9918–9919.
9. *Congressional Record*, June 21, 1972, p. S.9879.
10. U. S., Congress, House, Committee on Interstate and Foreign Commerce, *Report on H.R. 15003*, H. Rept. 92–1153, 92nd Cong., 2nd sess. (June 20, 1972), p. 22.
11. U. S., Congress, House, Committee on Interstate and Foreign Commerce, Subcommittee on Commerce and Finance, *Consumer Product Safety Act: Hearings*, 92nd Cong., 1st sess. (Nov. 30, 1971), Pt. 2, p. 301.
12. House Rept. 92–1153, pp. 22–23.
13. *Consumer Product Safety Act: Hearings*, p. 301.
14. U. S., Congress, Senate, Committee on Commerce, *Consumer Product Safety Act of 1971: Hearings*, 92nd Cong., 1st sess. (July 1971), Pt. 1, p. 339.
15. Ibid., p. 101.
16. Ibid., p. 143.
17. Ibid., p. 144.
18. Ibid., pp. 144, 145.
19. Ibid., Pt. 2, pp. 588–594.

20. Ibid., pp. 549–551.
21. Ibid., p. 249.
22. U. S., Congress, Senate, Committee on Commerce, *Report on S. 3419*, S. Rept. 92–749, 92nd Cong., 2nd sess. (April 13, 1972).
23. *Congressional Record*, June 21, 1972, p. S.9883.
24. Ibid., pp. S.9894, 9895.
25. *Washington Post*, June 22, 1972.
26. *Congressional Record*, June 21, 1972, pp. S.9916–9917.
27. Ibid., p. S.9917.
28. H. Rept. 92–1153, pp. 24–25.
29. House Commerce Committee, *Report on H.R. 15003, Dissent.*
30. *Congressional Quarterly Almanac, 1972*, p. 141.
31. *Congressional Record*, Sept. 20, 1972, p. H.8593.
32. Ibid.
33. Statement of the Commissioners, Consumer Product Safety Commission, 1973.
34. *Washington Post*, Oct. 14, 1973.

CHAPTER 3. SURFACE TRANSPORTATION

1. See Robert Roberts, "The New Look at the AAR," *Modern Railroads*, Sept. 1969.
2. Testimony of Thomas Gale Moore, Professor of Economics, Michigan State University, in U. S., Congress, Senate, Commerce Committee, Subcommittee on Surface Transportation, *Surface Transportation Legislation: Hearings*, 92nd Cong., 2nd sess. (May 1972), Pt. 1, p. 1079. In a 1973 report commissioned by the Joint Economic Committee, Professor George Hilton of the University of California at Los Angeles estimated that regulation by the ICC imposes a "$5 billion implicit tax on the economy."
3. Robert Fellmeth, et al., *The Interstate Commerce Omission* (New York: Grossman Publishers, 1972), pp. 257–273.
4. Cited in ibid., p. 133.
5. Ibid., pp. 136–137.
6. Ibid., p. 272. Note that three of the suspensions occurred after the 1970 Nader study of the ICC.
7. Article 1, Section 8(3).
8. Roberts, "The New Look at the AAR."
9. Ibid., p. 3.
10. Ibid., p. 3.
11. Fellmeth, *Interstate Commerce Omission*, pp. 26–28.
12. Quoted in ibid., p. 29.
13. Records of the Nader Congress Project, CP Archives, 1972.
14. *Washington Star-News*, Mar. 11, 1973.
15. Ibid.

16. See Royce Hanson, "Congress Copes with Mass Transit," in Frederic Cleaveland, *et al.*, *Congress and Urban Problems* (Washington: Brookings Institution, 1969).
17. U. S., Congress, Senate, Commerce Committee, Subcommittee on Surface Transportation, *Review of ICC Policies and Practices: Hearings*, 91st Cong., 1st sess. (1969), p. 59.
18. Ibid.
19. Ibid.
20. Ibid.
21. Letter to Senator Fred Harris from Lawrence Woodworth, chief of staff of the Joint Committee on Internal Revenue Taxation, Apr. 18, 1972.
22. *Congressional Quarterly Weekly Report*, Oct. 2, 1971, p. 2022.
23. Ibid.
24. "Smathers: Thriving Lobbyist," *Newsday*, Oct. 6–13, 1971, p. 31R.
25. *Congressional Record*, July 28, 1971, p. S.12367.
26. "Smathers," *Newsday*, p. 31R.
27. U. S., Congress, House, Committee on Interstate and Foreign Commerce, Subcommittee on Transportation and Aeronautics, *Transportation Act of 1972: Hearings*, 92nd Cong., 2nd sess. (Mar.–May 1972).
28. Ibid.
29. Senate Commerce Committee, *Surface Transportation Legislation*.
30. House Commerce Committee, *Transportation Act of 1972*.
31. Ibid., Pt. 3, pp. 1107–1114.
32. Ibid., Pt. 2, p. 604.
33. Ibid., Pt. 1, p. 229.
34. Senate Commerce Committee, *Surface Transportation Legislation*, Pt. 1, 1126.
35. Ibid., pp. 1123–1124.
36. Ibid., p. 1073.
37. *AAR Annual Report*.

CHAPTER 4.   AVIATION

1. Burton Bernstein, "The Piper Cub vs. the 747," *New York Times Magazine*, Mar. 8, 1969, pp. 34–35.
2. *Congressional Quarterly, Congress and the Nation 1945–64*, p. 536.
3. George Eads, *The Local Service Airplane Experiment* (Washington: Brookings Institution, 1972), pp. 1–2.
4. Ibid., pp. 128–129.
5. See ibid., Ch. 5–6.
6. U. S., Congress, Senate, Committee on Commerce, Subcommittee on Aviation, *Airport/Airways Development: Hearings*, 91st Cong., 1st sess. (June 17, 18, 19, 24, 25, 26; July 23, 24, 29, 30, 1969), Pts. 1–2.
7. *Congressional Record*, Nov. 12, 1971, p. S.18394.

8. "Howard W. Cannon," *Citizens Look at Congress*, Ralph Nader Congress Project (Washington Grossman Publishers, 1972), p. 17.
9. *Congressional Record* (bound edition), Dec. 3, 1971, pp. S.46760–46763.
10. U. S., Congress, House, Committee on Interstate and Foreign Commerce, *Aviation Facilities Maintenance and Development: Hearings*, 91st Cong., 1st sess. (July 21, 22, 23, 24, 25, 28, 29, 30, 31; Sept. 9, 10, 1969), Pts. 1–2.
11. U. S., Congress, Senate, Committee on Commerce, *The Role of General Aviation*, 91st Cong., 1st sess. (May 2, 1969), p. 69.
12. Senate Commerce Committee, *Airport/Airways Development: Hearings*, p. 595.
13. Ibid., p. 89.
14. Ibid.
15. Ibid., p. 173.
16. House Commerce Committee, *Aviation Facilities Maintenance and Development: Hearings*, p. 231.
17. Jeremy Warford, *Public Policy Toward General Aviation* (Washington: Brookings Institution, 1971), p. 59.
18. House Commerce Committee, *Aviation Facilities Maintenance and Development: Hearings*, p. 452.
19. Warford, *Public Policy*, p. 59.
20. *Congressional Quarterly Almanac*, 1968, p. 624.
21. Bernstein, "The Piper Cub vs. the 747," p. 35.
22. House Commerce Committee, *Aviation Facilities Maintenance and Development: Hearings*, p. 1.
23. *Congressional Record*, Feb. 25, 1970, p. S.4850.

CHAPTER 5.   COMMUNICATIONS

1. Ralph Lee Smith, "The Wired Nation," *Nation*, May 8, 1970, p. 586.
2. Bruce Thorp, "FCC Moves Toward Decision on Rules Vital to CATV Industry," *National Journal*, Jan. 2, 1971, p. 10.
3. Hamilton Shea, Chairman of National Association of Broadcasters' Television Board and Chairman of Future of Broadcasting Committee, quoted in ibid., p. 10.
4. *Television Digest*, June 26, 1972, p. 2.
5. U. S., Congress, Senate, Committee on Commerce, Subcommittee on Communications, *Community Antenna Television Problems: Hearings*, 92nd Cong., 1st sess. (June 15, 1971), p. 50.
6. Letter of Transmittal for Reorganization Plan No. 1 of 1970, dated February 9, 1970, in U. S., Congress, House, Committee on Interstate and Foreign Commerce, *Financing for Public Broadcasting, 1972: Hearings*, 92nd Cong., 2nd sess. (Feb. 1, 2, 3, 1972), p. 292.
7. Burch and Brown quotations taken from OTP, Notebook No. 4, The Network Project (Apr. 1973), p. 5.

8. *Broadcasting*, Feb. 16, 1970.
9. Cox, "Does the FCC Really Do Anything?," *Broadcasting* 11 (1967), pp. 97–104; see also William Wentz, "The Aftermath of WHDH," 18 *Univ. of Pennsylvania Law Review* 368 (1970), for a critical analysis of FCC renewal practices.
10. *Broadcasting*, Apr. 21, 1969, p. 60.
11. 22 FCC 2d 424, 427 (1970).
12. Dissent of Nicholas Johnson, 22 FCC 2d 424, 431 (1970).
13. Policy Statement on Comparative Hearings Invoking Regular Renewal Applicants, 22 FCC 2d 424 (1970).
14. *Citizens Communications Center v. FCC*, 145 U. S. App. D. C. 32, 41 (1971).
15. *Congressional Record*, Oct. 8, 1974, p. S.18504.
16. U. S., Congress, Senate, Committee on Commerce, Subcommittee on Communications, *Overview of the Federal Communications Commission: Hearings*, 92nd Cong., 2nd sess. (Feb. 1, 1972), p. 190.
17. Statement of Commissioner Nicholas Johnson in ibid., p. 189.
18. Interview, June 29, 1972.
19. Remarks before the 47th Annual Convention of the National Association of Educational Broadcasters, Miami, Oct. 20, 1971, p. 9 (available from OTP).
20. "Politics and Public Broadcasting," special report on National Public Radio, Jan. 12, 1972, p. 17 (text available from OTP).
21. Statement by Clay T. Whitehead before U. S., Senate, Judiciary Committee, Subcommittee on Constitutional Rights, 92nd Cong., 2nd sess. (Feb. 2, 1972), p. 8. (Available from OTP.)
22. House Commerce Committee, *Financing for Public Broadcasting*.
23. Ibid., p. 252.
24. Ibid., p. 284.
25. Ibid., p. 82.
26. Ibid.
27. *Congressional Record*, Dec. 17, 1971, p. H.13733.
28. Ibid., June 1, 1972, pp. H.5157–5158.
29. Ibid., May 31, 1972, p. H.5107.
30. Ibid., June 1, 1972, pp. H.5168–5169.
31. Ibid., June 22, 1972, p. S.10012.
32. Ibid., p. S.10014.
33. Ibid., p. H.5995.
34. *Television Digest*, Aug. 14, 1972, p. 2.
35. *Congressional Quarterly Almanac*, 1972, p. 358.
36. *Congressional Quarterly Weekly Report*, May 12, 1973, p. 1175, and June 30, 1973, p. 1749.
37. Ibid., Mar. 17, 1973, p. 593.
38. *New York Times*, Apr. 20, 1973.
39. Ibid. (editorial), Apr. 19, 1973.
40. Ibid., Apr. 20, 1973.
41. Thorp, "FCC Moves," p. 7.
42. Sidney Dean in U. S., Congress, House, Committee on Interstate and Foreign Commerce, Subcommittee on Communications and Power,

Hearings on H.R. 420, 91st Cong., 1st sess. (Dec. 12, 1969), p. 427.

43. Smith, "The Wired Nation," p. 584.
44. Clay T. Whitehead, speech delivered to National Cable Television Association, July 8, 1971.
45. Senate Commerce Committee, *CATV Problems*, pp. 1–2.
46. *Fortnightly Corp* v. *United Artists Television, Inc.*, 392 U. S. 390 (1968).
47. *Second Report and Order*, Mar. 8, 1966, 2 FCC 2d 725.
48. *Notice of Inquiry and Notice of Proposed Rule Making*, Dec. 12, 1968, 15 FCC 2d 417.
49. See *Official Report of Cable Hearings Before the FCC*, Vol. 1–10, Mar. 1971 (on file at FCC).
50. Senate Commerce Committee, *CATV Problems: Hearings*, p. 49.
51. Ibid., p. 107.
52. Interview, July 20, 1972.
53. Senate Commerce Committee, *Overview of the FCC: Hearings*, p. 114.
54. "Letter of Intent," *Television Digest*, Aug. 21, 1972, p. 116.
55. Ibid.
56. Ibid., p. 118.
57. House Commerce Committee, *Financing for Public Broadcasting: Hearings*, p. 292.
58. Interview, July 10, 1972.
59. Statement of Commissioner Nicholas Johnson Concurring in Part and Dissenting in Part, "Final Cable Television Decision," *Television Digest*, Aug. 21, 1972, p. 146.
60. Cable Television Report and Order, Feb. 3, 1972, in "Decision," p. 18.
61. "Letter of Intent," p. 119.
62. Senate Commerce Committee, *Overview of the FCC: Hearings*, p. 125.
63. Interview, July 20, 1972.
64. Dissenting Statement of Commissioner Robert E. Lee, in "Decision," p. 118.
65. Senate Commerce Committee, *Overview of the FCC: Hearings*, p. 167.
66. Concurring Statement of Commissioner Richard E. Wiley, "Decision," p. 151.
67. Senate Commerce Committee, *Overview of the FCC: Hearings*, p. 120.
68. *Filing of the Department of Justice Before the Federal Communications Commission*, Docket 18397, Sept. 5, 1969, p. 15.
69. Senate Commerce Committee, *Overview of the FCC: Hearings*, p. 152.

CHAPTER 6. HEALTH AND ENVIRONMENT

1. *Congressional Record* (bound edition), Oct. 11, 1968, p. H.30738. A sketchy account of the episode may be found in *Congressional Quarterly Almanac*, 1968.
2. See, for example, "Health's New Strong Man in Congress," *Medical World News*, Apr. 28, 1972, pp. 30ff.

3. Elizabeth B. Drew, "The Health Syndicate: Washington's Noble Conspirators," *Atlantic Monthly* CCXX (Dec. 1971), pp. 75–82.

4. See David E. Price, *Who Makes the Laws?* (Cambridge: Schenkman, 1972), pp. 216–227.

5. Lucy Eisenberg, "The Politics of Cancer," *Harper's Magazine* CCXLIII (Nov. 1971), p. 105.

6. U. S., Congress, Senate, Committee on Labor and Public Welfare, Subcommittee on Health, *Hearings on S. 34 and S. 1828*, 92nd Cong., 1st sess. (Mar. 9, 1971), pp. 30, 64–68.

7. U. S., Congress, House, Committee on Interstate and Foreign Commerce, Subcommittee on Public Health and Environment, *Hearings on H.R. 8343 et al.*, 92nd Cong., 1st sess. (Sept. 15, 1971), pp. 154, 165, 171–173.

8. U. S., Congress, House, Committee on Interstate and Foreign Commerce, *Report to Accompany H.R. 11302*, 92nd Cong., 1st sess. (Nov. 10, 1971), p. 66.

9. *Congressional Record*, Dec. 9, 1971, p. H.12113.

10. See coverage by John Iglehart in *National Journal*, July 10, 1971, pp. 1443–1452; Nov. 20, 1971, pp. 2310–2318; May 6, 1972, pp. 777–784; Sept. 2, 1972, pp. 1404–1408.

11. Ibid., Nov. 20. 1971, p. 2313.

12. U. S., Congress, House, Committee on Interstate and Foreign Commerce, Subcommittee on Public Health and Environment, *Hearings on H.R. 5615 and H.R. 11728*, 92nd Cong., 2nd sess. (Apr. 13, 1972), pp. 333–336.

13. Ibid., p. 355.

14. See the report from the *Cleveland Plain Dealer* reprinted in *Congressional Record*, Dec. 19, 1973, p. S.23432.

15. *National Journal*, Sept. 2, 1972, p. 1404.

16. Ibid., p. 1407.

17. See testimony before the Senate Health Subcommittee, reprinted in House Commerce Committee, *Hearings on H.R. 5615 and H.R. 11728*, pp. 357–362.

18. Richard C. Wallace, "Health Maintenance Organizations: Political Response to a Social Crisis" (unpublished paper, 1973), p. 40.

19. U. S., Congress, Senate, Committee on Commerce, *Report on H.R. 13324*, 92nd Cong., 2nd sess. (June 7, 1972), pp. 22–23.

20. See James A. Noone, "Legislation to Muffle U. S. Noise Still Alive Despite Senate Struggle," *National Journal*, Oct. 14, 1972, pp. 1596–1606.

21. See Cannon's statement in *Congressional Record*, Oct. 13, 1972, p. S.18004.

22. *National Journal*, Oct. 14, 1972, p. 1604.

23. *Congressional Quarterly Weekly Report*, Oct. 14, 1972, p. 2637.

24. See the discussion in Daniel Zwerdling, "The Environmental Rights You Don't Have (and Aren't Likely to Get)," *Washington Monthly*, June 1972, pp. 21–29.

CHAPTER 7. MARITIME AFFAIRS AND OCEANOGRAPHY

1. For an illustrative episode from the mid-sixties, see David E. Price, *Who Makes the Laws?* (Cambridge: Schenkman, 1972), pp. 65–69.
2. Data furnished by the U. S. Department of Commerce, Maritime Administration.
3. See Joseph Albright's revealing three-part coverage in *Newsday*, July 20–22, 1970.
4. U. S., Congress, Senate, Committee on Commerce, "The Goals of the Committee on Commerce for the Second Session of the 92nd Congress," Jan. 28, 1972, pp. 50–51.
5. U. S., Congress, House, Committee on Merchant Marine and Fisheries, *Report to Accompany H.R. 11589*, 92nd Cong., 1st sess. (Nov. 5, 1971), p. 6.
6. Reprinted in *Congressional Record*, May 2, 1972, pp. S.7121–7122.
7. U. S., Congress, Senate, Committee on Commerce, *Report to Accompany H.R. 11589*, 92nd Cong., 2nd sess. (Apr. 25, 1972), p. 6.
8. Albright in *Newsday*, July 20, 1970.
9. U. S., Congress, Senate, Committee on Commerce, *Report on H.R. 13324*, 92nd Cong., 2nd sess. (June 7, 1972), pp. 11–13.
10. See Theodore Lowi, "American Business, Public Policy, Case-Studies, and Political Theory," *World Politics* XVI (July 1964), p. 690.
11. *Congressional Record*, July 26, 1972, p. S.11933.
12. Senate Commerce Committee, *Report on H.R. 13324*, pp. 26–32.
13. *Congressional Record*, July 26, 1972, pp. S.11915–11916.
14. Ibid., p. S11930.
15. See Don K. Price, *The Scientific Estate* (Cambridge Belknap Press, 1965), Chapter 7.
16. For the background and passage of the 1966 act, see Price, *Who Makes the Laws?*, pp. 61–75; and Edward Wenk, Jr., *The Politics of the Ocean* (Seattle Univ. of Washington Press, 1972), Chapter 2.
17. Commission on Marine Science, Engineering and Resources, "Our Nation and the Sea" (Washington: Government Printing Office, 1969), p. 1. Emphasis added.
18. Ibid., pp. 229–230.
19. Wenk provides an account of the genesis of the NOAA proposal and its subsequent fate in *Politics of the Ocean*, Chapter 8.
20. PL 91–15 and PL 92–125. The council was allowed to expire for lack of funds in April 1971.
21. Quoted material taken from Commerce Committee news releases, May 1974.
22. U. S., Congress, Senate, Committee on Commerce, *Report on S. 3507*, 92nd Cong., 2nd sess. (Apr. 19, 1972), p. 1.
23. Commission on Marine Science, "Our Nation and the Sea," pp. 49, 53.

24. See ibid., pp. 56–57, 61.
25. U. S., Congress, Senate, Committee on Commerce, Subcommittee on Oceans and Atmosphere, *Hearings on S. 582 and Other Bills*, 92nd Cong., 1st sess. (May 5, 1971), pp. 115, 120, 131.
26. See ibid., pp. 131–132; and, on the controversy surrounding the land-use bills, *Congressional Quarterly Weekly Report* XXX (July 20, 1972), pp. 1874–1877.
27. See *Congressional Record*, June 21, 1973, pp. S.11654–11655.
28. Ibid., Apr. 25, 1972, p. S6671.
29. Senate Commerce Committee, *Hearings on S. 582 and Other Bills* (May 11, 1971), pp. 267–268.
30. This summary is taken from unpublished case material developed for the Congress Project by Peter Maier, Aug. 1972.
31. See Senate Commerce Committee, *Report on S. 3507*, pp. 48–54; and U. S., Congress, House, Committee on Merchant Marine and Fisheries, *Report on H.R. 14146*, 92nd Cong., 2nd sess. (May 5, 1972), pp. 56–64.
32. *Congressional Record*, Aug. 2, 1972, pp. H.7101–7104.
33. James A. Noone, "New Federal Program Seeks to Aid States in Control of Coastal-Area Exploitation," *National Journal*, Dec. 9, 1972, p. 1891.
34. Exchange of letters between House Oceanography Subcommittee Chairman Alton Lennon and CEQ Chairman Russell E. Train, Aug. 7 and 25, 1972.
35. Letter from Alton Lennon to Secretary of the Interior Rogers C. B. Morton, Oct. 10, 1972.

CHAPTER 8.   INVESTIGATIONS AND OVERSIGHT

1. See the testimony of K. Z. Morgan in U. S., Congress, Senate, Committee on Commerce, *Hearings on Public Law 90–602*, 93rd Cong., 1st sess. (Mar. 8, 1973), pp. 34, 46.
2. See the bureau's responses to inquiries from Chairman Warren Magnuson of the Senate Commerce Committee, ibid., pp. 305–306, 311–312.
3. See *Federal Register*, June 12, 1972, p. 15445.
4. Senate Commerce Committee, *Hearings on PL 90–602*, pp. 8–9, 297–298, 304–305, 308–309.
5. Ibid., pp. 13–14.
6. Ibid., p. 12.
7. Ibid., pp. 12–13, 23, 46. See also U. S., Congress, House, Committee on Interstate and Foreign Commerce, *Annual Report on the Administration of the Radiation Control for Health and Safety Act of 1968*, May 20, 1971, p. 61; Aug. 2, 1972, p. 63; July 19, 1973, p. 36.

8. Senate Commerce Committee, *Hearings on PL 90–602*, p. 33.
9. For sketches of the subcommittee's past ventures, see U. S., Congress, House, Committee on Interstate and Foreign Commerce, "Compilation of Activity Reports," Apr. 1971, esp. pp. 292–293, 388–392, 429–430.
10. See *Congressional Quarterly Almanac*, 1957, pp. 792–793; 1958, pp. 687–700.
11. For the subcommittee's own reports on its recent activity, see U. S., Congress, House, Committee on Interstate and Foreign Commerce, "Activity of the Committee on Interstate and Foreign Commerce," 92nd Cong., Jan. 2, 1973, pp. 45–50; 93rd Cong., Jan. 2, 1975, pp. 61–70.
12. Ibid., 92nd Cong. p. 46.
13. For a more detailed account, see "Harley O. Staggers," *Citizens Look at Congress*, Ralph Nader Congress Project (Washington: Grossman Publishers, 1972), pp. 16–20.
14. "Minority Views" in U. S., Congress, House, *Report of the House Interstate and Foreign Commerce Committee pursuant to House Resolution 170*, 92nd Cong., 1st sess. (July 13, 1973), p. 208.
15. Opening statement at hearings of Dec. 14, 1972, of House Interstate and Foreign Commerce Committee Subcommittee on Investigations.
16. See *Wall Street Journal* accounts of Dec. 16 and 18, 1972.
17. Letter from Daniel J. Manelli to David E. Price, Sept. 11, 1973. See also *Washington Star* story of Sept. 5, 1973.
18. Letter from Daniel J. Manelli to David E. Price, July 20, 1973.
19. U. S., Congress, House, Committee on Interstate and Foreign Commerce, Special Subcommittee on Investigations, *FCC Monitoring of Employees' Telephones*, Report, 92nd Cong. (Jan. 2, 1973), pp. 42–43. For the assurances received from other agencies, see pp. 31–41. See also *Washington Post* editorial, "Wiretapping as a Management Tool," Jan. 10, 1973.
20. U. S., Congress, House, Committee on Interstate and Foreign Commerce, *Inquiry into Alleged Rigging of Television News Programs: Hearings*, 92nd Cong., 2nd sess. (May 23, 1972), p. 143. See also the chairman's statement on May 18, when he was the *only* member present (p. 57).
21. Letter from D. Manelli to D. Price, July 20, 1973.
22. Letter from John Moss to members of the House Commerce Committee, Jan. 27, 1975.
23. House Commerce Committee, "Activity of the Committee," 92nd Cong. p. 3.

CHAPTER 9.   THE COMMITTEES AND THE FUTURE

1. For a more extensive discussion of this and other reform proposals, see David E. Price, "The Ambivalence of Congressional Reform," *Public Administration Review*, Nov.–Dec. 1974, pp. 601–608.

Index

344